PRINCE OF THE FAR ISLES

PRINCE OF THE FAR ISLES

The World is Waiting to Consume You...

T. M. ELZY

Seventh World Publishing

CONTENTS

For Dr. Carolyne 'Ezeese' Fuqua
My Clear and Present Muse,
Great Mother, Mekdes, Sun Womb
and Master of the Green Door

FOREWORD

The task of assimilating ancient knowledge into modern day wisdom is not one to be taken lightly. Stillness is required...a willingness to listen, and to be guided in that listening, until your steps are directed.

It's pretty easy to see the difference if what is inside of you is guiding you to contemplation, or to some outer display of self-glory...traits to which the world of effects will eagerly give its approval.

If you are willing to be an instrument, you have the potential to experience something rather remarkable.

The potential to be a clear and perfect channel for That which is longing to express Itself...a creative force beyond imagination and unlimited in focus.

Therefore, it is clear to me that TanyaMarie Elzy, one of my most talented and gifted students has been willing to be and do what was necessary to allow this creative endeavor to channel through...an offering of ancient wisdom beautifully illustrated in modern times.

Brava.

Dr. Carolyne Fuqua

AUTHOR'S NOTES

"What we have called matter is energy, whose vibration has become so lowered as to be perceptible to the senses. There is no matter."
~~~Albert Einstein

Some things you need to know as you read this story...

You have entered a world where millions of years ago, all men knew the truth, that time is not linear. Though the settings, people and clothing for this Hidden Age appears a cross between Mesopotamia, Egypt and Rome, the humans living on the planet during this time had access to knowledge that we would now consider lost. These same thought systems are now currently being presented as 'discoveries' to the present day. For this reason, it was possible for learned men and women to know the wisdom and teachings of all ages: past, present, and future.

That includes:

A profound knowledge of the human body (yes, including deoxyribonucleic acid: DNA)

The Periodic Table of Elements, known and unknown.

Lost and ancient languages to us were studied as future languages to them, such as Dead Latin, Abyssinian, Mu, Mesopotamia, and so forth.

Mythological theories of race based on physical appearance and geological location were unheard of and non-existent. Every man, woman and child knew that the people of the Earth were like flowers; many colors and varietals but still mankind beneath the
~~~

surface of the skin. Like the flowers, these differences were prized and appreciated. The DNA of mankind was unlimited then and all colors came from all peoples like Creation Itself; it was but one of the many gifts mankind would lose in its future fascination with separation. This too, was but a part of the cycle that followed the fall into modern day ignorance; an ignorance that one day, like our DNA would be healed by a return to our former glory.

No stories of a primitive man, no missing link, because for them there was none. In the same manner that carbon over time is pressed into diamonds, it was discovered long ago that human bones are pressed by the earth to resemble what future scientists will erroneously claim to be a type of prehistoric man. Yet Prehistoric man was not a deformed mixture of ape and man, it was simply the lifeforce of creation indwelling a body quite similar to the one you are wearing right now; that holds a DNA strand close to, but not identical to an upright ape. These so-called Prehistoric men and women were empowered by creation to move in sync with the elements and create what the future would call sustainable dwellings and clothing from the quantum field; and after use, return them to their former elemental compounds.

This would account for why no so-called ruins of civilizations pre-date certain eras; these aware humans followed the dictates of creation, only creating things that can be returned to the natural. (with the exception being structures designed for teaching and illumination, like in Ancient Kemet, Peru, Tibet, etc.). These ancient structures would be referred to as temples, literally for lack of a better word. No buildings designed to worship invisible, non-existent gods, but structures to inform and remind mankind during periods of ignorance and darkness that they hold within themselves the power and ability to change the world. Not with tools to destroy the planet, but with the conscious interaction (or creation if you will) with the elements by use of the mind. In contrast to The Sleeping Civilizations that followed, leaving their crumbling structures that eventually had to be abandoned for newer buildings that would in their turn, fall unabsorbed to the earth. Which leads me to my next point...

Why we are not aware of these possibilities in the present day.

The de-evolution of mankind began with tools.

I repeat, mankind did not evolve over time, we devolved.

We did not move up from zero percent of our potential over millions of years to ten percent, we devolved from ninety-nine percent to ten. The hypothesis is that once mankind invented the wheel, we lost the memory of how to move consciously through space and time, which is another construct of destructive imagination. With the wheel, man began to believe he needed a device to move from point A to point B, thereby forever dismissing any other way to move his physical body, which is at its core, a density of light particles that follow the law of physics, pulse, and wave, like everything else. The wheel effectively destroyed the concept of Relativity, where time is non-linear, meaning points exist anywhere and everywhere, so there is no 'place' you cannot be.

The invention of the wheel held up the concept of time, where one had to determine how long it would take for the wheel to deliver the physical body from where it now is to where it will soon arrive. Mankind then began to set limits for the world, and bound creation to these limits. Over time, his mind devolved from its once limitless capacity to barely ten percent of what it could now perceive and become one with.

The misuse of Science was the discovery of how to use tools instead of the natural tool of creation, the human mind. The purpose of mankind developing a reasoning brain was for the conscious use of the natural elements; once man turned away from the natural use of the mind for the unnatural use of tools to accomplish its aims, men and women forgot how to use the quantum field. They began to believe that bringing the invisible to the visible was unnatural, or magic, when in fact, they were given power over the invisible elements for that very reason. And magic itself, is the changing of the natural to the unnatural, for example, how mankind today takes natural elements and using chemical methods, changes these elements into polymers and then plastic, an unnatural creation that does not decay or return to its previous components.

Ancient so-called magic was merely the rendering of the natural to the unnatural, which is why harmful radiation, using a mixture of alpha particles emitted from the radioactive decay of naturally occurring uranium was the favorite weapon of choice for magicians. Magic, in fact, is the world we live in now, a world where we believe we need trains, boats, cars and planes to get from one place to another, androids and iPhones to speak to each other, and laptops, tablets, and wide screen television to entertain ourselves. We believe more in the power of the internet than the power of what made all these things, the reasoning mind.

Now we are a sad reflection of forgotten glory, in willing bondage to the empty heritage of the physical body: Eat, sleep, procreate and survive. Paying rent and mortgage and teaching our children to do the same, as though these were the only things of importance.

We walked away from the stars in exchange for nothing.

Therefore, the basis of this story and all the rest I will share with you, (including the **Trilogy of The Dark One**, of which this, **The Prince of the Far Isles** is the prequel, introducing most of the major characters of the Trilogy from Prince Rasdeter's viewpoint) are stories of how the world of magic and illusion won, and how the channels and holders of our original knowledge and power, also known as co-creators...lost.

Yet, the whole of it is written as both reminder and encouragement of how to reclaim what we have forgotten. Challenging us to re-ignite the dormant cells of energy and willingness that will bring the ten percent of accessibility in our minds and brains to 10.5 or more. Remember, we had Einstein and Tesla from ten percent, imagine what twelve percent or more can do. We may only need ten percent to reopen the quantum field and create the universes we were designed to.

From there, the other ninety percent is a given.

The road back may be long or short, but there is a path...you're walking it right now. Please enjoy these tales and while you're enjoying them, do dream again of your innate greatness.

Yes...and Thank You.

A TASTE OF THE BEGINNING OF THE END

"There is no energy in matter other than that received from the environment."
~~~Nikola Tesla

The moment she stepped away from him, she knew she was dying. She could feel it as time seemed to halt; her arms still warm from the embrace of his. Rasdeter's beautiful deep green eyes with flecks of warm amber were yet gazing at her with vulnerability and gentleness; he didn't realize why she pulled away. The cells of her body were screaming from the effort of holding back the radiation surging into them; the impossibility of how the molecules of air around her were being unnaturally changed into the sun's own fire.

"Saramis..."

In the seconds that passed from her moving away from him, the prince's eyes turned to puzzlement and wonder. He had instinctively tried to continue their joint embrace and found himself frozen in place.

She never took her eyes from Rasdeter; she didn't need to. Saramis knew the author of this attack was a being she'd been trained from childhood to avoid. Her people called them the Ancients because the years behind them had no number. It was beyond thousands and measured in the millions; most of them could not tell you the day they were born. As such, their power was
~~~

incalculable; he had entered the space they shared and bound them both before her own considerable power could detect it.

Saramis was a young woman who had built her life on love and service to others. The earth had often felt her submission to it; that's why she could also feel the reluctance of the energy surrounding her to burn and stretch her atoms to a point they could not return from. But the will of the Ancient was overriding it; without words she could hear the plea of the elements enfolding her:

Run...

But she would not. In that moment Saramis knew she could not willingly leave Rasdeter to his fate, no more than she could the first day she laid eyes on him. Saramis would watch him until she had no eyes to see with. Rasdeter's gaze had changed completely to that of abject fear as he saw her form begin to slowly dissipate. Veins bulged from every part of his body as he strained to reach her; he was roaring words she could no longer hear:

"Saramis!"

INTRODUCTION

He was born a prince and named Rasdeter. His father was Lord Altus, second born and brother to King Valtus, High King of the Far Isles, the most powerful nation in the known world. His mother was Princess Erami, who had the rare privilege of loving her husband, though the marriage was an arranged one. Erami cared for her child on their huge estates and ran a company of servants for the houses and lands, as she was trained to. The prince's most loved childhood friend was his cousin Sumter, the only son of King Valtus, who was always eager to see him. The boys learned and played together, and rarely turned down an opportunity to get into trouble, as boys often do.

Rasdeter had other influences on his life and adults who were important to him: Regent Polymus, who taught him the finer points of law, science, and politics. Lady Irisella, Mistress of the Hall of Women, who cared for Prince Sumter from birth. She found creative ways through music and the arts to distract the two princes from destroying everything in sight. And High General Aton, who taught Rasdeter how to seat a horse, defend himself with both a sword and the wooden boa staff, and how to correctly fire an arrow from a bow.

The prince had an amazing life, one that many would envy.

Two days before his cousin Sumter's twelfth birthday, Rasdeter's father, Lord Altus poisoned his wife Erami then raised his hand against his brother the king and slew him to obtain the woman he secretly loved, Queen Inka and the throne of the Far Isles. Lord Altus also tried to kill his nephew Sumter and failed. Prince Sumter was under the protection of Lord Brayten, a creator channel of great power and ability, who stepped through time and dimensional space to keep the young heir from certain death. Less than a week later, a pregnant Queen Inka would die from a broken heart. Of these events the young prince knew nothing; confined by force to his now dead parent's estates.

On the day of Queen Inka's funeral, the new King Elect executed his uncle.

Following the execution of Lord Altus, the High General of the Far Isles left the presence of his king followed by a group of his men. Though surrounded by the sound of hundreds of boots thundering the long halls leading to the outer courtyard, General Aton in this moment felt alone. His overwhelming grief at the passing of King Valtus was buried along with the rest of the emotions bombarding Aton, disbelief, and regret at the forefront. The words of Lord Master Brayten, that no one could have foreseen Lord Altus striking out at the brother he had clearly loved did not comfort the general. Lord Brayten's assertion that magic had been the underlying cause of Aton's inability to discern the threat to King Valtus also did little to buffer the pain in his heart.

King Valtus was dead. Nothing anyone said could change that fact; nor the fact that his High General was not present to either prevent his death or die with him, as Aton had vowed to do.

Aton was there when Valtus became king; already High General under Valtus's father. It was second nature to Aton to keep a close eye on the two royal siblings, no matter how obvious the affection between them. Yet...Lord Altus had passed the general on the way to slay his brother, and all Aton had noticed was how sickly Altus looked, how weak. General Aton knew that Altus was suffering from a lingering illness; how could he have known the root of it was poisonous magic?

The general shook his head to clear these thoughts, his mind now fixed on his present duties. Young Sumter was now his king, and as Aton turned his mind's eye to Prince Rasdeter, he could only see history repeating itself. Aton knew the two boys loved each other like brothers, and but so had the two men who had just died within days of each other; one of them a lord and one of them a king under General Aton's protection.

Aton was a soldier who had followed and enforced the rules of his kingdom all of his life. He'd just received a direct order from his king to spare the son of Lord Altus and send him into exile.

A king, who, like his cousin Rasdeter was only twelve years old.

Against the advice of all the men around him; regents, lords and military, young Sumter had followed his heart and exercised his right as the King Elect to send his beloved cousin Rasdeter away instead of executing him as party to his father's treachery.

Yet...General Aton was a seasoned man of war. In his long life, he'd seen many failed coups like the one of Lord Altus, and he was sworn to protect the bloodline of Valtus. He mounted his horse and rode to the estates of the dead traitor with a heavy heart. Although Aton loved Prince Rasdeter like his own son, the child was now a threat to the throne.

In his soldier's mind, there was only one remedy:

The Prince of the Far Isles must die.

LEAVING HEAVEN

"When men don't feel love, they destroy..."
~~~Dr. Carolyne Fuqua

The week following his cousin Prince Sumter's twelfth birthday was among the strangest days of young Prince Rasdeter's life. Over and over, day after fretful day, he ran to the main balcony of his father Lord Altus' estates, looking for him. He was, quite possibly, the only person in the kingdom who did not know for sure what had happened. The birthday celebration was abruptly cancelled, and his parents did not return home. That same day, the king's own soldiers came and occupied the estates and his father's personal guard summoned to the palace, where they were interrogated; none returned.

The prince soon realized he was under some sort of house arrest. He was not allowed to leave the main mansion of his father's estate. The eyes and visage of the soldiers who barred his way were cold and distant; they would not speak to him. Any requests he had were handled by the new housekeepers and staff; his own servants were also taken away and never heard from again.

Even his treasured Gervaise, who had once been his wet nurse, was removed from his side. Soldiers entered his rooms unannounced, led by General Ennis, a cold-hearted man who said nothing, merely pointed at Gervaise, who began to shake uncontrollably, the parchment of children's tales she'd been reading to the prince fell from her hands.
~~~

"No!" cried Rasdeter, as he leapt from his bed to prevent them; his mind could not comprehend how the men ignored his protests. He reached for Gervaise, clutching at her clothing. She was only able to stroke his dark wavy hair once before the soldiers surrounded her.

"Restrain him," said Ennis flatly, and the prince went rigid as their strong hands bound him; as a royal he had never been forcibly touched in his life.

Gervaise stared at the boy she had once nurtured in grief and great fear. She knew not her own fate and now felt dread for his.

"Fare you well, my prince..." she barely whispered it, but Rasdeter heard her.

"Stop!" Rasdeter shouted in desperation, "Not Gervaise! Please allow her to remain with me. What means this? Forbear, I beg you!"

With a gaze of pure arrogance and contempt, General Ennis turned wordlessly from the prince and marched away, his men escorting the hapless Gervaise through the doors of Rasdeter's rooms and out of his father's manse. Rasdeter watched helplessly from the outer balcony as they callously pushed Gervaise into a cage on a drawn cart with other servants. The former nurse and the prince watched each other until the road swallowed her.

"Gervaise!" The young prince shouted from his perch above the courtyard, "Gervaise!"

His tears soon blinded him and Rasdeter wiped his face. His parents were gone; now he had not even her to comfort him.

No one answered his questions; he did not know they were under orders to remain silent, upon pain of death.

Tearfully, the boy wrote letters to his cousin, Sumter, his uncle Valtus, the king, and his aunt, Queen Inka, who was always kind to him. They were taken and delivered immediately to High Regent Polymus, who decided to wait until after Lord Altus' execution to give them to the new young king, who might be swayed from his course by his only cousin's heartbreaking entreaties.

Rasdeter did not know the king's staff were watching him; looking for signs he may have known something, anything, of the assassination of King Valtus.

Of course, he knew nothing. He slept in fitful dread, alone in his rooms, constantly asking for information of the whereabouts of his parents. When questioned himself, he ever said the same: His parents left together for an outdoor luncheon in the afternoon, two days before his cousin's birthday, and his father Lord Altus said he could not go. His father promised he would return, and take Rasdeter to his uncle the king's palace, which he failed to do. So, now the prince worried, where is he, and why will no one say what has happened, and take him to his father and mother?

The young prince recalled how pale and sick his father looked, how glassy his eye. Rasdeter had clung to him, pleading to go; he could sense something was wrong. His mother Princess Erami, however, was calm, and tried to soothe him. Lord Altus wished time alone with his wife, she said, he would understand when he was older.

This, however, was beyond understanding.

During the afternoon following his father's execution, which his young son did not yet know, General Aton's soldiers rode onto his father's lands. Rasdeter watched from the balcony in horror as they rounded up remaining servants and village people, some who were put to the sword on the spot, due to information obtained from the interrogations.

The new young king's inexperience allowed High General Aton more sway than he should have. In his zeal to protect Sumter, and his anger at his own failure to protect King Valtus the general had men tortured, to locate the ones who may have influenced the fool hardy Lord Altus into treason. How sad the truth; that no one, even Erami had known anything. The ones Aton sought were beyond any normal man's reach.

The general had young Rasdeter brought down to him; even his soldier's heart constricted at the dark rings under the boy's eyes.

"General Aton," the young prince's lip trembled. "Please tell me what is happening; where is my mother, my father; no one will tell me."

The general nodded at this, satisfied that none of the staff would suffer execution for gossip.

"Come with me, Prince Rasdeter," said the general. "I will take you to your father."

The once confident and cocky twelve-year-old ran to the general, and threw his arms about him, terrified and shaking; the old soldier patted his back awkwardly. Rasdeter missed the silent looks exchanged between the general's soldiers. What did Aton mean, to take the child to the grave of the kingdom's traitor? Would this be kindness, or cruelty, seeing that he knew nothing of what transpired?

But the general had a horse saddled for the prince and indicated to his men he would escort the prince alone; they would return to their duties to secure the shamed lord's estates. His soldiers watched in puzzlement as the general and the prince headed off in a direction away from the palace, and his father's unmarked grave.

Once far enough away, the general began to converse with the young prince. Again, Rasdeter recounted all he knew; and the general's lips tightened.

"So, young prince," asked the general gruffly, "You've not seen your mother, the princess, all this while, or heard from her?"

That Rasdeter had no contact with his mother, General Aton knew. He'd been advised by Lord Master Brayten that Lord Altus had murdered his wife and disposed of the body where none could easily find it. Yet, old habits remained second nature to him. He could hear the truth in the boy's voice; no child could know of such horror and speak of it as though it were nothing. He was becoming convinced of Rasdeter's innocence, which made his task more difficult to complete.

"Is she well, general," asked the boy desperately, "And may I see her soon; today, perhaps?"

"You will see her," replied the general, his throat catching.

They stopped near a tree, twenty miles from his estates, in an area where his father Altus had frequently taken his son and his nephew Sumter hunting. Deer could be spotted in plenty on the grounds as they searched for food.

Rasdeter looked about him, puzzled. He had no inkling of personal danger, having been well treated his whole life. He turned back to General Aton.

"Where?" he began, then stopped at the look in the general's eyes. They were similar to his father's eyes, when last he saw him. Aton had the look of a man about to do something desperate.

"General Aton?" he said hesitantly.

"It gives me no pleasure to do this, Prince Rasdeter," said the general with a heaviness in his voice, "I see that you are innocent of the treason of your father, and his murder of your mother..."

Breath left the boy. His face held so many emotions, all at once, that it was difficult for the general to follow; shock, denial, pain, anger, and fear. But mostly denial.

"What...what are you saying; my mother is dead, my father a traitor? No!"

"Yes, my prince," continued the general. "Lord Altus slew his brother, King Valtus, two days before now King Sumter's birthday. And he admitted to Lord Brayten that before the attack on the king, he killed his own wife near the old seaport, and let her body drift to the open sea."

"No..." The prince doubled over in pain. Rasdeter wanted to deny what the general said, but it fit the picture of madness he'd been viewing over the past week and a half.

"He wouldn't...my father would never...he'd never hurt my mother. He was always kind to her, loving...!"

He drew his breath in a gasp.

"And my uncle Valtus, they were brothers; they loved each other!"

Through the haze of his agony, Rasdeter saw the compassion in the general's gaze, and something else. Then, finally his own eyes widened, and his young heart pounded in fear at last...for himself.

If his father was found guilty of treason, then, they must have executed him; and if his father was dead...Rasdeter stared in disbelief at the general.

"You don't think..." He choked out the words. "You...you're not going to hurt me, are you?"

But General Aton was silent; watching him still.

The prince looked about him wide eyed; there was no one to shout to for help, if indeed, help could come. Now everything made sense; his house arrest, and leading him out into the distant fields, far from his estates, alone. His eyes, as they returned to the soldier, this man of war, were filled with despair.

"If...if I try to run, you'll only shoot me in the back with an arrow..."

General Aton shook his head.

"You're a prince of the realm, Rasdeter..." said the general quietly. "I know you won't run from me, and shame your mother's memory."

The boy hung his head then and wept, broken hearted. Still, the general remained silent. He would give Rasdeter this, at least; a moment to embrace his fate, like the man he would never live to become. After a while, Rasdeter wiped his face on his sleeve, and dismounted his horse, still trembling, and trying to be strong, as his world came crashing to an end he'd never expected.

General Aton also dismounted quietly, his heart heavy with anticipated grief.

They faced each other before the tree; Rasdeter looked around him again, this time, for no one. Only to see the leaves waving in the trees above him, birds crying out, and the beauty of the clouds floating by, unaware of his personal tragedy. He looked again to the general. Aton slowly drew his sword, the metal singing as it left the scabbard; both were finding it difficult to swallow.

"And my cousin...Sumter?" The prince asked in agony, "He could not see to this himself; and look in my eyes, as you do?"

The general paused; his own body tensed in pain.

"We both die this day, you and I," said the general. "Your cousin loves you, my prince, more than he should. It is not his will that you die but be sent into exile."

"Then...why?" whispered the boy with hope, and desperation in his gaze. "Why won't you let me go, general?"

General Aton shook his head again sadly.

"This is the foolishness of a child, come to the throne too soon. If you live, you will rise against him; it is the way of kings, and shared thrones..."

"But I wouldn't, not if he spared me..."

The prince placed his hand on the tree behind him, to keep from shaking. He'd never been so much as cut by a blade, but he knew what it could do, in the hands of a master swordsman such as the general. Fear rocked his young body in anticipation of life ending agony.

"I wouldn't..." he repeated, his voice trailing away in the sudden quiet.

The general smiled grimly at his words, the reasoning of both boys; not yet men. It saddened Aton that he himself would not live to see Sumter rule his kingdom as a man. His hand tightened on his sword, and Rasdeter's face paled.

"Content yourself that I follow you in death," said Aton. "It is the only suitable punishment for what I now do, to protect him against his will."

He braced himself for the death stroke.

"You will feel little pain," Aton said, "If you do not resist..."

Rasdeter closed his eyes, his last thoughts on his mother Erami, her gentle face before him. He saw now the general spoke the truth, and he would soon be where they are. The birds overhead gave one final haunting cry...

The hooves of both horses thundered the ground as General Aton sped towards the palace of the Far Isles. He rode swiftly past his men without stopping. He did not look to their puzzled faces, lest they follow him; this pending doom he would share with no one. He had timed his deed perfectly; he knew Lord Brayten would leave after the execution for a time and wait for the young king's next summons.

Like any good general, Aton studied the behavior of all around him; it had served him well during times of both peace and war. The general also knew, Lord Brayten would prevent him, if he became aware of his thoughts. Even if he saw the wisdom of Aton's actions; Lord Brayten would follow any course that spared Sumter further pain.

Aton sighed; he was an aging soldier, though a high general. He knew more fighting days were behind than before him, and it was a soldier's duty and honor to die in service to his king. It was not the end he desired: One last glorious battle, the roaring of men charging forward to leave their names in songs and stories. Pitting flank, and regiment against a foe, while arrows sang overhead, his great heart finally giving out in struggle with a victorious adversary...no. This would not be his end. General Aton would be executed for disobeying his king; though in the end, it would save Sumter's life, and his lineage.

The general sighed again; he would have to be content with that knowledge.

His wife and sons would not see his death; they waited for him on the other side, in the shaded realms. One night the general came home, and she had died in her sleep, while he was off to battle with King Valtus. Aton found her cold and still in their bed, ever beautiful to him, and quiet. His sons had died in various wars of service and expansion. Each one made him proud as they took different pieces of his heart to the grave; he was puzzled as to how he had outlived them all.

Thoughts of Rasdeter pinched his soul; he was a good son, though his father Altus was a fool. Had his father accepted his place, his son would have grown strong and wise. The general could see his mother in him, now that, was a gentle soul. He would have married well, had his own lands, and children... General Aton could think no more of the child; lest the image of the small, lonely grave haunt him for the short time he had left.

He asked for a private audience with King Sumter, which he knew would be granted. The boy, now king, had always looked up to him, loved him; oh, such memories were a curse in this moment.

As Aton entered the hall, their eyes met, he and Sumter. The young king came immediately to his feet; it seemed the general had changed beyond recognition in the short time he was gone. Sumter remembered himself and sat again his father's throne.

Sumter did not know why his heart was beating so fast. But he knew the general was to bring Rasdeter to him, so he could explain to his cousin and childhood friend why they could see one another no more; and why his love for him spared his life.

"General..." began the young king, "Where is Rasdeter?"

The general cleared his throat, but no sound came out; he thought the truth would be easier to say than it was. As he struggled to speak, Lord Brayten appeared instantly next to Sumter's throne. After the new king's narrow escape from Lord Altus, Brayten attuned himself to Sumter's heart and thoughts; his fear was like a summons in his mind.

Lord Brayten looked quickly from the young king to his trusted general; his eyes full of wonder and dismay as he scanned Aton's memories.

If anything, the sudden appearance of Lord Brayten heightened the King Elect's fear; his voice as he spoke was not his own.

"General..." Sumter said again, and softly, "He...lives...does he not?"

It should not be that so much death, so soon, and so close to him, would cause him to fear the worst in any situation, yet now it did.

The general remained silent, and went to his knees, undone by his own deed. Sumter now rose from his throne, and approached his general, as some horror overtook him.

"Speak to me, General Aton; I command you--"

"If..."

The general's gruff voice was strained with grief.

"If he had lived, my king; he would have risen against you..."

The throne room was silent.

Then Sumter's arms lifted, and his hands went to his face, as though he might gouge out his own eyes. With this one blow, he was now alone; with no relatives near him, no one he could call his blood kin. Rasdeter's face loomed before Sumter, as when he last saw him, they were laughing like brothers. Who could do him harm, or think him capable of it?

All he wished for, was one last embrace; one time they could weep together; and now, nothing.

"Rasdeter!"

The Boy King's voice was raw as he screamed his cousin's name; it reverberated the columns of the hall. Lord Brayten looked away at this cry of mourning. General Aton could not lift his head, as he struggled with his own pain.

By the Sword

Lord Master Brayten and High Regent Galen conferred quietly in the halls leading to the rooms of the nation's new King Elect, young Sumter of the Far Isles. A mere boy, he had lost both his parents within a week of each other, due to the machinations of his once beloved uncle Lord Altus. Without the sure protection of Lord Brayten, (also referred to by men as a channel and Master Creator) he too might have died in the failed coup. Lord Brayten learned of the dark forces who took advantage of Lord Altus' misguided and unrequited love, the being known as Izar, the Twins. In pitched battle, Brayten destroyed them in sure payment for the near destruction of the Kingdom of the Far Isles. Brayten returned to the kingdom to assist the new ruler in the execution of Lord Altus.

All too soon, the Master Creator found himself again in the Far Isles for the sad betrayal of the kingdom's High General. It was a quandary. The treason of the king's brother required that his entire family be put to death, including his son, Rasdeter. As King Elect, Sumter's first act of policy was to pardon his cousin and have him sent into exile. The penalty for disobedience to a king is death, which Aton willfully did in order to protect Sumter's bloodline. Now under house arrest, the general languished while the desolate heir mourned the unfathomable loss of his parents and dear cousin, Prince Rasdeter.

"So," said High Regent Galen as he spoke of Rasdeter's father, "This was not the actions of a lone man, tempted by destiny, but the intrigue of dark power. What chance have we as men, Lord Brayten?"

The Master Creator clasped his hands behind his back and sighed.

"The tale of Altus is but a reminder of the hunger that awaits us all if we give in to the lower nature and its lurid needs and desires, High Regent Galen," replied Brayten soberly. "We can only be used by such forces if we are somehow willing to be. Lord Altus had much many men only dream of, but the hidden nature is never satisfied, never complete. There is a hole in it that only light can fill, and we must turn to it, or all is lost."

The High Regent nodded in agreement.

"Well said, my lord," replied Galen. "The light within us is indeed our only hope, and we must defend it daily. As you say, we clearly see the result of such unwillingness, our king and queen rest in the shaded realms, and horror upon horror is heaped on our young ruler's head. May the Great One protect him..."

Brayten did not respond aloud to this as his chest tightened in sympathy for the king. This may be only the beginning of sorrows was his only fear. Though he wished to, Lord Brayten knew he could not be there for every obstacle placed in the path of the son of King

Valtus. These were things that Sumter himself would have to work out on his way to his father's throne.

Lord Brayten waited respectfully in the hall with the High Regent until Lady Irisella, Mistress of the Hall of Women, and second mother to the new king, came out of Sumter's inner rooms to greet them. High Regent Galen excused himself.

"Is the king resting?" asked Brayten solicitously, and Irisella nodded sadly.

Sumter had wept bitterly for his cousin until he could weep no more and fell asleep.

He refused to make a decision about the fate of the general, and not a man but understood this. The boy loved General Aton like a father, and even though Sumter knew as king he must execute him, his young heart was broken. The new King Elect had hoped the general would be there to guide him in the years to come, and now he mourned this coming loss as well. Too much had happened too soon, and now Sumter pushed back against the horrid rules and regulations he felt were being thrust on him. He had lost his family; now must he slay the rest who are left to him?

"No, Irisella," he said between fits of tears, "I won't set the date, not yet. I know he has to die for disobeying me, for slaying my cousin. I know, but...but..."

And then the heartfelt weeping of a boy not yet ready to take on the tasks of a man returned to the room. Irisella stroked his hair gently, trying to hold back her own sorrow.

Brayten walked with Irisella as she spoke her heart, while he graciously listened. Then Lady Irisella extended her hand to Brayten, who accepted it in both of his.

"I have a thought that it is you he waits for, my lord," said Irisella quietly. "He needs a man's guidance now, he's had enough of our laws and policies..."

Brayten nodded to this.

"With your leave, Lady Irisella, I'll wait for him in the outer rooms..."

When young Sumter woke from sleep, he felt a warmth that always signaled to him that Lord Brayten was nearby. He rose quickly, washed his face, and tried to straighten his robes before opening the doors of his inner rooms. Sumter was comforted to find Brayten seated near the window.

"I'm trying hard to be brave, Lord Brayten," the young king admitted before seating himself across from his mentor. He restrained the urge to run to Brayten and embrace him, even though they were alone, and he could do so. Brayten smiled at Sumter's thoughts, to him they were so strong the boy could have spoken aloud.

"You're braver than you know, my lord," replied the creator, and the boy flushed at his mentor now referring to Sumter as 'lord'. It was a reminder of all that had happened.

"They, the regents, want me to execute Aton right away," continued Sumter sadly.

"You know you must," responded Brayten. "General Aton, most of all, would want you to. Everything he has done, even this, as horrid as it is, was done for you, my king. As a soldier and a general, he would not want you to delay. Aton knows you love him…"

These words brought tears again to Sumter's eyes, and he looked away. Finally, the young king spoke.

"But, what should I do, I mean, how should it be done? I don't want him to suffer…"

Lord Brayten now scanned the boy's mind to see his greatest fear in holding back from the general's execution. He found two things uppermost in Sumter's mind: That the king did not wish to humiliate the general with a traitor's execution, and most of all, he did not want to carry out the sentence himself, as he had with his uncle. Lord Brayten saw that the boy was sitting on a precarious ledge as a new ruler. Too much shedding of blood so early in his reign could desensitize him to another's suffering and make of him a callous king. Yet, he must not be seen to be weak; it would invite attack from envious nations. An idea came to Lord Brayten, something he had actually seen in the general's mind shortly after he struck down the king's cousin.

"My king," began Lord Brayten thoughtfully, "Consider giving the general what he truly wants, a soldier's death."

This statement interrupted Sumter's grieving. He looked at his mentor in puzzlement.

"A soldier's death?" echoed Sumter.

"Yes," Brayten responded emphatically, "Let Aton die in your service, as he has always wished to..."

The pair talked at length about Lord Brayten's idea, and how it might legally be done. The conversation appeared to ease some of the young ruler's pain. This idea might give some dignity to the general's death, and Sumter himself would not have to do it. Brayten could feel the boy's shoulders begin to straighten and his mind ceased its restless circle. He will make a good king, thought Brayten, should I live to see it.

Later that same day, Lord Brayten visited General Aton at his home. The king commanded he be confined there, despite the general's request to be sent to the jails. He wanted no special treatment for his crime, and Sumter's reluctance to treat Aton as he felt he deserved brought unaccustomed tears to the old soldier's eyes. And without the speedy execution he looked forward to, the general was left to torture himself with remorse and the humiliation of witnessing the grief of his former soldiers. They were not allowed to speak with him, but he could clearly see their anguish and his prize pupil Marcus was the worse of them. He stood outside, refusing to leave the general's door, and Aton could hear his quiet sniffles and coughing to cover the sound of his weeping.

Marcus opened the door for Lord Brayten. His men refused to lock it; they knew the general would not try to escape his fate. Many of them agreed with what he had done to protect the king; it was to them the ultimate sacrifice, the boldness of it took their breath away.

For his men, General Aton had shown them that he meant what he had taught them of service to the throne; it was a hard decision to make. All knew he loved Prince Rasdeter, though Aton had no respect for the boy's father. It was never anything he had to say; few of the military respected the king's philandering and abusive brother.

The general rose at Lord Brayten's entrance and stood at attention; the lord and master waved away this gesture of respect. Aton breathed heavily and again took his seat. Brayten sat across from him at the general's table.

"How fares the king?" asked Aton hoarsely, "I fear I've dealt him a horrible blow."

"You have, Aton," agreed Brayten. "The worse of which is how to execute a man who once lived to serve him, even against his will."

The general looked down at the floor beneath his feet and shook his head.

"He shouldn't hesitate this way, Brayten," Aton said heavily. "It may taint his rule..."

"I know," replied the creator, "But he's only twelve; less than a month ago, all he wished for was to run the hounds and practice archery."

Aton clasped his face at this and shook silently; Lord Brayten said nothing. It was one thing to know what should be done, it was another to act upon it. Aton was feeling all the pain of his decision and none could ease it for him.

"You know why I'm here, general," Brayten said finally, and Aton nodded.

"He's given you a week," continued Brayten, and at Aton's look of distress, he shook his head. "You'll need it to regain the strength you've wasted feeling guilty..."

The Master Creator came to his feet and looked down at the stricken general.

"Get up, Aton, wash your face and take nourishment, hone again your skills. The boy who loves you is giving you what you don't deserve, a soldier's death."

The Execution of Lord High General Aton

The day was a beautiful one, full of towering Cumulus clouds floating serenely against a deep cerulean blue sky. The winds were brisk and the air crisp; it was a day full of life and promise, without a hint of the sorrow to come.

Aton spent his time doing what he did best, preparing himself for battle. He was allowed the grounds outside his home to practice his skills. Despite his protest, Marcus insisted on working with him, to give his former mentor better focus. The general finally conceded; he realized this would help Marcus with his own emotions.

The two sparred in grim silence; only the occasional grunt could be heard as they battled. As always, the general did not spare his former pupil, and Marcus eyes held great respect; the general had survived numerous battles over the years for a reason. Marcus was excellent with a sword, and one day the general knew he would be unparalleled; he grieved this was one more thing he would not live to see.

Seconds later, Marcus sword was on the ground, and he stepped back quickly from his mentor, who followed the thrust and stood still. Their eyes met.

"You are ready, general," he said respectfully.

The general stood back in military formation and sheathed his weapon, breathing deeply. Then he shook his head.

"Do not mourn me, Marcus," he said finally, and watched as the man he treated as a son brimmed his eyes.

"I will not obey you in this, general," replied Marcus resolutely. "It is the only thing you have ever asked of me that I will not do."

Aton approached his grieving soldier and roughly clasped his shoulder.

"You will excel in all I have taught you," General Aton said in a strained voice. "Protect the king to your last breath. If you do this, my life is well served."

Marcus nodded and bowed his head, unable to say more. Aton then held Marcus roughly with one arm, his one and only display of deep affection towards his former pupil. Marcus gripped his general tightly and breathed deeply, he knew the general did not wish to hear his tears. Then Aton broke the half embrace and walked back to his home to await his final summons. The crisp air did not comfort Marcus as he watched his father figure march away from him.

Later that morning, the general heard a commotion outside his door. He came to his feet and looked at his sword, which was never far from him. Aton knew he could reach it if necessary.

But it was Marcus who held wide the door, and the general nearly gasped as he beheld the one who faced him with bright sunlight shading his form.

It was his king, Sumter of the Far Isles.

The boy had used the week to have actual armor fashioned for him in his official role as leader of an army feared by most of the known world. At twelve, Sumter was lanky and still growing, his arms and legs not quite filled out. Yet having the armor built for him gave the impression of the man he would one day become. The breastplate gleamed with the crest of his house, his boots were well made and suited for battle. His robe was short in the style of his military; across his chest were the straps that formed the setting for the belt that held his short sword, and Sumter carried a shield and helmet sized for him.

He looked every inch a commander and the general fell to his knees in awe and gratitude.

Sumter did not turn back to look at Marcus, he merely slanted his head and his soldier swiftly closed the door. It was a regal gesture, and the boy's eyes as he looked again at his general showed Aton that Sumter was beginning to accept his new station and the way he must appear before his men. The general lowered his head and coughed to contain his feelings.

"General..." began the boy and rested the tip of his shield on the floor. Aton moved forward to retrieve it, and the helmet; Sumter allowed this show of respect. The general placed these things on his table and returned to his knees before his king.

The young king took a deep shaky breath before speaking. He'd thought carefully about what he wanted to say, but now that he was in front of the man he once looked up to, Sumter grappled with his emotions. It was the last time they would speak to each other and his pain returned with the sight of the general.

"I've come..." Sumter paused and then said quickly, "I've come to tell you the things that will happen after your execution."

The general bowed his head in shame. Of all the things he expected to happen, this was not one of them, a private audience with the king after Aton informed Sumter of his disobedience. He had expected to be removed from the king's hall in chains and immediately taken to the courtyard and beheaded, his body then thrown outside the palace walls for the dogs to tear apart. In his ignorance and love, Sumter had done far more to punish his High General than he might have dreamed.

Aton waited in dread for his king's next words.

"I've decided to promote Marcus to the title of General and Forde over my personal guard," The new king said with difficulty. "I've watched him over the years, and he is the best of your former students. Once day he will command your ranks..."

The boy paused and breathed deeply at this; Aton could not raise his head.

"I'm having the remains of your wife and sons removed from the soldier's graveyard," Sumter said quietly to the horror of his servant, "And placed in a new sepulchre of marble, with your family name on it, and the order of your regiment. You will be interred with them on a hill overlooking the roads to the Kingdom of the Eastern Crest."

His body shaking, the general could hold back no more.

"My king, I don't deserve this honor..."

"No..." said the young king softly, "No, you don't..."

The silence between them deepened as the old soldier silently wept, sinking down on his crossed legs. Sumter swallowed several times as pain hammered at him. Then the grieving boy closed the space between them and placed his hands on the general's shoulders, a gesture of high honor.

"You were meant to stay with me, Aton," the boy said finally, speaking out his own despair. "You were supposed to guide me through this difficult time, show me how to lead these men. My father's gone, and I was counting on you..."

Aton now covered his face and wept aloud the tears of a broken man. They wept together, mourning a future they would now never share.

"Forgive me, Sumter," gasped the general in agony.

"No," whispered Sumter firmly. "I will not forgive you for slaying Rasdeter, and I will not forgive you for forcing me to do this, not now or ever..."

The boy took a deep rasping breath.

"But I will always love you, general, and I want you to know that as you render service to me one final time."

The general did the unthinkable then, and embraced his king, sobbing on the boy's chest from his kneeled position. No one would witness this, and the young king bowed his head on the general's, and they wept together one last time.

The king did not hide his tears as he left Aton's home, instead Sumter strode with purpose to join Lord Brayten who waited with the king's horse. The former general's men stood in a column at attention awaiting his orders. With the assistance of a soldier Sumter mounted his steed and held him steady as he turned to his men.

He spoke sharply.

"Bring him to the Debtor's Courtyard."

***

The place called the Debtor's Courtyard was more of an arena. It was so named for its original purpose, to allow those imprisoned for heavy debt to absolve their debt through battle. This was an old name for it, and the barbaric tradition was set aside hundreds of years ago when the site was turned into a training ground for troops. In the recent past it was used for private executions of nobility or captured kings who refused to surrender after a war was lost.

High General Aton could hear his blood pounding in his ears as he entered the arena; no one had told him his fate; he only knew he would be allowed to fight. Not knowing for sure what was to come made him uneasy. He gripped his sword tightly as he walked beneath the huge, shaded arch that marked the entrance to his death. He quickly noted archers standing at attention from one end of the oval shaped arena to the other; whoever entered here would not escape. His lips tightened as he gazed up at the main enclosure overlooking the multi-seated arena, with High Regent Galen, Lord Master Brayten, King Elect Sumter and his own Marcus, promoted to Forde General. Aton could see by his attire that Sumter had already placed Marcus over his personal guard.

This pleased the general as he saluted a farewell to his king.

Sumter did not respond to this salute; his hands gripped the railing with anxiety as his own blood pounded. He knew he must watch the execution; it was among the many things his father King Valtus had shielded him from. Soon enough, his father had planned to give his son his own Prince's sword that would signify the beginning of his training in the ways of war. Valtus did not wish to immediately drown his son's childhood fantasies of battle with the realities of spilled blood.

Little did King Valtus realize the first spilled blood his son Sumter would see would be his own.

Aton's eyes and body now turned sharply in the direction of the opening gates on the other end of the arena. He braced himself; the general expected huge hounds or spotted cats of great speed and cunning. He was startled for a moment to see criminals released from their bonds and given weapons; they blinked rapidly as their eyes adjusted to unaccustomed daylight.

Then a light came into his eyes and Aton grinned.

A brilliant solution, to have the general fight firsthand men who were already condemned to die. The general gave one last glance at the elevated enclosure; not to his king but to Lord Brayten, who returned this acknowledgement. Then the former High General of the Kingdom of the Far Isles released a great roar and charged. The men who faced the general were promised nothing, only a chance to die on their feet instead of their knees. Most of them recognized the general and howled at this double opportunity to slay the one who would normally oversee their own execution. The general waded into them, scattering their weak defense, and hacking away at limbs and torsos.

Sumter found himself watching the deadly artistry of Aton in amazement. He'd trained with the general who did not spare his station as a prince, but hurled him to the ground time and again, to teach him the unfairness of hand to hand battle. But to watch General Aton face a foe he intended to slay took the king's breath away. He closed his eyes frequently to calm his stomach, then for respite took the opportunity to ask Forde Marcus a question.

"Can the general prevail against them?" Sumter didn't mean to make his tone sound hopeful, but it did.

Marcus watched as the guards released more and more criminals who poured through the gates. He steadied his own voice before speaking.

"Not without aid..." answered Marcus, who also gripped the railing as he watched his mentor vigorously set about his task to sell his soul dearly.

The archers of the Far Isles had their orders; anyone who approached the general from the rear was shot dead for his trouble. Cowardice would not be tolerated; Sumter wanted the general to die facing his foe. Also, any incapacitated men dying from the horrendous wounds the general meted out were swiftly put out of their misery.

At one point, Aton was truly winded, the men facing him fell back at a command from one of them. The general panted heavily as he looked around him, unable for a moment to even close his mouth.

"Why waste our weapons?" A man shouted, "Wait a moment more until he tires, then we can finish him off--" The man paused in confusion as he tried to complete his sentence. He felt a sharp pain in his chest and looked down in wonder at the arrow growing out of it; his eyes rolled up and he went to the dirt. A few more arrows and bodies on the ground and the message from the king was clear: Stand still and die. The men screamed and charged the general who plowed into them again from his second wind.

Finally, Aton saw the men fall back again as another man pushed them aside to face him. The general recognized him.

"I never thought I'd have the chance to face you, Aton," The man said before spitting on the ground, "I've been shouting like a madman since this started for them to let me out..."

Aton wiped the blood from his face.

"Damn fool," The general gasped, "Spending your life in jail over a tavern brawl..."

"He was my brother, you bastard!" shouted the criminal. "Your men cut him down like a tree; he was defenseless...!"

"Before or after he gutted a tavern girl for not bringing him a drink?" Aton snarled. "He deserved hanging, he was a drunken idiot, just like you!"

The ground shook as the two met. He was a big man like the general, and not nearly as winded. He flung himself against the general's shield and pushed him back for the first time. Aton watched him warily as they circled each other.

The man pointed at him.

"You're gonna die today," He said in rage, "I'm gonna slit your throat and watch you choke..."

He was fast and strong; he charged the general, hacking at his shield and clanging his sword against Aton's blade, forcing him back until the general went to one knee. The man swung up and high without stopping.

"This is for my brother!"

The blow shattered the general's shield and sliced his arm, but the blood squirting was not only his own. Aton sliced down and across the man's leg as he went to his knees, and the scream from the man was high and shrill. Aton's next thrust went through the man's chest as he came to his feet.

Remembering the arrows of the archers, the remaining men rushed him.

It was like watching an aged lion fighting off a pack of younger ones. Finally, the tired general made a misstep, and a lucky criminal ran him through, pelted with arrows before he could proclaim his victory. The general grunted from the blow, unable to even cry out from the pain.

His king cried out for him, turning his head away from the lethal thrust.

Time slowed for General Aton. As his sight dimmed, he saw the arrows singing overhead, falling on the doomed men who survived the battle. He went to his knees again, gasping as his body cavity filled with blood, his great heart pumping out his life. Aton instinctively tried to pull out the sword in his gut, but his fingers weakened and failed him. He rested his head and body in the dirt, no longer able to feel the ground beneath him.

Young King Sumter found his voice at last.

"Bring him to me, Lord Brayten," Sumter asked hoarsely.

The general vanished from the field of blood and dying men, to appear at the top of the arena, in the private enclosure of the king. Lord Brayten rested the general on a raised couch the king had prepared for him; a servant rushed forward to wipe the blood from his face. The creator also held back the growing shock overtaking the general's body; Aton was able to turn his head and meet the king's brimming eyes.

Aton tried to speak but couldn't; Sumter shook his head and gently stroked the general's coarse, grey hair.

"It's alright," Sumter choked. "You don't have to say anything, I already know…"

These words seemed to comfort the general. Aton gave a last rasping sigh as his heart stopped; his eyes locked on his king.

Lord Master Brayten shielded the shaded enclosure from the view of all others, as the grief-stricken Boy King threw his arm over the general's body and sobbed his heart out.

THE WOMAN OF THE WOODS

"It is thought and thought alone that moves the Noumenal to the Phenomenal."
~~~Dr. Carolyne Fuqua

It was now nightfall, and leagues away two small figures huddled in the darkness of an old cave. Carved into the side of a huge mound of earth, trees grew tall on top of it; any men on horseback who passed by saw nothing. A tiny fire gave off a dim light that only the two of them could see. From time to time, one of them, a young woman, murmured words of healing and tossed seeds on the fire. The flames hissed and sparked, the yellow and orange colors mirrored against the darkness of the eyes of the other; a small and grieving boy.

Tears streamed down his muddied cheeks; occasionally he wiped his face on his sleeve. He'd begun the day a prince, his father Lord Altus, brother to the King of the Far Isles, his own uncle. His favorite playmate his first cousin, Prince Sumter, heir to the throne. The disappearance of his parents had frightened him, but never could he have imagined that the end of this day would bring answers that would leave him here, orphaned, a prince no more and presumed dead. His mind kept trying to make sense of what must surely be a nightmare he could wake from. He would open his eyes and see the warm sheets of his bed surrounding him, and his mother who was often the first to greet him in the morning. He would moan and pretend to yet be sleeping as she stroked his face and hair.
~~~

"Rasdeter, my son," Erami would say in that soft voice of hers, infused with love, "Why do you sleep? You must rise with the sun..."

This was the place he most wanted to be...

But High General Aton, who once showered him with gruff affection and instruction in the ways of men stood in his way.

The prince could not pass him; the dream of his mother's face faded away. Rasdeter felt again the rough bark of the tree he would soon die under and heard the words the general would say to him before Aton took his sharp sword and ran it through him.

The general braced himself for the death stroke.

"You will feel little pain, if you do not resist..."

Young Rasdeter closed his eyes, his last thoughts on his mother...

After a moment Rasdeter opened his eyes. The general yet stood before him, sword raised, his face contorted with determination and regret. But he wasn't moving, or even breathing. Prince Rasdeter backed against the tree in terror; did he strike already, and his spirit watched his execution? He feared to look down, lest he see his body there, reddened, and split. Then he heard a voice far away to his left.

"Child..."

The prince whirled in the direction of the voice calling to him. At a distance, he saw a young woman, cloaked as though she were cold. She held a small basket, as one who gathers herbs for cooking. She gestured to him urgently.

"Come to me, child, quickly...!"

Rasdeter patted his torso, then with trepidation, he finally looked at the ground, and saw nothing but grass, and tufts of flowers at his feet. He started again when he looked at the general, fearing he saw him. Then, self-preservation took over; he whirled from under Aton's arm, and bolted for the woman, thinking all the while, he would soon feel an arrow in his back from the general's bow.

But he reached her safely, and she gathered him to her swiftly, pressing him to the ground. When he looked up at her confused, she put a finger to her lips.

"Stay quiet, now, no matter what you see..."

Rasdeter watched in awe, as the air molecules shimmered around her hand and a small deer appeared where once he stood. Then Aton brought his sword down swiftly; the cry of the dying fawn almost human. The boy closed his eyes, afraid he yet dreamed a vision before death, of being somehow, someway, spared. He looked again, as the general knelt before the deer, and wept bitterly, thinking himself alone in the forest. Then the old soldier dug a deep, small grave, and placed the deer into it.

The general wiped his face as he finished the burial.

"You deserved better, young Rasdeter," Aton said, his voice raw. "Curse your father for bringing such dark days upon us; and such dark deeds, to force a man to slay a child. Curse him!"

The general wiped his face again.

"Rest now... I join you soon."

The two watched until the general mounted his stallion, took the reins of Rasdeter's horse, and galloped away, towards the palace of the Far Isles.

The prince looked up from the grass at the young woman, who looked also at him, her eyes filled with compassion.

"My name is Saramis," she said to his unspoken question. "I am a wise woman of the forests, with some small knowledge of creation; enough to save your life."

"Thank you, Saramis," Rasdeter whispered.

"Hold your gratitude, child," she responded. "For now I take you, where you can never return from. This is the last time you will see these lands you call home. If a man such as he felt bound to slay you, no one must ever learn you yet live; lest my impulsive work be undone."

Rasdeter nodded, as his inner pain returned. He watched the retreating figure of General Aton, riding away with the prince's horse, and all that remained of his former life.

Saramis watched the boy across from her and felt her heart ache. She didn't realize they were both thinking of the same thing; how differently the day had begun. Although her tribe had no boundaries, the grounds she walked that morning were not her normal ritual. There was an herb that only grew on Lord Altus' estates and only once a year. Morning was the best time to harvest them and she could not explain to herself why she lingered until the afternoon, picking other herbs and flowers she could gather later. Saramis stood still as the deer roamed around her; the songs of birds above her entranced her ears. She heard the hoofbeats of the general and the prince long before they came into view. Why did she render herself invisible instead of simply vanishing altogether? She could not say now or then. If they were hunting, perhaps she would save the deer tribe who stood boldly with her watching. A hunt does not always bring food to the table. A tiny baby fawn reclined at her feet; his white spots shifting back and forth with his breath. Saramis smiled down at him.

It was only curiosity that made Saramis listen to the words exchanged between the man and the child; her eyes widened as she began to understand what was happening. Rasdeter's sobbing for his parents ripped her soul and once he truly understood why he was there with the general, he first looked about wildly for help. She was invisible, so Rasdeter did not actually see her; the brief contact of his eyes with hers sent a shock through Saramis. She read the general's aura and felt no malice emanating from him, only deep and shattering pain. Yet it was clear he would slay the child. She covered her mouth as the two dismounted and the boy leaned back against the tree behind him, trembling.

The power within Saramis arched and branched out; she quickly directed it into the ground beneath her. Some of the deer around her scattered but when she looked at her feet the small fawn was still resting there, looking up at her with deep and beautiful eyes. Her breath caught as a thought came to her, a thought of sacrifice. She whispered to the little fawn:

"Run..."

But he wouldn't. He kept looking up at her as though to say:

Not without you...

She heard her mind saying, Don't do it, you don't have per-mission...

When young Rasdeter slowly gazed around again at the beauty around him and his head turned towards her, she felt her arm raise in his direction and her palm stretch out with fingers splayed. The power in her surged back up from the earth and through her body; it roared towards General Aton as he swiftly raised his sword and time stopped. Saramis knelt down and stroked the spots on the tiny deer.

Why, she asked him with her mind, Why didn't you run?

The fawn just stared at her and impulsively began to lick the salty tears on her face.

She rose then and called out to the boy she didn't know, but was about to save. Rasdeter didn't notice the deer beside Saramis as he tumbled beneath her, nor when she reached over and touched the fawn's smooth coat before she replaced him for the child. And he didn't notice when the mother doe stood under the tree where her baby was buried and looked at Saramis. Rasdeter was watching General Aton riding away with his former life, he didn't see Saramis and the mother doe staring at each other.

Forgive me, mother, Saramis thought. I know I will pay for this one day.

As though she understood Saramis, the mother deer lowered her head to the burial mound of her fawn and rubbed her nose across it.

The thoughts of Saramis returned to the cave she shared with her orphaned charge. She sighed; she would have to bundle him in her clothes. Even dirty his garments marked him a child of high station or noble birth. She had an extra cloak; perhaps she could modify his robes by removing the more expensive strips of fabric. The stars outside the cave seemed to also remind her that she needed to get them both far away from anyone who might see the boy and recognize him.

When her eyes returned to him, he was looking at her. She instinctively held out her arms and first Rasdeter hesitated; as a prince he was not used to being touched by strangers. Then he quickly crawled around the fire and returned her embrace; he was shivering.

"What is your name, child?" she asked in the darkness.

He tried to look up at her. He'd been silent all day and now he remembered his manners.

"My name is Rasdeter. I'm a…"

"Shh…" Saramis interrupted him. "Don't tell me more than your name, Rasdeter, nor should you tell anyone else. I can see by your clothing that you are nobility, but it might cost me my life if I know how high you've been born."

She lightly stroked his dark curly hair.

"It will cost your life as well, so no matter who you meet, pray don't boast of it."

He smiled a bit at her reprimand, the first time since his parents vanished.

"All right," he said finally. "It's just so much to get used to, so soon…"

Rasdeter rested his head on her shoulder.

"I still can't believe that I'm alive…" he whispered, and promptly fell asleep, exhausted.

Saramis cradled his head and drew her cloak around them both; he sleepily draped his arm around her waist and returned to his dreams of his mother.

THE ONE WHO MOURNS HIM

"There are some who would say that without the control of the elite and their man-made laws, chaos would reign. That, however, implies that the only orchestrator is operating in the human realm, and that there are no higher laws governing the universe..."
~~~Dr. Carolyne Fuqua

News of the near fall of the House of the Far Isles roared through the Nine Kingdoms like a summer blaze. Shock followed shock as the official parchments were delivered to each ruler. King Valtus is dead? Oh no, by treason? Surely not Lord Altus, his brother? Now Queen Inka has died, and her child not yet born? Prince Rasdeter assassinated by High General Aton? Now, the General is executed?

By the kingdoms, who will be left to rule, a twelve-year-old boy?

Of all the news circulating the world, the news most disturbing to the mage known as Enith was the death of Prince Rasdeter. The child's life was crucial to one of many secret plans the mage needed to succeed. Enith knew of both the mages and entities that had circled Rasdeter's father Lord Altus like vultures. It seemed Valtus was the only man in his kingdom who did not know his brother Altus was in love with his wife the queen. Enith never dreamed the schemes of Altus would result in his death, nor did he care. It was Rasdeter he wanted to mold and influence, but there were two things all the mages on the planet could not anticipate; the movements of Lord Master Brayten and High General Aton. Unfortunately, the pair had cancelled each other out and now only young
~~~

Sumter was left to rule. And while a master creator protected him the boy king was untouchable.

Yet something did not sit well with Enith. The general had wisely acted completely alone, leaving no one to say for sure where the prince was buried. High Regent Polymus and Lord Brayten had acted in concert to ensure that the general was executed without delay, before the young king's sentiments could get in the way of his judgment. Which of course prevented the mage from getting someone close enough to the general to remove his memories.

Enith clenched his fist in frustration. He could not rid himself of the thought: Was the prince truly dead? Or cleverly spirited away by Lord Brayten for his own designs? No...Enith thought, he would not leave such an open threat to the throne of the Far Isles; Brayten was a friend of Valtus. His thoughts drifted to the former High General. No, Enith scoffed sadly, That man of war could not think in hues of grey. If Aton had a chance to slay Rasdeter, he did so.

The mage gazed down at the parchment in his hands.

What I would give to know for sure of your fate, child, Enith thought. You would have made a fine king, and an ally of magic.

As Enith dissolved the parchment, he noticed a man approaching him. There were many men walking in his direction, but the energy of this one was different; the man knew him. In curiosity, Enith waited. His garb marked him as a regent of some stature, but his air towards Enith was that of a servant and when he drew close enough to the mage he knelt in deference. This gesture of respect held back Enith's power and his natural inclination to vaporize anyone who directly approached him without permission.

"My lord," said the man with his head still bowed.

"Do I know you?" responded Enith cautiously.

"You know my father," replied the regent, who could not conceal his fear. Only a dead man couldn't feel the power emanating from the mage. At his words, Enith instantly began to scan him; he could see the DNA in his cells of a man who once served him.

"You are Roane's son," said Enith at last.

"Roane is my ancestor, if it please you my lord for so saying," replied the man quickly.

Enith started in shock at the truth of his words. His own life spanned millions of years, and most people seemed to live and die around him as insects lived and died among men.

"I am...pleased to speak with a descendent of a man who served me well," said Enith. "What is your will?"

The regent's trembling increased.

"My lord, I have come across information that may be of use to you and in the name of my forefather I have risked my life to approach you. My ancestor had your name and likeness inscribed on his tomb with instructions given that should we ever have something you needed that we were to render it without fail. Even if said actions were to result in you wiping his bloodline from the earth."

The mage drew his breath in sharply. He enveloped the regent and himself in a soundless barrier while he racked his brain for memories of a man so devoted to Enith that he would bind his own family with a blood oath. Roane's face finally floated before him and the memories of his unwavering devotion came with it. Enith remembered Roane's tomb because he fashioned it himself. He nodded absently; Yes, here was a man who had gained the mage's respect. He looked down at the regent.

"Stand up, regent," he said firmly. "Your forefather has earned your life through his. I will hear you out."

The regent stood up but kept his eyes on the cobbles at his feet. He wasn't certain if direct eye contact was disrespectful and found it intelligent to leave nothing to chance.

He cleared his throat.

"As great father Roane has always cautioned us, there are hundreds between me and this information. There is a minor servant of The Far Isles who came to know that the Boy King asked General Aton for the whereabouts of Prince Rasdeter's grave before his execution."

Enith felt like he suffered a blow to the chest. He couldn't breathe as the regent continued.

"King Sumter wanted the prince's body returned for proper burial. Weeks after Aton's death the king sent men to scour the region and find the remains. Beneath trees twenty miles from the palace of Lord Altus, the remains of a fawn slain with a sword were recovered."

Now the regent dared lift his eyes to see if his news found favor or if he should brace himself for death. But the Ancient was not looking at him, his gaze unfocused on the distance beyond them. The regent continued.

"To...to this very moment, my lord, the body of the prince has not been found..."

The regent's pupils widened as the mage looked through him. He was next astonished by the touch of Enith's hand on his shoulder.

"Do not fear death by my hand, regent, and distant son of my servant," said Enith in awe. "Roane has yet served me beyond the grave and I have no reward for you great enough."

The mage once again turned his glazed over eyes to the horizon.

"General Aton has outwitted us all."

A Matter of A Name

In the days following their retreat from the cave, Saramis headed swiftly north with her young charge, who had initially protested the change of his name.

"But, Saramis," Rasdeter said stubbornly, "'Rasdeter'...it's not an uncommon name, and all I have left..."

The one who saved him slowed her stride and stood in front of Rasdeter, blocking his path. Her voice though quiet, still carried across the line of trees.

"And how long then," she challenged him, "Before you forget your seemingly meaningless name carries no weight with the people around you, Rasdeter? How long before someone who should not be looking for you matches name with age, and face with resemblance to those who once loved you?"

"Loved me?" Rasdeter echoed fiercely as he met her eyes. "All who 'once loved' me are dead, Saramis! No one who cares for me remains..."

At this last statement, he turned from her, no longer able to meet her gaze as his mind brought forth an image of his cousin Sumter, now King of the Far Isles. He'd been certain of his cousin's affection up until a few weeks ago. Conflicted thoughts and emotions railed at him. As a prince of the realm, as General Aton referred to him, Rasdeter was not ignorant of the basic politics of his nation. Even as children, he and Sumter had discussed the policies that would interest a child, such as succession, military coups and of course, what would happen should either of them die before manhood. These were things they spoke of as children do who consider the future written in stone. They'd grown up mostly in peacetime, certain their parents would live to be old and grey before Sumter took the throne. Rasdeter might move up the ranks of the military himself, perhaps one day become High General or annex a neighboring kingdom under the protection of his powerful cousin. How naïve those past conversations seemed to him in this moment.

Rasdeter raised his eyes finally to meet those of Saramis, who was silently watching every emotion that crossed his face. What she thought she saw there Saramis gave no name to, she felt the child's secrets should remain his own.

"'Pax', is a name common to the region we travel to," she offered quietly. "The rest...you can simply choose...to not remember..."

He shrugged and walked past her.

* * *

Hours later they stopped again. The boy saw people on the road ahead of them but the young woman beside him did not urge him to hide or change direction. He thought perhaps she used her abilities to shield them from view until he noticed the man who rode in front of the others locked his gaze on him unwavering.

Rasdeter's breath caught as the group dismounted a respectful distance from Saramis. After a moment, another boy approached her with his head tilted down and held out his arms; Saramis gave him her basket and the pouches she carried. The prince felt his face burn; he had never offered her assistance. His ears began to register the words spoken around him.

"Affi-Saramis," said the man who led them, "Forgive this intrusion; you were expected days ago, and when you did not return..."

Saramis lifted her head slightly as she gazed at the man who respectfully lowered his gaze.

"I am not deceived by this display of concern, Bowman," replied Saramis, "I have no doubt the other Elders advised you that I was under no threat of harm."

The man before her flushed as he raised his eyes.

"They said," he began hesitantly, "That you were accompanied by a stranger..."

Rasdeter felt himself start as the man's eyes now bored into his. He looked to Saramis, who now approached and smiled at him.

"He is no stranger, Bowman," she replied fondly, "But one I found alone in the forests. He felt like a brother, and so now I bring him home."

"What is your name...brother?" asked the Bowman in a voice strained under the tones of civility.

But Rasdeter did not look at the man who clearly hated him as he responded. He kept his eyes on Saramis, whose pupils widened at his reply.

"My name...is Pax."

The Council of Pacine

Between the Nine Kingdoms and the road to the Unnamed Lands stood a small nation of little stature called Everet. The nation of

Everet was annexed by a much larger one, the Kingdom of the Bright Forest. The capital of Everet was the city of Pacine, a place of winding streets with stone buildings filled with windows. One of the older dwellings had large windows only at the top and inside a group of men milled about speaking quietly of various topics. The servants moved with a sense of urgency, no one wanted to remain in the room for long. Even the dullest of them could feel the low hum of radiation coming from the gathered men. Pacine was a neutral city for the practice of magic, therefore it was not unusual for powerful magicians to meet there.

A young sorcerer named Ashlan stood outside the tall building admiring its considerable age. The people walking the streets around Ashlan barely noticed as he vanished from sight. Not unlike the celebrity sightings of the present day, these people were used to the application of his craft. As long as Ashlan refrained from harming anyone, no one on the street would recall his actions.

It was Lord Enith who called the meeting. Armed with information regarding the possibility of the survival of the Prince of the Far Isles, he was eager to restart his plans to overrun the Nine Kingdoms and bring them under the sovereignty of magic. Though hundreds of mighty sorcerers attended, it was the Ancient Eridon whom Enith wished most to sway. Eridon had long ago lost interest in the schemes of his brothers for humanity. Some felt that despite his great power Eridon was too distant from the cares of life and perhaps risked the danger all truly old magicians faced: The madness of continual separation. But in the last few centuries the lonely Ancient had located Ashlan, a blood relative. A near child compared to his new and powerful protector, Ashlan's zeal and passion for life had revitalized Eridon and brought him back from the brink. In turn Eridon indulged his youthful prodigy and allowed Ashlan to convince him to participate in things he normally cared nothing about.

Lord Enith, however, found Lord Eridon's cousin a two-edged sword: Ashlan seemed a child with too many toys to play with.

His cousin Eridon smiled warmly as Ashlan entered the room. His affection for his much younger cousin was well known, and as an Ancient of great power, few who wished to continue breathing would dare correct Ashlan for his late arrival. The young sorcerer, who loved his elder cousin dearly was not arrogant or abusive; merely idealistic and careless, traits that could prove dangerous in a profession that required discipline and precision. The mage Enith, himself an Ancient as powerful as Eridon, narrowed his eyes at the young mage who took his place at his blood relative's side. Any other mage who dared enter the room without permission would have been vaporized for impertinence. Enith however, would have words with Eridon afterwards, lest subsequent meetings result in the unnecessary deaths of those foolish enough to follow the example of his protected kin.

"Come, brothers," said Enith as he drew the attention of the group.

All gathered in front of a huge wall where the drapery and pieces of artwork were removed. Enith displayed an image on the wall of a detailed map of the five major kingdoms of the Nine: The oldest, The Southern Arc, its brother, The Eastern Crest, the facing nations, The Western Hills and The Northern Walls, considered by many to be the protective arms of the kingdoms, and at the topmost part of the land mass, The Far Isles, sometimes referred to as the Apex Kingdom.

"You are currently looking gentlemen," continued Enith, "At five of the most powerful kingdoms on this planet. Not one of them is open to or supportive of the practice of magic."

The mages began to murmur amongst themselves but Enith held up his hand for silence.

"My lord," said one of the men respectfully, "Many of the regents of these kingdoms practice magic as a letter of law."

"Only as a preventive measure I can assure you," responded Enith. "Very few of these same regents accepts magic as a way of life. They only practice our craft to ensure that the use of magic is detected, not promoted."

"Then why not simply conquer these rich and prosperous nations?" asked another. "Surely they cannot have citizens of great ability if their skills are so elementary as to merely require protection of legal documents."

Sounds of amusement followed these words, yet most were quiet as they pondered why they had not more fully focused their efforts on such ripe fruit.

"Well said, brother," answered Eridon, "Yet you must ask yourself if this is truly the case, why weren't these kingdoms taken over long ago?"

To their combined looks of confusion Enith gave response.

"The reason is simple, my friends. Because these lands are protected by creators."

Voices rose and clashed from this statement.

"These so-called creators are few in number," protested one sorcerer.

"And rarely seen," said another.

"How is it that we dominate the whole world except for these nations, and these nations are the most powerful?" asked one in anger.

Enith stepped forward.

"Because though we are legion, it only takes one of them, perhaps two, to hold off thousands of us."

He turned to point again at the map.

"And the most powerful of them is Lord Master Brayten, who guards the greatest nation, the Kingdom of the Far Isles."

One of the older ones scoffed.

"How strong can he be, this Brayten, Lord Enith? Did not our schemes bring down the House of the Far Isles?"

"Strong enough to save the son of King Valtus," replied Ashlan quietly. "And to bring about the death of the one we pinned all our hopes on, the king's brother, Lord Altus."

"Lord Altus was never the true goal, Ashlan," said Enith resolutely. "It was his son and heir, Prince Rasdeter."

"Rasdeter, Lord Enith?" echoed Ashlan, "He was but a child..."

"One we could have influenced naturally, Ashlan," interjected Eridon, "Without the use of poison magic as some did his father. Rasdeter would have grown up accepting our cause, and once on the throne of the world's most prosperous kingdom, all the Nine would follow his vision, and the hated creators ousted for all time."

"Then we have failed," said one.

"Not yet," began Ashlan passionately, "If we can destroy--"

"Stop!" cried Enith, "Say no more!"

Power flared from Enith, and all mages except Eridon fell back. He stood between his impetuous cousin and Enith who could barely contain his rage. Ashlan had raised his arms in fear but Eridon calmly pushed the dangerous energies away from him.

"You know he did not realize what he was saying, Enith," offered Eridon quietly.

Ashlan was among a growing new group of young sorcerers who were tired of hiding from the creators and working in secret; they wished to confront them directly, in hopes of wiping them from the earth. Lord Enith was wise enough to know that if their plans failed, the creators could trace any connections by magic to anyone involved in their schemes. He wanted nothing to do with such plans, or any discussions of it; this too, can be traced. Hence the interruption of Ashlan before he could speak the master creator's name, which might link Enith forever to Ashlan's schemes.

One elder silently disappeared from the room; this was not his fight and for him the meeting was over. One by one the others took his lead and soon the chamber was empty except for Eridon, Ashlan and Enith.

"Why will you not discipline him?!?" asked Enith in frustration. "He would not last a moment in front of our master."

"He will never see him," responded Eridon firmly. "I ask you not to place such ideas in his mind."

Enith controlled himself with effort; he risked pointing his finger at Eridon, whose own power flared in response.

"He will be the death of you, Eridon," said Enith, "Ensuring that all our plans come to naught. Take the centuries necessary to train him properly; it would be a help to us all!"

"I am training him, brother," replied the Ancient. "It requires patience, like all things. You must restrain the urge to hurt him, I promise you he will learn in time..."

Enith shot one last withering glance at Ashlan whose eyes widened in dismay.

"You hold him as the only precious thing in the world, Eridon," said Enith finally. "But we all have something to lose in this battle..."

Eridon's own patience began to thin. His power darkened the room and Enith knew he had said more than anyone could say to Eridon. Wisdom was required on his part; it would do little good if the two of them wiped the last neutral city in Everet off the face of the earth.

"I have said it, Enith," Eridon whispered tightly. "He will *learn*..."
The two Ancients locked eyes as Enith slowly faded from sight.

* * *

As Enith walked down the pathways of the city of Pacine, in the realm of the Unnamed Lands, he felt a shimmering beside him and instantly he blocked it. A wall of dimensional light wedged between him and the sorcerer attempting to communicate with him. After a moment, an image projected itself on the walls of Enith's barrier and the ancient mage gritted his teeth in barely repressed rage. Ashlan's persistence to force a conversation with Enith revealed his ignorance and immaturity. As well as the recent memory of how Enith nearly had to battle Ashlan's cousin Eridon over the same manner of ignorance rubbed an already tender nerve.

"Make plain your intent, Ashlan," growled Enith. "Before I forget who protects you."

The young mage answered Enith in equally frustrated tones.

"I fail to understand your hostility towards me, Enith," Ashlan replied, "I'm only trying to share good news with you."

"You've nothing to say to me that I am willing to hear. How many times must I explain to you how dangerous it is for me or anyone not directly involved to know of your plans for Lord Brayten?"

Ashlan sighed before continuing.

"All right then, I won't speak of it, Enith. Though I do wish you would help me with convincing Eridon..."

Enith stopped on the road and faced the image of Ashlan.

"Your cousin loves you too much, Ashlan," said Enith tightly, "And you're a fool. If not for that same love, I would reduce you to vapor and free him from your thoughtless schemes. But then I would have to fight Eridon for centuries while he grieved for you, and I just don't have the time to spare. Whatever it is you're planning, let it go for once."

Ashlan made a dismissive sound.

"There's a new age of magic coming, Enith, even you should consider embracing it."

Enith swiftly raised his hands and hurled Ashlan and his image into another dimension, unmoved by his plaintive cries of distress. He practiced controlling his breath as he strode down the winding street. As much satisfaction as the impulse had given him, he knew it would cost him time when Eridon learned of it. Ashlan is like spoiled fruit, Enith fumed to himself. Cloyingly sweet on the surface and rotten near the pit. He does as he pleases because of his cousin's protection. An ancient mage and a powerful one, Eridon was wise in all places except where Ashlan was concerned.

Eridon never should have sought Ashlan out, thought Enith, though he understood why. No magician can survive millions of years alone without going mad as some Ancients do, fighting insanely anyone without protection who crosses their path. Enith's thoughts turned without fail to Lord Iroh, his own ally through the recent ages. Without Enith, Iroh himself would have died at the hands of such men, driven to madness by centuries of loneliness.

An image of Lord Master Brayten interrupted Enith's musings. He's a master channel and co-creator, thought Enith sadly, Currently the most powerful human on the planet. If they face him, they will die. I cannot make Ashlan see that no trace of his energy or tachyons can attach to me or Brayten will follow it back and all my own schemes will be undone.

Iroh will also die, and that I cannot allow.

Thus, I must continue my plans alone, much as Eridon would add to it. The cost of his aid would be too high.

Enith blasted away his barrier and all atoms surrounding it.

THE INITIATION OF PAX

*"If something is possible **at all**, it is possible **for all**..."*
~~~Lord Falquin

The child who was once a prince surveyed his new world with trepidation. These people he now traveled with he had never seen before, never knew existed. They called themselves 'The People' or 'Humans' if he pressed them and they were different from other wanderers familiar to his previous life. They were not the Lourdes clan he was happy to learn. His father Lord Altus had terrified him as a small boy with stories of their mysterious and brutal ways. Rasdeter, now called Pax, recalled how even on simple trips to the borders of his kingdom his father had surrounded his precious heir with thousands of men. Rasdeter had often watched the trees for those that did not sway easily in the breeze, a tell-tale sign that a Lourdes archer might lurk nearby, ready to darken the sky with deadly arrows.

No, these seemed a peaceful group that spoke a language he found difficult at times to follow despite his extensive training in many tongues. Pax sighed at the thought; yet another trait about himself he must hide to survive. His savior had turned out to be something of a leader among her people; Saramis stood off some distance from him apparently engrossed in a meeting of importance, possibly concerning him. Pax held the small bundle of belongings given him by Saramis against his chest as though it protected him. Watching the people moving around him with purpose, going about their tasks he felt lost. The life of a prince was filled mostly with studies
~~~

and training on how to develop the skills needed to one day rule men. Everything else was done for him. For the first time in his life, Pax had no idea what to do.

From the corner of his eye Pax noticed someone approaching; he turned from watching Saramis to see another boy like himself.

"Good morrow," said the child shyly.

Pax's face burned again; it was the boy who had manners enough to relieve Saramis of her burden. But his eyes held no reproach, only curiosity.

"My name is Atoli," offered the boy. He was about the same height as Pax and also slight of build. He noticed with a start that Atoli too, was slightly apprehensive as well; he was offering peace that he did not know would be received.

Pax blinked rapidly.

"Good morrow, Atoli," he said finally. "My name is Pax."

"I know..." replied the boy as he turned his head slightly as though wondering if Pax was slow in his thoughts. "You said so this morning..."

Pax suddenly grinned. This innocent banter reminded him of his playful conversations with his cousin Sumter and it was the first memory that was not accompanied by pain. His new friend Atoli returned this grin but when he reached for Pax's bundle, Pax turned his arms and bundle playfully away. Atoli quickly covered his mouth to keep from laughing aloud in surprise. He looked around, but no one was paying attention to their discovery of one another.

"Well," said Atoli, his eyes crinkling, "Unless you wish to smell like that tomorrow, you'd best follow me to wash."

It was Pax's turn to cover his mouth in pure delight, the fabric of his bundle hid all but his eyes.

The pair took several hesitant steps together, then as though they had the same thought, they looked behind them at the adults. When it was clear no one was watching them, they began to run;

laughing, pushing, and shoving each other and stopping frequently along the way to retrieve pieces of clothing left behind.

Although he never found out for certain, Pax was right; the impromptu meeting was about him. There was no question of him staying with the people; the stature of Saramis was above reproach in this regard. Her gifts, power and wisdom were considerable, despite her words to then Rasdeter that her talents were modest. Anyone she brought to the people could be trusted to remain among them. The discussion was about where he would dwell. Despite her station, Saramis was not a true Second Elder. She had merely completed her ritual of ascension to a Wise One of the Forest at an early age. Saramis was still considered a First Elder; her ceremony of transition to true Human was four years away. She was unbonded thus far by choice and had shown no interest in bonding with another Human. Kha, as Bowman and First Elder, had a voice in the council. He argued strongly that Saramis should remain alone in her tent until she bonded; he felt the boy was too old to live with her.

Saramis of course, disagreed.

"How old is he?" demanded Kha, then flushed as Saramis responded to this with an even look; the elders were silent.

"Forgive me, Affi-Saramis," he recovered quickly. "You know my concern is always for you, your welfare," he then stammered as he corrected himself.

"I do not know his age," Saramis answered truthfully. She thought of his boyish face, thin frame with no trace of pre-adolescent hair and yet childish voice and shook her head. "He's still a child, and my tent has many sections to it. There's no harm for Pax to dwell with me," she concluded as she met Kha's gaze directly.

He stared as though he searched her eyes for something; when Saramis tilted her chin upwards, Kha looked away.

"Is there anything the child could tell us?" asked a Second Elder gently.

"No," Saramis responded truthfully again, "I fear his identity was lost through trauma of some sort," she continued as her thoughts turned to the grief-stricken armored man by the tree. Her gaze focused on the gathered elders.

"I pray you allow Pax to remain with me for now. Shall we add to his grief by separating him further? Should we imitate the kingdoms and their disregard for the needy and destitute? Let him grow with us and remember his humanity; there's plenty of time, years even, before we place him among our men…"

"He should stay with me," Kha persisted. "There are things only a man can teach a boy."

"You are not kind to him," said Saramis bluntly, and the elders turned to gaze at Kha's flushed face. "All the boys who look his age are yet with their mothers. What would you do but make him fear to be among us?"

"Is this true, Bowman?" asked Zema, a Second Elder.

"Are you unkind to the child?" asked another.

Kha the Bowman resisted the urge to stare resentfully to the ground. He kept his eyes now on the elders, raised his chin and respectfully softened his gaze.

"I meant no dishonor to Affi-Saramis and our new brother," he said after breathing deeply. "All know my zeal to protect our people from the influence of civilizations."

Affi-Tosla, the Second Elder of Second Elders stepped forward and all fell silent.

"The child will stay with Affi-Saramis. Her heart is soft towards him and this is what he needs most of all. Are we in agreement?" Her sharp eyes locked on Kha, who caught his breath and blinked quickly.

"We are in agreement," he affirmed deeply, and a sigh rose from those assembled.

They began to disperse but Saramis felt a gentle wave of energy from Affi-Tosla and turned back to her. The pair walked the short distance to Affi-Tosla's tent. Once inside, they sat together in silence as the Second Elder heated stones and tossed fragrant lavender and seeds that hissed in the sudden darkness. Saramis felt her heart begin to beat rapidly. Though she told the truth as she knew it, she also knew there were no secrets from Affi-Tosla.

But the Second Elder's words made her clench her hands in her lap.

"You know it is Kha's desire to be bonded with you, Affi-Saramis," said Affi-Tosla quietly. "It is the true reason his heart cannot know peace."

Saramis lifted her head in the darkness staring at the fine particles of ash floating up and through the open top of the tent. Her chest trembled as she breathed.

"Great Mistress," she whispered, "I know of his feelings for me. But I am only fourteen summers to his sixteen and all I wish now is to perfect my works. Why does he press me so?"

The Second Elder placed seeds in her palm with her fingers and rolled them together to warm them before tossing them to the stones. Once the hissing subsided, she spoke again.

"Your heart is not his," she said finally, "And he knows this as men do. He cannot petition for you for another two summers and during this time, he will suffer and start at any threat to his happiness..."

Affi-Tosla stared at Saramis whose pupils widened without light.

"Do you understand me?"

Saramis shook her head; she could not consciously accept her mentor's words.

Affi-Tosla continued.

"Kha sees clearly where you do not."

The Second Elder sighed.

"Any man can see the boy is near puberty. He stands the same distance from you as you from Kha. Your affection for him now is maternal..."

Affi-Tosla's eyes now bored into Saramis, they could both see each other in the dim light.

"His voice will begin to change in six moon cycles. You have until then to move him."

Saramis's own voice was small as she replied.

"Yes, Great Mistress, let it be as you say."

As the silence between them deepened, Saramis slowly moved to leave the tent; the words of her mentor stopped her.

"You did not have permission to save him, Saramis," said Affi-Tosla quietly.

The hissing of herbs and seeds began again as Saramis covered her face and silently wept.

The Story of Ghent, Son of Roane

The regent who met with the ancient sorcerer Enith was still trembling when he reached his home in a rural area near the city of Pacine. Though a regent of some means, he preferred to live in the more forested areas, away from the larger cities. Some who did not know him were puzzled by his choices but the reason for it was quite simple. Over the centuries since his ancestor Roane's passing, the borders and growth of Pacine had shifted eastward and away from its more ancient roots. The forgotten tomb that Enith built for his servant Roane rested near the center of an old sprawling marketplace and Hall of Magicians from a thousand years ago. An ambitious king in the distant past built another more prominent building far away from where Enith held his disastrous meeting with his brethren. The proud descendants of Roane remained where their progenitor was buried and kept up the grounds. They built several estates, planted huge gardens and fountains around it. Many of them became regents so they could periodically return to the palace of The Bright Forest and remind the current court and king of the great service their ancestor Roane had rendered both kingdoms and their inhabitants.

Some of these family members in the distant past also learned magic, but the regent known as Ghent was more interested in the application of the law and the letters that formed it. He listened with interest to his father's tales growing up of the adventures of Great Father Roane, even imagined himself growing up to be a powerful sorcerer. But his introduction to law instantly captured his heart. Ghent spent hours poring over the works of men who set up the standards and principles that governed the kingdom and debated endlessly with other young men of letters into the night. His father Ordant sighed at this and focused on his other children; at least Ghent would keep a roof over their heads when he was no longer able to.

Ghent's father was part of a society that kept watch for any developments that might be of interest to mages and sorcerers, thus it fell to Ghent to approach Enith when the House of the Far Isles did not fall as intended. His father, now aged, had taken his son to Roane's tomb to remind him of his duties. Ghent listened to this now old tale with respect and a growing sense of fear. It was all well to speak of a mage millions of years old with power beyond reckoning; it was another thing altogether to approach him. As eldest, Ghent would approach Enith first. If the mage vaporized him, his father would send his offspring one by one to render service and if unsuccessful, at last himself, barely able to walk, to accept the fatal blow.

The reality was not nearly so romantic as the story. The regent considered himself a brave man, but this task was among the things that fools do before dying. Ghent had been beside himself, offering every prayer he knew as he sought out the Ancient.

Ghent was shocked that the mage had even allowed him to speak, but it was his deference that gave the mage pause. To kneel to Enith was easy for Ghent; his knees were shaking so badly at the display of the sorcerer's power that Ghent could barely stand. Yet it was Enith's scan of Ghent's DNA that saved his life. Once the mage released him, the regent quickly made his way home. There was a part of him that doubted he yet lived; from time to time he looked down at his sandaled feet and touched his robes to be certain as he returned to his estates.

But Enith had been greatly moved by the devotion of Roane's family. It stood out in contrast to the disappointing lack of vision displayed by Ashlan, a promising sorcerer hampered by his over-protective cousin Eridon. Had Ashlan been as diligent as Roane, thought Enith, He and Eridon would make an unbeatable force for magic. Yet Enith had to admit that it was Ashlan who brought back Eridon's will to live. Without Ashlan, only loneliness and inevitable madness were in Eridon's future.

Unaware of these things, Regent Ghent entered his home, immediately overrun by his children who could not restrain themselves, despite the pleas of their mother.

"By All Things Good," she cried out, "Can you not allow your father to enter and be seated?"

But after Ghent's close brush with death, he was more than happy to be mobbed by his treasures. He gathered the two smallest ones to his chest, Iason and Midlin, enjoying their squealing and squirming. His eldest son Carn wrapped his arms around his father's waist and received a tussling of his hair for his efforts. Round they went, a tangle of arms and legs until Ghent found his seat, laughing loudly as his little ones pummeled him with love.

"Have you any sweet reeds, father?" asked his youngest son Iason as they searched the pockets of his robes, drawing a stern reprimand from Dru, their mother. Ghent looked up at her as though drinking in the sight of her, causing her to pause and blink rapidly. Dru had no doubt her husband loved her, but after three children and a huge estate to run, it was gratifying to see him gaze at her thus every once in a while.

She had no idea just how happy Ghent was to see her and their children.

He nuzzled the neck of his smallest, drawing a delighted squeal, then set her down and roughly grabbed his eldest son to tickle and wrestle to the floor, causing the other two to pounce in abandon on his back. Dru covered her cheek and shook her head in resignation at his apparent madness, then signaled to her servants that supper would have to wait until the battle died down.

Later that evening, once his exhausted children were well-fed and sound asleep, Ghent made sure that Dru felt appreciated and loved. Drowsy and warm, she placed her head against his chest as he drew the covers over her. The regent shared his day with his wife, unconcerned that she was almost too heavy eyed to hear most of what he said. He spoke in soft tones as he brushed her brow with his fingers and stroked the hair behind her ears.

Dru repeated her question as Ghent lightly pressed his lips to hers.

"Husband," she murmured from a faraway place, "What if this sorcerer requires your services again?"

Regent Ghent sighed with a heavy heart. He looked about their spacious rooms as though he never fully noticed it before. Now the tapestries stood out in vibrant color on the windows; every drop of condensation on the water pitcher was precious and unique. He gazed down at Dru, who was fast in dreams and answered her.

"Then I must go and do all he asks of me, up to and including my life."

Ghent watched the candles in the room burn down until the room darkened. Eventually, he slept.

The Answered Question Unspoken

Affi-Tosla was not given to walking randomly among the people; she mostly kept to her tent. Sighting her outside of a council was a rare event. Though she shunned no one the people did not approach her without permission. All knew the work she did among them was important; she was not given to idle conversation. Her tent was smaller than even the least of the wise ones, yet no one questioned why. If you were invited inside, any thoughts you entertained about the size and circumference of her dwelling were dispelled to the point you could not speak of it.

On a rare day, the Second Elder was seen in the general area. Saramis and Pax were passing through on their way to pick herbs and fruit for meals. Pax had insisted on carrying the baskets. Saramis had smiled without comment; she remembered his reaction when Atoli first approached her. She listened now to his words.

"I confess, Saramis," Pax said quietly, "I had no idea the care and feeding of people entailed so much labor..."

As his mentor chuckled to herself, his gaze drifted beyond the people passing them and met those of Affi-Tosla who stood in the center of the general area alone. He stopped and when Saramis noticed the subject of his gaze, she reacted with alarm.

"Pax," she said as she took his arm, "You must not stare at her..."

But he could neither hear, nor feel her restraint. It seemed all sound around Pax ceased and all the people faded. Affi-Tosla did not turn from his eyes and the people began to notice. Soon an empty space was between them and Saramis looked to the Second Elder in dismay.

In the ensuing gathered quiet Affi-Tosla opened her arms to Pax.

Without hesitation he dropped his baskets and ran to her, hugging her tightly. The people sighed as Affi-Tosla returned his embrace and kissed his dark curly hair. This was a great blessing. Bowman Kha stood rigid as he beheld the gift; a small girl standing beside him watched wide eyed. Unconsciously she removed her thumb from her mouth and wiped it on her robe; she would never suck her thumb again.

The Great Second Elder felt warm to Pax; the beating of her heart soothed him like nothing before it; he raised his head to look at her again.

"Mother..." he said it without thinking. The ones who heard him caught their breath collectively and began to murmur and look at each other.

Affi-Tosla stroked his face as his eyes brimmed.

"So..." she replied kindly, "It appears you are not completely asleep..."

She looked up and across the space to Saramis who came quickly.

"We will initiate him without delay," Affi-Tosla said to the stunned gathering, "His soul has asked for it..."

The rest she said directly into the mind of Saramis.

The part of him that knows is ready, Saramis, but now that you have taught him to forget who he is, we must wait until the remainder unfolds.

Becoming Human

"Who is she, Atoli," asked Pax, "...and what is an initiation?"

When his name was Rasdeter, Prince of the Far Isles, he attended his first King's Summit with his father, Lord Altus at the age of nine. His uncle King Valtus went every year and on this year, he brought his own son and heir Prince Sumter, Rasdeter's cousin. Though the boys were excited, for a great part of the trip they were mostly subdued. This event marked the beginning of their training for manhood and the future leadership of men. It would end when they both demonstrated mastery of politics, languages, education, and weaponry. Rasdeter would receive from his father a sword forged uniquely for him, as would Sumter. The difference being that upon ascending his father's throne, Sumter would also inherit a legendary sword handed down through generations, the Legacy Sword of the House of the Far Isles.

It was the only ritual for manhood Pax knew of, and his father had died before giving Rasdeter the sword. There were also rings, fine robes and a smaller crown that marked his station in life, things left behind when young Prince Rasdeter mounted a horse and rode off with General Aton to find his parents.

"Are you remembering something, Pax?" asked his friend kindly. Pax had drifted off in memory, and Atoli's words disrupted the illusion in his mind of the chest in his father's rooms that held his inheritance.

Pax looked up at his friend with eyes that glistened.

"It's gone..." he answered truthfully.

Atoli patted his friend's shoulder in sympathy.

"Her name is Affi-Tosla," said Atoli, "She is the Grand Elder of all elders, both First and Second. She has dedicated her life to us, and all living things."

Atoli appeared to lose himself in thought as he gazed around the tent he shared with Pax and other boys who were of the age of training to be warriors. He watched the sunlight streaming through the flaps, spilling light on the simple beds the boys slept on.

"She's always been here for us," Atoli continued quietly, "I feel sometimes that even once she has left us and returned to Source, she will remain in our hearts..."

Pax was respectfully silent as he waited for Atoli to speak again.

"She will show you what it means to be human," he said after a moment.

Atoli shrugged and smiled at his friend's puzzled expression.

"It is something you already know, but have forgotten; that's why we call it an initiation..."

He clapped Pax shoulder again and came to his feet.

"What you choose after that is up to you."

His Father's World

As the boy who was once a prince waited for his initiation ritual to begin, young Pax stirred uncomfortably in his new robes. The fabric, though plain was very fine to the touch; the child marveled at how it rivaled in quality the clothes he was used to wearing. He pulled gently at his sleeves and smiled to himself. If the colors were different, brighter perhaps, he could pretend he was back home and his mother the princess would chide him to hurry, as she often did when his father returned for the evening.

Pax thought of his father Lord Altus and blinked rapidly. The general never told him why his father slew his only brother, the king. And Pax didn't know why his father killed his mother. Did he also slay Queen Inka, his aunt, while heavy with child? Had some horrible affliction possessed him? If Pax had gone with his father and mother on that fateful day, would his own father have slain him as well?

These actions didn't match up with the man he remembered. Pax knew his father loved his mother, loved him. What changed him?

He looked up to see his new friend Atoli smiling at him. Behind Atoli stood Saramis, her gaze compassionate and gentle. Pax flushed and tried to return their hopeful offering. His mind turned to the woman who had held out her arms to him; who he'd unconsciously run to. He felt peace in her embrace; a peace he thought he would never feel again. These were his people now. They wanted him, accepted him and that was all that mattered.

"I'm ready," he whispered.

Remembering the Hidden Sun

Pax remembered very little of his initiation into the tribe called Human. Near twilight, Atoli led his friend into a large tent, followed by Saramis. Inside, the elders were gathered, both First and Second; behind them and through a second flap leading outside stood his new people, the Humans.

Atoli explained to Pax that children are considered closest to the Source of Creation when born. All children who show both interest and promise are invited to become First Elders, where they will learn mastery over the four lower bodies (the physical, emotional, mental and the intellectual) and speak in the council. Second Elders are those who have given their lives to the spiritual advancement of all people living, and once they reach a certain age they are now closest to the return to Source, hence the title Second Elder.

Pax listened to these explanations wide-eyed. His previous world was completely different. The only thing his father was concerned about was the physical and the mental; how to train his child and himself on how to rule over other men. Pax was educated in languages, numerical equations, science, even philosophy. But he knew what his friend Atoli spoke of was beyond anything his education had prepared him for.

The voices of the elders brought Pax crashing back to the present moment.

"Child of the cities," began one of the elders, "You can only be among us because you are ready to."

"And you can only see us because you want to," said another.

"This is a path anyone can find," said the smallest elder, "And you can leave us when it so pleases you. But if you stay, it is because you are called to."

Looking from face to face of those speaking, Pax tried hard to follow what was being said. Was he supposed to respond, he thought in panic, What was he to say?

"Yet only you will know if any of this is true for you," stated Affi-Tosla. She stepped forward and Pax's heart began to beat quickly.

"We are the people called Human," she said firmly. "We only exist to remind mankind of what all people have turned their backs on. As such we have no creed but peace and the universal laws all things are governed by. We were born to create universes, yet most men you see only feed the concerns of the lower nature: Lust, greed, envy, sloth, anger, covetousness, and pride. Do you understand me?"

Pax thought of his father and his eyes tightened as he gazed at Affi-Tosla.

"Yes..." he whispered.

"You have recognized me, one called Pax," said Affi-Tosla, "By calling me 'Mother'. By these words I honor your soul's request, and offer this, a way to rise above your baser nature, the only inheritance you have in this world."

The child locked his gaze on the older woman as his emotions of loss hammered at him.

"Do not despair," she said kindly to the tears in the boy's eyes, "If your parents knew these things, they would have taught you. But you can refuse it..."

Affi-Tosla now stepped back and turning, she pointed to the flap of the tent behind them.

"Through that opening stands the People, fellow humans like yourself. You may join them and be initiated on the path they walk on the journey to the higher plains. Or you may stay here and return through the door you came in from. You will remain among us and be loved by us, no matter what you choose..."

Without hesitation the boy called Pax walked to the door flap Affi-Tosla indicated and stepped through.

The Initiate

Once outside, Pax was told to lie down on several blankets and when he lifted his eyes upwards all he beheld were stars and planets that seemed close enough to touch. A fire was burning; he smelled citrus and herbs.

A First Elder spoke into the gathering twilight.

"Whose child is this?"

Saramis stepped forward.

"He has neither father nor mother; his life has no beginning to us, and unknown is his end. I will be sister to him and speak for his blood..."

"You have no children, Affi-Saramis," said another First Elder, "How will you vouch this? What will bind him?"

Reaching up into her bound hair, Saramis removed a strand and taking a blade, she cut it and dropped it into a bowl held by a Second Elder filled with herbs, roots, river water and citrus.

"This hair has been nourished by my blood; it will hold and second him."

"What will be his name among us?" asked another.

Affi-Saramis took a deep breath.

"Among the Humans," she said, "Also called, "The People", he shall be known as...Pax."

The people began to sway back and forth, then they moved along in concentric circles around each other in a wider circle, imitating the rotation of planets and their satellites around Pax as though he were a central Sun. They began to hum softly, and the combination of their voices caused the ground beneath Pax to vibrate.

Second Elder Zema placed the bowl on a pitted fire dug into the ground. Once hot enough, she dipped her fingers into it as it glowed from the flames. The glyphs that were etched on the sides of the bowl blazed with yellow light; the symbols followed his eyes into the night sky above him and whirled around the planets. The elder smeared a thick mixture of the herbs and roots onto his forehead, forming the four directions.

It made Pax feel sleepy; he heard Affi-Tosla chanting from somewhere.

"You are Human. When the Great Breath touches flesh it is quickened..."

The Great Elder seemed to be everywhere at once, Pax murmured incoherently and stopped when he felt Saramis touch his arm.

Her eyes Pax remembered. Saramis was looking at him and Pax had a moment where he felt certain he had known her before; long before he met her in the forest on his father's estates. His heart thumped wildly; it was true, he knew it. He stared at her then, with all the love in his heart, lifetimes of it, and watched the pupils of her eyes widen. She moved away from him and Pax heard again the comforting sounds of Affi-Tosla chanting.

"When you call to What breathes you, It answers..."

The people began to circle Pax; they chanted blessings as they removed flowers, leaves, small stones, and seeds from another bowl and covered him with it. Even Kha's eyes softened as he laid a small white stone over Pax's heart and gave him the blessing of the people. He tried to hold Pax's gaze and for a moment the boy saw an infinite sadness; his own eyes brimmed. Then it appeared Kha faded into Atoli; and Pax began to weep again as he felt the heart love of his cousin Sumter in Atoli's loving eyes. Atoli covered Pax with a handful of leaves; he whispered a blessing and touched Pax's lips with two fingers. The elders did the same; their fingers sent a bolt of fire through his body and Pax relaxed against his blankets.

"What you have Forgotten, you will one day Remember..."

Affi-Tosla did not touch Pax; she stood over him and spread her arms. When she lifted her arms upwards, Pax followed them. He felt his body leave the ground and vault to the sky where he slowly rotated above the people while they chanted. The constellations moved with him, in the direction of an ancient sundial, speaking sacred things he would not recall except in his deeper dreams.

"And when you Remember, you will dance on many planets, and the Sun will be your Heart..."

He saw the Sun, he was holding it, and when it sank into his chest, Pax fell asleep.

The Remembrance

When Pax woke up, it was morning. He still felt drowsy; his eyes opened to find Saramis kneeling beside him. She was quietly wiping the herb mixture from his forehead and rinsing it away in a small bowl. Atoli stood behind her, holding the robe from his friend's initiation against his chest. Atoli had dressed Pax in his usual robe while Saramis waited outside. He breathed deeply in relief as Pax's eyes opened; it was a good sign that Pax came back with the morning light. As a newcomer, Atoli was concerned that the initiation was too much for his civilized friend; he was greatly comforted when Pax met his gaze.

"Do you remember anything?" Saramis asked gently and drew his eyes to hers.

Pax tried to answer her question, but a different response came out.

"Why do they call you Affi-Saramis?" he murmured, and Atoli covered his mouth in amusement as he thought of the herbs an elder had rubbed into Pax's skin.

Saramis smiled at his sleepy request.

"It is a title, Pax," she responded, "Given to the wise ones and the Second Elders, mostly. 'Affi' means 'uniting a common means', an 'affinity' between Life and Spirit... Simply an acknowledgement of the work I've done among our people."

She paused at the look in his eyes. It was not the gaze of a child. Pax spoke from another place.

"I remember you, Saramis," he whispered, "I've always remembered you..."

Before either of them could react, Pax drifted back into his dreams where the Sun waited for him.

The Death of Eridon

Magicians do not sleep in their robes. Magic is a practice, a profession even, but it is not everything in a mage's life; even they are called to do mundane things, such as live in an ordinary dwelling, and sleep. After millions of years, Enith obtained many homes, some by magic, some by gifts from nations that sought his favor, and some purchased with the coin of the realm. Thus, it came about that the mage was sleeping in one of these homes, perched on the summit of a mountain, a favorite place.

Enith suddenly came to his feet with a shout, but this sound went unheard as the mountain he slept on shook to its foundations from a blast heard across the hemisphere. Wrapping his bedclothes about him, Enith ran to the nearest window facing what seemed to be the origin of the devastation. Millions of years old, Enith was an Ancient not easily impressed, but even he gasped at the rearrangement of the line of great mountains running from southwest to where he stood. Instantly, the mage took himself back in time to view the blast from the beginning and watched in awe as a great blinding light met the coursing power of thousands of magicians. He looked to his right as the massive roof of a building hurled through the air and smashed into a nearby mountain, blowing a huge hole clean through it. The tons of earth of this mountain shuddered but held its new formation.

Enith knew that a great meeting of thousands of sorcerers had transpired at the Hall of Mages in the Kingdom of the Far Isles, one he had no intention of attending or supporting. He also knew that the Ancient Eridon also, had refused to attend. His heart began to beat rapidly; Enith did not need magic to know that every magician in that building was dead. He knew the deadly signature of Lord Master Brayten. The mage had warned Eridon that if he faced the powerful creator, he would die.

"What fools..." The mage whispered with heat, his heart filling with unaccustomed sorrow. He didn't always agree with Eridon, but Enith had fondness for him; long had Enith feared he would one day find the Ancient frozen in time on a hill or mountainside like so many before him.

Suddenly, Enith's eyes widened in alarm.

"Ashlan..." the mage recalled that Eridon's favorite cousin had sworn to attend. He turned his face from the flashing skies, his mind whirling. Did he dare to use magic to see for himself? Breathing deeply, Enith waved his hand across the earth and skyline and a faint light pulsed near the crest of the devastated hill leading down to the pierced earth. The mage raised his arms and his outer robes appeared and covered him. Seconds later, Enith vanished from his house.

After scouring the mountains by way of magic, Enith found Eridon standing on a hill facing the now destroyed Hall of Mages. Enith blinked rapidly, the changes in his old friend were profound; the life had left his eyes, and he stood with his arms at his side unmoving, though his robes billowed gently about him.

Enith followed Eridon's line of sight; he was staring at the epicenter of the blast miles away, whereby using magic, Enith could make out the form of a small child sitting in the midst of dissipating radiation. A man, probably a minor regent, stumbled along blinded through the wreckage; the child ignored him. There was no sign of Lord Brayten, yet Enith knew the creator was supposed to be in the Hall with the magicians. The two Ancients stood in silence for a time while the twilight deepened.

Then the child vanished.

Eridon did not react to this development; he remained unmoving; his gaze vacant. Eventually, Enith chanced a word with his silent friend.

"Ashlan..." said Enith, by way of a question more than a statement.

Eridon did not respond for a moment; then finally he took a shuddering breath and spoke.

"You were right..." Eridon began, his voice cracking, and Enith felt his chest constrict in sympathy. Tears began to stream down the face of the Ancient, and now Enith felt dread.

"I should have--" Eridon's breath caught in mourning, then he forced himself to continue. "I should have taken him away to train him; isolated him from others, until he could learn discernment--"

Lord Enith felt his own chest collapse at this confirmation of Ashlan's demise.

"Eridon," Enith said in pain, "I cannot share how regretful I am for you..."

However vehement the mage had been during the Council of Pacine, this was not something Enith wanted to be right about. He too, hoped that Eridon would eventually rein in his wayward protégé and show him the ways of wisdom in his craft. Like Eridon, Enith also believed the Ancient's power could protect Ashlan, but that was only if he stayed away from the only thing his powerful older cousin could not shield him from, Lord Brayten. Creators did not seek out magicians to destroy them, that was not their way. But if you attacked them, few would hesitate to unleash their ability to turn a magician's own power against them.

"But..." Eridon continued with slumped shoulders, "I was so fascinated by him. Ashlan was so full of light, and foolish ideas. I wanted him to enjoy his life; I thought I could protect him..."

"Come with me, Eridon," said Enith gently, "We can decide what to do from a safe place. Come with me now..."

But the Ancient shook his head sadly.

"She will find me," Eridon responded with a sigh. "She must find me; my love for him is too strong. I will not move from this place."

Eridon turned his head slightly to gaze upon Enith's grief.

"You should go, Enith," said the Ancient. "It would not do for her to find us together. In her grief, she may not distinguish the lack of intent in you..."

Enith saw the wisdom in this; he said one thing more as he vanished.

"I will mourn you, Eridon," he said sadly, "Possibly for centuries..."

But Eridon was not concerned with Enith's grief, or the grief of any others. He locked himself on the hill, which trembled from the power beneath his feet. Soon he would remember the cave behind him, but for now he focused on his cousin Ashlan's fiery grave.

You know nothing of grief, yet...thought the broken mage. I will wait an eternity for her if need be.

Tears came back to his eyes as he thought of Ashlan.

And then I will give her the keys to death and destruction, and fling wide the gate to escort all of you in.

A TRIBE CALLED HUMAN

"We were created to be an organic whole, each one of us resonating a certain frequency on a particular ray. Together, we are a living rainbow, expressing all the possible colors and sounds harmoniously..."
~~~Dr. Carolyne Fuqua

The year that Saramis marked sixteen summers Bowman Kha petitioned to bond with her in her eighteenth year. Eighteen was considered by the people to be a year of possible mastery over the four lower bodies: The physical, the emotional, and the mental, with the last one, the intellectual, occupying the lower realm of the heart. On the other side of this was the higher heart and the pathway to ascension. This made the eighteenth year of life an ideal time to bond with another and begin the Initiation of the Battle for the Heart. The petition was a lengthy process, and because Saramis was already a wise one of the forests she did not require permission from her parents who lived with another tribe months away.

Saramis could speak for herself and she asked to remain unbonded.

Normally this ended the petition but Kha requested his right to an answer or explanation. If there were another one that Saramis wished to bond with, Kha had the option to face this other in debate or single combat. Most males chose combat. Even then Saramis, as a wise one, could still decline the bonding. But that would leave her unable to bond with anyone else if Kha did not eventually choose another. If there was no one else that Saramis wished to bond with, she faced the decision to remain single the rest of her life. This was
~~~

not a bad thing; there were many among the wise ones who did not choose to bond. The energies of the lower body organs were merely channeled into the higher regions near the lungs and heart; it made them more powerful. It was another way to protect the people and maintain a higher vibration for the planet, so it would not be so easily overrun by the lower vibrations of survival and greed.

These principles did not comfort Saramis as she waited for the council to summon her. Telling her childhood friend that she did not love him was a thankless task. She knew Kha well, he would not accept her words of non-affection. She could not fathom why he saw fourteen-year-old Pax as the threat to his happiness and not her lack of intimate feelings for him.

Her thoughts of Pax made her sigh. He looked a child to her still, she was unable to see past his lanky frame and thin, boyish face. Despite his efforts to bind his unruly dark hair back from his fore-head, a strand always managed to escape and make him look even younger. It was possible that Saramis did not realize that she had locked this image of him before her eyes as he grew; it prevented her from seeing the changes in Pax that everyone else, especially Kha, could not fail to notice. Sometimes Saramis felt older than her sixteen summers.

For his part, as Pax grew from a boyish twelve summers to a more adolescent fourteen summers, his initial puzzlement at Kha's hostility towards him began to make some kind of sense. Saramis called Pax 'little brother', and the way she carried herself from the beginning had made her feel older to him, so he watched Kha's misery with the amusement that only an awkward teenager would. Pax missed few opportunities to torture Kha with his seemingly unlimited access to Saramis. Pax sought her out for the most trivial of needs and requests; things he could easily figure out on his own. Bowman Kha watched these antics with narrowed eyes and clenched fists.

One day Pax's playful foolishness backfired. He entered Saramis' tent unannounced, idly thinking of what he should say today to get her attention and annoy Kha. He'd seen Kha in the distance accompanied by others, no doubt heading in her direction; it was another opportunity to have a little fun at the older man's expense.

"Saramis?" he called out; but heard no response. Pax could not say later why he walked toward the first flap in her tent, dividing the common area from the space beyond and pulled it back, but he would never forget what happened next:

Saramis wore her official robes, with tiny shells that glanced the sunlight. She was kneeling before a small fire preparing herself for a ritual. A young girl was lovingly stroking her thick hair as she began the process of binding it in ropes that she would wind around Saramis' head. A long strip of fabric hung over her arm, ready to finish the process.

Pax had never seen Saramis's hair unbound. As a wise one she kept it wrapped like many others; it was not required, but she preferred to wear it thus. Now it spilled in beautiful, fluffy waves of dark brown ash; and as she turned to meet his eyes the sun blasted the red gold colors trapped beneath the brown.

His jaw dropped.

"You're a goddess..." he whispered, awestruck.

Before Saramis or the younger First Elder could respond, all heard a deep clearing of Kha's throat behind them. They both looked past the flustered Pax to see the Bowman with a contingent of elders. But Pax could not tear his eyes from Saramis until he heard the barely concealed anger in Kha's voice.

"So..." the Bowman said deeply, "You see her now with a man's eyes..."

Kha now looked past Pax to Saramis, who returned his gaze with distress. She knew full well what Kha would do with this situation with elders to witness. When Kha looked again to Pax, he could see clearly that the boy understood him and also realized in the same moment that Pax had never understood him before. The look behind the boy's eyes changed along with his disturbed innocence.

Kha nodded to this and spoke again with authority he knew would be unchallenged; he heard the murmuring of the elders behind him.

"And as a man," Kha continued firmly, "You will never enter her tent again alone or without permission. She is a wise one, and you will treat her with the respect of a man, and not a child."

Pax blinked rapidly as he swallowed with difficulty.

"Let it be as you say," he agreed hoarsely.

The elders made way for Pax as he exited the tent with haste, his face burning. He faintly heard Saramis calling out to him, but he knew better than to turn back. Kha watched with satisfaction as the figure of his future rival grew small in the distance.

* * *

Pax avoided Saramis for days after this incident; he was embarrassed beyond words. The sight of her now made him uncomfortable and too aware of himself. His robes seemed to never be arranged correctly; the urge to fidget in her presence made Pax want to run for the trees. The nights were worse, no matter how he tossed and pulled at his covers he could not remove the image of her sunlit hair, the flecks of dark satin in her warm brown eyes. His voice frequently cracked when he tried to share his dismay with Atoli, his fast friend.

"What's wrong with me, Atoli?" Pax lamented, "I don't understand myself anymore. She's my mentor, isn't she? She shouldn't look..." he gulped awkwardly, "I don't know...beautiful to me, should she?"

Atoli scoffed with the air of a young man who thinks himself much older.

"She's only two summers older than you, Pax," he reasoned. "Saramis just dresses herself like the older wise ones so the people will take her more seriously."

Atoli shrugged before continuing.

"It is her great power that has earned her place. She dresses older... What of it? Do you care for her?"

Pax shook his head vehemently, then covered his eyes with his fingers pressed firm against his face.

"I can't think about that, I can't think about that," he chanted. "Oh, I'm so regretful I walked into her tent, Atoli. I just wanted to irritate Kha; he's such a dark cloud about her..."

"Well, you may not have to worry about it," confided his friend, "Kha has petitioned to bond with Saramis when she reaches her eighteenth summer..."

Atoli continued speaking but Pax heard nothing else. He removed his fingers from his eyes and stared blankly at them. Kha wants to bond with Saramis? Like a husband? Like...

Reaching a level of misery, he could neither understand or put words to, Pax came to his feet and walked away from his suddenly puzzled friend.

* * *

Enith and the Child of Prophecy

Not long after the demise of the Ancient known as Eridon, the mage known as Enith found himself walking the roads of the Kingdom of the Western Hills late at night. He wasn't certain what had drawn him to this particular realm, but it was his way to wander the Nine Kingdoms late in the evening, searching his mind for ideas to bring about their collective downfall.

The Western Hills earned their name for the mountainous region and the great rolling hills that both surrounded and ran through it. Many roads gently rose to steep heights and then sloped downward; it was not unusual for a hill to appear to drop off a ledge in the distance. This made travel through the nation a slow one for caution; those unfamiliar with the trips and turns of the road could come to harm in the evenings of a new moon.

These warnings did not apply to an Ancient, of course. Enith walked these roads easily no matter what the day or night might bring. His steps were sure as he almost glided on the winding dirt road beneath him. Nor did he fear any men of ill purpose who waited behind grassy hills on the path; it amused him for those too dull of their senses to realize the power that coursed through his form. Any foolhardy enough to leap from the shadows soon learned there was much to fear in the darkness; neither knife, sword, or arrow could pierce the mage's defenses, and daylight often revealed charred and blasted corpses to morning travelers.

Often Enith passed other magicians on the way. Were he or she an Ancient, Enith would incline his head towards the mage in a respectful manner and receive the same. Sometimes a discourse would ensue or not, it depended on the needs of the moment. If the mage were not an Ancient, Enith would generally ignore their existence, this being a boon to both parties. However, if said mage did not offer Enith a bow or gesture of respect for his power, as he or she passed him, one of two things would follow: Either Enith would vaporize the ignorant mage on the spot, or Enith could send a bolt of power through the mage's bloodline to his mentor. If the mentor were strong enough to withstand such a blow, the pupil would be severely chastised upon his return. If not, the confused mage would return home to a pile of smoking dark grey ash, and the horrid prospect of finding another protector. No easy feat since all would know how he or she came to be in such a vulnerable position to begin with.

That said, it was Enith's way to perform the latter action. Vaporizing a rude mage was seen by him as the easy way out, without a sure lesson learned. Also, this served to retain respect for the power of the Ancients, they were already too many stories circulating of ancient mages creating trees of themselves in the forest. People needed to remember why they were feared to begin with.

These were among the thoughts Enith mused on as he neared the top of a steep hill. He noticed the light approaching him on the opposite side distractedly, it was not uncommon for an Ancient to reveal himself as such late at night; it was an encouragement to avoid him.

But all such musings left Enith in a rush as he felt not the familiar hum of radiation coming from the small, illuminated figure approaching on his left, but a power of such light it seemed the sun itself would yield to it. In terror, Enith flattened himself to the grassy wall of the hill beside him. He'd instinctively tried to flee and found himself blocked on all sides and bound to the earth.

A small child came into view, a female of barely nine years. She wore robes of light blue, that seemed almost white in the light that surrounded her. Fluffy, soft waves of amber brown hair floated around her face and past her shoulders. If one believed in ghosts or angels she appeared so, yet there was nothing about her power that spoke of worlds unable to affect the physical. As she turned amber gold eyes upon the Ancient, his own widened; he recognized her.

"The Dark One..." he whispered, and the child smiled.

"Amusing, is it not, for men to refer to me thus," she said as light filled the countryside, "Yet I suppose I understand it to be a metaphor for what I can do to magicians..."

Enith did not respond to this as he thought of her other name, 'The Destroyer.'

The mage stiffened as he felt The Dark One scan him; she was holding back her might, so she wouldn't annihilate him in the process; Enith blinked rapidly.

"Enith," she said at last, "You were on the hill with Eridon after my father died."

The Ancient found his voice.

"I did not--" he began, but the child smiled again at him, a corner of her mouth lifted, and he fell silent.

"I know you had nothing to do with Lord Brayten's death, mage," responded the child, "It is the only reason you're still breathing..."

The child, whose secret name was S'ateegra, lifted her hand and the mage beheld a tiny ray of soft green light reveal itself. With stark contrast to the deep blue behind it and the grey night clouds above it, the ray stretched from beyond his line of sight into the sky and vanished beyond the horizon in the direction of the Far Isles. The other end of it attached itself to Enith's chest, and he could not contain his amazement.

"The Bloodlines of the Mages," Enith gasped in shock, "Eridon gave you the secret? No!"

"He offered it willingly, mage, I did not know to ask," she replied, "I believe his exact words were: 'Destroy them all.'"

Undone, Enith turned his face away in grief at this betrayal. The Ancient's love for his cousin Ashlan not only brought about his own death, Eridon would see to it that all who had a hand in Ashlan's seduction would die by default.

The child called The Destroyer continued as though speaking to herself.

"Usually, the color of the bloodline between magicians is a deep red. But the color shared between Ashlan, Eridon, and yourself is green, Enith, the color of the heart, and love itself. Your friend loved you, mage..."

"And I him," choked Enith, "It makes this betrayal more painful... No mage will be safe from you now..."

Lightning crackled around the child's aura.

"They were never safe from me," responded the girl darkly, "Eridon but saved us both time and effort in my quest to avenge my father's death. Yet in this moment it occurs to me that you may be wondering why I revealed this to you..."

Instinctively, the mage lashed out at the Dark One, who, fortunately for Enith, had learned a few things. Instead of allowing the Ancient to vaporize himself against her barrier, she lightly grasped his deadly vault of radiation and held it in her hand. She studied the swirling energy trapped between her fingers, then raised her eyes to Enith, who blanched at this casual display of her power.

"As I was saying, Enith, you may be questioning why I do not now return this to you, and watch you burn. And I confess myself tempted to. You have done great harm in your vast lifetime, eons of shattered dreams and destruction, yet you tremble at me. And I see in the future, you will do much evil, to those I have yet to meet and love..."

Enith had nothing to lose by asking, so he chanced a question.

"Is this future you speak of written in stone, Dark One? Can you be so sure I will harm those you will care for?"

S'ateegra held out her hand with Enith's radiation tight within it, and Enith began to sweat his brow in dread.

"It would be very simple," she said softly, "To end your schemes and quite fitting to do so with your own power, magician. But I would need permission from every single person involved, thousands of them, including creation Itself, and I do not have it. Whether they realize it or not, each one of them needs the pain and devastation you will bring to their lives in order to grow and I must respect their choices. Therefore, I am bound to allow you to leave my presence alive. However..."

The hills lit up with daylight and despite his fear, the mage looked around him in wonder. Enith returned his gaze to the child at the sound of her voice.

"You have sown a great harvest, Ancient, and be assured, you will not escape it. Go your way and choose your steps wisely, Enith, or they will lead you back to me..."

She took his energy then and rendered it inert; Enith's heart pounded as he watched her crumble it like dust. She turned her hand over and it struck the ground with a dull thud and vanished.

The child then allowed the terrified mage to fade from her sight.

* * *

The Petition of Life with Saramis

Throughout the petition process, Pax took up a vigil behind a rather large tree. He was beyond view of anyone approaching the council tent, but he could see the comings and goings of all concerned. His friend Atoli had explained to Pax that as a First Elder of the people, Pax could request to participate in the proceedings. However, it might result in Kha issuing a challenge, naming Pax as a suitor for Saramis, and this alarmed Pax more than any insight he might gain from listening in.

But he couldn't stay away. From the safety of the tree, he stood, then he sat down and got up; in short Pax did everything he could to burn off his excess energy and distress.

Pax didn't want Kha to bond with Saramis. That was as far as Pax could reason it; he'd never experienced jealousy before so he didn't recognize it. The thought of Kha taking Saramis for his own made Pax wish he were older and stronger. An image came to him of Kha touching Saramis's hair and the youngster clenched his fists to keep from shouting his frustration out loud. Pax now understood why Kha hated him from the beginning, but he was too young to do anything about it. As he stormed about the tree Pax was completely unaware that he was thinking the thoughts of a man in love with someone out of his reach. He had more in common with Kha than he realized.

Inside the private council meeting of Kha's petition for Saramis, emotions were understandably strained. The people knew of Kha and Saramis's predicament; they had all watched the pair grow up. Saramis had always been quiet and off to herself and Kha became an early leader of young men. His affection for her was well known, as was Saramis tendency to study hard at her craft when she was not off somewhere, gathering herbs and daydreaming. She never seemed to show any interest in relationships; many felt she might choose to remain unbonded for life. Others wondered what would happen when young Pax came of age and if his childish adoration of Saramis might change to something more. All felt some sympathy for their predicament.

But not every petition for a lifemate among the people was fraught with drama. At fourteen, all knew Atoli and Nea desired to be bonded when they were old enough. They had already rather shyly begun to perform tasks for the tribe together. When in council, they did not sit near one another and kept their eyes and minds focused on the process at hand. But their energy towards one another was strong and made the elders smile with approval.

When Atoli's mind did occasionally drift during the petition process, it was towards his friend and brother Pax. He could feel his brother's misery through the drapes of the council tent and his own heart ached for him. Atoli refocused his gaze when he noticed one of the Second Elders looking at him. He was present only as a witness; his relationship with both Kha and Pax prompted Atoli to ask the elders if he could remain silent. The elders agreed to a point; if there was something he should share; they would know it and request it be spoken into the circle so that the pain around it would heal those gathered.

Saramis sat with her hands tightly together in her lap. She fully expected Kha to be angry and demanding in his petition and felt herself armored against his railings. But as Kha began to speak of his lifelong love calmly and earnestly for her, Saramis felt a blow she could not counter. Blinking rapidly, she began to breathe in shallow shuddering breaths.

Bowman Kha spoke of his value to the people, of his diligence in learning their ways and how he had proven himself as a warrior and potential mate. He would be able to care for Saramis and protect her; Kha felt himself ready to support her work as a wise one among the people; he would die defending her if need be.

"And it would be an honor to father her children," Kha added quietly, as he met Saramis gaze, "I would make it my lifelong quest to ensure her happiness..."

The gathered elders sighed collectively.

He meant every word. This was no attempt to manipulate or force Saramis; it was simply a man pouring out his heart with the hope of winning hers. The silence deepened as they looked at each other, both trying to restrain the urge to weep.

"I love you, Saramis," said Kha deeply, "You know this..."

"Kha..." Saramis responded in misery, "Please don't..."

"You must answer him, Affi-Saramis," stated a First Elder firmly, "Bowman Kha deserves it, for such an earnest plea."

Saramis took a deep breath.

"I cannot bond with you, Kha," she said painfully, "I cannot return such love, I do not feel it..."

"Why?" he asked, heartbroken, "Why, Saramis? You loved me once..."

"No, no, no," Saramis shook her head with each word, "It was a child's affection, like a friend, nothing more."

"You were mine once," Kha persisted, "Your heart was soft towards me, like Nea is to Atoli, I could feel it..." He pointed to the two First Elders, who blushed jointly and looked down at the floor of the tent.

"And then it changed..." he said accusingly.

"Stop!" cried Saramis, "Don't bring him into this, it isn't right!"

The gathered elders gasped as Saramis power flared with her emotions. Bowman Kha's pupils widened at this apparent threat; he stared at Saramis in shock. Affi-Tosla came to her feet, and Saramis hung her head in shame. Her energy sank back into her body, the light from it swirling around her chest.

All looked to Affi-Tosla, who spoke firmly.

"Bring him into it."

The Ascendency of Kha

Pax paused his pacing around the tree. He could not hear or see anything from the council tent, but he felt something; an energy coming from the tent and it hurt. He felt suddenly afraid for reasons that had nothing to do with his own pain. He looked towards the tent, his thoughts on Saramis and her alone. He could see the faint light from the council fire making the skin of the tent glow, but that was all. Pax now regretted his decision to not participate in the petition council; he could not know it was the smartest thing he'd ever done in his life.

Inside the tent, you could hear a pine needle drop in the silence. Saramis could not open her eyes for a moment. She knew she'd made a grave mistake in losing control of her emotions before the council, and age was no excuse. The council could bar Saramis from contact with Pax if she were found to be an unsteady foundation for him and Kha would have a victory of sorts, even if he did not win her. And worse of all, Saramis had failed the confidence of her teacher. She kept her eyes lowered.

"You will speak the truth now, to each other," stated Affi-Tosla, "So you may heal what is hidden."

Saramis spoke first.

"Why, Kha?" she asked him pleadingly, "Why do you insist on making Pax the reason we cannot bond? Why can't you see that he's too young to feel that way about me?"

"Because you saved him, Saramis!" Kha bellowed, "What choice does he have but to love you?!?"

Silence returned to the council tent as Kha and Saramis stared at one another. As it lengthened, Saramis spoke again, her voice small and full of despair.

"What do you want me to do?"

As usual Kha did not hesitate.

"Leave him," he said passionately, "Leave him here and come with me. If the sight of him pains you, we can go to your parent's tribe, or mine. Pax will be safe here with Affi-Tosla; she will teach him the Law; there is no greater safety than this. Her eyes are not clouded as yours are..."

When Saramis remained silent, reeling from his offer, Kha continued.

"Come with me, I beg you," he asked, "Let go of this obsession you have with him. Already he causes you to make mistakes you never have before. Please see that what I'm offering you is life without fear. Come with me, Saramis...please..."

For a long time, all was quiet. The woman Kha loved searched her heart. This time when power came from her, it was softened, and the elders sighed in relief.

She met his eyes.

"I will not leave him," she answered calmly, "My blood is bound to him. I must refuse your request."

Kha took a deep breath finally and nodded. He looked to Affi-Tosla, who met his gaze with an unreadable expression.

"I am answered," he said, his voice cracking, "I request permission to end my petition, Great Elder Affi-Tosla..."

"Granted, Bowman Kha," she said simply, "If you wish, you may go."

Kha nodded again his respect and waited for Affi-Tosla to rise before he took his leave. She did so, entwining her fingers together in front of her. Coming to his feet, Kha exited the tent without turning his back to his teacher. The Great Elder said nothing else, she didn't need to; everyone rose and backed out of the tent, murmuring their thanks for her great wisdom.

Saramis, however remained kneeling on the floor of the council tent, her head now bowed in misery, drowning in shame at her actions.

"Will I be punished, Great Mother?" she asked in a whisper.

"Civilizations deal in punishment, Affi-Saramis," Affi-Tosla responded quietly, "You know this. I cannot stop you from punishing yourself, however, and I see this is your intent..."

The fire crackled in the tent as the power of the elders faded; it was now possible to see the shadows of the two women on the sides of the tent.

The Great Elder spoke again.

"You will no longer sit in council with us, Affi-Saramis," said Affi-Tosla as Saramis snapped her head up and looked in despair at her mentor, "Can you tell me why?"

Saramis took a long breath and released it.

"I have demonstrated no mastery over the emotional body, Great Elder," Saramis replied as her eyes brimmed, "I have threatened harm to a Human and felt no remorse…"

"And what have you shown your fellow elders, both First and Second?" asked her teacher quietly.

"That I have no regard for them…"

"Therefore," continued Affi-Tosla, "Should your judgment be trusted?"

"No…" answered Saramis, "It should not…"

Saramis now bravely met the Great Elder's eyes and stilled herself.

Affi-Tosla nodded her approval of this effort at self-control.

"You will return to council…If…you once again demonstrate mastery."

The Great Elder turned to her place on her small chair and seated herself.

Saramis lingered.

"Why do you ask me for direction that you will not follow, Affi-Saramis?" asked her teacher to the unspoken question that hung in the air.

But her pupil remained silent, and after a moment, her teacher answered her.

"Kha is right, you should leave him."

The Hand of His Brother

Pax was reluctant to approach Saramis after the council meeting; the energy of her sadness was palpable, and he could not discern the reason, himself or Kha. The First Elders hugged her often and she held them tightly. The Second Elders offered comfort with words and walked with Saramis as she went about her tasks; Pax watched this with great trepidation. Pax knew that Saramis had refused Kha, but this did not bring him comfort. It seemed she was making up her mind about something and she did not approach him, so he waited.

It was inevitable that Kha would either voice or act out his frustration, this also Pax knew. And with a man's instinct, Pax felt it would be directed towards him, not Saramis, so he braced himself for a storm.

However, it was a storm with no warning.

The morning dawn was breathtaking and after his tasks, Pax desired to walk and clear his thoughts, so he did so. The land where they camped seemed endless; hills rolled away and back to him, the flowering trees and bushes spilled their petals on his path and Pax felt a peace uncommon. Recent dreams of his mother pained him less and less; she appeared to comfort him and remind Pax of her love for him more than her absence. Many times, he awoke recalling only that she held him awhile and whispered how proud she was of him. This memory was bittersweet; Pax leaned against a tree with one foot against the bark behind him, watching white and pink petals drift from its branches to the ground.

I miss you, he thought, and I wish you were here with me.

He sighed at the impossibility of this request; Pax reached out his hand and smiled as a few petals rested in his palm briefly before floating away. Princess Erami had loved flowers like this one, white with pink in the center. When the former prince saw them it never failed to bring his mother to his mind. He pressed a few between his fingers before absently allowing them to slip to the ground.

He took a different path back to his people, so deep in his thoughts that Pax didn't realize that he approached Bowman Kha who was practicing his swordplay alone. It was too late to change his path; Kha would see him. Pax was learning the ways of men, and he knew such an act would draw Kha's contempt, so he slowed his gait and walked carefully towards his apparent adversary.

Pax felt his heart pounding in his ears; Kha was viciously using his sword on the tree in front of him, no doubt imaging Pax as the recipient of his rage. The man paused in his attack, breathing heavily as he stared down his invisible enemy. Kha raised his sword to renew his attack and from his peripheral vision he noticed Pax approach. His gaze changed from curiosity to astonishment at finding Pax alone; his eyes narrowed.

"Why do you seek me out?" he asked Pax gruffly as he lowered his weapon.

"I do not seek you," Pax responded calmly, "You were on my path. Are you well?"

Kha paused at this cordial greeting; disarmed by the lightness of it. When he did not respond, Pax shrugged and appeared to continue on his way, but Kha's countenance changed and he stepped into the path Pax walked on.

The two stared at one another. Kha's gaze was piercing; but Pax countered it without aggression, he simply refused to look away. After a moment, Kha broke the silence.

"You do not fear me..." he mused.

When Kha lifted the sword he was still holding, Pax stepped back from him, his pupils widening. Kha boldly pointed it at Pax, the blade flat and directed at his chest.

"You should..." he continued.

As the silence between them deepened, Kha took note of Pax determined gaze, startled breathing, and clenched fists. His eyes narrowed again.

"You are no farm boy, separated from his parents," Kha speculated as he finally lowered his arm, "A tiller of grass would fear a warrior, or soldier with a blade..."

The man set down his sword on the husk of a broken tree behind him; he did not trust himself with it, alone here where no one could see his actions. Kha was trying to remember the laws he swore by as he gazed on the one who stood between him and his heart's desire. He touched his finger to his forehead.

"But, yes, I recall now, you don't remember your parents..."

Kha smiled thinly as the look in Pax eyes changed to anger.

His jaw worked as though he would say something, but the boy remembered he was weaponless; it would do little good to provoke an already angry man. His face flushing, Pax wisely decided to continue on his way, but Kha gripped the front of his shirt and pushed him back. Pax now planted his feet and took a defensive stance.

"What are you about, Kha?" he asked firmly.

Kha grinned broadly.

"So, you are a man," Kha responded, "I was of the opinion that you preferred to hide behind the skirts of Saramis..."

Spots flared before Pax's eyes, he was so wrathful, but still he tried to restrain himself as he sized up his opponent. Kha was four years older than Pax and already an accomplished bowman and warrior. He was taller and well-muscled; it was highly possible Kha could flatten Pax with one blow. He spoke to calm himself.

"I ask again," he replied tightly, "What are you about, Kha?"

The smile on Kha's face was smug.

"You are no farm boy," he repeated, "You would not face me so. I believe you are the child of a soldier, a man who would teach his son at an early age to defend himself and his family..." Kha reached confidently for a wooden staff leaning against the tree husk near his sword.

He tossed it to Pax who caught it easily. Kha laughed at this movement.

"Even if you do not remember your father, you remember what he taught you..." Kha reached for another staff.

"If not," he said as he raised his eyebrow, "This will be your first lesson..."

Kha swung at Pax and was surprised at his expert parry. When Pax, still silent with rage took the offensive, Kha grunted as he warded off the boy's blows. He stared at Pax with renewed respect.

"Good," Kha said gruffly, "I won't have to go easy on you..."

Pax, as it turns out, was very good with the wooden boa staff. He was taught by General Aton, who did not spare his students, whether high born or not. Pax called on every single thing the general taught him as he sparred with Bowman Kha. The battle between Kha and Pax went on in the quiet glen, disturbed only by grunts and labored breathing. Neither noticed the approach of Atoli, who knew Kha's battle moves. The boy felt alarm as he watched the bowman become more and more aggressive with Pax, who was soon reduced to mostly defense.

"Kha!" Atoli cried out, "What are you about? Stop!"

Kha was overpowering his rival and his intention was becoming clearer by the moment; he had already displayed his dominance. For his part, Pax was beginning to think he faced the general once again, who had only one goal: His death.

But Pax would not back down. He saw again the general looking at him and heard his words when the prince realized his intent:

"You're a prince of the realm, Rasdeter. I know you won't run from me and shame your mother's memory..."

If he were to die today, Pax would meet his mother in the shaded realms with his head held high...

Neither fighter noticed Atoli running for a spare wooden staff; he barely had time to reach them as Pax lost his footing. Kha swung back in a high deadly arc meant to crush Pax's boa against his chest. If such a blow struck the boy's head, it would surely slay him. Atoli planted his feet just in time before Kha's staff came crashing down; it split Atoli's boa and sent him sprawling on top of Pax, who still held up his boa; his arms cried out in agony as the wooden staff cracked but held against the finish of Kha's swing.

With the defeat of his enemy, Kha's eyes cleared, and he saw with dismay that Atoli was on the ground beneath him, staring up at Kha in utter shock. Kha's weapon slipped from his fingers as Pax met Kha's gaze with fear and hatred. The Bowman could not know that Pax was staring through him in this moment at General Aton, whom Pax also knew as a twelve-year-old boy he could not have defeated.

Atoli came to his feet in rage and pushed hard at Bowman Kha's chest. Kha yielded to the much smaller boy in shame, even as Atoli pushed him again and again in grief.

"Why?!?" Atoli screamed at Kha, who could not meet his eyes.

"Brother..." said Bowman Kha in misery.

"No!" roared Atoli, "This is not possible. How can I be your brother if he is not?!"

Bowman Kha had no answer for this question. He remembered the laws he had lived all his life by, and the principles of peace he stood for. The people had accepted Pax as one of them and Kha had treated him as an enemy and a stranger. Kha had allowed his lower nature to blind him. He realized now that if he had been willing to show Pax how the people lived he would never have reacted like the people of the civilizations he frowned on. Perhaps, his actions may even have found favor with Saramis. Now Kha felt he had committed a deed that could not be undone. He looked to Pax but there was no forgiveness there.

When Kha spoke again it was with great strain.

"I pray you, do not judge the people by my actions, Pax," Kha said with difficulty, "We are better than this..."

The man who had suited Saramis and lost turned from the two boys and walked away.

Pax released a huge breath as Kha disappeared on the path. His hands, back and arms hurt so badly that it was almost impossible to think. His friend had saved him; that much was certain. The two looked at each other finally, both in a pain that encompassed body and spirit.

"Thank you," said Pax sincerely.

"You shouldn't have to," answered Atoli, who then covered his face with his arm, heartbroken.

* * *

The Judgment

Days after his encounter with Bowman Kha, Pax was awakened at dawn by Atoli and asked to follow him. Rubbing sleep from his eyes Pax trailed behind his friend as they walked a familiar path to the common area then past it. At the edge of their camp where dogs and sentries stood at attention, a puzzled Pax saw the gathered elders. Sleep completely abandoned him as beyond them were Saramis and Kha, dressed for what appeared to be a long journey. His steps quickened, and Pax left his friend Atoli behind. Saramis held out her arms to Pax but he stopped as he neared her, looking in dismay from her to Kha. But his adversary did not look victorious or smug; instead, he appeared to be both resigned and wary.

"What's happened, Saramis?" Pax spoke in a whisper, "Where are you going?"

At fourteen, Pax was barely taller than Saramis, who was herself a tall woman. She was in the grip of some emotion Pax could not identify; perhaps because his heart was beating too fast to contain his own. She drew his eyes from Kha to hers when she touched his face. Pax stared down at her, drowning in her warm brown eyes.

"I'm going to stay with my parents, Pax, some months from here. I..." she had a hard time continuing her words. Dread filled his body, and Pax felt his stomach tilt.

"You're going to leave me here," he offered, feeling like a child.

When Saramis nodded, Pax felt his chest constrict. Kha and the elders moved away from them and Pax heard himself pleading with her.

"What must I do to contain my offense?" he asked her. "Am I remiss in some duty, or something I've failed to learn..." his babbling stopped, and Pax grasped her hand.

"There's no fault with you, Pax," she whispered, "The fault is with Kha and me; the council has spoken..."

"Don't bond with him," he blurted out, unable to stop himself. Saramis touched his lips with two of her fingers and Pax became completely still.

"I won't..." she said, and he began to breathe again. "He's only coming with me until I reach my parents, then he has to go on to another tribe. He's volunteered to do it, he feels great shame for attacking you, Pax."

"Then you can both stay," Pax reasoned, as he looked up to meet Kha's eyes, who looked away. Kha could not hear their words, but it was not difficult to guess what Pax wanted. "I can forgive him, I completely understand..."

He was babbling again, angling for a way to keep her there, or go with her. Saramis reached up slightly on her toes and touched her lips to Pax's face, who stiffened in pleased shock, his mind totally derailed by this act.

"Promise me you will stay willingly," she said quietly, "Learn everything Affi-Tosla, Atoli, and all the elders can teach you. Promise you will study as hard as you can..."

He gripped her hands in his tightly.

"Only if you promise to return," he said deeply, "If you won't stay, and you won't let me go with you, you must promise to come back to me..."

His green eyes darkened as he looked at her.

"If you don't, I'll come looking for you, I swear it..."

She nodded.

"I promise..."

Saramis sighed as Pax pressed his lips to her forehead; he didn't dare do else. How he wished he could touch her hair before she turned from him, but it was bound like always. Shared pain came between his glance and Bowman Kha as Saramis neared him and Kha fell in step beside her. Pax breathed deeply as he watched her figure grow smaller in the distance, followed by the warriors who would accompany them and eventually return. He would keep his promise and another he did not share with Saramis.

Pax would grow in strength as well as wisdom; if he had to face the Bowman again, he silently swore the outcome would be different.

Unlike Saramis, Pax was certain that if Kha truly loved her, he would not let the matter of her future lifemate be left to chance. His eyes now open, Pax was certain Saramis was the one he wanted to spend his life with. He stared at an empty horizon, both heartbroken and determined.

As the group quietly walked together on the road, the Bowman could feel the unhappiness coming from Saramis. She was trying to do the right thing by leaving Pax, but her heart was not behind her actions. The council was right; she would cripple his progress as a man if she continued to use her power to protect him. Saramis told herself she felt responsible for Pax, like an older sister, perhaps, nothing more. Yet Kha had no illusions regarding Pax's growing feelings for the woman he loved. It was Saramis' blindness to Pax that made some small hope fan in his heart.

Kha knew what Pax did not, that it would be years before Pax saw Saramis again. The elders had decided it would be best for all concerned to split the three of them up and give time for the past events to heal. The Bowman would keep his word and not pressure Saramis with his constant presence. He would go to a tribe only weeks, not months away. Kha would give her the space she needed, for memories of his transgressions to dim and perhaps all memory of Pax to be forgotten.

* * *

Remembering Rasdeter

Some months before Saramis and Kha returned, some new people joined them from a neighboring tribe. Some of them were completely new to their way of life, the way that Pax himself had been over six years ago. A pair of them, brother and sister were among those unlearning civilization, Cord and Aylin, respectively. They could not be more different these two; Cord's frizzy, dark blonde locks and warm brown eyes were a contrast to Aylin's sleek raven hair and bright blue eyes. The elders and the people greeted them and introduced them to everyone; Pax, Atoli and Nea were trailing behind, holding bundles of clothing dried by the clean winds of the day before.

Aylin started as though she'd been struck as Pax came into view, his unconscious male beauty prominent as the sun lit up his dark hair and deep green eyes. His once lanky teenaged body had morphed into a warrior's; broad shoulders and muscled arms from hunting and fighting made an impressive sight, and young Aylin flushed as she stared at him.

Pax, of course, completely missed this stunned admiration. Had he remained at his old home he would have grown up at the court of his uncle King Valtus; no doubt pelted daily by shy giggles and bold flirting from adolescent ladies and princesses hoping to make a suitable match with such a handsome specimen.

His friends Atoli and Nea, however, did not miss the reaction of Aylin and gave each other knowing glances. Finally, a bemused Atoli nudged his blind friend and subtly pointed out his new admirer, who flushed even deeper and looked away from Pax's puzzled gaze.

"She's quite a beauty, Pax," offered Nea with a smile, "And she seems to like you..."

The former prince appraised the newcomer and shrugged. Her beauty for him was not in question to his mind, it was how she compared to Saramis, and by that measure all others fell short. However, Pax flushed as she tried to meet his eyes again. It felt like Aylin was looking right through him and he didn't know what to make of it.

They were eventually introduced, and Pax for once was glad he was not in his old kingdom. Custom might dictate that Aylin offer Pax her hand and he would be obliged to kiss it, something in this moment he was heartily glad he didn't have to do. Yes, Aylin was beautiful, but Pax didn't wish to encourage her affection; he was very clear about the woman he wanted. His people did not hold with multiple partners and he would be expected to do the honorable thing by Aylin if he claimed her.

That would never happen if Pax had any chance to win the heart of Saramis.

Thus, the prince was polite, but he felt his heartbeat faster as Aylin took the opportunity to drink in the sight of him. He watched her pupils widen as she gazed at him rather breathlessly and Pax almost stepped back from her. He had no skills when it came to females, and without the overwhelming attraction Pax felt for Saramis, he wasn't quite sure how to react to this blatant display of Aylin's feelings. He was grateful when Nea stepped between them and spoke kindly to Aylin, who summoned the will to turn away and resume breathing.

From that moment, Pax did everything he could to avoid Aylin, who tried every way she could to cross his path. The girl was awestruck, innocently enough, and made attempts to refocus her fascination but it was difficult for her. Nea and the other women took Aylin under their wing and helped distract her. The girl had no mother figure to guide her in how to be with others, much less a man she was attracted to. Aylin was shy and bold by turns, not knowing what to do with herself. Her brother Cord, who was even less equipped to deal with her, had spent most of his time protecting her from assault while they wandered through various kingdoms. He knew most men would not hesitate to take advantage of her ignorance. The boy was thankful he and Aylin had found refuge in such a loving and embracing society.

Cord fell in easily with the men, happy that he and his sibling were no longer destitute. Without family, practical skills or land, the world of civilization was not kind. Cord was eager to learn anything that would assist him in earning his keep among the people. It would take a while for the pair of them to learn a system that was not based on commerce, but sustainable living through barter and trade.

However, the day Saramis and Kha returned was painful for both Pax and Aylin; it was simply for different reasons.

The sentries heralded their approach, as they did for everyone the people recognized as family, so Pax did not immediately know who joined them. In the four years of Saramis' absence, the people who called themselves human had wandered the known world, and Pax had seen wonders. Even in his previous life of privilege, the former prince had never seen all the nations of his world. His father Lord Altus, like his uncle King Valtus had been protective of their heirs and did not travel everywhere with them. Then, as now, a prince of any nation was a target for intrigue and control; a future king was great currency for those with the means to exploit them.

The time apart had been challenging for Pax, but as he promised, he spent the time well. The older warriors trained Atoli and his now dear friend, so Pax learned the more advanced lessons he might have gained from General Aton, had things gone differently. He also learned the ways of peace, things no one in his old world knew of, though some longed for it. Often a king fought many battles not only to extend and preserve his kingdom but to hopefully gain a reign of peace for his son, the future king. Many times, this was not the case. Generations of battle lie ahead for most kingdoms, and for some the end of a bloodline entirely as men struggled for riches and dominance of the world around them.

But these thoughts were not occupying the mind of the former prince at the moment. Pax was enjoying a period of play as he taught games to a gangly puppy who could barely walk, as his mother watched serenely. Loaded down with hungry pups who drank themselves into a stupor, she looked relieved at least one of them was distracted. She only turned her head at a playful yelp from the frustrated pup who could not hold on to the finger Pax stuck in his mouth, moving his knuckle back and forth to encourage a growl. Pax lifted his head idly at the commotion near the common area; he came swiftly to his feet at the sight of Saramis's distinctive headdress. Pax bent down once more to give a caress to his new friend and placed him gently next to his mother. At the smells and sounds of feeding, the pup remembered his hunger and waddled happily over to his mother, who laid back in resignation. Pax gave her a comforting stroke behind her ears and then straightened his back, trying to fit his heart again into his chest as he approached the people gathered around his beloved.

Four years...Pax felt his whole body was one gigantic heart as he strode cautiously in her direction. He could hear nothing but the pounding of it; the excited words and murmuring of the people faded away and he only saw her wrapped in light and beautiful beyond any memory of his fevered dreams. Atoli felt Nea's hand tighten on his arm and he looked down into her troubled eyes in sympathy. Who could miss the yearning of his friend's face and eyes as Pax drew nearer to Saramis? Had she accepted Bowman Kha while she was gone? Pax would be devastated.

Yet the truth was even worse.

Saramis was in complete joy as she greeted the tribe she called home. Kha had wisely separated himself from her as they were surrounded. He had no rights to Saramis, and he knew with a man's wisdom that if he stood between her and Pax it would be difficult for Kha to release the position. His own heart increased its beat as Kha noticed the huge changes in the boy left behind four years ago. This was a full-blown warrior, not a child learning his craft. The boy had shown promise before the Bowman left; Pax lasted longer against Kha than he had expected. It had increased his need to win decisively, to Kha's own detriment. Apparently, Pax had not forgotten his defeat and appeared ready to challenge Kha if necessary.

But it was Saramis Pax was focused on, and when she finally noticed his presence, she turned to him in great joy.

"Pax!"

He flushed with pleasure at her brilliant smile and twinkled eyes. Then she closed the space between them and touched his face.

"Little brother..." Saramis said with great affection, and the expression on his face turned from supreme happiness to puzzlement.

Did she just call him--'Little brother'?

The former prince blinked rapidly to contain his dismay. Did she not see him, Pax could not help but think, being now at least a foot taller than Saramis.

"It is well to be home again," she proclaimed, and took his hand in hers. Pax stammered something unintelligible and allowed himself to be dragged along with her as Saramis continued to greet everyone else.

Perhaps it was merely something to say, Pax thought as he accompanied her. It was good to hold her hand this way, he mused, a distinct change from the last time the prince was in her company. I have to allow Saramis time to adjust, he reasoned finally, I was fourteen when she left, and I was never able to express to her the seriousness of my feelings.

His eyes met Kha's for a moment and the expression of both men was unreadable. Now he knows, the Bowman thought, of how Saramis shields herself from intimate emotions. There's something inside Saramis that doesn't wish to hear or see the changes of life all around her. It is a barrier I have faced most of my life with her.

Yet, as the Bowman watched how Saramis still clung to the hand of the confused young man who walked with her, Kha did not dare to hope the blindness of Saramis would last.

Aylin also noticed this exchange between Affi-Saramis and the young warrior who troubled her dreams from the day they met. With a woman's wisdom, she could tell the difference of how Pax looked at Aylin and the clear emotion in his eyes when he gazed on Saramis. She saw gentleness and a guarded protectiveness that lashed at her burning heart. Aylin looked at Saramis and marveled. How could she not see that he...

The girl breathed deeply and looked away.

No, Aylin told herself, It cannot be love between them or she would not look at him so. She doesn't feel for him the way that I do...

The girl watched in misery as Pax and Saramis walked together, surrounded by loving friends. Presently, Aylin noticed the sympathetic eyes of Nea on her from a distance. But when the be-loved of Atoli made to approach Aylin, the flustered young woman turned and strode quickly away.

* * *

The brokenhearted Aylin did not go far, however. She sought out her brother Cord for support and advice. Aylin found her sibling at the edge of camp with the sentries. They were discussing a favorite topic: How to make drums and furniture from discarded wood and toppled trees. The older men had many unique ideas on the best ways to separate good branches and trunks from rotted ones; ways to mix stains and carve soft or hardened bark, the list went on and on. Cord found this craft fascinating; he had many questions, which of course made the older warriors wax proud and endless on their answers.

From the corner of his eye, Cord spied Aylin and took note of the seriousness of her disposition. Feeling immediately protective, Cord turned respectfully from the discussion as his sister drew closer, while the men happily continued without him. In a univer-sal symbol of despair, Aylin pressed her forearms against her chest and bowing her head, she leaned into her brother's chest, who gently placed his arm around her shoulders. Cord squeezed her in a brotherly fashion and pressed a kiss to her forehead, then made a sound of dismay as he felt her shaking.

"Whatever has distressed you, sister?" her sibling asked kindly, "Is there anything I can do?"

His sister heaved a great sigh of misery.

"I don't know...Well, it's about Pax, I think..."

Cord's voice took on a note of alarm. He'd thought Aylin's crush on Pax harmless, and he seemed a good man, but now...

"Has he hurt you?" Cord asked firmly in an older brother voice, and his sister hastened to calm him.

"No, brother," Aylin reassured him, "I mean, he hasn't touched me or anything like that..."

"Oh..." Cord responded in a different tone, "You've made your feelings known to him then."

"No..." Aylin said as she now stepped back from her brother's embrace. She didn't wish to set Cord's mind down the wrong path. Aylin knew her brother acted like a father sometimes towards her and she didn't want him to decide that he knew what she was going through before Aylin told him.

"Well, what is it then, Aylin?" Cord replied, "You've been wandering around our new home like a love-sick pup. I told you a man won't respond well to that; unless, of course he's the love-sick one."

"I saw him with someone else," Aylin blurted out in misery, "I think he likes her!"

"Aylin, Aylin..."

Cord sighed deeply and crossed his arms. He hated giving out love advice to the sister he adored, mostly because he knew Aylin wouldn't listen. He sometimes marveled as to how he'd been able to protect her innocence for so long; Cord knew he wouldn't be able to much longer. Aylin seemed determined to have her heart broken by someone who couldn't see her value, most likely because Aylin herself couldn't see it.

"Does this woman that Pax loves return his affection?" asked Cord.

His sister blinked rapidly.

"I'm not sure...She seemed not to notice..."

Cord narrowed his eyes at this; he wasn't sure if Aylin was telling the truth, or the truth as she wanted to believe it. If the woman didn't return his affection, why would his sister be upset?

He took his sister by the shoulders to get her attention.

"A man can only make a decision if he's aware of his choices, Aylin," her brother stated firmly. "You'll just have to let Pax know how you feel. And..." This Cord said after raising his forefinger for emphasis, "You'll have to accept his decision, whatever it is. There's nothing worse for a woman to do than to insist a man accept her. You won't like the consequences of such an act, trust me on this..."

Aylin nodded bravely and then hugged her brother tightly. As she made to leave, Cord suddenly grabbed her shoulder and turned her back to him.

"Consider well your actions, sister," said Cord gravely, "You're a child no more, I realize that, and I like Pax as a man and perhaps a mate for you if that is what the future holds. But if you give me cause to defend your honor, I will do so without hesitation, and you may lose either your suitor or your brother. Do you understand me?"

Her eyes wide, Aylin nodded contritely. She knew her brother meant his words, and seen too, the results of his vow. She stepped back from Cord and nodded again, and he crossed his arms, satisfied that she'd taken him seriously.

Cord watched his sister until she disappeared on the path leading to their tents.

As his gaze wandered to the tree line above them, the man known as Cord sighed. Because of the needs of his sister Aylin, his mind turned to things remembered, and Cord spoke to his father in his mind.

On your death, I swore to look after my sister Aylin and protect her, father, but there are some things no man can protect another from. Mother had less than minutes to hold her and name her Aylin before she died, and my sister has suffered for her absence ever since.

I've done things, father, that I'm not proud of to keep that vow...things I hope you understand.

His thoughts turned to the object of Aylin's affection, the warrior called Pax, and his eyes narrowed.

Upon meeting him, he seemed to me to be a man of his word and high morals, father. Not one to weaken a woman's mind with words of love to cover his lust. I hope I've not misjudged him. I will keep a closer watch on his dealings with my sister. Aylin seems to enjoy this place, as do I. It would not be well to be forced to wander the kingdoms again because of my sister's lack of discernment.

Suddenly Cord noticed the conversation behind him had become more animated, so he turned again to join his new brothers.

* * *

Months went by after Saramis and Bowman Kha's return with very little change. Saramis settled back into her routine as though she'd never left. Pax had seen to the upkeep of her tent while she was gone, oiling the skins regularly so they would not thin or crack. She was beside herself with happiness; such that it made him abashed. The men helped Pax assemble her tent and Saramis held his hand again tightly in appreciation afterwards. But this display of affection had a different effect on Pax. It reminded him too much of the adoration shared by Atoli and Nea; this served to increase his yearning to change the nature of their relationship.

Sometimes Pax would find Saramis gazing on him as he went about his tasks. But when he returned this glance in hope, Pax would find the woman he loved would change expression and call him to her side to speak of mundane things. He enjoyed her attention, of course, but without some indication of deeper feelings, their time together caused Pax more pain than contentment.

It was not lost on Pax that Aylin appeared to seek from him the same things he sought from Saramis. The girl did not bombard him with her presence, but he could feel her attraction for him as though she stood next to him. It made him marvel that Saramis was as blind to him as he wished he could be to Aylin.

Equally clear was her brother Cord's gaze as Pax moved among the people. He groaned at the thought of Aylin speaking to Cord about him. And if he added the Bowman to his list of troubles, Pax felt as though the whole camp stared and followed his every move. Little wonder that the former prince spent more and more time away from his home. He found every excuse to go hunting or even foraging for plants, roots, and herbs; anything to keep his mind distracted.

Unknown to him, the elders watched all the tangled threads of Pax's life in silence. Whatever needed to happen regarding this state of affairs would happen soon, they reasoned. A climax to such things was unavoidable. Second Elder Zema kept a closer eye than the others. She was the one all turned to if the Great Elder was not present, which was often, as Affi-Tosla visited all Wanderers of the Plains across both the known and the unknown world.

Her eye fell on Cord as he bonded with the people; his happiness could be felt across the common area. Since his father died he had never lived among men without suspicion and a fear for the welfare of his sister Aylin; he appeared to be relaxed with them...almost.

The reason for Cord's apparent lack of tradable skills was simple: he was a mercenary. He earned his and his sister's keep through war and strife, a trade he was forced to ply when his own kingdom fell to a larger one. Cord and Aylin's father had been a general. Determined to follow orders during the final battle before the kingdom burned, his father fought his regiment to the last man. They defeated their foes then watched in horror as more and more troops marched in their shattered gates. He turned to his son Cord, who fought beside him, just as determined as his father to die with him. But his father grabbed Cord's breastplate roughly and shook him.

"Your sister!" he bellowed, "Find Aylin and flee this place!"

Cord stared at his father in dismay.

"No, father," said Cord, "We die with you in honor, as you taught us..."

Cord was shaken by the look in his father's eyes.

"Your mother died for her, Cord," said his father fiercely, "You will obey me, and protect her with your life. Now go...Go!"

He pushed his son hard; and for a moment they stood staring at each other. Cord then rushed to his father and held him tightly; he felt a rough kiss from his father on his hair. Then he pushed Cord away again and without a backward glance, marched with his last group of men against a grimly advancing troop that thundered the ground with their approach.

All this and more Zema saw as Cord sought fellowship with the warriors of the people. The Second Elder kept her counsel to herself and spoke of what she learned only to the Great Elder who in turn advised Zema to keep watch. Zema thought of Aylin and sighed.

Your brother thinks he knows you, Aylin, but he still has much to learn.

* * *

One evening as Pax returned from his anguished wanderings, he came across Aylin sitting alone in the common area. Everyone else had just dispersed for the evening, and she seemed lost in her own thoughts. She held a small reed in her hands, breaking it repeatedly. Aylin started as she noticed Pax; he approached with the full moon behind him; his hair looked like dark silver in the moonlight.

"I'm sorry," Pax murmured politely, "I didn't mean to disturb you..."

He meant to walk past her, and Aylin meant to let him, but something crossed her mind and she spoke to it.

"May I ask you a question?" She asked, and Pax gave a nod as his heartbeat increased; he had no idea what she might ask of him.

Aylin hesitated a moment, then got it out.

"Do you dislike me, Pax?"

"Why no," he stammered in dismay, "No, of course not..."

Pax felt immediately awkward; he hadn't meant to convey that impression at all. He turned towards her in a conciliatory movement, horrified at the idea she might think him rude or unmannered.

Aylin offered her hand to Pax to help assist her to her feet, and reluctantly he did so; the warmth of her fingers sent a shock through him. The moon made her blue eyes a strange color, and he suddenly found himself paralyzed by the deep pool in her gaze.

"You haven't spoken to me since we were introduced, and I wondered if there were some offense in me..." her voice trailed away.

Pax didn't know what he said after these words from Aylin. It was a combination of apology, excuses and soothing phrases that made no sense. She shook her hair slightly as she listened to him and a river of moonlight spilled down the length of it. Unconsciously, Aylin lowered her lashes as she tried to think of what else to say, and Pax swallowed hard at the reminder of her beauty.

"You must forgive me," the flustered prince stuttered, "I didn't, I mean I don't..."

Aylin could be shy or bold, depending on the moment, and as she looked at Pax trying to find the right response, she decided on the best way to advise him of her feelings.

She stepped forward, and drawing his face down to hers, she kissed him.

As their lips met, the completely inexperienced Pax felt his body ignite like a bonfire. He couldn't breathe for a moment from the softness of Aylin as she gently pressed herself against him. Pax didn't know what had happened, but he wanted more of it; his arms betrayed him with a will of their own, embracing Aylin and pulling her closer. As her sweet kiss became more passionate, Pax marveled at how he had imagined holding another in this way, this close...

Saramis.

The thought was a bracing cold wind, and Pax broke the kiss, using his traitorous arms to hold Aylin's shoulders and push her back.

"Please..." she whispered, her hands caressing his forearms to draw him back in.

"I can't..." Pax gasped, "Aylin, I can't. You mustn't press me this way, my heart belongs to another...It would be wrong..."

The moon shone in Aylin's eyes as they pleaded with him.

"It wouldn't be wrong, Pax, I promise...Just stay with me please...I'll help you forget her..."

He'd never felt such agony. Blood pounded in his ears and neck and behind his eyes. The imprint of her lips was still fresh in his memory and the temptation to experience it again was driving him mad. To give in, however, would cost Pax everything he'd sought for the last four years, a life with Saramis.

Saramis...

Pax strode angrily away from Aylin, trying to recover his mind. But Aylin was not yet defeated by his attempted departure. She took a deep breath and gave it her best; her words struck his back like arrows.

"She is blind to you, Pax," Aylin said urgently, "Blind to anyone, any man who wants her..."

He turned slowly to face her and paused at the rawness of the desperation in her eyes. Did everyone know he loved and desired Saramis? And this woman; was the look in her eyes any different from his?

Her body trembled with exertion as Aylin tried to physically will Pax to come back to her. She tightened her cloak around her neck.

"Perhaps I'm not the only one wasting their time and efforts."

Blood pounded in his ears again. Her challenge was direct, but a thought came to him before he answered her as she so eagerly wished. Confrontation and force were now tools he himself could use. It had worked amazingly well with him, but with Saramis... This time as he turned from Aylin, they both knew there was nothing more she could do to provoke him in her favor.

Her pain followed him into the darkness between them.

"Pax!"

* * *

Saramis felt his emotions hammering at her long before Pax stepped without permission into her tent; she came to her feet at his entrance. They stood a moment staring at each other; his gaze one of determination, hers of questions and confusion.

He studied her face, searching for some indication of mature affection, anything at all...

His breath exited his lungs in despair.

"She was right," he said finally in agony, "You cannot see me..."

"Why do you say this, little brother," whispered Saramis, "Of course I can see you…"

His brows came together as his face darkened.

"You are not my sister, Saramis," Pax responded quietly.

He said the words deliberately and something in her gaze shifted but not enough. Pax realized that there was actually something wrong about the way she looked at him, something about him that Saramis could not see. He moved closer to her and her legs locked in place instinctively. She was in her place of power and it was impossible for her to step back. Pax's body stance and arms rigid at his sides was a challenge she could not back down from.

He stepped closer.

"Pax," Saramis whispered again, "What are you about?"

"I want you to see me, Saramis," he repeated, "See me as I am right now in this moment…" he did not dare raise his hand to point at her, but his fist tightened, and he saw her gasp at this movement.

There was something disrupting in her and he saw pain in her confusion that mirrored his own. But he would not stop his advance.

"Pax," she replied softly, "You are my little brother, but I cannot allow this disrespect…"

"You're not my sister…Saramis," he said deeply, "You have…never…been my sister…"

With his next step, her power soared around her, but she did not direct it at Pax, instead she contained it behind her. He felt no fear though it seemed a storm raged around them. He watched her pupils widen as she seemed to recognize the emotion that was the strongest of all the tidal waves surging inside him.

"Pax…" she said as she took a shuddering breath.

"My name…" he said tight with anger, "Is not…Pax!"

She slapped him, hard.

The sting of it pierced his body as his cheek turned from the force of her hand. He closed his eyes as though he savored the violence of it; every cell in his body roared to life. Saramis gasped as the tall gangly boy she imagined every single day for the past six years vanished and a man strong and vibrant instantly took his place. His eyes as he slowly turned his face back to hers were almost black as his pupils pushed back the color of his dark green irises. Yet there was no anger behind his eyes, only triumph as Saramis saw clearly what she could not un-see again: That his feelings for her were not brotherly, and he was not a child she could easily dismiss.

"Rasdeter..." the name came softly as Saramis tried to calm herself. The sound of his name ran chills down her arms; Saramis felt a ring of warmth around the crown of her head. She blinked quickly to keep her eyes from watering; she was yet in her place of power.

Pax, his goal accomplished, stepped back as slowly as he had advanced, his eyes never leaving hers. He felt the same ring of warmth from the sound of a name unspoken for the last six years. Pax knew in that moment that though she would continue to call him Pax, from now on her eyes would say Rasdeter when she looked at him, and for now that was enough. He paused at the door of her tent.

"Good night, Saramis," he whispered in kind.

Her hand went to her throat as soon as he was out of sight.

A Throne in Dreams

Despite his victory with Saramis, Pax did not sleep well that night. He sought refuge in the tent he shared with his friend Atoli, tossing, and turning through feverish dreams. One dream was a recurring one that never failed to puzzle him. In it Pax saw a girl in various stages of growth. In some dreams she was a newborn, placed into his trembling arms; he often kissed her sleeping cheek, a small tuft of red hair smoothed against her forehead. In others, she had just begun to walk; Pax saw her standing in a field of grass and white dandelions with a stem in her tiny fist, offering it to him as the seeds began to blow away. Sometimes the little toddler would laugh, other times she would run to him crying because she lost the seeds; Pax would always wake up before he could hold her in his arms and comfort her.

In another dream he imagined himself crowned king by his father Altus, who could not answer why he was king instead of his uncle Valtus. People were weeping everywhere, and no one could tell Pax where Queen Inka and Princess Erami his mother were. His father turned away when Pax pressed him for response.

When he thought of his cousin Sumter he found himself in the forest at the border of his former estates. Nameless fear enveloped him, and he started running towards a lone tree. General Aton stood with his back to Pax; against the tree was Sumter, his eyes full of desperation and dread. Sumter looked over the general's shoulder and met Pax's eyes.

"Rasdeter!" Sumter cried out, "Please help me, cousin, don't let him kill me!"

Pax ran as hard as he could, shouting to the general to relent. Pax was king, he must not disobey him. But the blade came out, the sun glinting as the metal rose and fell.

They both shouted the same word.

"Cousin!"

Pax woke with a start, rolling away from his friend's touch. Atoli held both hands out in a calming motion.

"Steady, my friend," he said in a soothing voice, "I was but trying to rouse you from shouting in your sleep."

Horror shaded Pax as he recalled his most recent dream. His chest heaved as he looked to Atoli.

"Speak, Atoli," he asked hoarsely, "What did I say?"

But his friend shook his head.

"I couldn't make out most of it, Pax," he responded, "You just shouted 'cousin' various times..."

Pax lowered his head and gripped his woven blankets as grief overcame him. His beloved cousin Sumter would remain part of a past he could not return to. Did Sumter mourn him as bitterly? Atoli remained respectfully silent while Pax quietly shuddered his pain into the bedclothes beneath him. Eventually his friend Atoli spoke.

"My heart is heavy for you, Pax," he said with strain, "How difficult it must be to not remember the ones who loved you..."

Atoli's friend did not respond to this offering, he simply continued mutely shaking his pain into his covers. Atoli watched Pax until finally he exhausted himself to sleep again.

***

The day following Pax's dream of his cousin King Sumter, Saramis was walking through the forest searching for herbs and confused at her feelings. Pax seemed a completely different person to her now and of course he was. She felt remorse for striking him and yet, she reasoned, what else could Pax do to shock Saramis out of her self-induced spell to keep him a child? She hugged herself tightly as she walked. She didn't know what she wanted, Saramis thought in despair.

The Woman of the Woods stopped in amazement; she almost walked right into Pax, who did not see her, also lost deep in his thoughts. She blinked as she noticed his flushed skin. Before this moment, the young man couldn't imagine a scenario where he would not notice her presence immediately.

We're alone, the thought thundered like a chant in his mind.

"I'm sorry," Saramis stammered but Pax didn't speak, he just looked at her, dazed by her beauty. Gone was the confident man who stepped into her tent the night before, replaced by a man who simply couldn't breathe at the thought of being alone with her. Pax's pupils widened, and he stepped back; Saramis misunderstood this movement.

"Please forgive me for striking you, Pax..." She offered as her voice trailed away.

"You had no choice," he finally said and then added with a twinkle in his eye, "You can do it again, if you like..."

This drew a small smile and deepened the blood to her warm brown skin; was he flirting with her?

The quiet in the glen deepened as Saramis began to walk in a circle, thinking. Pax followed this movement in the opposite direction, his eyes riveted to her face. She was struggling to speak with him as an adult; he could see this, and his mind whirled as he prepared himself.

"You've changed so much, Pax, and I feel as though I've remained the same..."

"You're not the same," he replied urgently, "And neither am I..."

Saramis shook her head.

"I just keep seeing the little boy whom I comforted in the caves..."

"Let him go," said Pax firmly, drawing her eyes to him in surprise, "I have."

Her shoulders sagged.

"What do you want of me, Pax?" she asked in despair.

"A life with you," he said without hesitation, "Forever if that's possible..."

He watched in wonder as her hand went to her throat and she tried to catch her breath. Pax saw something different then; the truth buried under her blindness, the barrier holding her emotions back from him.

He spoke to this.

"Saramis," he whispered, "What is it that you hold against me, truly? Is it that you wish to remain unbonded for life, like some others of our people? Why do you hold me back from you when you know that I love you?"

Pax said this last thing breathlessly. Nothing studied or rehearsed, just the truth of what he felt for her. Saramis looked at him then and he saw something behind her eyes; it made him hold his breath again.

She shook her head in honest confusion; an unspoken fear she had never addressed herself.

"I just…"

She hesitated.

"I just don't understand why I'm older than you…"

Pax boldly crossed the space between them and holding her face in his hands, he pressed his lips to hers. He closed his eyes and didn't move, though he ached to. He just held her, feeling the trembling of them both. They could hear the hush beneath the birds who suddenly stopped chirping, and the leaves drifting slowly to the earth. Pax's blood pounded in his ears as he felt Saramis's hands gently cover his and her lips tentatively returned his gentle press.

Then Pax kissed Saramis with all the tenderness of four aching years apart.

* * *

As the day deepened, Pax and Saramis were not the only people meeting in the shaded areas that sheltered the tribe called human. Cord was walking with Atoli and Nea, listening carefully as Atoli explained the various fauna and vegetation that the people gathered for nourishment. At some point, Cord began to explain what he understood of Atoli's words, with encouragement from Nea. The fellowship between them was warm and Cord felt his heart expanding; perhaps he and his sister had finally found their forever home.

Presently, they came across Aylin, who was off moping and feeling sorry for herself. Cord politely excused himself from his friends and moved to join his sister.

The siblings stood in silence for a while. When Aylin began to wipe her face on her sleeve, her brother sighed and broke the quiet.

"Will you tell me what ails you, Aylin," said Cord, "Or must I speculate that the warrior Pax is somewhere at the center of your misery?"

At this, Aylin covered her face and broke into full blown sobs. Strangely enough, her brother did not move to comfort her as in the past; Cord merely crossed his arms and watched this display with narrowed eyes.

Finally, between gulps and restrained weeping, Aylin spoke her mind to her brother.

"I did...as you suggested," she stammered, "I told Pax my feelings..." she looked up to Cord's face at this to check his response and her eyes widened at his unreadable expression. Aylin expected her protective brother to be tensely waiting for her story to unfold, yet Cord was not. She wiped her face again, not sure how to continue.

But her brother waited in silence.

"Well, I...I tried to tell him, but he...he..."

Aylin then fell on Cord's shoulder, sincerely weeping her heart out, but Cord did not respond to this, instead he stared off in the distance, trying to keep the tension from his jaw. As his sister became fully aware that her brother would not react to her drama, Aylin stood back from Cord in puzzlement.

"What means this, brother?" Aylin asked in amazement, "Do you care not at all what has befallen me?"

When her brother's eyes slowly turned in Aylin's direction, she saw at last the anger he was barely holding back from her, and she blinked rapidly, for she knew not the cause of such rage.

"But you've not yet told me what has befallen you, Aylin," replied Cord tightly, "If anything has..."

"Why do you say this, brother?" Aylin exploded in frustration, "I...I'm trying to explain my distress!"

"Perhaps you're having trouble explaining your distress, sister," said Cord tightly, "Because you cannot form your words without saying a lie..."

Unwisely, Aylin tried to strike her brother across the face for this insult, who easily caught her wrist and squeezed it painfully.

"You have no honor to defend, sister," Cord said with emphasis, "And you cannot tell me what you said to Pax because you used no words to convey your feelings."

The blood drained from Aylin's face.

"What are you about?" she asked weakly, though Cord's sister was beginning to fear that she knew exactly what her brother was speaking of.

"You've probably forgotten Lathan, Aylin," Cord said quietly as he released her wrist, "Some years before, but I have not. And you know it is my way to make certain you are safely at rest before I close my own eyes..."

Aylin flushed and turned away in shame from her brother. Lathan was a man the siblings met early on in their journey through the kingdoms. Cord had believed Lathan to be an honest man, a ruse Lathan presented to bring himself closer to a much younger Aylin. This dark chapter ended with Cord having to slay the older man in order to save his sister, an event that scarred them both.

"In truth, I only wanted you to speak with Pax, brother," Aylin said in great remorse, "It was not my intention for you to defend my honor..."

Cord did not respond to this offer but waited a moment. When his sister had trouble going on, he continued in a lowered tone.

"Such hope I have that you mean that, Aylin...To think you might place me in harm's way on a selfish whim..."

Aylin now turned to Cord in misery.

"But I would never do this, Cord, you must believe me..."

The former mercenary scoffed.

"You are capable of many things, sister, that I have seen first-hand. And one thing more I have learned..."

Cord now paused to consider a thought, then gave it a voice.

"My protection has crippled you, Aylin. There is now a belief in you that whatever comes your way I will stand between it and you; and this is something that no one can truly do for another..."

It seemed that Cord would say more to his sister, but he shook his head sadly and walked away from her.

Aylin leaned against a tree and hid her face. She did not know it then, but in the morning, her brother would be gone.

***

Bowman Kha stood on the crest of the Pacine mountains, considering the turn his life had taken. His long quest to win the heart of Affi-Saramis had ended in defeat, both of body and spirit. In the years that Saramis was separated from Pax, Kha had come no closer to the goal of making her forget his rival. At first, he was encouraged by how her blindness to Pax's growth remained intact on their return to the tribe.

Kha's vision, however lacked nothing; he was startled to see the changes in Pax, a boy no longer. He was taller; his chest and arms were much stronger than years ago. Pax's gaze was confident as their eyes met; he had not forgotten their impromptu battle long ago and was clearly prepared for another.

Something else happened, to Kha's great disappointment. He did not see the exchange between Saramis and Pax on the evening the young man entered her tent, but the next day, Kha noticed the look in Saramis's eyes had altered. She clearly saw the same man everyone else did, and when Pax submitted his petition to bond with Saramis, she did not immediately say no, as she had with him.

Bowman Kha issued a right of challenge, which was accepted by the council, since he did not bond with anyone after Saramis's refusal years ago.

To their mutual surprise, the Great Second Elder added another requirement before the petition could proceed, she would have an audience with the three of them.

They did not meet in her tent, however. Once the trio gathered in respectful silence before her, Affi-Tosla led them outside of the boundaries of their camp. They walked in silence until she paused before a huge tree, hundreds, perhaps thousands of years old. In the early morning light, the leaves on the tree looked radiant. Saramis, Kha, and Pax felt as though they could see every single leaf, as though it stood out and called to them. They each heard her voice as though she spoke to them alone.

"Every choice you make creates a lifetime; each decision is a leaf on the Tree of Experience. Just as the leaves of a tree appears without number, so are the possibilities of the lives you move through. The present moment can only be experienced once, so all your lives move at the same time, just as you see all the leaves of this tree at once..."

The Great Elder turned to look at each one of them, they were riveted on her gaze.

"If you create a lifetime through a decision and then say no to it, you merely create a new lifetime where you must repeat the decision until the lesson is learned. There are no branches without leaves. Nothing you create returns empty; all words are spoken with power."

In their stunned silence, Affi-Tosla turned her piercing gaze to Saramis.

"You three have done this dance for lifetimes. When you turn from your power, pain will come to remind you of it. This time, Saramis, you will learn why you did not listen to the wisdom of your inner voice."

Saramis covered her face with her hands.

Pax longed to comfort her, but he did not dare to. He started as he noticed the Great Elder's eyes on him.

"The World is waiting to consume you, Rasdeter..." she said quietly.

His eyes widened; how did she know his true name? Before his mind could turn to Saramis, the elder said something he knew Saramis did not know, because Pax had never told her.

"You want to see your cousin again," the Great Elder said as Pax's chest constricted. "As long as you want this, they will find you. They believe that the only way they can kill him is through you and in some ways, they are right..."

Pain ripped through the former prince, who could not contain the brimming of his eyes. Questions roared in his mind: Who was looking for him? Did his cousin know he was alive? Could he truly go home once more? And most importantly, who wants to kill Sumter, and why do they think that he, Pax would help?

Affi-Tosla's eyes were filled with so much compassion as she gazed on Kha that his heart nearly burst in sudden sorrow. She approached him, and Bowman Kha went to his knees. She placed her hands on both sides of his face, and he knew it was over for him as she spoke softly.

"On this tree, Kha, there are thousands of leaves, perhaps millions, that belong to you and Saramis. You have won many times, and perhaps it is this memory that drives you in the present moment. Yet, you, too, gave permission for this lifetime to experience loss, though you have tried to change your mind over and over..."

She lifted his chin and wiped the tears from his face like a mother would, looking deep into his eyes.

She whispered.

"Saramis has given up all notion of safety in this life, Kha. You cannot save her."

Bowman Kha leaned his face into her bosom and his body shook with silent sobs.

* * *

The lavish beauty of the mountainside pulled Kha back into the present moment. His horse nudged him with affection, sensing his sadness, and Kha stroked the stallion's mane. Though his hurt pride lashed out at him, the Bowman withdrew his challenge to Pax's petition and gathered his things to leave the region for good. He shared with Affi-Tosla that he realized he had been following the urges of his lower heart in pursuing Saramis. He would honor the laws he had always abided by and allow the woman he loved to live the life she wanted. Before he left, the elder had said something strange to him, that he didn't understand.

"You have my protection, Bowman Kha."

But he felt the love behind it, so he nodded to her and knelt to receive the farewell blessings of the people.

When Saramis approached him to say goodbye, Kha couldn't help himself, he crushed her to him, savoring their first and only mutual touch. She returned his embrace in sorrow.

He whispered in her ear.

"If you ever need anything, I will know it..."

The woman Kha loved sighed as he pressed his lips to her forehead, then he turned from her and left, never looking again behind him.

* * *

His horse nudged Kha again and he smiled at this continual lapse into memory. Kha leaned slightly against his stallion's neck as he drank from his water pouch, then mounted him and rode away.

* * *

The mercenary known as Cord had also left the Tribe called Human; he was making his way in a different direction than Kha, on the roads to the Unnamed Lands. His heart was heavy as he strode through the forest on an unmarked trail. Cord wanted to stay with the people but feared his sister's immaturity and hunger for adversity might place him at odds if he remained. The former mercenary wished to lay down his sword for pay but there was no place for a man without skills other than bloodwork. He thought of his father with remorse. He knew what his father thought of mercenaries and now he was one. But how else could he feed himself and his sister as a man of no kingdom? Cord had planned to watch over Aylin until he could find her a respectable husband but his accidental viewing of her interaction with Pax clearly showed Cord that his sister was not concerned about her respectability.

His mind turned to Lathan and Cord's chest constricted. He didn't know for sure what had happened between them and Aylin was too young at the time to say. Cord had often feared his sister was affected somehow by the older man; she was never the same afterwards, but then neither was he. Cord had killed before Lathan, but that was in wartime. To slay a man outside of battle in defense of another was completely different. He wondered if when he finally met his father in the shaded realms and told him of his life, if his father would have preferred his son and daughter had died with him than to have lived in shame.

The former mercenary turned swiftly at a sound behind him, with crouched knees and drawn sword. Cord started at the sound of a familiar voice.

"Brother, where do you go in such a hurry," asked Atoli kindly, "It took us most of the day to catch up with you. All is well?"

Cord could not speak for a moment.

"I am ashamed to say I left without warning, Atoli..." he shrugged after a moment, unable to say more.

One of the young men with Atoli spoke quietly.

"You are a brother to us, Cord, and brothers do not travel alone. Even Bowman Kha is shadowed where he walks to another tribe."

"Another tribe?" echoed Cord in a hopeful tone. This idea had never occurred to him.

Atoli pointed to four of the seven warriors who walked with him.

"They will go with you, to the kingdoms or another tribe, wherever you travel, you need only to say it."

The former mercenary was overcome, he bowed his head as his voice cracked.

"I've never had friends, Atoli, the cost was too high..."

"Now you have friends and brothers," responded a warrior as he stepped forward to clasp Cord's shoulder, "And should brothers not care for one another?"

His lips tightened as Cord nodded mutely. The men of the tribe gathered around Cord and roughly jostled him as men do to calm their emotions; Cord responded with unaccustomed laughter and returned their harmless banter. The group then became two groups; Atoli waved farewell to Cord.

"Fear not for your sister Aylin in your absence," said Atoli warmly, "The women will tend to her. Be well, brother, until we stand under the sun again together..."

Cord returned this gesture, his heart greatly lifted as he walked his path in the company of those who loved him.

Life with Saramis

In his eighteenth year, Pax and his people once again wandered near the kingdoms. Now well versed in their ways, he knew the reasons for avoiding them, not the least of them was to veer well away from the Lourdes clan, a group of marauders who fought to overrun kingdoms and any groups who did not embrace their stern and warlike ways. Pax, like all members of his tribe were warriors and quite able to defend themselves. It was simply their way to live peacefully on the land. His people claimed the whole earth and so moved freely on it. They did not believe in staying in one place, setting boundaries around it that needed to be defended.

Kingdoms rose and fell for that reason. If you claim one nation and place borders around it, eventually you must protect it and once you outgrow it, you must extend and absorb other nations by battle to maintain it. This logic became sensible to Pax, especially when he considered that his present predicament came about as a direct result of his father's desire for his uncle's throne.

They were very close to the Kingdom of the Bright Forest. Pax and Atoli stood on a hill overlooking the eastern borders that surrounded the kingdom with great tall trees. The king's palace stood on the topmost hill with huge gates and walls. Beyond it were smaller mansions and buildings until finally you could see just before the tree line the boulder huts and tents of the general populace. It was beautiful in the afternoon light, and the pair stood mesmerized until Atoli's mate caught his gaze and he moved away.

Atoli was allowed to bond with his first love at eighteen but he did not leave his tent with Pax until he demonstrated his ability to care for Nea and provide for any possible offspring. Pax had watched with interest as Atoli drew his plans for their lifemate tent in the dust and discussed it with the other men. Like most of the people he included space for members without family who might come to live with them, the elderly and the young. Atoli wanted skins lined with fabrics for extra protection from high winds and took his time to select the perfect branches culled from trees with flexible and supple limbs. It was designed to fold up quickly with all things inside intact in the event the people must move to another location.

He spent months carving his own furniture from discarded and fallen wood. Atoli carefully mixed the natural dyes he used to draw symbols of his and Nea's ancestors on the outside; Nea would paint the symbols of love peace and longevity on the inside once the couple took up residence. The men worked together to assemble and erect the finished tent; Atoli beamed with pride as he wiped the sweat from his cheeks. The people gathered to bless their bond and Nea covered her face, overcome at the final product of his labors. This clear display of his feelings for her affected them both. Atoli was unable to speak for most of the ritual; he merely held her hand tightly and gazed into her eyes.

Pax's musing about Atoli and Nea brought him back to the present moment as his friend moved away from Pax and down the hill. Nea was now great with child and naturally Atoli's thoughts were on her and their coming offspring. Nea was strong and capable but this was their first; their interactions drew smiles from members of established families.

The smile that came from Pax was bittersweet. Though he had bonded with Saramis, it would be many years before he could build her a tent. The one she occupied had been built for her by the people when she became a wise woman and designed to last.

As before, Pax recalled little of his own ceremony of bonding with Saramis. The beauty he found displayed in her robes of the Marriage Knot had left the former prince mostly speechless. He was required to complete a ritual of cleansing himself that lasted three days. On the last day, his brother Atoli entered his secluded tent with a basket that held several pounds of white beads; Atoli asked his friend a simple but puzzling question:

"Do not count the beads, brother Pax," said Atoli, "Only tell me the first number that entered your thoughts when you saw them."

Pax hesitated as he recalled his thoughts when he first beheld the beads.

"Twelve..." he answered with a look of confusion and watched as Atoli smiled.

"Does it mean anything, brother?" asked Pax, who suddenly felt afraid.

"There is no wrong answer," responded Atoli, "The meaning of the beads only deepens with each stage of your life with each other. Elder Zema will explain..."

Two First Elders began to chant as they entered his bonding tent. Atoli helped Pax string the beads; his hands had begun to shake as he tried to thread them together.

The Second Elders entered his tent followed by Saramis; whose slight trembling matched his own. The beads she strung for him were black and knotted between; his brothers would tell him later that it was to keep them silent, to mirror the quiet of a seed pushing up through the earth. His skin warmed at her touch, and Saramis frequently looked away from his gaze of intense and burning wonder.

She stiffened slightly when Pax brought forth his own beads; it was then he noticed that the beads from his new lifemate numbered the same as his: Twelve.

His breath quickened, he had no idea if this were a good or bad thing, until their eyes met, and he saw her widening pupils with brimming eyes full of love. Pax was spellbound as he fell into their depths; his brother had to prompt Pax to kneel and tie the second string of beads around her left ankle. The act of touching her soft skin threw his mind completely off course; Saramis smiled shyly as

Atoli again directed his best friend to sit and wait while his soon-to-be lifemate gently tied her second string of dark beads around his own ankle. Pax would not remember how this shared intimacy felt; he would only remember that from this day forward, he would be separate from Saramis no longer.

Second Elder Zema calmly explained to Pax that the number of beads represented all the lifetimes Pax could effortlessly recall knowing or remembering Saramis, and she to him. The former prince did not understand what this meant, but Pax recalled the words of his brother Atoli, that one day he would understand; that was enough for him.

The future lifemates both felt their hearts pound in their chests as Elder Zema moved to pull back the flap of the tent and the Great Elder entered. The pair were directed to sit across from Affi-Tosla who waited patiently while the First Elders stoked the flames of the small fire pit with fragrance and seeds.

"This feeling that you share for each other is bound up in mystery," began the Great Teacher, "And many believe that it is because you are male and female; that men and women are supposed to mate with one another and reproduce to ensure the survival of the human species."

She gazed on the warrior known as Pax.

"You have been told this…" she stated, and Pax nodded soberly, unsure of what the Great Mother would say next.

"My…father…always said that a man should marry, and bear children," said Rasdeter softly as he glanced from Affi-Tosla to Saramis, "That a man's word…and his lineage was everything in this world…"

"Yet if this were all to the reason for it, then your heart would draw you to anyone, any female, and you would feel no preference over another," Affi-Tosla continued, and Pax's mind flew immediately to Aylin, who was beautiful by any standards, yet his heart did not yearn for her.

As the Elder's eyes fell on Saramis, the woman of the woods flushed and looked down at her hands.

"Would you say that your attraction for Rasdeter is merely physical, Affi-Saramis?" asked the Great Elder, and Saramis shook her head as she now met her mentor's gaze.

"I am drawn to him," she replied and looked shyly at Pax, who could not easily look away.

"You are energy," answered the Elder as Pax respectfully returned his gaze to her, "And just as the lodestone pulls and repels, the male and female energy pulls at one another. You will be drawn to the one you have the most to learn from, and this is stronger than any outside appearance."

Affi-Tosla held out her hands, and the pair placed their outside hand in hers; Pax his left hand, and Saramis her right hand.

"We call your bond 'Lifemate', not because you must remain physically bonded for life, but because you will be spiritually bonded until you have mastered everything you need to learn from each other. This can take days, weeks, months, years, or lifetimes, and when you are finished, you will move on to another lesson, with either another soul or another lifetime together. You have already agreed to bond before this moment; before you met in this life; that is a part of the mystery. Yet because we are here in this tent, I must ask you both aloud: Do you, Rasdeter and Saramis, agree to be bound to one another until all lessons are learned?"

"I agree," said Pax strongly, and heard Saramis give her own earnest reply.

"I agree," she echoed, and both watched as the Great Elder bound their hands together with her own.

"Who of our tribe will second the vows of these two humans?" asked Affi-Tosla, and Atoli and Nea stepped forward.

"I have heard my brother Pax and I stand by his word," said Atoli firmly, and Pax felt Saramis fingers tremble in his palm as Nea spoke for her.

"I have heard my sister Saramis and I stand by her word."

The Great Elder looked to Second Elder Zema, who spoke with a trace of a smile behind the seriousness of her voice.

"This bond is recognized by the Tribe called Human," offered Zema, "And cannot be undone."

"So be it," said Affi-Tosla as she squeezed their hands together, "Let the earthly rituals begin that the world requires; all else is complete."

As the formalities, feasting and celebrations of his people began, Pax felt everything fade from his mind. He reached for the hand of Saramis as they stood before their now shared tent and tentatively brought her fingers to his lips. Saramis could not know in this moment that her new husband's heart nearly stopped as Pax watched Saramis reach up with her other hand and slowly draw away the bonds on her hair.

* * *

Thoughts of the lovely colors trapped in the dark amber strands of Saramis's hair brought Pax gently back to the present moment. The former prince sighed at the feelings these memories evoked in him; Pax had felt himself reconciled to his new life and filled with peace now that Saramis was his. Soon he hoped he would see the fruits of his union with the woman he loved, and Pax could truly press roots deep within the family he grew up in. Yet thoughts of children made his chest tighten with anxiety; what would he tell a son, or a daughter about himself? The symbols on Atoli and Nea's tent filled Pax with pain; could he paint the symbols of his true ancestors on the skins and include an image of his father the traitor and murderer?

As Pax stood on the hill, he was suddenly immersed in a cloud of dandelion seeds; they caught in his hair and clothing and he recalled the child from his recurring dream. A faint image of her blowing on the white seeds made Pax smile. She's learning, he thought, then mused to himself if he should speak with Saramis or one of the elders for the meaning of the dream.

Perhaps it's just something I've made up to make myself happy...

He breathed deeply as he focused his vision on the trees of the Bright Forest. The sun's light was beautiful as it danced on the leaves and branches, it eased somewhat his now heavy heart.

Pax scoffed at his own childish train of thought.

"What is done cannot be undone," The former prince said aloud to himself as the image of the names of Lord Altus and Princess Erami inscribed on the sides of his future tent with Saramis came to mind. "For all I may wish it..."

His eyes returned to the home of the king and as he gazed the walls and gates became a more familiar place: his old home, the Kingdom of the Far Isles. Pax imagined his cousin Sumter, now also eighteen, sitting on his uncle Valtus throne. He couldn't help himself as he began to wonder who was left to assist his cousin: was High Regent Galen still alive, did Polymus or Lord Brayten yet guide Sumter, and what of Lady Irisella?

Pax caught his breath as the image of General Aton came before him. Though now a grown man the memory of his near demise almost caused him to step back. Certainly, the general covered up what he did. Sumter wouldn't let Aton get away with slaying him...would he?

Six years have passed, he thought, surely no one was talking about what his father had done. But a young king on the throne of the Far Isles...

There had to be news of his cousin...

More impulse than thought, the former prince straddled his horse and rode swiftly down the hill and towards the roads leading to the Kingdom of the Bright Forest.

A Great Prize

Pax strode uneasily through the marketplace of the Bright Forest. His clothes marked him clearly as a Wanderer and he gripped the reins of his mount tightly as he made his way. Once he noted there were many strangers mingling among the common folk he calmed himself. He felt all eyes were on him as he headed towards the local tavern, but it was not for the reason he thought. The Wanderers were mostly tall and easy to look upon, so he fit right in. But among the ordinary folk of the Bright Forest his great physical beauty stood out, even with the robes of the Plains draping him. Finally, Pax noticed that it was mostly women, particularly the rather young who stared openly at his dark curly hair, chiseled features, and deep green eyes. His face burning, Pax drew his cowl over his head to ward off their glances and shivering giggles.

The atmosphere of the local tavern assaulted him. Six years of open-air living and before that the pampered breezes of a palace ill-prepared Pax for the sights, sounds and relative darkness. His people of the woods kept themselves clean and their robes neat. In the Kingdom of the Bright Forest many of the people who were not among the nobility or proud of their station in life as masons or tradesmen cared little for personal hygiene or well-worn clothing. Some walked in tatters and shredded sandals, eager to blame anyone but themselves for their appearance. The smells also appalled him; mongrel dogs lapped up scraps and pre-digested food from the floor while men who neither noticed nor bathed themselves idly scratched at neglected sores. His eyes widened at young boys and girls serving fermented and strong-smelling beverages to people from all places and times. Several older men and women shouted orders to these children from behind a covered table while all others talked in a loud discordant hum.

He nearly walked out; this was more than he could bear as either prince or common man. Then Pax overheard some men of nobility conducting a rather heated discussion of local politics. He decided he could bear the stench a while longer, but he checked his chair before seating himself. He noticed some men relieving themselves on the walls before being forcibly removed by what passed for protection of the premises. An old woman in particular shouted threats to discourage any more indignities inflicted on her establishment.

His small table removed the idea of company; he used coins to purchase something he had no intention of drinking. The thought of what these people might do in preparation of food and drink made Pax feel nauseous. He was just close enough to overhear what might be shouted; he wisely decided not to appear to be openly listening.

Three men who looked to be nobles were in a tense debate; a fourth leaned back on his chair in a detached and bored manner. He wore something like the robes of a regent, as Pax recalled them; he dared not stare to be certain.

"Why do you keep bringing up The Kings Summit, Atrello?" bellowed one man, "This is old news and unsubstantiated. King Ruan did not assault the High King of the Unnamed Lands, N'Goth wasn't even there!"

"I heard the First Hound of the Circle of the Earth fought a dark angel and brought down one of the summit buildings, killing hundreds," said another man as he lowered his cup.

"That didn't happen either, Busso, I know someone who was there," said the first.

The one called Atrello sneered over his brimming cup at his verbal opponent. His red bleary eyes marked him as one who would argue a point whether it was documented or not.

"Well," said Atrello haughtily, "Do you know why King Sumter did not attend his first summit as a king of the world's most powerful nation?"

"Perhaps he was too young to go?" offered Busso.

"No one knows why he didn't come, Busso," said Gorm, the noble who first spoke, "But I'm sure Atrello will tell us anyway."

Pax started as though an armored fist struck him at the mention of his cousin's name. He gripped his cup tightly as waves of emotion surged out from him.

What Pax did not realize was that the bored man seated at the table with the other three nobles was both regent and mage. He shared a purpose with thousands of mages seated in taverns across the earth scanning for reactions to conversations regarding young King Sumter. In fact, they desperately searched for anything that would lead them to the true name of The Dark One or even more immediately urgent, to him, whose true name was Rasdeter, the Lost Prince of the Far Isles.

The mage could not see Pax, the protection of Saramis covered him. But he could feel the former prince's emotions; his gaze suddenly changed from bored to alertness. He sat up carefully and scanned the room slowly, trying to pinpoint the source.

Atrello drank deeply from his cup, slamming it to the table for emphasis. A young boy hurried to the table with more ale at this summons.

Atrello grinned.

"I have it on good authority that the true reason Sumter did not attend was not because he was too young. King Ruan is sixteen to his eighteen years and she attended. It was because a family member was murdered on the roads to the Western Hills."

Pax was having trouble breathing; he was trying to still his wildly beating heart. From the corner of his eye he noticed the change in the fourth man sitting at the table. He was not listening to his companions; he was scanning the room. Pax could feel the tentacles of his power waving out, he couldn't sense him, not yet...

I was a fool to come here, Pax thought in alarm. Of course a mage could sense the disruption of my emotions...

"An easy remedy," Gorm countered arrogantly, "Surely his High General would execute criminals in place of his king."

"Well, it wouldn't be Aton," Busso said with a laugh, "Sumter killed him for slaying his cousin, in a rather gruesome way, I might add."

The others laughed at this jest, while the one called Pax tried not to groan at the mention of Aton, the man who should have slain him. He tried to restrain his emotions but failed as waves and waves of them branched out from him like an explosion. The mage came to his feet in amazement, no longer hiding his intent to find him. Power arched from his hands as his companions looked to him in alcoholic confusion.

The regent and mage still could not see Pax, which made him narrow his eyes. His assumption was correct: someone of power was either cloaking someone or a group of people from his sight. The sorcerer made a sound of frustration, but he wasn't giving up.

Sweat broke out on Pax's brow; how can he escape without alerting the mage? In slow motion, he noticed the boy who could see him approaching to offer him more brew. His eyes widened in terror; if they caught him...

He had to risk it. Pax released the slightest thought.

Saramis...

She responded instantly and everyone in the tavern stood still...

Except the mage.

He was strong, braced by the energy of others and now that he felt power surrounding him, his own heart thudded wildly in his chest. This was a great prize indeed, and he must find it. He concentrated and shook off the might of Saramis, but he could not yet see the source of the emotions hammering at him.

Time to narrow my focus, the mage thought. If I cannot see the person, let me see if I can ascertain the empty spaces...

He let his power blanket all the people he could see and suddenly the table in the corner stood out, not because no one appeared to be sitting there, but because his power could not penetrate the space. His gaze locked on and through Pax, who now looked at him in open fear.

The mage still couldn't see him, not yet...

The regent and mage called on his brethren, who instantly linked together to augment his might; they would all appear there if he needed them. Pax watched as his power seemed to fill the world...

Saramis could not help him, Pax thought in despair; she wasn't strong enough. He felt her surge; she was about to join Pax and possibly die with him. His terrified thoughts finally brought forth the only help that seemed infinite to him among his true people...

The name blazed in his mind.

Affi-Tosla!

Pax vanished in a roar of light. The mage was hurled backwards against the wall behind him, losing consciousness. Now that Pax was safely gone, the tavern and its people returned to normal. The mage's three companions looked about them in confusion; wasn't he just standing next to them? Gorm gazed to his right and squinted as he spied the mage lying on the floor behind them.

"Well," Gorm grunted, "I never imagined the regent was drunker than you, Atrello."

"What was he having?" asked Busso, "It must have been good..."

"Tavern boy!" shouted Atrello as he pointed, "Bring us more of whatever he had and make it a double!"

The men roared with laughter and raised their cups.

* * *

The Report of the Mage

The regent and mage who faced the power of the Great Elder recovered in his rooms at the Hall of Regents in the Kingdom of the Bright Forest. His drunk but wealthy friends had the unconscious regent tied to his horse by their servants and delivered safely to his quarters. The mage whose name was Keoni returned to his senses in a panic; the last thing he remembered was a wave of power he had no answer for; his brethren who sent their magic power in support of Keoni were also hurled backwards by the might of some sorcerer they could not see or identify.

"It must be an Ancient," Keoni fearfully muttered to himself as he swiftly checked to make sure all his body parts still existed. Encounters with Ancient magicians were at best unpredictable and at worst they were deadly. The blast of light had been a warning, the mage thought, had the Ancient intended to, he or she could have slain Keoni and all the mages supporting him, such was their power. He was glad in this moment that he himself was under the protection of an Ancient.

A few hours later, Keoni was ready to travel. As soon as he stepped from his rooms, he saw another mage anxiously waiting for him, a regent called Abner. Abner was trustworthy and unambitious, a trait that made him valuable to their mutual master. Some regents looked down on Abner for this but Keoni was not one of them. In an organization filled with power hungry, grasping mages, Abner was prized simply for not being one of them.

Abner fell into step with Keoni as he made his way through the halls.

"I'm glad you are well, Keoni," said Abner sincerely, "I heard about what happened--"

Keoni made a gesture calling for caution, by placing his forefinger to his lips; Abner nodded. Living in a hall full of powerful regents who practiced magic naturally called for discretion. They made their way in silence, not speaking again until they were outside and mounted on horses. Afternoon light spilled on their path as they rode through the gates of the outer cities of the Bright Forest Kingdom. A mixture of dark and light green leaves blew from the limbs of trees in their way, scattered by their speed and quiet.

"He's waiting for you, brother," said Abner finally, watching as Keoni gave a great sigh.

"I know, friend Abner," replied Keoni, "...and I fear to give him my report; that I failed to secure an invisible person or persons, guarded by great power."

"Our master can be reasoned with, Keoni," said Abner soothingly, "Provided what you tell him can be used in his favor. Even a regent without skills in magic was able to assist our lord--"

"I know," responded Keoni more tersely than he meant to. He'd heard the talk of a mystery regent from another city (completely powerless!) who approached an Ancient and lived to tell of it. After he, Keoni, had been scouring the earth for seven years, eager to bring his master the great prize, proof positive that the lost prince either lived today or died as a child.

Keoni softened his tone as they neared the mountains.

"Forgive my sharp tone, brother," said Keoni contritely, "You, of all the regents, know how hard and diligently I've worked."

"Of course, Keoni," replied Abner with a shrug. "And none knows it more than our master..."

The pair continued on their way, speaking in this type of coded language until they reached the safety of the mountains. There the mages dismounted, preparing to transport both themselves and their mounts inside when they noticed the approach of another of their kind, coming towards them from the mountain.

The hooded mage held up his hand; Keoni and Abner paused in their spells.

"Thank you for coming, brother," said the man to Abner, "But the master will speak with Keoni alone."

Both hearts increased their beat; neither knew what this change meant. The men exchanged glances; Abner tried to make his an encouraging one.

"As you say, brother," replied Abner, and reached for the reins of both horses. Wordlessly, Keoni turned and followed his fellow mage, his stomach churning as he tried to appear brave. An image came to him of the wave of power coming from the supposed Ancient in the tavern, and he tried to hope that the future did not hold a similar event in the presence of his master. Keoni clenched his hands and breathed deeply as he climbed the summit.

On the way, Keoni was suddenly transported from the side of the summit and into his master's presence. A vast hall was carved into the topmost part of the mountain, giving it vaulted ceilings and a massive platform meant to hold thousands, if needed. Many steps led up to this platform to give the people approaching a rather intimidating viewpoint. On this stage was a lone chair, fashioned to look like a throne, and on it sat the master of Keoni, Abner, and thousands of other magicians, the Ancient known as Lord Enith. Behind him, his image was amplified and enlarged on the wall; it looked as though the mage towered over all those standing on the floor beneath him.

Having never been summoned to this place before, Keoni was terrified.

Enith wore robes of dark blue, almost black, and deep within the fabric, stardust twinkled like the milky way; it faded and came back to the foreground, and Keoni had the thought that his master had trapped dimensions in the fibers.

The voice of his master shocked Keoni from his reverie.

"You have news for me, regent."

"Yes, my lord..." he answered and gave his report. What the mage did not realize was that as he told his tale, his master scanned his mind, seeing everything: What Keoni remembered and all the things he overlooked in his retelling. Enith's eyes lit up at the same moment that Keoni stood up in the tavern, excited with possibility; and Enith came to his feet when he saw through Keoni's mind the force that slammed him into the tavern wall.

In the present moment, this movement by Enith froze Keoni and stammered his speech; he had no idea what it meant.

"Continue," said Enith firmly.

Keoni heard himself babbling.

"That's all I can recall, my lord..."

Enith remained standing, his eyes scanned again and again the power that froze everyone in the tavern, and the power that slammed Keoni and thousands of his brethren back from the invisible person in the tavern. That it was only one person shielded by this power and not many was all that Enith himself was able to detect. The mage was astonished that anyone other than an Ancient was able to block his own piercing gaze.

But there was another possibility...

His master was not looking at his servant but through him. Keoni did not know this, and it took everything he had not to fall to his knees and beg for his life. Lord Enith went down a mental list in his mind:

The nobility at the table were speaking of King Sumter when the first wave of emotion manifested itself, and the second.

They were speaking of General Aton when the strongest wave struck.

The Ancient's breath quickened; it cannot be...

Keoni stepped back and raised his arms over his face as Enith's power flared forth. The Ancient rumbled the mountains as he strained to overcome the energy protecting the one he could not see through his servant's mind. He had never pushed this hard, he never needed to, and to experience something other than The Magician's great strength brought unaccustomed sweat to his brow. Finally, Enith gasped in amazement and stepped back himself.

His face became a mask as his vision focused and he saw Keoni on his knees, waiting for death.

"Rise, Keoni," said the mage in wonder, "And do not despair, for you have fallen on my favor..."

Keoni came to his feet with difficulty.

"Feel no shame for your encounter in that humble tavern, for you have stumbled on great power..." Enith felt himself transported to that fateful moment when an unknown regent approached him with two gifts from a long dead servant.

His eyes focused again on his trembling follower Keoni and unconsciously the Ancient sorcerer made a fist.

"All this time I have searched for emotional reactions to King *Sumter...*" he shook his head. "Only the prince would feel dread at the mention of the man who tried to kill him..."

Keoni's own eyes widened; it was the prince himself who escaped him?

Enith bade his servant approach him and Keoni did so, still unsure if he would survive the night or not. Once close enough, his master placed both hands on either side of his servant's face. Power flared again, and Keoni felt a warmth surround his brain.

"On your life, Keoni, say nothing of this to anyone until I have announced if it is true or no. This energy I have placed around your mind will protect you from anyone trying to glean memories from you..."

The mage's gaze darkened.

"My seal will discourage anyone other than The Magician himself."

Lord Enith released his servant and stepped away, still holding his gaze.

"Should I be able to verify that you, Keoni, have delivered to me my heart's desire these last seven years, I will reward you handsomely. I know what you long for..."

Keoni blinked rapidly.

"Master..." the mage said then stopped, unable to say more.

"You shall have it," continued Enith, "...and things you have never dreamed of..."

Keoni bowed to Enith over and over, his heart bursting with gladness.

"Now go, faithful one," said the mage, and Keoni vanished.

He appeared again next to a startled Abner, who had just turned away from the moment Keoni vanished on the summit, scant seconds ago. The two men looked at each other in amazement and glanced again at the summit; the mage who escorted Keoni was gone.

"Brother..." said Abner, but his friend took his arm and firmly shook his head.

"On your life, ask nothing of it," stated Keoni firmly, "Nor search my mind for anything, or you will die..."

Abner nodded quickly and cast a spell on his own mind, so he would not be tempted to unconscious or careless death. The mages searched out the now darkened road in silence and rode without speaking until they reached the Hall of Regents, where they spoke earnestly of mundane things.

* * *

Deep in the mountains of the Bright Forest, the mage Enith brooded in near darkness. Torches on the walls of his retreat hung unlit, a few candles on the table next to him dared to offer light.

So close, he mourned, so close...

Enith knew what his servant did not; that the power that froze the tavern occupants was vastly different from the power that struck down thousands of mages. His fist pumped his throne in frustration as his mind turned frequently to the wave of light that hurled all his dreams to dust. He could not see past it, try as he might, and he did try, almost killing Keoni in the process.

An unnecessary death, he mused. He needed Keoni for the next step...

You are not an Ancient, the mage spoke in his mind to his invisible adversary, but you are a being of great power, with a force that I cannot penetrate...yet...

The mage looked about in the darkness and sighed deeply.

You have forced me to play a hand I do not wish to, in order to gain my aims. To secure the truth of the prince, I must do what I have spent millions of years avoiding; placing myself in debt to another. And not just any other, but the only one more powerful than any Ancient, the one all magicians are subservient to...

The Magician himself.

Little wonder then, that his servant Keoni's information brought Enith instantly from elation to despair.

A moment later, the last candle died out.

An Audience with The Magician

Long ago, less than a millennium after his decisive victory over the hated creators, the being known as The Magician removed himself from the world scene. You might think that after such a life-altering success at the very dawn of mankind's memory, that he would set up his throne and build a city around it. From there he would rule over men, and every child born on earth from that moment to now would grow up knowing his name.

But his mind didn't work that way.

The one who had learned the secret to confound the once in-vincible creators was not given to overconfidence. The Magician's vision was a long one; he wanted the earth and its inhabitants for all time, not just a million years or so. He had broken the trust and faith that man had in the creators; they no longer flocked in droves to learn the universal laws and science that governed all of creation. Instead, man feared them, leaving their halls of learning abandoned and desolate. Fewer and fewer creators were born or developed; most men doubted they ever existed; the stories of them were relegated to myth and speculation.

It appeared to be a glorious victory on the surface.

When The Magician faced Lord Master Theron and the remain-ing creators on that faraway day in the distant past, he revealed to Lord Theron that he, The Magician had learned far more than just how to destroy them. He had discovered the creators most cherished secret, that one day a child of prophecy would be born that would be greater than all of them. One that would break The Magician's stronghold on the thoughts and hearts of men. Mankind would once more embrace the inheritance of creation; they would understand quantum physics and the elements on levels unheard of. They wouldn't need his magic; man would create their own universes without the need to unnaturally change the chemical properties of the earth and elements around them.

It was a brave dream, one that The Magician was determined to destroy.

Mankind has always loved and been influenced by legends. Stories of adversity and bringing forth the best in man's own spirit were the things that inspired and drove mankind to greatness. So, the one who first showed man the dark side of his nature decided to become a story himself, to all but those of his inner circle, those who loved power and corruption as much as he did. To them he granted his own dominion over the earth, by use of magic and illusion, a way to separate men and women from their own innate power. The Magician wanted man to rely on the tools he made more than the Invisible Intelligence that inspired man to create them.

A brilliant strategy, that once The Magician set it in motion, he need do nothing else. It ran smoothly on its own, enticing man to greater and greater inventions, while his most marvelous tool, his mind, shrunk more and more from disuse, until only ten percent of its potential was available to advance the progress of mankind.

There was only one threat to this strategy; a fully aware creator with the ability to reawaken man.

The mage and Ancient known as Enith did not know the whole story of the battle between The Magician and the creators, nor did he care about it. What mattered for him was his own dreams of power and control; it was the only thing that kept him engaged and alive. Without this need to meddle in and subvert the dreams of others, Enith himself would fall prey to the bane of every ancient sorcerer: Madness. He refused to see, as did all others like him, that the longer he lived, separated from the call of creation, the more he would become like the source of his power, The Magician, who was completely insane.

For all Enith's great power, he was like any other man who needed stimulus and growth to develop. If he wished, he could stand on a hilltop, and watch the centuries fly by him like a breeze. He would watch cities and kingdoms rise and fall, men scurrying by like ants, building, fighting, dying, until just the sight of it would entrance him.

The mage shuddered at this thought; he'd seen it before. An Ancient would stand on a high place, like a hill or a mountain, and after a while, he or she would grow still and unmoving, seduced by the tapestry of life unfolding. The earth and trees would grow up around him and fall again as the land masses shifted, and still he would stand there, watching everything and now seeing nothing.

Enith had approached such mages, and gently waved his hand before their faces; few responded. Some had actually shifted their gaze to look at him briefly. One had shed a tear, and Enith knew then that there was no offer he could make that would cause them to move and rejoin him in the flow of natural time. Enith had walked away from these encounters with sadness. He knew eventually, he would return one day to find them gone. They would finally close their eyes and just let go; the particles of the body no longer held together by sheer will, and they would fade away to dark grey ash.

It was either that, or unrelenting battle with any and all who crossed their path. Enith's mind turned to his former pupil and now partner in his schemes, Iroh. The mage had saved Iroh from a maddened Ancient who had broken the one cardinal rule among magicians: Never attack a student who was under the protection of a mage or sorcerer. The insane Ancient had lashed out and destroyed Iroh's mentor, who was not an Ancient or as powerful, for the sole purpose of slaying Iroh, a fledging of much promise.

Enith had watched the battle with interest and stepped in at the last moment to save Iroh, who should have died immediately with his hapless mentor.

Lord Enith's deep reverie was interrupted by his arrival at The Magician's retreat. Enith had made a request for audience with his master and was gratified that it had been accepted. The Ancient had wisely also included a request for protection from The Magician's bound servant, The Rook. This was also granted by his master's word, which was the only reason Enith resolved to come.

The Rook was a former creator, now bound by a blood oath after The Magician's discovery of a creator's only weakness, the knowledge of their true name. The Rook, who once went by the name Michael, was a prize from the war near the beginning of time. Although The Rook was no longer connected directly to the source of creation, he cannot be killed by magic, and his power seems to yet be without limit. He takes out his pain on any follower of The Magician, who in turn is unaffected by either The Rook's rage or the decimation of his mages.

Yet, none can deny The Rook's value to his master: Any task The Magician sends him on is fulfilled, typically in the most destructive way possible. Hence, it behooved Enith to ask for protection as he sought his audience; he had no counter to The Rook's massive power.

The Magician also had a High Regent named Alaric; it amused the creature to mimic the ways of men. This High Regent met Enith at the entrance to his master's retreat. It was a courtesy and an indication of The Magician's favor; this move made Enith breathe easier as he followed the other mage through the torchlit halls that led to his audience.

The throne room of The Magician dwarfed any room that Enith had ever seen, including his own. Filled with light, it was difficult not to admire this tribute to the ages. Enith saw some reference to every civilization ever known, and some that were not yet known. The mage watched the comings and goings of thousands of mages, running errands for their master. There were some humans who dared to serve this great company, their minds sealed against any memory of whatever tasks they performed.

Yet the closer Enith came to The Magician's ornate and shining throne, the more he marveled at the raw power emanating from the man who stood to the right of his master, the former creator known now as The Rook.

Enith was millions of years old, and secure in his power. He had even faced down and destroyed other Ancients; the one who attacked Iroh came to mind. Before this moment, the mage had been sure that no one other than The Magician could separate him from his body before he could strike back. But now that his eyes met those of The Rook, who returned his gaze without emotion or interest, Enith was certain he was in the presence of one who could summon force without end. The mage breathed deeply to contain his alarm. Surely, without the bonds of The Magician surrounding him, this man could level this entire mountain, and the plains beyond it, blackening the hemisphere.

The voice of his master brought Enith back to the present moment.

"Well met, Enith," said The Magician, "It has been long since we spoke last, eons even."

"Yes, my lord," replied Enith with a deep bow.

"As you know, I am intrigued that such a powerful sorcerer as yourself would need anything from me, as evidenced by said lack of contact," continued his master, "Yet, here you are. Speak to me then..."

And Enith gave his tale, well aware that his master now scanned his mind as Enith did Keoni. It was a lesson in humility, one that Enith had lived millions of years without. He noticed the creature on the throne above him reacted in the same places Enith himself had done, and he worried that perhaps he would lose this enterprise that meant so much to him to another, even The Rook.

He worried needlessly. The Magician was fascinated by the story, that was all. But he had questions for his servant Enith.

"Is the child a creator?" he asked the mage, and Enith blanched; such a thought had never crossed his mind. He could not help but glance again at The Rook, who almost smiled at this...almost.

The Magician sat silent a while, thinking.

"If the child lives, Enith, what do you plan to do with him?"

The mage considered his answer for less than a moment. It was best to speak plainly of his desires; The Magician was very good at discerning a lie.

"It is my hope to place him on the throne of the Kingdom of the Far Isles," Enith responded softly.

After a moment, The Magician did something rare; he laughed aloud. The mages in his retreat paused at this unusual sound. The creature's eyes twinkled as he appraised the Ancient.

"It would be well if the Nine Kingdoms fell *before* the great battle at the end of the age, mage Enith," said his master, "Providing of course that the first cousin of King Sumter lives..."

Silence again took over the hall as The Magician searched his mind, sifting through the images he gleaned from Enith. Then he spoke aloud to the Ancient.

"You have stumbled across someone protected by a creator, Enith..."

The Magician nodded as the mage both flushed and blanched from his head to his feet. His master thoughtfully stroked his chin as he considered his words.

"Nothing can be seen that they do not want seen," he continued, "Such is their power. Whoever it is, I cannot learn the identity for you...without the aid of another."

Enith couldn't help himself, he gazed at The Rook, but his master shook his head. Then lifting his head slightly, the creature gave a meaningful glance at his High Regent, who immediately vanished.

The Magician came to his feet, and all turned to him.

"I will help you, Enith," he said simply, and the Ancient blinked rapidly before he nodded quickly.

"I owe you great thanks, my lord--" he began, but his master stopped him.

"You will owe me far more than that, mage," The Magician said with a slight smile. "For now, I seek the company of one who has shunned my presence far longer than you yourself have been living. In order to learn the truth of the prince, Enith, my hand cannot be seen. My schemes for this world lie in the beginning of it, and there are many things I do not wish for those now living to know..."

The Ancient felt the subtle shift in energy, and he looked in alarm at The Rook, whose black hair and robes began to move as he stood still. Enith could see certain elements become visible around his master's servant, and the atoms enlarged themselves and spun rapidly.

Millions of years in the future, scientists would 'discover' plutonium, a transuranic element derived from uranium and create isotopes from it suitable for use in nuclear reactors. It is said that when a uranium-235 atom absorbs a neutron and fissions into two new atoms, it releases three new neutrons and some binding energy in what is known as a chain reaction, that can cause a massive explosion. The Rook did not create the plutonium and uranium elements that danced before his eyes. He summoned them, from deep within the earth and from comets hurtling by in outer space, along with radium, mercury, and phosphorus. The only true joy he could now know The Rook experienced as the deadly particles paused at his mental command.

Many of those in the hall stopped their pace and looked to their master, suddenly uncertain. The mage turned back to lock eyes with The Magician, who watched Enith with an unfocused gaze.

"I will find her, of course," the creature seemed for a moment to be speaking to himself. "I have always found her, no matter where she roams this planet. From time to time, she leaves earth to be free of me, but it calls to her as I do..."

"Enith..." The Magician now said softly to regain his attention, "Stand still..."

The mage felt the power of his master enfold him. Seconds later, Enith was blinded by a bright light; it took everything in him to remain unmoving. But he did so, and when the Ancient could see again, he gasped:

Every living thing in the building, other than himself, his master and The Rook had been vaporized. At his feet were piles of dark grey ash and above him, a mushroom cloud blossomed and crackled with the energy of split atoms and nuclear dust. Everything else was unharmed; the fronds of palm trees waved in the transformed air; gold twinkled from the painted artwork in the ceiling, an uncaring witness to the devastation.

From what seemed a faraway place, Enith heard his master's voice.

"Have you ever watched the sun descend into the ocean, Enith? No doubt you've seen that lovely final flash of green light as the very top of that great ball of fire appears to vanish beneath the waves. It is a reminder of creation, what the Egyptians will one day call the cackling of the goose that brought forth creation at the speed of light, and future scientists will refer to as the Big Bang that started it all..."

The Magician pointed to his servant The Rook.

"This is but a taste of what these people we call creators can do. In the future, man will build machines to do what The Rook can do with his mind; call forth the elements in the combinations necessary to reduce the cells of the human body to the state before the zygote, to the flash of light that signals the possibility of life..."

"This..." The creature continued passionately, "Is among the skills and powers that the creators want to place in the hands of farmers, wanderers and...sheepherders, Enith! Do you not see that the only possibility, the only way the world can be safe is for these creators to be either controlled or destroyed!"

The Rook added nothing to this discussion. His eyes became blank again after fulfilling The Magician's will, focused inward to the agony of the distant past. The Rook cared not one whit for his master's plans or his forced execution of those same schemes. His thoughts were his own and they boiled with only one thing: Revenge.

The Rook's mind turned briefly to the mage Enith who supplicated his master for the domination of men with this thought:

It matters not your plans and schemes; I will see you all dead along with him. The Magician will die if I have to crack the earth in half to accomplish it.

His hair and robes returned to their former state as the winds of radioactive destruction dissipated at The Rook's command.

"Go your way, mage," said his master to Enith, "I will send word of what can be learned of your precious prince..."

Enith turned swiftly to go, unnerved by this display of raw power. Willfully destroying a cavern full of hundreds of people to both keep a secret and make a point was more than enough for the Ancient. The High Regent of The Magician reappeared at Enith's side as promptly as he left, and the mage breathed deeply at the reminder of his master's protection.

He heard again the creature's voice as he reached the hall doors, still sparking and tinged with smoke.

"Do give my regards to your former pupil Iroh, for me, Enith," said The Magician smoothly, "I look forward to meeting him."

"As you say, my lord," replied Enith more courteously than he felt.

The Ancient turned back to offer his master a final bow, then vanished as he crossed the threshold.

* * *

Moments later and leagues away, Enith stood atop his own mountain, trying with difficulty to control his emotions.

His audience with his master merely confirmed Enith's wisdom: It was right to keep away from the direct source of all magic, The Magician. And not just because of his exceedingly powerful servant, The Rook. Even though the creature was not human, the laws of the universe still applied: Separation from creation eventually leads to madness and more separation until the will to dominate and control others is all that is left.

Enith's thoughts went without fail to Iroh, whom he warned early on to stay away from The Magician, for just such an event as Enith had witnessed; the wanton annihilation of hundreds of able and talented sorcerers to prove a point about the creators. More than once The Magician had boasted that he could raise up mages and followers from the mud and dust of the ground, so eager was mankind to embrace his illusions. Little wonder the creature cared not how many died as he pursued his plans to dominate the earth for all time. Enith, in his turn had his own schemes and had decided to have Iroh spearhead their conquest of another kingdom, The Circle of the Earth. It had a direct bearing on Iroh's life and Enith's future plans, so it was an assignment important to them both. In this moment, the Ancient was glad his friend Iroh was distracted, and did not ask to accompany Enith to offer support.

For all the good it did.

The price for my request has been set, the mage thought sadly. Of course, The Magician would ask of me the only thing I cherish other than the destruction of the Nine Kingdoms, my prized former student and present ally, Iroh. I have dared much for this enterprise and now everything that matters to me is at stake.

The mage gazed down at his hands which now burst into flames.

If the prince is alive, Enith thought grimly, and I learn the name of the one who cloaked him from me these seven long years, that same one will feel my pain, to their extreme detriment.

The flames followed the lines of the Ancient's body and the mountain side erupted in fire.

The Protection of The People

The Magician sat again his throne in the deafening silence following the exit of the Ancient known as Enith. His High Regent Alaric used magic to gather up the dark grey ash of hundreds of sorcerers foolish enough to remain in the room while their master spoke his secret plans aloud. He then left the room himself; the regent knew The Magician wanted to speak with his bound servant alone.

After another moment passed, his master broke the quiet.

"Well, my Rusch, you know I cannot read your mind. So, tell me your thoughts on the quest of Enith."

The Rook did not respond right away, instead his eyes narrowed. He knew The Magician was not curious to learn his evaluation of Enith. The request made him wary.

"I have no thoughts of it," responded The Rook finally, "You know I care not what befalls the Nine Kingdoms."

It was the manner of The Rook to use familiarity when speaking to the one who held his life. The Rook had no fear of either The Magician or his possible death. His master in turn was amused by this disrespect; he knew his servant hoped he could bait the one who controlled him into destroying him. Followers of The Magician, however, could not bear The Rook's lack of manners and from time to time one of them would attempt to take him to task for it. The former creator's usual response to this was to vaporize the mage who corrected him before he finished speaking.

Hence, unless his master gave his servant a direct command, he typically addressed The Rook in private.

"I find myself intrigued as to the mage's attempts to shield his protégé Iroh from me, my Rusch," stated The Magician as he gave a sideways glance at his servant, "Why do you think this is so?"

The Rook did not return this glance, instead he studied the yet smoking doors across the wide expanse of his master's hall. As usual, his response was a blunt one.

"The mage Iroh does not know who he is," replied The Rook in a bored tone, "Enith is of course afraid that you will tell him."

His master's smile was a thin one.

"And why would I do that?" the creature queried to no one, "Iroh's ignorance is a boon to all of us. It will only provide better leverage to control the Ancient. I admire Enith's ambition...to a point, of course..."

The Servant of The Magician was not fooled by this seeming banter. He knew there was an objective to every conversation with the one he was bound to. His master was testing the waters; there was something he wanted from The Rook, something The Magician knew his powerful servant would not easily give.

As expected, his master changed the direction of their dialogue.

"Do you think the lost prince is a creator?" asked The Magician.

The one who gave away his soul for love scoffed at this question.

"A creator needs no protection, you know this," The Rook replied.

The Magician leaned forward on his throne as he studied his bound servant.

"Yet, it was energy from a creator that saved our unknown prey in the tavern..."

The Rook felt the invisible chains that bound him to The Magician tighten around his neck. His breath sharpened as he looked sideways at his master. He watched carefully as The Magician made a fist, and The Rook's chest constricted in pain.

"I know you can see what I cannot, my Rusch," said his master softly.

Then his voice hardened.

"Who was in the tavern?"

The Rook's power flared in response to this attack, but he could neither protect himself nor harm his master; the building and mountains shook from his efforts. The Magician knew his servant would eventually try to use The Magician's own power to kill himself, so his master used the only true weapon he had to coerce The Rook's obedience.

"Carefully consider your response to me, my servant," said The Magician calmly, "Remember your uncle, Lord Peder..."

His eyes brimming, The Rook released a shaky breath as sweat dampened his brow. Eons of enslavement to the creature had not dulled the remorseless agony of the past, sharper than the pain his master inflicted.

A wise one and a mystic once said that when men don't feel love, they destroy.

The Rook, who was once named Michael was the epitome of this concept. His relationship with the monster who formed him was a complicated one. His bondage to The Magician came about from the betrayal of his uncle, Lord Peder. The creature's only motivation in keeping The Rook alive is so that he can use the former creator in the final battle at the end of the age against the creators and the child of prophecy. Yet, if you believe that The Rook co-operates with The Magician in order to spare his uncle's life you would be wrong. The only leverage his master has left is the promise of Lord Peder, whom The Rook has sworn to eradicate in sure payment for his crimes. The Magician watched as the mention of his uncle shifted the struggle between them and changed the demeanor of his servant.

"I cannot see everything...master," The Rook replied in a tight but more measured tone. "You already know there were two of them, one more powerful than the other. No creator can override the will of another. The weaker one is a Woman of the Woods; her power is directly connected to the earth itself. I can see her easily, but the other..."

The Magician interrupted him.

"Where is she, then, this 'Woman of the Woods'?"

The Magician marveled as The Rook's destructive power flared again. The Rook was bound to assist his master against his former kinsmen, the creators. Despite his seeming aloofness this agenda did not sit well with him.

His master waited in patience; he knew his servant must answer him.

The powerful Rook's voice was full of strain, though he tried to speak calmly.

"She lives with the Wanderers of the Plains..."

The Magician snapped his fingers and his High Regent instantly appeared at his side.

His master did not even look at Alaric.

"Summon the Legion," The Magician said to his regent as he stared at The Rook, who slowly closed his eyes.

The Protection of the People, part II

In the months after Bowman Kha left the Wanderers of the Plains, life settled down again. Atoli and Pax successfully led the warriors in repelling the attack of the Lourdes clan on the people. Pax taught his fellow warriors what his father Lord Altus taught him; the tell-tale sign of their archers in the trees, and their wolves on the ground. Saramis and the other elders were also a formidable defense, and the clan scattered.

The Great Elder was not among them, though her tent remained. Pax himself carried her tent, after the elders packed her things. It was not unusual for Affi-Tosla to vanish while amongst them. A First Elder was usually the one to enter her tent to make sure of her absence.

That evening, the warriors not on sentry duty sat gathered around a small fire talking quietly of the day's events. Affi-Tosla's tent was assembled by Pax after the battle, and Atoli built the fire not far from it. Her tent offered a subconscious comfort to the people; it was not unusual for children to fall asleep near the entrance late at night. The elders soon joined the warriors and formed a circle with them, calming herbs were passed out to the people to chew. A small one cautiously sniffed his before giving the stem a hard bite, drawing a smile from the others. He found the aroma and the taste pleasing; he gave the elders a grin as he chewed on the bark.

Saramis sighed in contentment at this respite; it was nice to have a moment to savor the company of her tribe. As she gazed around the circle, her eyes fell on Pax, now her lifemate, and she looked away shyly. He had more trouble than she did in turning away; now that Pax had obtained permission to be with her, the urge to stare at his fulfilled dream was ever present. His face flushed at a nudge from Atoli, who grinned at his brother's unabashed happiness. Atoli raised his other arm as one of the little ones crawled into his lap to get closer to the fire, his eyes already heavy with the need to sleep. Before long, most of the smallest tribe members had found a spot within the circle; the older members lowered their voices and gestured their communications.

Pax found himself distracted for a moment; a tiny dandelion seed floated across his fingers and rested on his hand. He smiled to himself as a thought of the little child with red gold hair from his dreams came to mind. Pax had searched among the people and never found a child who matched her description, though the people of the Plains were of every hue and color imaginable.

Perhaps you've yet to be born, little one, Pax mused as his gaze returned to Saramis, whose pupils widened as their eyes met. A thought unconsidered began to form as his own pupils dilated, then was interrupted by a shiver that seemed to envelop the entire camp.

Suddenly, Saramis felt the hairs go up on her neck; she looked at the Second Elders, who had similar responses. Four of them came to their feet, just as the flap of Affi-Tosla's vacant tent flew open, and the Great Elder came into view, carrying a staff and striding rapidly in the direction of the circle. They swiftly made a way for her; she stopped and pointed at a stunned Pax.

"You," the Great Elder said curtly, "Into my tent, and do not come forth until I call for you."

A confused Pax came to his feet, just in time to be shoved towards the tent by Atoli.

"Do it, Brother," he said sharply, "These are words of life..."

As Pax vanished in the folds of Affi-Tosla's home, Saramis also came to her feet, in time for a sharp rebuke.

"Stand fast, Saramis!" cried her mentor, "His energy is all over you, you cannot help us!"

Saramis caught her breath tightly, stung by Affi-Tosla's words.

The First Elders gathered around her, using their energies to dampen hers. Never had there been a threat to her people she could not respond to. What was she now, a liability to her people and not an asset? She turned to look at the Great Elder's tent.

And what do these events have to do with Pax?

Affi-Tosla stepped away from the light of the circle and vanished, reappearing at the camp borders past the line of anxious sentries, who gripped their weapons in alarm. The dogs were baying and barking viciously at the dark line of the trees beyond.

The darkness gave itself form and moved away from the shadows of the tree line. A group of creatures shaped like men walked silently towards the Great Elder. They seemed to have no number and they multiplied rapidly, standing behind one who appeared the leader, though he looked no different from the others. He had no features, yet a sound came from the complete absence of light within him.

"Give us the child, and we will leave you in peace." Its voice hummed.

The Great Elder scoffed.

"What child do you speak of, and what do you know of peace?"

The humming sound became louder.

"You are all children to us, even you, Sun Womb, and Mother of Immortals. Give us the child, the one your people call Pax, and we will leave here..."

The ground began to rumble beneath the Great Elder's feet.

"If you could take him," said Affi-Tosla calmly, "You would not ask permission..."

For answer, the darkness again multiplied and surrounded the camp. The dogs began to whimper and shiver as the light from the sky was blotted out. The warriors raised their weapons ready to make a last stand. The four elders appeared around the camp in the four directions, Zema took the position facing south behind Affi-Tosla. All four crackled with power, the only light against an ocean of darkness.

The humming sound from the leader took on a tone of anger.

"You know not what you face, Great Elder."

Affi-Tosla took a step forward.

"Nor do you."

They rushed her then, and the camp. The four elders held a wall of light the darkness crashed against and the First Elders screamed from the backlash. Saramis gasped as she felt the darkness speed through the air and slam into her body, tracking down the DNA of the prince like a lodestone. The dread humming exploded in her ears and she cried out as she heard voices shriek insanely, babbling words that had no language yet clearly commanded her to give up the prince or die. For answer Saramis pulled power up through the planet and used it to force the darkness back in a nimbus of radiant light, encircling the First Elders who surrounded her. They leaned on Saramis and gathered their strength. The other Second Elders formed an inner circle around the remaining members of the compound. They chanted words of creation to hammer back at the humming that caused all others to cry out in pain.

The leader of darkness rose himself in the air to smash down Affi-Tosla, who in turn raised her staff and slammed the base of it onto the ground.

Megatons of energy struck the darkness, and the hemisphere was under temporary daylight as an earthquake shook the nearby mountains. Every single stronghold of darkness was obliterated, the camp was now surrounded by a wall of flattened dust.

The earth and sky were quiet now; dandelion seeds floated in the air as the normal night returned under the moon's unblinking eye.

Affi-Tosla finally turned to look behind her at Second Elder Zema, who nodded at her unspoken question; the warriors who stood ready to give their lives were safe. Breathing deeply, the Great Elder began to walk back towards the camp; the dogs ran to greet her and jump up to be petted. The four elders fell in step behind her as she came into view of the common area. Her sharp gaze noted the bravery of the First Elders, who also rushed to her for hugs and kisses, which she gave profusely. Saramis all but wrung her hands when she met the eyes of the Great Elder, who did not rebuke her further, but held out her arms to her wayward pupil, who ran to her like the others.

The aim of all their efforts, the Lost Prince named Pax waited inside the Great Elder's tent. He had been in her tent alone only once before, four years ago, when he was despondent over the absence of Saramis. Her home at that time had been filled with light and young Pax had marveled at the hidden lands within its walls. But now, the tent was filled with darkness so deep he feared to step further in, afraid he might step off the edge of a cliff unseen. Soon, he began to see something in the inky blackness, a vision of sorts of a city with white grey walls and buildings that morphed into other cities, gates and doors of ornate depth and design. The city came closer and closer to him with its endlessly opening gates and the prince felt he actually walked the streets of this amazing place.

He suddenly forgot why he was in the tent and all his questions.

Pax was mesmerized by it, he watched the secret beauty of this endless vision until suddenly, he felt the ground beneath him tremble and then shake in a massive upheaval. Before he could fully react, Pax felt a soft hand on his shoulder, and he looked up from where he was seated into the deep compassionate eyes of Affi-Tosla.

"Mother..." he said warmly, and she smiled down at him.

Later, as the evening gave way to dawn, Pax, Saramis and the elders sat in council. Pax was full of remorse for the attack on the people, but the Great Elder would hear none of it.

"There is no one here who did not agree to take arms against the darkness; therefore, everyone here agreed to be attacked," stated Affi-Tosla firmly. "However, Rasdeter, I no longer have permission to stand in your defense, nor does anyone else here."

"I have to leave," offered Pax resolutely, "I have to work this out on my own."

"Not without me," replied Saramis quietly, and Pax took her hand in gratitude.

"We're coming too," said Atoli, but the Great Elder shook her head.

"They must go alone, Atoli," she responded, "You do not have permission to go..."

She paused at the questioning glance of Pax.

"Great Elder," Pax said respectfully, "Many times I have heard you speak of permission being asked, granted or denied, and I have never quite understood the meaning of it. "Who is denying Atoli permission to come with us?"

"You are," the Great Elder answered to his stunned face.

"Nothing in your life happens without your permission, Rasdeter, and this is something all those who are blind to their choices deny. By choosing the world and the emptiness it represents, you have denied the part of you that longs for peace. Once you reach the goal you seek, you will know why we must stay here and why when you call for me again, I cannot protect you."

"I don't understand..." Pax shook his head in bewilderment, but Affi-Tosla smiled.

"You will never understand peace while you turn from it..."

All sat in silence for a time, then the young Woman of the Woods spoke to her mentor.

"Have you no words for me, Great Elder?" Saramis asked in quiet anguish.

"I have given you the Law and all the principles of it," replied Affi-Tosla, "And you have refused to apply it to your life; what more can be said?"

The fire in the small pit crackled and spit as the rays of dawn filtered in from the top of the tent. Saramis braved to speak once more.

"When should we leave, Great Mother?" she whispered.

The Great Elder whispered in kind.

"Now."

* * *

Atoli and Nea wiped their faces as they watched Pax and Saramis grow small in the distance. His lifemate had weighed the couple down with dried food and things for the road. Atoli had checked and re-checked Saramis's tent; finally, Pax had stopped his brother's anxious movements. Atoli was miserable; he could not imagine life anymore without his brother Pax. They embraced, then struck their spears together in farewell. Nea had clung to Saramis, who spoke softly of a planned reunion they both doubted would happen. She placed her hand over Nea's, who held her growing belly and giggled shyly about her apparent fertility. Second Elder Zema flung seeds and flowers over them and gave the blessing of a peaceful road ahead while the Great Elder stood and watched. Their last hugs and kisses the pair offered to her and felt her love as they departed.

Zema joined Affi-Tosla on a hill overlooking the road Saramis and Pax traveled. Zema could feel the energy of the Great Elder surrounding them, but she knew Affi-Tosla could not hold this protective light over them for long.

"Destiny has overtaken them..." Affi-Tosla said almost to herself, "The hounds are gathered to feast..."

"How much time do they have?" asked Zema, and the Great Elder scoffed.

"Rasdeter is done with wandering, Zema..."

After a moment, the pair vanished over the horizon and Affi-Tosla finished her thought.

"Seven is the number of transformations, Second Elder, but I doubt they have that long."

THE DEATH OF STARLIGHT

"Our entire biological system, the brain and the earth itself work on the same frequencies."
~~~Nikola Tesla

The sorcerer Paza had always trusted her dreams. They had guided her from her very first days on the planet, back when time was not measured by days, or even years, but ages. From the very beginning she had a dream that her life on Earth would end in a blaze of light and fire. Paza didn't fear the dream when she was young; she watched it with peace and wonder. It felt like creation, like how the stars are born and burn out. She thought of herself as a living sun. Everything has a cycle of transformation; what was there to fear?

But that was before she met the one who would change her life forever. Once he taught her how to see death she feared it; she would never again awaken peacefully from her dreams.

She recalled the day when she came to realize that her body was separate from those she knew as parents or progenitors. Before this time, Paza knew she was a part of everything she saw, the people, creatures of the Earth, even the stars and planets. Because Paza saw both the microcosm and the macrocosm she recognized no distance between herself and the star bodies; if their light could touch her, well then, she could touch them. She danced dimensions and wove stardust molecules into things she could use. Paza watched as the Earth impregnated itself and brought forth life. She loved to sit on the shores at night and watch creatures crawl out of the seas and
~~~

send images to her mind that she translated into thoughts of beauty and wonder.

Her dreams had told her that soon she would see a phenomenon outside of eternity.

It happened that she was among those precious few now living who witnessed two beings who looked like men step away from a massive burst of light. They were huge and beyond comprehension. One stood still as the other moved quickly across the planet. Paza sensed one was waiting for the other to return so they could both go back into the light. She waited also but the one who moved away did not return. Finally, Paza turned again to her favorite pastime; watching the birth of stars and planets. She loved draping herself with starlight. One evening she was thus engaged when the being who first moved away from the light approached her. Smiling, she held out her hands to him, offering a robe of starlight to adorn himself.

He returned her smile as he accepted the garment.

"Paza," he said, and her hands flew up to her ears in astonishment.

Human communication was mostly telepathic back then; human sound was used only for creation. Didn't he know this?

She gazed at him in confusion. Why did he call her Paza?

He answered her question aloud.

"One day, millions of years from now, Paza will mean 'golden' in a language that will be spoken by the tongue and not the mind. I prefer to speak to you, Paza, I like the power that it gives me."

She had no place for the concepts he was offering her, so she mentally asked him something else.

The one you came with; he is waiting for you at the light that never dims. Are you going back?

The being smiled again at her.

"No," he answered, "I like it here. The contrast is...interesting."

He looked around at all the people and creatures moving around the land. Then, he pointed at the ones that began to approach them.

"So..." he said in curiosity, "You see yourself as everything around you? Nothing is separate?" He now raised his head and looked up at the same stars and planets she danced with. "The idea seemed so much easier to me when light surrounded everything," he mused, "When there was no contrast. Now...I want to see, touch and learn..."

Paza's brow furrowed.

Learn? Separate? You say very strange things. Is it because you are using sound to communicate? If you use your mind it will be easier for me to understand you.

There was a strange look in his eyes as he gazed at her; almost as though he could see something hidden inside of her that she was unaware of. The thought of this made Paza step back; how could something be in her that no one knew of?

"I like you, Paza," the being said as he appraised her, "But your eyes need to be opened like mine. I now see things that you cannot, things that I am willing to teach you."

He looked down at the robe she had offered him, and with a thought, he shrunk down his body from its great height to seven feet and placed her robe around him. It morphed to fit him as her mouth gaped. The people gathered around them silently, drawn to him by his deeds and the vibrations coming from his lips.

Sound without creation; how was it possible?

What they failed to see was although it was not creation, he was making something; a world apart from what they now lived and moved in. A world that, if they entered it, would exchange knowledge for learning and creation for tools, causing them to forget everything they once knew.

He closed his eyes and listened for the last time to their collective thoughts.

"You think of me as the First Brother," he mused aloud to their astonishment, "Very well, let it be as you say."

He looked around at the people.

"Say it," he commanded firmly.

After a moment, to Paza's amazement, the people began to repeat his words aloud. They began to laugh and chatter words they were thinking. It became a canopy of noise she could make no sense of. It was so strange. When people thought telepathically it didn't matter how many thoughts were streaming it all flowed perfectly because the mind was infinite. Paza again covered her ears as order faded into chaos. As he began to walk away, they followed him. Then he stopped and looked back at Paza.

"Paza," the being now known as the First Brother said gently, "Follow me and I will teach you the right way to see this world."

He stretched out his hand to her. "Come."

It seemed the cells of her body exploded with light as Paza looked at him, but the truth was her cells were dying. She was about to enter the world of time where everything bound by it eventually dies. She took one last look at the stars raining light for her to gather and make garments, music, and other things with. Stay, they begged her, but the sound of his words rang in her ears. She was beginning to question whether sound should only be used for creation; perhaps there were things beyond it. Lifting the hem of her gleaming robes Paza turned her back on the stars and ran to join the one who would teach her the meaning of separation.

* * *

Now in the present day of the Nine Kingdoms, the sorcerer Paza could feel the press of time on her life. When she was alone, she sometimes wept for what she had so eagerly turned her back on. Now when she stood among the stars they were silent. If perhaps they spoke to her, she could no longer understand their music. Paza could sense creation but she could not interact with it. Each age she depended more and more on the power wielded by the mysterious being she had once been enchanted with.

With overpowering dread, Paza saw the slow but steady transformation of the First Brother into The Magician, how he began to go mad under the heavy burden of separation. He was angry that he could no longer hear the thoughts of others; that the power of creation he had discarded with arrogance would not now return to him. The Magician was convinced he could force his brother to give back what he must have somehow taken from him. Paza remembered how he demanded that his followers help him find the one now known as the Second Brother.

At first, The Magician said he needed his brother to return to the light. Then he decided that his brother was keeping him from the light, and finally he determined that *he* was the light, and once his brother was dead, all power would belong to him.

Paza's dreams warned her to flee while the First Brother was occupied with the initial search. When she beheld him use his now twisted powers to slay the followers who failed him, Paza experienced something never felt before in all her eons on the Earth: Fear.

Those who could see tried to tell The Magician where his brother was, but he did not believe them. And this was but the beginning of his fall into madness. When Paza witnessed The Magician slay his most trusted advisor for telling him the truth, it was at last too much for Paza. She fled to the Rim of the World, and from there, she vaulted herself among the stars. Perhaps now was the time of her death, perhaps now she would find the peace denied her. But Paza only floated in the emptiness alone.

* * *

It sometimes took centuries to find her, but The Magician always did; he was connected by darkness to everyone who used his power. The older Paza grew the more powerful she became; eventually Paza shone like a dark star no matter where on the planet she stood. She spent eons on other planets and solar systems where The Magician could not go. Like the humans he longed to control, The Magician was bound to the planet Earth until he found his brother. Yet, Paza too, felt a pull irresistible to the magnetic force of her home. Sirius and Orion's belt did not look the same from other galaxies and she loved the way Earth's moon pulled at the iron particles in her blood.

The Magician eventually found her walking the edges of the sea at night. Paza had gone as far back in time as she could yet it was impossible for her to return to a time where she did not know The First Brother. Once on the path away from the light, one must walk the full journey back to it; she could not return to union without fully realizing what had first separated her from it. Paza was weeping because the creatures now crawling from the waters in the darkness didn't speak to her. She found no images in their minds of beauty, only blind survival. But Paza didn't try to run from her former mentor, instead she wiped her face and waited for him.

The Magician was uncharacteristically gentle with Paza. Not because he felt compassion; he was incapable of loving emotions. It was because she was one of the few living who remembered him and one of the first to follow him that he was lenient with her madness.

Like The Rook, Paza was his plaything; it amused him to indulge her.

"First Brother," Paza whispered faintly, "I want to go back..."

"You cannot go back, Paza," replied The Magician, "If you mean before you joined me in time, you can only go forward."

The creature stepped closer to her.

"I need you to stand with me, Paza, like you did before. If you'll see this through with me to the end, and help me defeat my brother, then I'll be free of this planet, and I can take you anywhere you wish to go."

Paza tilted her head a bit as she gazed at him. Why was it so hard to understand him at times?

"You know that I'm going to die here, my lord," she answered, "You know I've told you my dream."

"But you don't know when, Paza," said The Magician with a shrug, "And neither do I. Perhaps I'll bring you back here when the planet dies if that's what you want. Just say you'll stand with me, that's all I ask."

His words brought a smile to her lips.

"That's not all you want," Paza said wryly, "You always say you want one thing, and then it turns out to be everything."

He held out his hand to her, and suddenly Paza felt like they were standing on the Earth when it was new.

He's so good with illusions, she thought.

"That sounds like a 'Yes'," he offered.

She placed her hand in his and gasped as she felt herself again bound to him. The darkness in The Magician roared through Paza and temporarily dispelled the madness running her mind. The look of satisfaction in his eyes confirmed her thoughts.

Such a fool to return where he could find me, Paza thought, I should have died in space between the moons of Saturn.

Paza looked up at The Magician sadly.

"You're going to make me kill someone, aren't you? Why do you enjoy causing death so much?"

"I wouldn't call it enjoyment," The Magician replied in a nonchalant manner, "Everything here has a cycle of birth, growth and decay. The earlier they start, the sooner they can return; it's all one to me."

They walked together along the shore quietly for some time before Paza spoke again.

"You didn't answer my question."

"I'm uncertain you'll have to kill anyone for me, Paza," mused The Magician, "But I do want you to help my people find someone, or at least determine for sure if he's dead. He's a prince of the Nine Kingdoms...his name is Rasdeter."

The Sacrifice of the Fawn

Paza walked the Earth several times before she came to the Kingdom of the Far Isles. She walked through time and dimensions, long before Saramis and Rasdeter were born. She did not need to meet with the mage who faced the power of Saramis in the tavern; as soon as The Magician thought of Keoni, Paza saw him. Through the mind of Keoni, she saw everything that transpired. When she beheld the mage hurled against the wall, Paza knew it was not Saramis who defeated his enhanced might.

Her breath quickened, but she said nothing of it to the First Brother.

"I see the one who cloaks her abilities and confounded the mage who serves Enith," Paza had stated, "A Woman of the Woods, the Wanderers of the Plains People. A child really...and yes, these emotions are connected to a memory of Sumter, High King of the Far Isles."

The Magician already knew of Saramis, he'd learned it from The Rook, so Paza's confirmation merely allayed his constant suspicion of his bound servant's motives. But the failure of his Legion made The Magician cautious; his hand must remain unseen to those who could confront him before he was ready. The light of a creator can pierce any darkness; for now, he needed to remain unknown and unsuspected in the doings of the world.

Yet he was intrigued by the Quest of Enith; anything that might affect the outcome of the final battle must be controlled by The Magician and he alone. There was only one question uppermost in the mind of the First Brother, and he voiced his concern to Paza.

"If you find the prince alive, Paza," asked The Magician quietly, "...and he is under the protection of this child of power, will they be able to escape you?"

The woman who dreamed of Starlight met The Magician's gaze and shook her head sadly.

"No, First Brother," she replied, "They will not."

* * *

Paza stood cloaked in the dimensions as she watched time roll before her from her perch on the mountains facing the Far Isles.

People swarmed in ribbons below her; the pageantry of ancient kings ebbed and flowed before her eyes. Paza stopped the river of years as she beheld the destruction of the Hall of Mages. A lonely figure stood at its epicenter, a girl of nine years. That this child was the cause of the massive detonation, Paza knew; she watched the grieving child fall to her knees, stunned by her loss. The daughter of Lord Brayten, unknown until this moment. With a wave of her hand, Paza quickly rewound time and watched Lord Altus riding up to the palace gates, on his fateful, tragic errand. The Ancient from the Time of Starlight did not gaze into the palace to witness the death of King Valtus; this was not her focus. It was the aftermath and the events that unfolded.

This was why The Magician sent her, Paza was the only one who could approach and not be detected. Yet still the Ancient Starchild took precaution to cloak the dimensions. Had the daughter of Lord Brayten not been so distraught with grief, she would have detected Paza's power, and the story would have a different end.

Soon enough, High General Aton gathered his men and left his new king for the estates of the nation's traitor, Lord Altus. Paza calmly watched the general's men round up and slay the innocent, named as conspirators by Lord Altus' guards under torture. Though it disturbed her, these were events she could do nothing about, and she knew The Magician cared nothing for such lives. He cared only for what threads of fate might affect the outcome of his future battle with the so-called child of prophecy; nothing else concerned him. When young Prince Rasdeter came to the courtyard under escort, her eyes brightened. The boy threw his arms around the general's waist and Paza's heart finally constricted; the light of the child's innocence burned brightly, and the Ancient was reminded of the stars she long ago turned her back on.

Paza followed the general and the prince, the horses they rode could not leave her behind. She listened intently to the words they exchanged, and when the boy dismounted, her own heart thundered as hard as his. Could she watch the general slay the child?

Should she change these events? The Magician only asked her to find out what happened to the prince, not save him. Paza saw the stars again in memory, pleading with her to take their light and make music with it; the dimensions around her shimmered with her indecision.

Paza's eyes widened as Saramis appeared from nowhere; the general and the prince could not see her. Paza gasped as power flared from the young girl; she watched it arc and stop the flow of time.

The girl is powerful, thought Paza, Such promise...

Events, as before, unfolded quickly and soon Paza watched the deceived general ride away.

Clever girl, thought the Ancient, Lord Brayten will only see what the general saw, and he will not have opportunity to verify it, for his own time has run out...

She watched the fallen prince and his protector walk quickly away, the power of Saramis causing the miles to vanish under their feet.

Paza sighed.

Poor, gifted Saramis, thought the Ancient, You have meddled in the affairs of great monsters, and you will not escape their wrath.

She wiped tears from her face.

The prince will not thank you for the fate you lead him to, child of power. Hard as it was, Paza grieved, You should have let that beautiful, sweet child perish.

* * *

The Dreams of the Lost

Ghent was restless for months after his encounter with the mage Enith. He spoke again with his wife Dru regarding the mage his family was bound to, holding her tightly as she vented her grief. So many generations had peacefully passed that most family members other than Ghent's father never expected to serve the mage during their lifetime. But the payment was now due, and it fell to Ghent to fulfill the oath since his father was too old to be of much use.

His father Ordant had nodded with pride as his son recounted his meeting with Enith, and the mage's pleased response. He patted Ghent's shoulder and reminded him that now his name would be among those etched on the inner wall of Roane's tomb; a great honor. As before, Ghent listened carefully to his sire, outwardly calm and inwardly horrified. A man of such power is not committed to mundane tasks, thought the young regent, Surely, he will ask something of me I cannot perform. I will pray this is not the case, yet I worry. My father did not see what I saw, he thought sadly as his father waxed broadly on the virtues of the family blood oath.

In the months that followed, the regent spent more time with his wife and children than he had before. Those days of blissful ignorance are gone, he reasoned, and Ghent wanted as many memories as he could of them. Dru tried not to cling to her husband but every time a visitor was announced they both looked to the other in dreadful anticipation. His children remained unaware. The gratitude of his eldest son Carn shone in his eyes as his father spent quality time with him, showing him the tasks and value system of a good, responsible man. Ghent's throat tightened as his young daughter Midlin, barely a toddler, looked up to him with adoration, bringing her dolls to him when torn or injured. In the past he might have sent Midlin to Dru for comfort, but now he knelt down to her level and patched her toys, giving sage advice on how to keep them well. His middle child, Iason, also a son, he frequently carried on his back, to the child's delight, down to the pond to dunk him in with shrieks of imaginary protest.

The evening his life changed forever Ghent was walking from his father's library, his arms loaded down with parchments and old books of law. His fellow regents had protested his many absences and he wished to smooth things out with them. They agreed to research together a particular codex, one that would hopefully shed more light on a decree the king wanted passed concerning widows and their offspring.

A breeze came through the trees and suddenly blew the parchments and books from Ghent's arms. He made a sound of protest and then stopped as the papers organized themselves into neat piles on a stone bench on his path. The regent felt the hairs go up on his neck, but still the sound of Enith's voice startled him.

"Are you well, son of my servant Roane?"

"Yes, my lord, and you?" Ghent asked as he recovered his breath.

Enith did not reply to this polite query, he stepped from the darkness onto Ghent's path, his hands clasped behind him. He seemed to be sizing up the regent, who tried to appear far calmer than he felt.

"I have not rewarded you for your great service to me, Regent Ghent..."

"My reward is to serve you," replied the regent sincerely over his fear.

The mage gazed at Ghent appraisingly.

"I believe you mean that, regent," said Enith, "Yet to reward you is the reason I am here."

"My lord," Ghent responded with a bow to his new master. This gesture pleased Enith; the regent was as he appeared to be, a man with a good heart and a desire to be of service. Ghent wanted no gifts or betterment of his station, which was precisely why the mage wanted to reward him with those things.

"I have a prince in my employ, regent, who has a kingdom and a government to run. It would please me if you would take the position. This prince has a great need for a man who loves the letters, and I know of no one who loves the law more than you, Regent Ghent..."

"As you say, my lord," replied Ghent sincerely. "May I ask the name of the kingdom you wish for me to serve in, and the name of the High Regent I should confer with?"

The mage Enith grinned broadly; he liked such an earnest young man. I am loathed to corrupt him, he thought, an event unavoidable if he stays too long in my company.

"To answer your question, young regent, the kingdom you will serve is the very one that Everet is annexed to, the Bright Forest, and its High Regent is now you."

Dreams of the Lost, part II

Saramis stood outside her shared tent with her lifemate Pax, gazing at the heavens but unable to focus on the wonder of it. Faraway in the distance, the torches of a northern kingdom flickered. How she wished in this moment that she and Pax were among them, common and unknown. Saramis had begged Pax from the beginning never to tell her who he really was. But the former prince could bear the burden of his hidden identity no longer, and the night they bonded he told her.

Pax could not understand why Saramis had covered her face and wept at his words. Try as he might, at first, he could not comfort her. Saramis now clearly saw everything the Great Elder had gently tried to show her. But she knew that even if she saw all things possible on that day seven years ago, Saramis still would have saved Pax.

She loved him. The massive tree her teacher had shown her came into focus in her mind. Hundreds and thousands of leaves, perhaps millions, over the lifetime of it, and every single leaf a life, and a decision made during that life, that led to so many lifetimes and dimensions where so many things were simultaneously possible.

And in every one of them, Saramis had loved him. Whether she met Pax or did not meet him; if she loved him or spent her life with Kha, Saramis had always loved Rasdeter, and he had always loved her.

But this love would not save them.

The world wanted Rasdeter, the Lost Prince of the Far Isles, and whether the man called Pax realized it or not, he wanted the world too. The whole world was looking for them, and now Saramis knew it would find them. Pax never released his old life, he was always thinking about it, and a part of him longed for it. The energy of such longing was strong and sooner or later, events in his life would draw back to the source of it, which was him.

All dreams manifest, Saramis thought in sorrow. I knew when I saved him he didn't belong to me. Blindness to the truth is but temporary, and now I must pay for my arrogance.

"Saramis..."

She placed a brave smile on her face as she turned to him.

Pax held open the flap of their tent, and she was taken again by his strong form and deep green eyes. Wordlessly, she closed the space between them and wrapped her arms about his waist, sighing as he kissed her forehead in his customary manner.

"My goddess," Pax whispered as he returned her embrace.

She tightened her arms around him, listening to his heart as he chuckled deeply.

"I sense your mind is again filled with complicated thoughts," Pax said to her, "Will you share them with me now, or can it wait until morning?"

Reluctantly she nodded at the darkening of his eyes.

"We should speak now, beloved," she said quietly to his disappointment, "There are things we must decide before we rest."

"Very well," Pax replied as he drew her into their home, "Let us speak, decide, and rest," and the corner of his mouth turned upwards in a mischievous manner.

It seemed Pax would never be happier than he was in this moment; Saramis was his. The former prince didn't realize that this was the only thought he had that did not contain some element of fear; all else in his life was uncertain.

"I'm not sure where we should go, Pax," said Saramis, "I thought the plains would be safe for us, as long as we stayed away from the kingdoms..."

She hesitated as he held her gaze.

"This is my fault, I know this," admitted Pax, "I should never have sought out word of my cousin Sumter..."

Saramis touched his lips with her fingers, it always calmed Pax and filled his eyes with love.

"They would never have found you if not for me..."

"No," Pax responded firmly, "You must never say thus..."

He pulled her into his arms again and held her tightly. It was meant to comfort, and she received it so, resting her head on his strong chest. They lingered a moment, and then Saramis drew gently away from Pax to keep his mind on the task at hand.

The moment Saramis stepped away from him, she knew she was dying. She could feel it as time seemed to halt; her arms still warm from the embrace of his. The prince was yet gazing at her; he didn't realize why she pulled away. The cells of her body screamed from the effort of holding back the radiation suddenly surging into them. In seconds, the young woman was on the defensive, in the fight of her life.

"Saramis..."

The prince's eyes turned to puzzlement and wonder. He had instinctively tried to continue their joint embrace and found himself frozen in place.

She never took her eyes from Pax; she didn't need to. Saramis knew time for them had finally run out. The Ancient known as Enith had entered the space they shared and bound them both before her own considerable power could detect it.

This moment now belonged to Enith.

He had waited seven long years for this victory. His irritation at Saramis, this young woman who was not even a fraction of his life-span who dared to stand between him and his most fervent goal, was high. If she did not flee from him, Enith would simply erase her from existence. He was impressed with her resistance even as he smiled in contempt.

Saramis enveloped herself in a shrinking instant of time; a place she could try to hold off the overwhelming power of the Ancient. Any lesser being would have been reduced to ashes between the beats of a heart. She actually felt the reluctance of the energy surrounding her to burn and stretch her atoms to a point they could not return from. But the will of Enith was overriding it; without words she could hear the plea of the elements enfolding her:

Run...

But she would not. In that moment Saramis knew she could not willingly leave Pax to his fate. Saramis would watch him until she had no eyes to see with. Pax's gaze changed completely to that of abject fear as he saw her form begin to slowly dissipate. Veins bulged from every part of his body as he strained to reach her; he was shouting words she could no longer hear:

"Saramis!"

The sorcerer known as Enith nodded his respect for Saramis as he built his power well past the point she could hold on or return from. If she wished to die for the prince, he thought, so be it.

Pax now saw their attacker, and without taking his eyes again from Saramis, he cried out.

"Do whatever you want to me, only spare her! I'll do anything you wish, please!"

This plea distracted Enith for but a nanosecond; then he released his deadly radiation at the hapless Saramis, who stretched out her arms to her prince one last time.

* * *

Pax fell to his knees roaring out his pain. Still bound, he could not even crawl to her remains, all he could see was the fallout from the blast that Enith protected him from. His anger now spent, Enith looked at his prize, a fallen prince, who hung his head and wept without shame. His work would be harder now that he dealt with a man instead of a boy, he mused, but eventually Enith knew he would have what he most wanted, a king to control.

And not just any king, but a ruler of the most powerful nation on earth.

It would be well for the prince to see what becomes of those who resist or stand in my way, Enith thought grimly as he waited for the dust to dissipate. Finally, the man known as Pax sorrowfully lifted his head to view his beloved, his heart deadened, his soul destroyed. They waited in silence; Pax knew nothing else that happened to him after this would matter.

When the dust and smoke cleared both men stared in shock; only Enith knew what to say.

"Paza..." he declared in frustration and wonder.

The Starchild stood calmly between Enith and the unconscious Saramis, the destructive radiation completely absorbed by her. Few that walked the earth were as old as Paza, and Enith, for all the millions of years behind him, was not one of them.

He clenched his fists as Paza answered his unasked question.

"He will die without her, Enith, what then of all your plans and schemes?"

With a slight wave of her hand, Paza freed Pax from the bonds of Enith and he immediately rushed to his lifemate as the Ancient Starchild stepped from his way. Pax could not contain himself as he pulled a limp Saramis to his breast and sobbed in relief on her neck and bodice.

"Release, I pray you, your anger at her cleverness," continued Paza as Enith struggled to hold his fury, "He has already agreed to do whatsoever you will as long as you do not harm her. Can you not see this will be easier than torture and force?"

Enith nodded finally.

He knew that his temper could make hasty decisions for him, and he had to admit that Saramis had achieved the impossible when she unknowingly bested him.

"As you say, Paza," he agreed reluctantly as he watched the grateful Pax holding what he cherished most in life. The prince's hands shook as he smoothed Saramis's soft fluffy hair back from her face. The warmth of her skin comforted him as he fought to regain his sanity. Though Pax gave Paza a gaze of profound gratitude, his eyes were wary as he looked on the mage who almost slew his beloved.

"I have your word, then," he asked in a strained voice, "That you will not harm her?"

"You have it," said Enith, "...and I will not deceive you in this promise, provided you keep your word, and obey me in all things."

A moan came from Saramis as her spirit once again animated her body. Pax cradled her closer to him, his heart skipped a beat at her sluggish movements.

"I will obey you," he said deeply as the lids of her eyes fluttered.

"Very well," replied Enith in a pleased tone.

Enith flared his power upwards and around the tent; it vanished in a blaze of light. When Pax could see again, he and Saramis were on the tiles of an inner courtyard of a palace. Servants, soldiers, and staff members moved about in their duties, they could neither see nor hear them. Paza smiled sadly as Pax met her eyes, she knew the prince felt safer with her between Saramis and the mage.

Enith pointed to a draped couch; the prince hurried to place Saramis there. She tried to stir, but the ordeal of her battle with Enith had gravely weakened her. Saramis gingerly touched her temples and tried to rise; Pax restrained her.

"You must try to rest, beloved," he whispered as his hands gently pressed Saramis against the cushions beneath her. She carefully turned her head towards Enith and Paza. Her body stiffened, and she looked up at Pax in dismay; he could not see the dark power rolling from the pair in cresting waves. The light coming from the two lovers were faint against such towering deep waters. If these were the ones who sought the man she loved, Saramis knew their plight was beyond all hope. The words of Affi-Tosla to Pax before they left the people came back to haunt the young woman:

"The World is waiting to consume you, Rasdeter..."

Saramis had never doubted that Pax was of some high station in life, his clothes betrayed that from the beginning. She hoped all those years that he was the son of a regent or general, someone with potential to rise higher, judging by the man who tried to slay him. She never dreamed that her gentle loving Pax was the first cousin of the most powerful king in the known world. When the general left the woods, believing the prince dead, she felt that was the end of it. Saramis thought she could handle any magician of the courts who stumbled upon their secret. It was why she didn't fully understand the reason the Great Elder suggested she leave Pax behind for nearly four years.

But when Pax faced the mage in the tavern, and Saramis felt the power of thousands of mages behind him, she began to realize that more than humans were searching for this humble, suffering boy. Saramis also knew she and Pax would have to leave after the camp was attacked and Affi-Tosla was called upon to save it.

Even then, she had no inkling of the heights of darkness that wanted her lifemate. It was when the Ancient nearly destroyed her that Saramis fully realized the degree of trouble that awaited them, and now that she laid eyes on Paza, an Ancient Starchild, her heart pounded at last in fear.

She had no level of power that could help them both escape; she felt Paza acknowledge her thoughts with a simple nod of assent.

The Woman of the Woods felt her lifemate stroking her cheek; she turned her face into his palm and kissed it. Saramis tried to mask her despair from Pax as he embraced her; it would not be long before they both learned the reason for such a relentless and prolonged chase they had unknowingly endured.

From the corner of his eye, Pax saw a regent approach them.

"This is Ghent," said Enith, "He will serve as your High Regent."

"My...I don't understand," Pax stammered.

The mage known as Enith laughed with true mirth.

"You must forgive my lack of manners," he said finally, "In my haste to obtain you, I'm afraid I've left out all introductions..."

He stretched out his hand towards the woman who saved Saramis.

"This is Paza," he said softly, "A woman nearly as old as the planet itself. As you have witnessed, she is a being of great power..."

The mage's eyes darkened, and Pax's heart began to beat faster.

"As am I," he continued with emphasis, "You may call me Enith, one of the Ancients, a sorcerer of no little means. You," Enith said as he pointed at Pax, "Are Prince Rasdeter, formerly of the Kingdom of the Far Isles. This..." he indicated with a sweep of his arm, "Is the palace of the Bright Forest, your new home."

As the mage spoke, other magicians entered the courtyard, one of them carrying a silver tray with curved blades on it. Blood pounded in Pax's ears so that he could barely hear what was being said.

Enith began to pace the tiles.

"You will rule here," the mage said almost to himself, "...temporarily. One day, you will seat another throne much higher than this one. But for now, this will do..."

Pax found his voice.

"My lord, I am not the one you seek. I am one of the people, the Wanderers of the Plains. My name is Pax..." he stammered.

Enith smiled thinly.

"And so, you were," Enith replied, "And so you are. Did you never inquire as to the meaning of your name in the region in which Saramis claimed to have found you?"

Stunned silence met this question; Pax had never asked the meaning of his name. He realized now that it was because he'd always resented it; resented having to change his name, his identity.

"It...it's a common name..." he began.

"Yes," answered Enith, "Because in that region, the people are very attached to their nobility, and find every excuse to name their children after them. I'm sure your lifemate chose it subconsciously..."

Enith now looked to Ghent, who cleared his throat, drawing the prince's eyes to him.

"The name, 'Pax' means 'ruler', my lord," The regent offered in a subdued tone.

The blood drained from Pax's face. He turned to Saramis, who looked as shocked as he was. It seemed the mage had drawn an invisible noose around the neck of his valuable prisoner. Now it began to tighten, so Pax could feel it.

"Now you see, 'Pax'," Enith said snidely, "You could never escape your destiny."

The ancient mage scoffed.

"Hiding your nobility with plainsmen and commoners. As a confession, I admit to you that it was rather ingenious; I never thought to search for you there. All the while, for the seven years that thousands of mages scoured the earth, I imagined you were in the company of ambitious men like myself; subject to dreams of ultimate power."

The mage stared off in the distance, back to the day he suspected the prince was alive. His voice turned far away.

"I could have raised an army to attack the Far Isles years ago, but with an ordinary king of another nation, I would have little support from the neighboring kingdoms. It ran the risk of destroying what I needed most to control the known world..."

Now his eyes lit up as he almost grinned at Pax, who met his gaze in horror. Attack the Far Isles? His cousin Sumter?

"However..." Enith said with emphasis, "Imagine an army led by a legitimate heir to the throne of the Far Isles; an heir with a sympathy for magic? With one great battle, I could slay the sole obstacle to the plans of any magician; a High King who rejects everything we stand for, King Sumter!"

The man called Pax felt his eyes brimming. He thought only moments ago that he'd faced the worst event of his adult life, the near death of Saramis. But...to be used, as a pawn to topple his beloved cousin, to be directly responsible for his demise?

"No..." Pax whispered in alarm, "No, you cannot ask this of me..."

"No?" asked Enith as he looked meaningfully at Saramis, who was too overcome to be in fear for her life.

She was responsible for all of this, her mind reeled, Death now would be a kindness...

"Wait!" Pax cried out desperately, "Wait, I pray you!"

But the mage only smiled and looked to Ghent, who in turn signaled to the mage holding the silver tray to approach.

"Fear not," said Enith, "I anticipated your reluctance to slay a blood relative, one you grew up with and once held dear..."

Enith drew one of the shining blades from the tray, admiring the candlelight glancing off of it. He held it forth, then stepped away from it and it hovered alone in the air.

"This," said Enith, "Is an enchanted dagger. It will embed it's magic deep in your heart, my prince, and help you overcome your tendency to think higher thoughts of noble actions..."

The dagger seemed to sing with light exploding from it, but this was deception; there could be no true light coming from a source of utter darkness.

Paza spoke into the frightening silence that followed.

"You will submit to this, Prince Rasdeter," she said evenly, "It will become a buffer for you, in the horrors to come..."

"Why?" the prince said with an ache in his voice, "Why would you do this?"

"All of your life," Paza said gently, "You have ever only wanted two things; to either die or go home. These two emotions have brought all the people you see before you, we are here to supply that wish you left untampered by anything else."

As Pax began to weep in earnest, a group of mages pulled him from the embrace of Saramis, then surrounded him and held his arms. One of them ripped open his shirt, exposing his bare chest.

Another took the other dagger and approached Saramis, but Paza shook her head.

"It won't work on her," said the Starchild, "And you won't need it. She will not leave him, no matter how deep what you do to him scars her soul."

Paza looked at Saramis, who returned this gaze with hollow eyes.

"Pride, Saramis," said Paza, "Your only downfall. You placed more faith in your power than your willingness. Now you must watch as they destroy him with what he wants most of all; the throne denied his father."

"No!" shouted Pax, "No, it's not true! I never wanted it..."

Enith calmly looked at Ghent, whose eyes widened.

The mage wanted him to do it; take a blade and slay another man's soul. Ghent could not hesitate. His eyes tightened as he stepped forward; he cannot fail the memory of his ancestor Roane. Yet his wife Dru and his three children came before his eyes, in particular his eldest son Carn, who looked up to him. He imagined the boy turning from him in shame; Ghent had raised him to shun the wicked and protect the helpless.

What would he think of his father's actions?

The enchanted blade floated in the air beside the regent; Saramis felt her power flare and strike an unseen wall. In desperation she looked at Paza, who shook her head.

Paza spoke directly into her mind.

You are powerless here, Saramis, and powerless you shall remain if you stay with him.

Saramis sobbed openly as she watched the man she loved turn pale as the dagger moved nearer.

Ghent's eyes also brimmed as he walked towards Pax; could Ghent take his soul without losing his own?

The prince struggled wildly as the regent approached, all promises forgotten. The mages held him fast; one behind him pulled his hair painfully as he wrapped his other arm around the prince's neck. The son of Lord Altus hurled back again in time and stood in front of the tree in the forest, General Aton before him.

He pleaded with the dead general.

But I wouldn't rise against him if he spared me, I wouldn't...

He knew Affi-Tosla, the Great Elder would only help if she had permission to do so. The man who lost his name cried out in his mind to the Second Elder and only stillness greeted him. Her words returned to him:

When you reach your goal, you will know when you cry out to me, why I cannot protect you...

For the first time in his life, Pax was without aid. No one to take responsibility for what happened to him. Too late, his mind was re-solved to accept his place among the people who called themselves Human. Too late he realized he only wanted to be Pax, a Wanderer of the Plains.

The prince cried out to the Invisible.

"By the Great One, spare me!"

Paza's voice was barely heard over the prince's cries.

"God cannot save you from what you want..."

Regent Ghent buried the dagger in Rasdeter's chest.

Both men screamed.

THE TRANSFORMATION OF PAX

"I believe it to be an invariable rule that tyrants of genius are succeeded by scoundrels."
~~~Albert Einstein

Ghent awoke on his stomach, sprawled on his bed in the Hall of Regents in the Kingdom of the Bright Forest. He was in great pain all over his body, the bulk of his agony concentrated around the area of his heart. He could barely raise his head; when he did so his temples throbbed in protest and he returned his face to the pillows beneath him with a groan. Two women ministered to him while unconscious; they removed his outer robes and wiped the sweat from his limbs and torso; he was relieved to find his nether regions still bound.

A voice stirred him from his preoccupation with his pain, it was his master, the mage Enith.

"A wound to a man's soul is felt in the body," stated Enith thoughtfully, "...and the damage done is quite similar to slaying the body. Just as a murderer cannot erase the deed his hands have done, so must a man who slays a soul must feel the slain soul's pain..."

Ghent began to weep.

"You are a good man, Regent Ghent, I know this," continued Enith, "So too, is Prince Rasdeter. Your ancestor Roane was also a good man. You have sworn a blood oath to serve me, and I know you will do so..."

The mage stretched forth his hand and a flame appeared above his open palm.
~~~

"However, a good man has a wall of light around his heart, and sometimes this light will cause a good man to betray his word in order to protect it. Your ancestor Roane was the one who taught me this, and I loved him for it..."

Enith began to pace the room he provided for Rasdeter's new High Regent, gazing at the windows and furnishings, and seeing nothing, as he recalled a time long gone.

"You see, betrayal for me is not so simple as it is for other men. As a man of ambition, I expect those who appear loyal to me to yield to their own desire for control, for dominance. These things are quite easy to detect; most men wear their greed and lust on their faces, and after millions of years, it has become nearly impossible to deceive me..."

The Ancient paused in his pacing and looked to his regent, who could not see him over the lancing misery that forced Ghent to grip the sheets beneath him, praying for death.

"But a good man is different, son of Roane. A good man does not actually betray you; rather, he is holding fast and faithful to an ideal; a belief system that the world can be better than it seems. More importantly, he believes that the loss of his own life is worth this ideal, and he will lay it down gladly and embrace his death content..."

Enith began to absently disrupt the flames above his palm as he thoughtfully continued.

"A corrupt man is incapable of this, regent. He will slay everyone around him to preserve his own skin. Such a man is useful to a point; after that moment he is expendable. This is why I was loathed to slay your ancestor when my tasks for him struck this wall of light inside him. And I felt Roane's reluctance to oppose my will; he truly loved me; I could sense it. This love he felt for me was also inside this wall of light around his heart. I was fascinated by the experience; in all the centuries I can recall, I have never had such a man serve me."

The Ancient fell silent a moment as his mind drifted in time to recall the features of Roane, whom Ghent faintly resembled; Enith marveled as the image faded.

"Therefore, I searched a way around this obstacle, so I would not be forced to kill him. As with you, Ghent, I kept my servant ignorant of my motives. It came to pass that Roane also stabbed a man with a soul blade in my service, and from that day forth, the wall of light around his heart was breached. His intent to follow my wishes now matched his zeal, without the coarse ambition of lesser men. Roane's conscience, however remained intact along with his obedience. You will suffer, Ghent, from time to time, I cannot change that. But you will not betray me now, as you watch what I must do to the prince in order to gain my aims..."

The mage reached down and drew back the hair from Ghent's forehead, so he could see his face.

"You have reminded me of my great love for my servant Roane," Enith said quietly, "It grieved me when he finally died, and he was the only man I built a tomb for in recognition of his sacrifice."

"You, too, will die in my service, and so will your son. Perhaps I will prolong your life, as I did Roane's, until my power could not sustain the renewal of his cells."

Enith fondly patted Ghent's cheek.

"We shall see. Rest now, regent, it normally takes a few days before you can move around with the pain inside you."

Once the Ancient left his rooms, Ghent blacked out from his agony.

The Price

Prince Rasdeter was taken to the king's chambers and laid upon an enormous bed covered with silken sheets and warm fluffy blankets. The rooms were beautiful, filled with fountains and urns full of fruit trees and flowers. Gold, silver, and fine jewels were strewn everywhere alongside fine fabrics and painted vessels. Children waited with handwoven fans to comfort the prince, but Saramis sent both them and all other servants away.

The prince frequently woke up screaming from the wound in his heart, and it would not do to terrify those ignorant of the cause.

While Rasdeter was unconscious she bathed him. The sweat that poured from his straining body soaked the bedding; she had the servants change it frequently; it gave them something to do besides wring their hands and weep for him.

Saramis also wept. The power she could not use to free him she used to ease the frightful changes in his body. The screaming came from the disruption of his soul, and that Saramis could not ease. Hours she spent flowing power from her body to his, in an effort to keep the prince from going mad from the pain. Exhausted, she bathed and changed her own clothes during his periods of unconsciousness. His screams upon waking brought her running, sometimes barely dressed as Saramis hurried to help her lifemate endure his wounds to both soul and body.

On the third day he stopped screaming and finally slept.

Nearly mindless from her own ordeal, Saramis slumped on the bed beside Rasdeter and welcomed oblivion. The servants removed the last of the soiled bedding and buckets of water used to bathe the prince. After cleaning the rooms, they brought fresh flowers and trays of bread and fruit. Then they closed the massive doors to the king's chambers and quickly returned to their lower rooms in the palace where other staff members waited to hear the latest news.

One of the servants, a female, unrolled the length of her sleeves and shook her head in sympathy.

"I feel sorry for the poor thing, he's been screaming his head off for days now," she said as she wiped her forehead, "It seems the worse of it is past, he's finally sleeping, thanks to his wife..."

"Do you know who the young man is, yet?"

"Dunnan said he heard the young lady who helps him, call him Pax."

Dunnan, a man of the house staff, nodded to this. They were all weary from their labors, but eager to discuss it. Another man who helped the chamber maids added to the report.

"Well, I overheard one of the mages call him a prince."

The ones who were not present for the discourse murmured together at this comment.

"A prince..." said an old hunter in wonder, "What need have we of a foreign prince?"

A light came into Dunnan's eyes at this statement. He recalled the sorcerer the others deferred to, all save the unnaturally tall, silent woman, whose gaze made him uncomfortable.

"The older mage called him Rasdeter," said Dunnan, who did not know he spoke of Enith. An adolescent boy who heaved the buckets of dirty water into the drains added to the conversation with a question of his own.

"Well, who is he, then? A prince named Pax or Rasdeter?"

As the group pondered the mystery of the suffering young man's identity, the maids placed the soiled bedding from the king's rooms into a tub to be cleaned. Later the following day the linens would be rinsed again and hung to dry by the morning staff. The conversation continued while they worked.

"I'm thinking he might be Prince Rasdeter of the Far Isles..." Dunnan said thoughtfully.

One of the women who helped clean the chamber turned in surprise and scoffed.

"Impossible! Prince Rasdeter died as a child..."

"Murdered, you mean," said one, "There's an old story they buried a fox where they killed him; a hunter found it..."

"Lord Altus's estates were overrun with deer, not foxes..." replied the old hunter who felt he should know. "I can't verify it, but I'd agree with Dunnan; I think he's the Lost Prince Rasdeter."

But the servant was unconvinced; her hands went to her hips to emphasis her position.

"Why would you believe such tales?"

"Two reasons," the old hunter stated thoughtfully, "One: He was brought by the mages, and the young lady who came with him didn't seem too pleased about it. You know magicians are usually up to things that bode ill for others."

"And the other reason?" interrupted the awkward teenager.

"The king's missing," continued the old hunter soberly, "And his family; the whole lot of them, right down to the littlest..."

None gathered could dispute such musings. Their thoughts turned to King Templin, who disappeared shortly after Enith and his magicians took up residence in the Hall of Mages. The Bright Forest was a kingdom that promoted the practice of magic. The comings and goings of magicians had never been a problem for the king, he even had the Hall built to appease them. He was of the opinion that the mages would offer additional protection for his people, as did his father before him.

The day King Templin disappeared his High Regent vanished also. Soon after, his queen and their children were reported missing; the servants who cared for them wept and could not be comforted. The other regents rushed forward to fill the gaps in government, watching the movements of the mages in helpless dismay.

"You'd do well to watch what you say from now on," said a soldier from the door; all turned in alarm to look at him.

"We deal with men no longer," the soldier continued, "But those who can cast a spell to listen through walls. Your tongue holds your life, be sure of it. I'd say no more of the young man or the lady in the king's chamber, were I any of you..."

Silence followed his departure, then sounds of hurried feet and closing doors.

* * *

Comes the Darkness

The whole of the third day, both Rasdeter and Saramis slept. On the fourth day, Saramis rose first, and ministered to her lifemate. The day went by quietly as the prince reclaimed his strength, at least, what strength he could. He could not speak after days of straining his vocal cords, and his attempts to communicate with his beloved by writing were met with shaking fingers. Rasdeter indicated his desire to flee with signs and symbols in the air; finally, he pointed to an open window and the rolling hills of the Bright Forest. His lifemate shook her head.

"We cannot risk it yet, beloved," Saramis said, "You're not strong enough…"

Rasdeter made a dismissive motion with his hand and tried to rise; she barely reached him in time before he tumbled from the bed.

"Only rest a moment, my love," she soothed him, "Such wounds require it…"

His head once again against his pillows, the prince fell swiftly into exhausted sleep. Saramis bowed her own head against his slumbering chest and wiped her face.

Her words were meant to lull the prince to peace, she knew escape was impossible.

On the fifth day, the couple received a visitor, Regent Ghent.

His gait was careful as he entered the chamber, and this confirmed the fears of Saramis; that the regent was also affected by the power in the enchanted blade. Ghent's face told the rest of the story, with sorrow, grief and guilt pouring from him as he neared the bed.

"Is he…?" the regent's voice trailed off weakly.

"He's been stabbed through the heart, Regent Ghent," said Saramis more firmly than she meant to, "If not enchanted, his story ended days ago. I see you have suffered for it," she continued in a gentler tone, "But you walk today; Pax cannot even rise…"

Saramis turned from the regent to stroke the hair and face of her beloved; Rasdeter stirred fitfully. After a moment, his eyes opened dimly, and as he noticed the presence of Ghent, Rasdeter crashed into consciousness, his hand instinctively moving to cover his wounded chest.

The regent stepped back.

"Forgive me, my lord," Ghent said hoarsely, "It was never my intention to harm you..."

Rasdeter's voice was rasping and slow.

"Get away from me..." he said weakly, "Leave us alone..."

All three turned at a voice from the door.

"I'm afraid leaving you alone will prove impossible, Prince Rasdeter," said a mage as he entered the room, followed by another. "After all, we must prepare you for your future coronation."

Saramis felt Rasdeter's hand tighten on her arm; at the look on the prince's face the mage began to smile in acknowledgement.

"So, you remember me from the tavern, my lord. I'm flattered, especially since I was unable to see you or make your acquaintance more fully at the time..."

His gaze slid over to the prince's lifemate, who glared at him.

"And you must be Saramis," he continued, "The 'Woman of the Woods' who rescued him from me." He bowed from the waist.

"I am pleased to finally meet you both. Please call me Keoni."

The mage smiled warmly at the hostility of Saramis, who came to her feet despite the weak protest of Rasdeter. She placed herself between Keoni and his prey and stood in a defensive stance. Regent Ghent, who knew no magic, unconsciously backed up near the head of the royal bed.

"You will leave us alone," she stated in a warning tone.

Keoni stepped to the side, admiring her. "I can see that you mean that," he said, "After all, you froze an entire building full of people, and bravely faced down not only myself, but several thousand of my brethren..."

The mage's power flared and filled the room; Ghent heard himself moan under the hum of it. He could feel the heat of the mage's radiation burning his already weakened cells.

Rasdeter whispered.

"Beloved, no..."

"But now we stand face to face, 'Woman of the Woods'," sneered Keoni, "Well outside your place of power."

Saramis stomped her foot on the tiles, and power came roaring up from the earth, through the foundations of the palace and into her body. A shield of light blazed around her, the bed where lay her husband, and the helpless Ghent, who had no protection.

"And what do you know of power, and where it comes from?" she snarled and pushed forward, lancing the field of radiation the mage held barely intact.

Keoni fell back in shock; fear came into his eyes as he recalled the force in the tavern that hurled his body into unconsciousness. He roared at the mage Abner, who stood next to him, also cowering in terror.

"You fool, I thought you said her power was gone!"

The other mage stammered.

"It's what they said..." Abner cried out, "She can't take him away from here..."

Saramis didn't wait to hear more; the skies outside rumbled and darkened; she pulled every ounce of power she could take in that moment and exploded the room. Her power blew the doors open and Keoni wisely fled her.

The hapless Abner screamed as the blast struck, vaporizing him.

Saramis fell to her knees, spent. The prince's wife was still recovering from her near death at the hands of Enith, ready to give that life in defense of her husband. Ghent hobbled quickly to her side to offer whatever aid he could. Rasdeter could see nothing of what transpired, he only felt the massive aftermath of the blast that Saramis shielded him from. He cried out hoarsely from the bed.

"Saramis! Where are you? Answer me, I pray you..."

"She is well, my lord," answered Ghent, "She needs rest, as do we all. I only hope we receive it..." the regent coughed roughly and then sighed as he tried to hold Saramis, who turned her head against Ghent's shoulder and restrained the need to weep.

"I'm here, my lifemate," Saramis whispered. She allowed the regent to help her up, then crawled back into bed with her husband the prince, who embraced and held her as tightly as he could in his condition. He kissed her forehead.

"You mustn't risk yourself again for me," Rasdeter said softly, "You are all that I am living for..."

Saramis was too weak to reply, she placed a kiss where she could reach him, then slipped away to troubled dreams. The prince now looked at the regent without fear, who nodded at him, blinking rapidly. Rasdeter closed his eyes and joined his wife.

Regent Ghent drew the covers over them both, then hobbled through the blasted door.

* * *

Enith listened without comment as Keoni raged and complained about his encounter with Saramis. When his master did not respond to his rant, the mage's furor died down as he began to wonder if he had made a mistake in coming to Enith. Yet Keoni must say something, seeing that a mage in Enith's service had vanished and could not be found. Enith said nothing for quite some time after Keoni completed his report. He stood with his back to the mage, his forefinger and thumb on his chin, one arm resting on the other as he watched the clouds floating by in the distance. The uncomfortable silence lengthened, then finally Enith spoke.

"I warned you not to approach the prince and his wife before the seventh day," said Enith quietly.

Keoni made a slight startled movement; this was not the response he expected, but he quickly rallied.

"Your servant Abner informed me that Regent Ghent had entered the king's rooms; I merely meant to chastise him..." Keoni's voice trailed away.

"Is 'Ghent' another name for 'Keoni'?" asked Enith as he finally turned to face the mage who now blanched in fear.

"Have you gained my confidence, Keoni," Enith continued calmly, "That now I must tell you all the things I am thinking of or planning to do?"

"Forgive me, my lord," said Keoni desperately, "I moved instinctively to protect what I erroneously saw as your best interests..."

Sweat broke out on Keoni's brow as his master smiled thinly.

"No doubt you did," Enith replied.

The window Enith stood in front of was elevated on a platform and several steps led up to it. Enith stepped away from the curtained window and came to the edge of the steps leading down to his servant, who could not contain his trembling. Keoni had seen firsthand what his master could do to those who displeased him, and he knew his first mistake could be his last.

"Master," Keoni began, but Enith raised his hand for silence.

"You have worked hard and faithfully for me, Keoni," said Enith, "...and you were the one of the thousands in my employ who first found the prince. For this I have elevated you above the others and placed you in a station where I felt you could...almost...be trusted..."

Enith's hand returned to his chin, his eyes appraising his servant. The sins of Keoni were neither lust nor greed, but pride and ambition, traits that Enith prized in those he selected for the upper levels of his organization. Keoni's zeal to impress Enith was a key factor in his receiving the assignment to help Enith shape and mold a lost prince into a regal king.

An assignment failed before beginning it.

Pride has swiftly turned to arrogance, mused Enith as he continued speaking.

"This move has placed you in a train of thought that has made you careless. So, I've made up my mind..."

Keoni slowly closed his eyes and prepared himself.

"I will not slay you for this mistake, Keoni. I want those who serve me to remain encouraged; finding the Lost Prince was a huge achievement, and I want my servants to reach high for fruit above their reach…"

The errant mage's eyes flew open at this remark, his gaze humbled and full of gratitude. His master nodded at this.

"And I will not demote you. However, you have caused the unnecessary death of Abner, who also thought he was acting in my best interests when he approached you, my elevated servant, to inform you of Ghent's movements…"

Enith's hands began to flame and Keoni fell to his knees.

"You should recover by the seventh day, Keoni, a sure reminder of the wisdom of listening and obeying my wishes to the letter…"

Keoni could not help himself, he cried out.

"Mercy, master, mercy!"

As the withering blast came from Enith's hands and Keoni screamed and twisted in agony on the ground, his master scoffed.

"This is mercy, fool," Enith said with just a trace of the towering anger he felt, "Anyone else would be a pile of ashes as soon he finished his report."

Keoni's howls of pain could be heard throughout the building, a lesson no one who served Enith would easily forget.

The Offer

On the seventh day after Rasdeter's ordeal, the mage Enith requested an audience. Although Saramis was not deceived by this formality, she had little choice but to accept on behalf of her husband. The prince was able to walk, though painfully, and he made his way to the sitting rooms outside the king's chambers. Ghent came in before the mages to make sure the prince was comfortable. Dressed in warm robes and blankets, the prince still shivered as one with a fever. Saramis found robes for herself in the queen's dressing rooms, trying not to weep at thoughts of the previous owner's hopes and dreams. Nothing good has become of them, the prince's wife mused, I pray the end for them was swift and without warning.

Enith entered the sitting rooms with a bow, accompanied by two mages carrying a large wooden trunk. Saramis relaxed the tenseness in her body when she noticed the mage Keoni was not among them. Rasdeter sensed her unease and reached for her hand, bringing it to his lips. He received the smile he sought and the deep love in her eyes. Seconds later, all realized that Paza had joined them; Enith bowed to her as well.

"What means this, Paza?" Enith asked, "I have given my word not to harm Saramis."

The Starchild glanced at the mage as though the answer should be obvious.

"You had an audience with the First Brother, Enith," said Paza, "...and requested his assistance to find the Lost Prince Rasdeter. Now, he is interested in your quest, and you know what that means..."

The mage known as Enith could not help a sigh.

"You are his eyes and ears, then," said the mage, and Paza nodded.

"Very well," concluded the mage with a shrug and turned his attention to Rasdeter and Saramis. If the matter could be dealt with, it would have to happen later. The Ancient pointed to the wooden trunk. "I've brought you presents, my lord."

"I want nothing from you but my freedom," replied the prince in a weakened but resolute voice.

Enith placed his hands behind his back and shook his head.

"What lies within this box you have wanted all your life, Prince Rasdeter..."

"My name is Pax," said the prince firmly, followed by a short fit of coughing. The mage waited respectfully for the rasping to subside, then Rasdeter spoke again in a stronger tone.

"I want to go home, Enith, to my home on the Plains."

"This is from home," said the mage, and with a wave of his hand, the pine lid of the trunk freed itself from its hinges and lifted up. Rasdeter gasped painfully as the beautiful golden chest of his father Lord Altus came into view. The light of the morning sun struck the front of it and the gold filigree woven around his family crest flashed from the brilliant casket like fire. Saramis felt her free hand go to the neck of her robe, crushing the fabric as she gazed on this gaudy temptation, the beauty of the world and its works.

"This has haunted your dreams from the moment you lost your true home, my lord," said Enith with a touch of triumph in his voice. "When the enchanted dagger pierced your heart, it revealed to me all your past hopes and dreams, the pain of separation from your father and his house; your inheritance, my prince. Will you deny your father now?"

"Yes!" cried the prince with tears in his eyes, "I deny him, a murderer, and a traitor! I want no part of him!"

Saramis tried to back away but her husband held her fast, his grip stronger than it should be. "Please, my love," he whispered, "Don't turn from me, I'm not like him..."

But his wife saw what the prince could not yet see.

"Be careful my heart," she whispered in return, "He will offer you everything..."

"You are a prince of the realm, Rasdeter," said Enith with a gleam in his eye, watching the prince go pale as the mage repeated exactly the words of the dead General Aton. Without taking his eyes from Rasdeter, he waved his hand again and the chest opened. From inside it floated the rings that sealed his duchy and princedom, the crown ordained for the firstborn male, and the gilded robes that bore his crest and sigil.

"The inheritance of a prince, and not just any prince, but a son royal born of the most powerful kingdom of the world. These are things not just handed down from your father, Rasdeter, but from his father, and generations untold; the Kingdom of the Far Isles has stood for thousands upon thousands of years...!"

"Stop!" cried the prince, but the mage was relentless.

"These things cannot be sullied by your father's mistakes because they come before him. Centuries of tradition, cumulating in this, promised you and untouched by your father..."

From deep within the golden casket, rose a gorgeous shining blade, forged in fire, and hammered with the seal of the Far Isles.

"The Prince's Sword," exclaimed the mage, "Made by a master swordsman, especially for you, Rasdeter. Lord Altus died before he could give it to you; no man has touched this blade, other than the one who forged it."

Try as he might, Rasdeter could not take his gaze from the hilt or the length; the light blasted the irises of his eyes. His own sword; made only for him...

Enith turned the sword in the air until it hung vertical, the crown hovered above it, the rings slowly circled the hilt of the blade like satellites. Rasdeter tried to speak but couldn't. His wife Saramis lifted her chin and held her breath. She looked to Paza, but the Starchild and everyone else was looking at Rasdeter.

He hesitated.

"It..." The prince stammered, "It's beautiful..."

Then turning his head down and away to his right, Rasdeter shook his head.

"No," he said finally, "You cannot tempt me with it, I know what it means..."

"Do you?" countered Enith.

The bright and shiny jewels of the prince's inheritance slowly lowered back into the casket and the lid of it closed with a light click. The chest then lowered in the wooden trunk that housed it; the hinges also made clicking sounds that could be heard across the sitting rooms as the lid fell in place. The two mages silently walked away, leaving the box on a marble table that could bear its weight.

"No harm to ponder on it, my lord," said the mage Enith smoothly, "Remember, no one has touched it..."

With a last bow, the mage and his companions took their leave.

Rasdeter stared at the box a moment and swallowed hard. The mage was right; the casket and its contents had marked the prince's thoughts years ago and he believed it was among the things he would never see again. He clenched his fist and gazed up at Saramis, who met his eyes with all the love she had.

He gently squeezed her fingers with his other hand.

"I think I'll rest now, beloved," he said quietly, and Ghent came swiftly to assist. As the prince left the sitting rooms, Saramis gazed sadly at Paza, whose chest tightened in sympathy.

Both women were waiting for Rasdeter to call the mage back; to remind Enith to take the box with him.

But the prince did not.

* * *

The Shadow of the Sword

The prince called Rasdeter slept fitfully that night, and the ones following. Every night, he found himself alone in his father's house with High General Aton. The general stood before Pax, holding a wooden boa staff in one hand and a sword in the other. Aton seemed to be asking the prince to choose between them, but Pax was too afraid. He looked to his right and saw a mirror, and when Pax looked into it he saw himself as a boy again. He was dressed in the coronation robes of the Far Isles, a huge and heavy crown sat awkwardly on his head. The general seemed to notice the mirror as well; Aton lowered his arms and looked sadly at Pax.

"You've forgotten me, Prince Rasdeter," he said, and Pax began to tremble.

He would awaken from these dreams with a start, looking about him for his familiar tent on the plains. The heavy ornate drapes and stone windows did not comfort Pax upon awakening, nor the huge bed of the king with its fine sheets and blankets. Some mornings Pax would search with his eyes for the general; these trappings of wealth were a part of his memories of the man who tried to kill him. It was also a reminder of his captivity and the horrible things the mage Enith wanted Pax to do.

The only comfort Pax had was Saramis, the girl who saved him, whom Pax had grown to love and as a man fought for to win her heart. These were mornings he was grateful that Saramis had returned his love and married him. If she were yet asleep Pax would not wake her, he would reach out and stroke her long thick fluffy hair across her pillow; he frequently marveled at her unbound beauty. If she were awake, however, and turned at his sudden movement, Pax would do what husbands and lovers had done for untold ages; he would reach for her warm and sleepy form, drawing her to him for comfort at dawn.

But his wife was lost in her own dreams, so the prince moved away from his rest and prepared for the day.

His bath was drawn and ready for him. The servants of the palace already treated Pax as though he were truly their king, and the former Wanderer of the Plains wasn't sure what to make of it. Pax had no illusions about the fate of the man who once ruled here; surely, he did not simply step down from his throne and hand it over gently. He tried not to think of how old the man was or if he had a queen and family. Enith had Ghent stab Pax in the heart to control him; the prince shuddered at the thought of what the mage might do to someone he considered in his way. Instinctively, Pax covered the wound in his chest, a consistent reminder of the mage's ambition. That Pax should not have survived such a wound brought tears to his eyes; tears of rage and futility. Even if escape from the mage was possible, what would be the cost?

Thoughts of Saramis made Pax shake his head in defeat; with that threat, Enith had the prince, body, and soul.

As Pax approached the sitting rooms he could feel the presence of the wooden box, waiting for him. He'd not gone near it since the mage left it there weeks ago, but the memory of it haunted him. It also disturbed Pax that he could feel the absence of Enith; his fingers unconsciously touched the edges of his pierced skin. Pax remembered the mage said the enchanted blade gave Enith access to the prince's past thoughts and desires; he felt a tremor of fear that the magical bond between them might flow both ways. It also hurt Pax that Enith had used the prince's memories and longing for home against him. Pax was blinded by this; what could be wrong with wanting to go home?

Ghent stood waiting for Pax in the king's outer rooms, holding parchments from the morning court, which he resided over in the former king and High Regent's absence. It was inevitable that Ghent and the prince might bond over their shared near-death experience. Pax could feel the corruption in everyone else who served the mage, and the regret and sincerity of Ghent won the prince over. The two had started a pattern of spending the morning and the evening together; this also included Saramis when she was willing to attend. The government must go on, whatever had happened, and this showed the wisdom of Enith; Ghent had a love for the law from his heart.

"Good morrow, my lord," said the regent with quiet joy; Ghent was relieved that the prince was regaining his strength.

"Good morrow, Regent Ghent," responded Pax, who was looking forward to this distraction from his present thoughts. "How went the morning court and the ordinance for the building taxes?"

The regent's eyes shone with respect for his new lord. Pax remembered much from his former teachers in his father's house and understood the basic concepts of the ordinances his new regent brought to his attention. Many days Saramis would enter the outer rooms to find her husband and Ghent lost in animated discussion over how things should progress and be done.

Saramis was no stranger to the law, it was simply that the ones she followed were universal, and included the welfare of all mankind, not only the interests of a select few to the detriment of the many. She listened to these conversations carefully and only added to it if some aspect of the common man seemed overlooked.

But this morning they were alone. Saramis often remained awake late at night protecting her husband's rest. More than the effects of the enchanted blade waited for the prince, and unknown to Pax she frequently did battle with unseen forces that lurked to penetrate his helpless subconscious. These battles left Saramis exhausted and unable to rouse herself until late morning.

This new day found the prince curious about the background of Regent Ghent and how he came into the service of Enith. Pax politely inquired and was soon spellbound by the humble regent's tale of the blood oath taken by his family centuries before he was born. Once the regent finished, Pax turned his head away in pain at the thought of Ghent's family. It reminded him of Atoli and Nea, who was pregnant when Pax and Saramis left. Pax missed the man who served as the only brother he had ever known after his separation from his cousin, and his mind turned to Atoli often during the day.

"Regent Ghent," asked Pax finally, "Have you seen your family recently?"

The regent's chest constricted at this inquiry and Ghent shook his head, unable to speak.

"Why, you must go straight away then," responded the prince in dismay, "Such absence is unseemly."

Regent Ghent hesitated, then shook his head again.

"My lord, I must obtain permission..." Ghent stared down at the polished oak table, so the prince would not see the anguish in his gaze, "This is not given easily...the mage is quite clear on it..."

The prince came to his feet and his regent rose in horror; his arms outstretched with palms out in a beseeching manner.

"Lord, I beg you, make no contact or communication with the mage!"

Pax turned to him in confusion.

"It's but a simple request, Ghent..."

The regent now moved around the table to approach the man he served.

"He will use it against you, my lord," The regent whispered as though Enith could hear them, "Don't you see, he does not rest while he waits for you to recover. Enjoy this time while you can."

Pax was stunned, he didn't know what to say to this revelation. Amazed, he turned from the regent willing to sacrifice his time with his own family to give the prince this respite. Clearly, the mage was waiting for any indication that the prince was ready to take on his regal duties. He thought of Saramis, who now that the prince was getting better seemed slower to recover from her own injuries. Tightening his lips and blinking rapidly, the prince placed his hand on Ghent's shoulder and shook it gently.

"I will not forget this, regent," the prince whispered in return. Then the prince walked through all the rooms of his quarters to check on the welfare of the woman he loved.

However, this cautious idyll did not last. Three days later, Saramis rose from her rest to find her husband the prince in the sitting rooms standing before the wooden box. He had removed the lid and now gazed on the golden casket within it. The prince smiled as she approached. Saramis was a vision at morning, her waves of lovely dark brown hair shot with amber by sunlight floated over her dressing gown. She wore her headdress less and less in the palace and simply braided her hair with pressed flowers before others. Pax held out his arm to his wife and Saramis wrapped her own around his waist in greeting, which pleased him. She hid the distress in her eyes as Pax ran his other hand over the gilded metal.

"Have you opened it?" she asked softly, and the prince shook his head.

"Not yet," he murmured without thinking.

Saramis caught her breath at this. She still held hope that he would not; she buried her face in his neck and Pax tightened his arm around her.

"What harm can there be in claiming what is mine?" he questioned to no one, and his wife sighed deeply in despair.

"Come back to rest with me," she said suddenly, and Pax turned his head to meet her eyes. The prince had missed her embrace while she rested this past week and his pupils widened at the comfort he had gone without. When he hesitated, she stroked his face and drew her other hand across the one he rested on the box.

"Very well, my goddess," Pax responded deeply, "You've persuaded me..."

Saramis took both his hands then and gently pulled her lifemate away from his destiny.

That same evening, as Saramis, Pax and his regent dined together in the king's private hall, the mage Enith joined them, trailed by a considerably more subdued Keoni. When the three came to their feet in alarm, Enith waved his hand and Keoni stepped back into the corridor leading to the hall. The mage Enith bowed graciously to the trio and shook his head to the servant's offer of food.

"Wine, perhaps," Enith said cordially as he took the prince's measure.

"You look well, my lord," the mage offered after a nod of respect to Saramis, who lifted her chin at this. The prince's wife knew the source of the nightly attacks on her husband and narrowed her eyes at Enith's slight smile.

The mage continued.

"I see you've opened the wooden box, my prince," Enith stated, and raised an eyebrow at their amazement. The Ancient touched his robe over his chest and Pax paled.

"We have a bond now, Prince Rasdeter," continued the mage, "I'm certain you've felt it, during the time I've been away..."

Saramis looked in dismay at her husband, who flushed at this revelation spoken aloud.

"My name is Pax, mage," the prince replied sullenly, "You'd do well to remember it."

Enith could not help but smile at the unconscious regal tone in the prince's voice. He took his seat and waited for his cup to be filled before speaking again.

"Very well, Pax," echoed Enith, "But the box belongs to Rasdeter, who I'm beginning to see more of each day. You've done well, High Regent Ghent, in steering our future king in his new duties. I've heard nothing but good reports and the general happiness of the people."

"And the king, mage," responded Pax tightly, "In whose hall we sit and on whose food we dine, where is he and his family?"

The Ancient studied the workmanship of his goblet as he replied.

"We will speak of it, rest assured," said Enith calmly and set down his cup. "Today, however, I am more interested in speaking of your father Lord Altus, and what you know of him."

The prince did not expect the conversation to turn in the direction of his father, his heart skipped a beat in his wounded chest.

"Is it your intention to shame me before my wife, mage?" asked Pax as he flushed in anger, "I have told her of his treason, and Ghent, all know he slew his brother the king."

"But have you told her why?" responded the mage softly, who now placed his hand to his chin as he studied the prince.

"Why?" echoed Pax as he blinked rapidly in confusion, "For the throne of the Far Isles, Enith. Why do you question me thus, what are you about?"

"There is much you do not know of your former home, Pax," said Enith, "Many questions you have no answers to and do not know to ask, being only a boy when Lord Altus changed your life forever..."

Pax tasted a tang in his mouth as he watched the smug countenance of the mage. In truth, he only knew what General Aton was willing to tell Pax in the moments before Aton tried to end his life. Pax felt the comforting touch of Saramis on his shoulder, but he knew Enith was building up to something, a way to destroy what little innocence the prince had left.

"Speak plainly, mage," blustered Pax in fearful anticipation, "I cannot guess at your mind."

But Enith was enjoying drawing out the suspense; he rose from the table and began to slowly pace the tiles.

"It occurs to me in this moment, Pax, that you are indeed a better man than your father Lord Altus. He was never able to obtain the woman he truly wanted..." Enith now turned and faced the prince directly. "...and had she survived the death of her husband the king, the throne of the Far Isles would merely be an added benefit."

The silence was deafening.

Ghent and Saramis held their collective breath as the words of the mage sunk in.

The prince's brow furrowed, as though the mage spoke to him in an unknown language. His father...desired to marry...Queen Inka...the prince's aunt? The image of his mother Princess Erami floated before Pax. The murder of his mother had never made sense. Then Pax remembered how the general had looked at him when he protested how much his father loved his mother.

"You...you're lying..." choked out the devastated Pax, who then struck the table beneath him and came to his feet with a shout.

"You're lying!" he roared.

"The general told you your father murdered your mother and left her body to float out to the open sea," stated Enith calmly, "Yet still you doubt my words?"

"You're both LIARS!"

The prince had never fully grieved his mother. Pax had wrapped her in the soft gauze of altered memory, where all was well and perfect until some horrid disease took over and drove his father mad. The prince recalled how ill his father looked, the sweat on his brow. What else could have driven him to murder his defenseless loving mother?

His hands rested on the hall dining table and his head hung down as a silent howl of pain shook the prince; Pax relived again the moment he learned of his mother's death and his father's treachery. Erami had loved her husband, and trusted him with her life, a life Lord Altus had callously discarded in his lust to have another man's wife.

"Your mother was a good woman, Pax," said the mage softly, "A princess of royal blood. Now she's gone, with no one to defend her honor but a twelve-year-old boy."

This Enith said deliberately to remind the prince that he was now a man and how a man defends himself...

The prince's mind flew without error to the crate, which housed a man's defense...

"No, my lord," said Ghent, but Pax roughly pushed him from his path.

"Pax; Stop!" cried Saramis, but the prince could no longer hear her pleas.

As Pax rounded the corner past the open doors of his suite, the mage Keoni backed away from the prince's stride, who no longer feared him, so caught up was he in rage. Pax marched to the sitting rooms, determined to gain his sword, and attack the nearest source of his pain, the Ancient known as Enith.

Saramis materialized between her husband and his goal.

"Pause a moment, my love," she pleaded, "Can you not see how he baits you to folly? Consider his purpose in saying these things!"

The prince could not see Saramis and could barely hear her, so blinded was he by bloodlust. His gait paused but an instant as he literally looked through her to the wooden box with its golden chest inside. When Pax stepped forward again, Saramis pulled power from the earth beneath them to hold her husband back.

The touch of her energy shocked Pax, so that he started as his head cleared.

"Saramis..." Pax said in wonder, "Why do you stand in my way?"

Tears brimmed her eyes.

"I must," she whispered, "I must...until I no longer can..."

The prince crushed her to him, tangling his hands in her hair and kissing her frantically. She returned his embrace and they held each other tightly.

Yet as Pax held her close, he did not turn his back on the casket; from time to time he gazed at it as he kissed her hair.

* * *

From then on, the mage Enith joined the trio for supper on the seventh day of each week. He brought no new revelations, however. He spoke only of the day's news and things going on in the kingdom, in an attempt to lull the prince once again into complacency. His wife Saramis was not deceived by the mage's overtures of peace. The one thing a mage of Enith's power and age has is time and patience, running plots and schemes that take hundreds of years.

She could not guess what devices the mage had to gain the co-operation of the prince, but she knew all of them hinged on the Prince's Sword. There was some reason Enith wanted Pax to wield it, but it was not discernable to Saramis. There was no energy coming from it and she knew the sword was real; no taint of magic disturbed the metal; all was as it should be.

Yet the nightly battles continued. The prince's wife was smart enough to know Enith used this to tire and distract her, but she could not risk Pax being poisoned by magic while he slept. The former Woman of the Woods changed her routine and took rest during the day while her husband spent more time with his regents.

The people of the Bright Forest were slowly adjusting to the change in rulership; as Pax grew stronger he allowed himself to be seen by the court. Sightings of him spread like fire, everyone wanted to know more about the young couple who had replaced King Templin and his queen.

On the day Enith planned his final move against Saramis's checkmate he did a curious thing; he gave High Regent Ghent permission to see his family. This offer from the mage was greeted with both elation and fear, the regent knew Enith wanted him out of the way for a reason. The regent packed nothing for the trip; he simply saddled his horse and left for his home.

Saramis found a short note from Ghent; he realized his absence would be warning enough.

The day at first went better than planned. The regents organized a tour of the inner kingdom for Pax and Saramis, who were surrounded by guards as they made their way through the populace. Pax recalled his initial visit to the Bright Forest Kingdom and found himself delighted by the implementation of his suggested improvements. He requested to tour a portion of the outer kingdom as well, and his regents reluctantly complied as the soldiers tightened their guard. The tavern where he met and escaped from Keoni looked completely different and cleaner. The owner met him at the door with a pleased and mostly toothless grin. All was well as they made their way to the main gates of the courtyards leading back to the palace.

Some people were allowed to greet the prince and his lady, mostly children who were considered harmless. Not yet a king, it was permissible for some to touch him, and the children took full advantage. Soon, a throng of them surrounded the prince and his wife, pushing and jostling one another in an effort to be the closest to the couple. Their laughter and shouts for his attention pleased the prince and made his eyes sparkle. At one point, Pax felt a small boy place his tiny hand in his, drawing a smile from Pax as the child looked up to him.

"What is your name, my lord?" asked the boy in careful practiced language, no doubt the influence of his mother, who stood by anxiously hoping her child would not offend the prince.

It was an innocent enough question, yet Pax looked to his wife as though not sure how to reply. Another boy did not wait for an answer but shouted his own at the top of his lungs.

"They say your name is Pax Rasdeter, the new king!" shouted the boy, whose friends then pummeled him for his lack of manners.

Saramis covered her mouth to hide her laughter. Pax again felt the small boy pulling at his hand.

"Is it true?" he asked with huge eyes, "Are you the king?"

"Well, I don't know, to be honest," answered Pax kindly, "I was born a prince; I believe one has to be crowned to be a king."

The loud boy came from under the restraining arms of his fellows to shout again.

"He's Prince Rasdeter!"

At this proclamation, the children came as close as they dared to question the prince.

"Are you the Lost Prince Rasdeter, the one the whole world is looking for?" said one in wonder.

"From the Far Isles?" piped in another child, a girl with wild red hair.

The little one next to her popped his thumb from his mouth and spoke.

"Cousin to High King Sumter?"

One rather overexcited child repeated gossip he'd heard from others older than him.

"The king made a huge marble grave for you, have you seen it?"

This child, of course, received a severe cuffing from his father for his rudeness, who then dragged him away.

With this startling comment, the regents began to move the children and the people away from the prince and Saramis; the guards closed in to block the children out. His heart beating quickly, Pax did not know how to respond to these words, and his hesitation made the loud boy bold.

"What about General Aton's grave, my lord? They say it's almost as big as yours!"

In slow motion, Saramis finally beheld the cunning of Lord Enith, as a cresting wave of emotion exploded from Pax, who gasped and staggered from the onslaught on this unexpected revelation.

Traitors and criminals were given an unmarked grave; that is, if anything was left after being thrown to dogs or ravenous pigs.

While not quite a traitor, General Aton had disobeyed a direct order from his king; there should be no marked grave to find, much less a place of honor in a marble building. Once Pax had learned in the Bright Forest tavern of Aton's execution, his heart was mostly quiet. He felt defended by his cousin, and certain that Sumter had not ordered his death.

But in a kingdom, marble buildings were given to heroes...

Pax turned his shattered face in his wife's direction, his eyes wide and sightless. He would not see things properly from this point on, she knew this. They murdered his mother, executed his father, and sent the general to kill him. This was the only truth he would now believe.

There was only one thing that could change the look in his eyes.

"The grave, the sepulchre," Pax whispered to her, "Can you see it?"

Saramis nodded quickly, afraid to breathe.

"The inner courtyard, my love," she whispered in kind, "I can try from there."

The pair moved swiftly, surrounded by guards who pushed back the crowds. Saramis placed herself in front of a large fountain with the sky above her and earth at her feet. Her husband stood off to one side, his feet apart and his hands clenched into fists. Saramis quietly said a prayer to see the truth. She then pulled fire from the core of the planet; it roared up through her and she directed it to the sky above the scattering crowds of people.

"Think of what it should look like, beloved," said the prince's wife and Pax searched his memories of his home, The Far Isles. The Fire of Saramis then opened a portal and the prince's breath caught:

On a hill facing the west, a gigantic marble building stood, gleaming in the sunlight. The image rotated slowly so Pax could see a name inscribed in huge letters on the façade over the magnificent columns:

RASDETER

The prince covered his mouth with closed fist as he saw within it two raised tables with marble coffins; one that housed the re-covered remains of his mother, the other was empty with one word carved on it:

Cousin

Pax covered his face at this display of his resting place, and Saramis sighed as she felt his wounded heart open again. She closed the portal as the prince turned away, but after a few steps he stopped.

"Open it again, "he asked quietly, "Search the burial grounds..."

Saramis complied, and in the late afternoon light they looked until at last they found it; a small marble building facing the east. Saramis brightened the fading light until they could make out a name chiseled in the stone:

ATON

The beloved of Pax watched in despair as his face changed and the brief light around his heart began to shrink and fade to noth-ing. Saramis could almost see the heat coming from the enchanted wound in Pax's heart as the magic crackled and spread throughout his body, undoing all the works of light she had poured into him. His jawline became rigid and tense as the last bit of light warred with the darkness growing inside him. Then belief became real. He turned from her and marched with the remaining regents into the palace; Saramis sadly followed a few paces behind.

* * *

It was the seventh day and Enith stood silent as Pax marched past him without a word. Pax pointed at two soldiers who fell in behind him as the prince entered the king's sitting rooms. The prince's wife soon heard the shattering of wood as the soldiers hacked away the wooden box. As Saramis drew closer, she saw her husband lift the lid of the golden chest from his father's house.

He paused a moment.

"Pax, husband..." began his wife, but Pax raised his hand for quiet.

"No, Saramis," said Pax resolutely, "The time for words has passed..."

He lifted first the rings, admiring them before placing them on his fingers, flexing his hands into fists. Then the prince's crown he'd longed to hold. His fingertips brushed over the filigree and stones like a caress; he smiled to himself as he set it down on the dark etched marble table beside the chest. As Pax lifted the royal robes the mage Enith snapped his fingers and two pages hurried forth to assist the prince in the proper fastenings. Finally, the prince reached deep into the gold casket and brought forth the Prince's Sword. Freed from the rich fabrics surrounding it, the blade shone with fire and Pax grinned as he gazed on it. He laid the flat of it against his robed sleeve and admired how it hummed with life. It was a glorious instrument of death and royalty, and Pax loved how the hilt fit his now man's hand perfectly. He turned to display himself before his wife who almost couldn't bear to look at him. The pages approached him timidly with his crown and Pax nodded; they placed it on his head.

The assembled regents and nobles murmured in awe at this transformation.

The mage Enith waved his hand grandly.

"I give you the Prince of the Far Isles, noble regents," said Enith with enthusiasm, "And soon King of the Bright Forest."

Saramis now approached her husband, who gazed on her with proud and loving eyes.

"Pax..." she whispered, but the prince shook his head and placed his hand beneath her chin.

"No, my love," he answered gently, "You must call me Pax no more. He is a Wanderer of the Plains, and he cannot bring me the justice I deserve. Only the prince can save my mother's name and tear down the shameful grave of the general. Rasdeter will do it, and he will not leave one stone atop another. His name alone will bring me peace..."

The prince turned from her and faced his regents and soldiers, who swiftly bowed to him.

"All hail Rasdeter," they shouted, "King of the Bright Forest!"

Under the roar of cheering men, Saramis heard the words of Enith as he stood next to her and spoke softly:

"He is mine now, Saramis, you know this. Subconsciously, he was ever looking for a reason to do it, and the general was always the key to his door. And while he seeks to clear his name, I will have both his life...and Sumter's."

Saramis could not hide her pain from Enith, and he gave her one last word.

"You can stay or leave, Woman of the Woods, I have won either way."

Enith then vanished from the hall and reappeared in the corridor outside the sitting rooms, where Keoni waited for him. The pair stood a moment savoring the true beginning of Rasdeter's damnation. Then the mage turned his head slightly towards Keoni and spoke in an undertone.

"The child took quite a beating for his impertinence, did he not?"

"Yes, my lord," agreed Keoni, "His friends took him quite to task for the embarrassment he caused our future king. A shiny eye and bruised lips for his trouble..."

"Pay him gold," said Enith firmly to Keoni's startled glance.

"And leave him alive?" asked Keoni incredulously.

"Of course," responded the mage, "Such enthusiasm as he displayed today may make him useful again to us in the future. Go..."

As Keoni immediately vanished to fulfill his master's will, Enith clasped his hands behind him and relished the realization of his fondest dreams.

King Sumter will fall by your hand, Rasdeter, thought Enith. You are his only weakness, as the general was yours. And then I will place you on the throne of the Far Isles and cover it in dark magic that will last for centuries...

The mage breathed deeply; his gaze focused on the future.

Although by that time, he mused, I may have to find you another queen...

Saramis did not linger to watch while her husband raised his sword in triumph, she sadly returned to their private rooms. She then searched until she found a covered box of the proper size, then Saramis slowly unwrapped her headdress from her hair, folded it neatly and put it away.

KING OF THE BRIGHT FOREST

"Everything is moving; nothing, no matter how dense, is still. There-fore, life is movement."
~~~Lord Master Theron

There is a thought system on this planet that wealth, power, and prestige convey some sort of barrier against the lessons of life. That if you have enough material things you will somehow dodge the arrows of fate and the flow of time. Wealth will protect you in some fashion from disappointment, pain, sickness, missed opportunities or bad decisions.

Young Sumter was born the heir to the highest throne on Earth in his day. The army he inherited from his father King Valtus, the troops, legions, regiments, cavalry, and chariots counted in the thousands and hundreds of thousands. His archers could blacken the skies with arrows, and the ships the king could launch were an impressive and intimidating sight if a warring nation were approached by him from the sea. The lands held by the Far Isles took months to travel from one end to the other, and there were parts of it neither Sumter, his father or his grandfather had ever seen in their lifetime.

Even without the army and the military, his people numbered in the millions. In his father's day, thousands of regents flocked to his country seeking coveted positions in the government. Libraries and halls of learning flourished, and King Valtus's library was the envy of many educated men, including fellow kings.
~~~

Sumter came from a line of rulers that stretched back beyond memory, thousands of years. Only Lord Brayten remembered the beginning of the Far Isles, and he had shared many stories with Sumter's forefathers, and then the young king himself. King Valtus had a rich legacy to hand down to his son Prince Sumter, and he proudly looked forward to the day he could begin in earnest Sumter's transition from young prince to future king, as did his father before him.

But the future is promised to no one.

Two days before his twelfth birthday, Sumter lost the man he loved and looked up to more than anyone, his father. The day his mother, Queen Inka, died less than a week later, he was an orphan, and barely saved from death himself. His uncle, Lord Altus, General Aton, and Prince Rasdeter soon followed as blow after blow of sorrows were heaped on the young boy's head.

Those who loved him surrounded the young prince to protect him: Lord Brayten, who literally saved his life. Lady Irisella, who bravely placed herself between Sumter and a determined Lord Altus. Forde Marcus, who took General Aton's place with zeal and devotion. General Hesta, who was then a sub-general under Marcus. Regent Polymus, who took on the duties of High Regent Galen, who fell deathly ill from grief shortly after the failed coup of Sumter's uncle.

Although Sumter did not realize it at the time, the loss of his beloved mentor and protector Lord Brayten changed everything. On the day Lord Brayten died, his daughter S'ateegra burst onto the world scene, fully armored with the power of creation; indeed, more powerful than any creator ever born, including her massively powerful father. What no one knew at the time was that Brayten had added his might to that of his child, the exact event that magicians all over the planet had feared would happen. The Master Creator had hoped this sacrifice would serve to help protect the Earth and it did.

What Brayten had gambled on was that his child would be ready to handle his demise, but he was wrong.

In her towering grief, the nine-year-old set off on a quest of vengeance against any and all magicians involved in Lord Brayten's death, a journey that would soon earn her the name The Dark One, The Destroyer. Yet while she lived, any kingdom that did not hold or develop the practices of magic was safe from the intrigues of magicians. This stand brought the child of prophecy many enemies, who plotted to either control her or slay her, as they had her father.

It also meant that the Far Isles was loved by her, having been precious to Lord Brayten.

The child of prophecy came to visit Sumter, and this lifted his heart for a moment. However, not long after Lord Brayten's daughter was gone, the once prince became melancholy and began to ignore the morning court as he rode about the lands of his kingdom seeking solace. King Sumter turned these neglected duties over to Regent Polymus, who was well able to fill in for him. Forde Marcus, as head of the king's guard accompanied Sumter everywhere, not only as his duty, but in care for the young man General Aton treated as he had his own sons.

This day, young King Sumter rode out to the estates of Prince Rasdeter, renamed after the treachery of his father Lord Altus made it impossible for the king to refer to it thus. The only reason Sumter did not have the buildings razed to the ground was because of his first cousin and former playmate. He was clearly sentimental about it, although he had no qualms about demolishing and rebuilding the rooms of Lord Altus.

The grounds were well kept and tended. The king hosted visiting nobles there occasionally, with the proviso that no one disturb the prince's rooms or that of his mother, Princess Erami. Like his father King Valtus's library, the new king preserved these rooms, so he could visit them and remember a happier time in his life. The king also kept guards before these rooms to ward off temptation from his guests. Yet these fears were groundless since the king issued a stern proclamation of imprisonment or war against those persons addicted to the lure of gossip.

Clouds floated serenely overhead, the air was crisp and full of drifting leaves. The two men rode in silence as their mounts matched their cantor on the familiar road leading to Prince Rasdeter's home. Sumter unconsciously caught his breath as they rounded the bend of majestic trees sheltering the gates of the sumptuous main house.

King Valtus had spared no expense for the homes of his beloved brother Altus. Instead of the ancestral homes of all princes not slated for the throne, Valtus had built for his only sibling an estate that was the envy of many, much larger than the home Lord Altus should have inherited. Five homes, a huge manse and a stable worthy of kings awaited a visitor, with a separate servant's quarters and farm to grow vegetables for the Lord's kitchen. Men talented with the breeding of stock made sure the finest meats were available for the table; herds of sheep and goats grazed happily on ample fields. Though Lord Altus often traveled other lands in search of fine grapes and wine, his own winery boasted fine vintages that he often brought himself to the king's own table to sample.

Little wonder then, that the mages who enthralled the king's brother used this act of trust decades old to poison the unsuspecting king.

This information of course, did very little to soothe the suffering young monarch as he approached the gates, swung wide for him by the staff who waited for him. Marcus communicated the wishes of Sumter as he wordlessly dismounted and nodded mutely to his people. Not many days went by that did not include some thought of his departed cousin Rasdeter, and today was no different. But the king usually rode out to the estates on his cousin's birthday, and thus the trip. Other than a respectful greeting, the staff and servants knew to be quiet as their lord and master made his rounds on the prince's birthday.

The children of the servants, on any other day, would run to the king, who allowed this; it reminded him of Lady Emmia, who also loved children. It was a rare privilege; to touch a king without permission was punishable by death. But for the children who served Rasdeter's house it was permitted; their cries of joy, endless questions and adoration healed his heart. Sumter loved to embrace the little ones as they begged to kiss his cheek, it made him laugh out loud. He would tousle the hair of the older ones, as his father had him. Sometimes he brought them presents, causing the children to shriek as their parents clasped their hands in pride and trepidation, hoping their precocious offspring would not irritate their king.

But even the children knew not to approach the king on his first cousin's birthday.

Not because the king would hurt them, but because Sumter knew he might be too emotional to handle it, and he did not wish to weep in front of them. As the king passed into the corridor leading to Rasdeter's rooms, a very little one stood still by her parents, but chanced to wave her small hand to him, slowly and tight to her body. Her mother blanched at this mistake, but the king smiled at the tiny girl and gave a quick wink, to discourage her mother's sure punishment.

Forde Marcus waved off the guards in front of Rasdeter's outer rooms as the king passed them, he would watch the doors himself and give the soldiers an early respite.

Sumter walked at a measured pace as he made his way into his cousin's inner rooms. Though the rooms were dusted and clean, wherever his childhood friend had dropped his wooden toys and soldiers they remained there. Sumter wanted to imagine Rasdeter turning from the last place he stood in the room, the window. He knew his cousin had watched the forces of Aton from his balcony, had watched in horror the unnecessary executions done in Sumter's name without the Heir Elect's knowledge. Sumter knew this because had he been in his cousin's place, it was what he himself would have done.

The king approached the window, to the only spot in the room that would never be cleaned while he lived, the place where his cousin stood for the last time. In his hurry to join the general, the young prince had discarded his bedclothes and stepped out of them, rushing to gather his garments and outer robe. Sumter turned in his mind's imagination, watching his cousin hurriedly dressing and wiping his face, racing past his things as he followed the soldier waiting for him at the door.

Neither Rasdeter nor the soldier knew the boy was rushing towards his death.

Sumter turned back to the window and as always, he saw it: the barest imprint of his cousin's small hand in the dust on the balustrade. The king took a moment every year to place his hand in the air just above this imprint; to imagine he could still feel the energy and heat from the skin of his cousin. It was all he had left; no small body to press to his and weep, nothing to mourn over, nothing to bury.

Sumter looked down on the courtyard, where none dared to walk on this day. He would see the image of young Rasdeter, the same age as he all those years ago, rushing into the general's arms, whom he thought had finally come to save him. With mounted horses, they would ride away from his home into the distance and all physical evidence of the doomed prince would be erased from the earth.

And now King, Sumter would turn away from this tortured re-fabrication, lean against the sheltering wall and far from listening ears give vent to his shattering grief.

* * *

Over the years, many would come to the Far Isles with tales of the prince and his impossible survival. The first time the then Boy King heard these tales, hope did not spring into his heart, as some might mistakenly believe. His first reaction was incredulous disbelief; the general had confessed the prince's murder to Sumter himself. Why would any sane person make such a claim knowing the penalty was death?

Sumter felt himself grow angry that anyone would approach him with such fantasies while he grieved, and soon orders were given that the fallen prince would not be discussed in his presence. Well-meaning pages and regents who came with news years later were kindly intercepted by the king's staff who asked those demanding an audience with the king a simple question:

Is the information worth your life?

This soon earned the king the peace he sought regarding his cousin.

The discovery of the faun buried in Rasdeter's supposed resting place did not shake Sumter's belief. It only confirmed for him that someone had taken his cousin's body, likely to fuel the stories and increase his pain. The only news he welcomed was the whereabouts of his cousin's remains, so that the king could properly bury Rasdeter and deal with the criminals who dared touch him.

When the king came back into the corridor, he asked for the mother and the child who waved at him. The mother was visibly trembling as she approached with the king's soldiers behind her until Sumter reached out his hand to the little girl who promptly came running. Sumter picked her up just as she was about to awkwardly bow to him, causing the staff nearby to nervously smile. He motioned for the still frightened mother to follow him and the king led the group to the rooms of the late Princess Erami. With the child on his hip, the young king explained the history of the rooms to the enchanted little girl who listened as carefully as one her age could. Occasionally, she would remove her finger from her mouth and point as Sumter mentioned an item of interest. Her mother covered her mouth in tearful joy as this honor was bestowed on her daughter, and the king found himself comforted on Rasdeter's birthday for the first time in many years.

However, if you imagined that these scenes of compassion and understanding meant that Sumter was a benevolent, soft hearted king, reconsider. For his people trembled in his presence for good reason.

Being forced at twelve years of age to execute both his uncle and one of his dearest father figures taught Sumter hard lessons of what was expected as a future leader of men. He experienced his first battle at fifteen and by eighteen was a seasoned warrior. King Sumter was fair, but he enforced his will on his soldiers and his subjects without hesitation. And because he came to the throne so young, any sign of disrespect to his position as Lord High King was met with a discipline that was strict and unforgiving.

His people loved him, but they kept their backs straight and their demeanor alert in his company.

So, it came about that Sumter was in a somber but lifted mood as he returned to the palace. Regent Polymus was waiting for the king outside his library, one of Sumter's favorite places to have private discussions with his esteemed advisor. Marcus stopped at the door; he would only accompany his king if invited. Sumter frequently did this, but at the look on Polymus face his Forde General did not need to be told to wait until summoned. Polymus bowed deeply before his king, but Sumter made a wave of impatience with his hand as he passed the regent. He could tell when Polymus had something difficult to tell him; he was always more differential than usual. Marcus closed the doors behind them with a firm click.

King Sumter breathed a sigh; he had hoped the day would end well.

"My Lord King..." began Polymus but his king interrupted him.

"Polymus," replied Sumter gravely, "You need not ask for your life every time you have something difficult to tell me. I trust that you would not bring anything to my attention that was frivolous or unwarranted. Speak, I grant you."

"My lord," responded the regent, "Since this news has a history of the penalty of death hanging over it, I felt I should at least give warning..." his voice trailed off as the king paled under his warm gold skin.

More news of Rasdeter alive and well in the world? Who would dare... Sumter felt his jaw tense as he struggled with renewed emotions he thought long dead.

"Tell me but the source of such information, regent, and I will decide from there," the king said tightly.

His High Regent hesitated.

"The parchment bears the seal of the Kingdom of the Northern Walls, my king," Polymus responded quietly.

His mother Queen Inka's kingdom. His grandfather King Garrin, a trusted source. Sumter was devastated. The young king placed his palm and fingers to his forehead and walked across the library, thinking.

His grandfather must be ailing to send him such news. The old king had firsthand knowledge of what transpired during those days. How could he believe these tales?

"Read it to me, Polymus," said Sumter finally. The older man's hands shook slightly as he retrieved the parchment and began to read aloud:

To my grandson Sumter, High King, and treasured child of my daughter Queen Inka.

It is my hope you are well in these troubled times. We both have had many occasions for mourning these past years and I am strengthened by the knowledge that you have ruled your parent's kingdom wisely and with great endurance for what you have suffered.

Thus, I do not bring this to you lightly but as a warning.

There have been disturbances in the east these past six years, and many rumors of nations that have no love for you. The magicians of the world need but a reason and a weak one will serve to make war with you, and if you fall, the Nine Kingdoms fall with you.

So, make not light of my words, High King.

The kingdoms in the Unnamed Lands are amassing an army, and they rally behind a young man your age, one with dark hair and green eyes, whom they have crowned King of the Bright Forest.

As you might ask, King Templin and his whole family have gone missing.

The mages who placed him on the throne have called him Rasdeter and say boldly that he is the Lost Prince of the Far Isles.

I know what you have told me, and I believe you.

But it is my fear that they have made some abomination of the prince's bones and bring it against you, that the world may tremble. Therefore, do not dismiss my words, but take action, my king.

Know that I stand beside you in power and love.

Your grandfather, King Garrin.

The king stood silent a moment, then stretched out his hand for the document, which his regent gingerly placed in his palm. Sumter recognized immediately that his grandfather used his own hand to write, which also meant that no one other than his grandmother Queen Orsa had possibly seen it.

This disturbed Sumter greatly.

The king walked over to his desk and gently laid the parchment on it, then crossed his arms and turned to the window. He made a slight movement as though he remembered something.

"Where is the emissary?" he asked, meaning the regent who traveled from the Northern Walls to deliver the message.

"Awaiting your response in the Hall of Regents, my king," replied Polymus.

No doubt shaking in fear of his life, thought the regent somberly.

"See that he or she is well treated as I prepare my reply, Polymus," stated Sumter. "Do summon a scribe to fetch stain, wax, and parchment for me and ask Marcus to bring Lady Irisella to me without delay."

"At once, my lord," said Polymus, and took his leave quickly.

Lady Irisella was the Mistress of the Hall of Women. This was an elevated position in the kingdom, one that Irisella was well qualified to do, as a member of nobility. She was born and raised in the Western Hills Kingdom, and other than his own mother Inka, the king could not recall another female from his past that was closer to his heart. Lady Irisella helped Queen Inka raise Sumter, and his earliest memories was of her face, ministering to him and lovingly enduring his boyish antics. She also embraced Rasdeter, sharing with the boys their growing milestones in times of peace and times of turmoil.

Of course, the then young prince thought these happy events would last forever.

Sumter was nearly a man before he began to wonder why his dear friend had never requested a marriage alliance or expressed a desire to return to her home. Lady Irisella never offered much detail to her answers, only that she earnestly wished to serve her former charge for the remainder of her life.

It was Sumter's way to treat Irisella like a friend when alone with her. She had helped him with his grief, and the former prince did not like the idea of treating Irisella as a servant, though protocol required it. He wanted to be himself with someone, and in the absence of his parents, she was the closest Sumter would ever come to it.

Lady Irisella was too humble to realize this effectively made her the most powerful person in the kingdom. She had the ear of the king and could say to him what others could not. Yet Irisella was smart enough to know her place, and her devotion to Sumter was unmatched; she would always act in his best interests.

Therefore, the king summoned her to discuss what he would never say to anyone else.

The conversation lasted longer than intended, and at some point, the young king requested refreshments for himself and his honored guest. Though the doors to the king's library were heavy and thick, Forde Marcus placed himself before them to discourage anyone walking by who might be tempted to linger.

Lady Irisella was trying her best to soothe the distressed young monarch, but for the most part, it wasn't working.

"Sumter," she asked him patiently, "Why do you have such resistance to this information?"

"Because it makes no sense!" he exclaimed in exasperation, his forearms outstretched, and his fingers curled in a classic gesture of frustration. "Yes, Aton was a High General and well versed in politics and government, but at his heart, he was a soldier. Aton was loyal to my father and swore an oath to protect his bloodline. He knew I wanted Rasdeter to live. He wouldn't take him somewhere and pretend to have slain him knowing what it would cost, his reputation, his heritage, his life!"

Irisella gazed thoughtfully down at the missive from her king's grandfather. Sumter had given it to her to read for herself, an act of trust between them that neither questioned. She sighed.

"Is it possible the general was under some enchantment?"

The young king paused at this to look at Irisella but shook his head.

"Lord Brayten saw everything in the general's mind, Irisella," Sumter responded in a calmer tone, "He watched Aton deliver the lethal blow. Rasdeter is dead..." his voice trailed off in pain.

The Mistress of the Hall of Women met her king's eyes.

"Yet...he saw what the general saw..." she persisted.

"No magic can cloud the vision of a creator, Irisella," said Sumter softly, but Irisella continued to hold his gaze, and suddenly his eyes widened.

"Another creator..." Sumter could barely breathe. "But...why?"

"Could you watch a grown man slay a child and do nothing?" she said by way of answer, her own heart twisting at the thought.

"But...but yet..." replied the king in wonder, "would not Brayten, as the most powerful channel of creation, be able to see it?"

At this, Irisella approached her suffering ruler and spoke kindly.

"Brayten was not looking for a lie, Sumter, but the truth as the broken heart of the general saw it. He was focused on you, as we all were," she continued as Sumter turned away in mourning.

Lady Irisella shrugged in despair.

"Had Brayten lived..."

King Sumter swallowed hard at this; the death of his mentor and last father figure nearly broke him. If not for the appearance of the creator's daughter, and the final words of Brayten's love for Sumter that she gave him, the young king feared his own heart might have been irreparably broken.

"So..." whispered Sumter as he struggled with his emotions, "So you think the root of this was an act of compassion from a source of creation, rather than the intrigues of magic..."

"I do not know, in truth," replied Irisella gently. "But these rumors have persisted for years, Sumter, despite all your efforts to silence them..."

She gazed at the young man she loved and would give her life for.

"Is it so hard for you to hope, Sumter?" she offered quietly.

The library was silent for a time as the king leaned both hands on his desk and bowed his head, trying to suppress the pain in his heart. As always, the woman who loved him as a son and raised him as a child could see into the thoughts behind his actions. Finally, he looked up at Irisella and nodded.

"Yes," he answered her. "Yes, Irisella, it is hard for me to hope. That of all the people that I have lost over the years, that one, even one might be restored to me..."

He breathed deeply.

"I must reject such hope, my lady. Even the seed of hope is poison to a man in my position."

The king held his arms out to the one he subconsciously treated as his mother, and Irisella quickly returned his embrace. Eventually, they both turned to gaze out the window behind his desk and the king finished his line of thought.

"The threat of war is real, Irisella, so that I will investigate; this will please my grandfather and place my regents and military at ease."

"What of the child of prophecy?" offered Irisella, as a last attempt to bring Sumter peace. "Would she not help you solve this mystery?"

But the young king smiled and chuckled deeply, remembering the last time he saw Lord Brayten's daughter.

"Perhaps," he replied as the corner of his mouth lifted, "If it were possible to tear her away from the Great Lizards she so loves..." Sumter now gazed down in merriment at his foster mother, his mood restored. He gave her a squeeze with his arm and released her.

"Away with you, now," he said playfully, and pointed at her attempt to plead innocent. "You think I do not know your mind, but I do. No matter what the topic, some angle for a queen for me is always beneath your artifice..."

"Sumter..." Irisella protested as she blushed. "This is not always the case, I was serious. You know I wouldn't..."

But Lady Irisella did not press the point; she knew this was but a deflection, another way for the king to dismiss the topic of his cousin without making a clear decision. She gave in to him, as a parent would and played his game.

"Very well," Irisella said with a slight toss of her head. "She may be young for you yet, but she's quite a beauty and in a few years, you'll agree with me."

She watched as her king smiled to himself and slowly turned from Irisella, and she knew their lengthy talk had ended. The Mistress of the Hall of Women excused herself and left the library. At the sound of a click of the heavy doors, Marcus pulled it open for her. The soldiers at the end of the corridor hurried their steps to replace their leader as Marcus escorted Lady Irisella on the long journey through the palace and back to her halls.

The King of the Far Isles sighed as he gazed out from his library. He could not admit to Lady Irisella or even to himself that his heart held constant hope of reunion with his first cousin. In this fantasy Rasdeter would still be twelve, as he was in Sumter's dreams, where he could not perceive him as a grown man as himself. He always came running into the palace alone and safe, with horns blaring in welcome behind him.

"Sumter, cousin, I'm here, I'm alright!" he would cry, and Sumter would scoop him up and crush him to his chest as everyone cheered. Rasdeter would kiss his cheek and in his dreams the king could feel it; sometimes Sumter would awaken from these dreams and touch his face in pained wonder.

In darker dreams however, the king would see the general standing in the background. Aton would look at Sumter sadly and shake his head. At the increased pounding of the king's heart, Rasdeter would turn and notice Aton; he then stared at his cousin in great fear.

"No!" he cried in terror, "No, Sumter, don't let him take me, I do not wish to go..."

But the general would reach for the prince and Sumter could not find his voice to stop him. He desperately held on to Rasdeter, but the child would slip from his grasp. Sumter would strain to reach him and something invisible would hold him fast as his young cousin continued to cry out as Aton dragged him away.

"You're the king," The boy screamed as the pair disappeared into the suddenly silent crowd, "You're the king!"

The High King shut his eyes tightly at the memory of this recurring dream. When he opened them again, his jaw was set as his amber colored eyes stared over the landscape. I will do for you what I could not do in life, cousin, Sumter swore in his mind. I will find the author of these lies and the ones who took your remains...they will die together. Then we both can rest.

From his balcony the king could see the emissary passing through the inner gates with a guarded escort, on his way with Sumter's reply to his grandfather, King Garrin of the Northern Walls.

He watched until there was nothing left to see.

A King in Borrowed Robes

Saramis viewed the fitting of her husband's new robes because he asked her to. Rasdeter was secretly hurt by her disinterest but he wanted her there; his discontent was transferred to his servants. The best robemakers in the land were on hand but nothing they offered pleased him. In truth, it was the colors of his homeland that the prince wished for, the deep purple, gold and green, but he could not wear them for his coronation. It must be the standard of the Bright Forest, a rich sable brown, bright white, and deep red; the prince was very unhappy. Rasdeter looked to his wife, who wore an unreadable expression as she stood to one side, waiting. He vented his frustration.

"I don't like the colors," he said as he waved the pages away from him. "They don't suit me..."

The Head Robe Master paled at this comment, as he worked to keep himself from wringing his hands. The High Regent spoke gently to the future king.

"Once you are crowned king," said Ghent evenly, "You may change the colors of the kingdom as you wish, my lord..." Rasdeter's expression brightened at this and the regent's sharp eye cut off the beginning of a protest from the Robe Master, who flushed and lowered his gaze.

"However," Ghent smoothly continued, "You may wish to consider the confusion a change of colors may cause on the battle-field..."

Crestfallen, the prince turned away from the polished mirror and removed the unfinished robes, dropping them into the arms of an anxious page who tried not to grunt from the weight of it.

Then a determined look came into Rasdeter's eyes.

"Leave us," he said quietly, and led by Ghent, his new subjects left the room.

The prince walked over to his wife, who met his eyes as he gazed down on her.

"You make me feel like a disobedient child when you look at me thus," he said softly though no one remained in the room with them. "Pray tell, how have I displeased you?"

For answer, Saramis flung her arms around Rasdeter's neck and clung to him. Surprised by her embrace, he returned it tightly and whispered against her cheek.

"Oh, no, beloved, do not weep. Are those tears for me?"

Sunlight filtered into the wardrobe room and sprayed the tiles with warm light. When Saramis still did not respond to his words, the prince began to stroke her hair and arms.

"You're unhappy about my cooperation with the mage, I know this, Saramis. But no real harm will come of it, my heart. It is my destiny to restore my family name and if I must take the throne to accomplish it then I must. Please don't be angry with me for it..."

Yet Saramis was not angry. The former Woman of the Woods was trying to hold back her grief as she listened to the man she loved speak the words of the magic coming from the wound in his heart. She was fighting for Rasdeter's soul, as Enith waged war with her every step of the way. All the mage needed was a point of agreement, and with the prince's rage at the discovery of General Aton's grave, Enith had the catalyst necessary to poison Rasdeter's heart against his cousin King Sumter.

The secret nightly attacks on the prince continued and Saramis felt her strength to hold them off wavering. She feared to inform the prince, that it might encourage Enith to attack Rasdeter directly, causing more harm than good. The prince's wife now tried to speak but couldn't. Confused at her mysterious condition, he watched the working of her facial muscles in puzzlement and growing fear. Overcome and exhausted, Saramis slumped in her husband's arms, and Rasdeter cried out.

"Beloved, no...!"

Regent Ghent came immediately at the prince's distress and hurried before him as Rasdeter quickly carried Saramis to the king's bed. Despite the efforts of the nation's healers, she could not be roused.

The future king was devastated and refused to leave her.

Later that same day, Keoni reported the collapse of Saramis to the mage Enith in his mountain retreat. Enith met this news with quiet joy. Though he said nothing, his eyes sparkled with triumph. He'd worried the child was inexhaustible and had begun to plot something far more drastic than his sorcerous nightly poison. Despite his boast to Saramis, Enith knew the prince was far from ready to plunge his sword into his cousin's chest. The seed of Rasdeter's anger needed fuel to grow and this is what Enith desired, a harvest that his wife's loving resistance denied him.

"If she fails to rise before nightfall, report this to me at once," said Keoni's master. Keoni turned to leave then paused. His master acknowledged him.

"Speak, I grant you."

"Forgive me, master, but it seems to me that the regent's heart is soft where the prince is concerned."

"Of course, his heart is soft towards Rasdeter," his master scoffed, "They were pierced together, Keoni. Why do you think I separated them when I moved against the prince? Say or do nothing to warn Ghent, and all is assured..."

"Yes, master," replied Keoni dutifully, yet his master sensed something behind his servant's words.

The news Keoni brought Enith had placed him in an expansive mood, one that allowed him to tolerate this extended discussion. The mage appreciated Keoni's competitiveness and had a fondness for his servant, therefore Enith offered him wise council that he might not give another.

"Stay careful, Keoni," his master now said softly, "I have plans for Ghent that do not concern you. Do not allow your jealousy of the regent to cause another misstep. My patience and your value may not always be in alignment. Do you understand me?"

"Yes, my lord," Keoni whispered.

"Be gone, then..."

Keoni vanished swiftly.

The mage sat in silence for a while savoring his new victory over Saramis then finally came to his feet. He spoke aloud his thoughts as he watched a molten sun drift serenely towards the horizon, the floating clouds forming a darkening blanket behind it's coming rest.

"Well met, my prince. It seems your last battalion of defense has fallen. Time to begin in earnest. Sweet dreams..."

High General of the Bright Forest

The road to the position of High General of a nation is a long one. A series of successful battles can lead a talented man to the rank of first general. This is also a road many sons of the privileged can travel. Unlike the current day, however, an unseasoned man cannot lead thousands of men into a full-blown war, no matter who his father is.

It is a king's desire to win, not waste the lives of his soldiers. A leader who both survives a battle and brings gold, jewels, horses, and livestock back to his king can expect a promotion, in the hope that future conflicts will yield even more. The general who brings down a nation, no matter what size can nearly name his own price, for land, palaces, and slaves is worth more than precious metals. Thus, a warrior who attains five or more successful campaigns and wars will expect at some point to be promoted when the current High General dies. Many in the military as they rise in the ranks make moves to keep themselves from harm's way. There must be, after all, some men of both age and experience to engage a possibly superior foe.

Yet, there is wisdom in a general who does not distance himself too far from the conflict. The rank of High General has many privileges, not the least of which is creature comforts such as fine food and the rewards of foreign women. With such favors for the taking it can be easy for a man to lose himself in overindulgence. Every kingdom has in its history a story of a battle that turned against them, and an aging, heavy general who relied more on his soldiers for his defense than himself.

The Bright Forest had a similar story in its recent history, one that lead to the promotion of its current High General, Lord Brennan.

Like High General Aton of the Far Isles, Brennan was not born to nobility, it was bestowed on him by his king, Templin of the Bright Forest.

Lord Brennan was loyal to Templin and he warned him against the construction of the Hall of Mages and the encouragement it would bring for mages to gather there. But Templin and his High Regent were unaffected by this advice and proceeded with the project, which took several years. Brennan attended the dedication of the structure because he was required to; he watched the mages with narrowed eyes. As a man who worked his way up the ranks of power, Brennan was accustomed to the smell of ambition and to his mind the Ancient known as Enith reeked of it. When the mage by chance met his eyes, the general felt an eerie chill over his back and shoulders and his soldier's heart knew his king had made a grave mistake.

The Kingdom of the Bright Forest was called so for a reason, it was large, wealthy, and beautiful to the eye. Brennan knew the mages that Templin kept on staff were no match for such a man as Enith, and when the king introduced the mage to the general, Brennan stepped back rather than take Enith's hand.

Though his king flushed in embarrassment at this natural impulse, the Ancient was not offended. Enith spoke smooth words that neither man listened to as the pair sized each other up. The Ancient nodded his respect for the general's wisdom, yet his gaze also held a warning that made the general's own eyes widen.

When the Ancient finally turned away from Brennan, the general realized he'd been holding his breath.

Shortly after these events, the High Regent was rumored to have vanished. Lord Brennan was one of the few who knew this to be not rumor, but fact. The lord and general had returned with his men from a skirmish with the Broken Meridien and arrived after the morning court as one might expect. On a whim, Brennan entered the hall before freshening up, he was wearing his actual armor, not the ceremonial weapons reserved for the morning court, which was usually full of regents and diplomats. Members of the guard were always present, but few in number once the officials disperse for the latter part of the day.

The general and the few men who accompanied him passed through the doors and stopped in shock. The entire staff of Templin's mages and their High Regent were in pitched battle with but four of Enith's sorcerers and on the other side of the door, the men standing guard heard nothing.

The slamming of the heavy doors behind him told the general all he needed to know. The mage Enith had made his move and begun his coup; he would start with the only true defense the kingdom had against his might, these meager fools who called themselves practitioners of magic.

Brennan and his soldiers charged to the aid of these men, who were yet subjects of the king, and if they fell, would the kingdom itself be far behind?

The High Regent made a good showing for himself as his regents and magicians died screaming from the radioactive blasts of the four rogue mages, though outnumbered by over a hundred. The High Regent brought down two of the four mages himself, with the general and the only military with real weapons keeping the others from attacking him, he was soon all that was left of their magic defense.

The High General was a man of strategy; he knew well what would come next. The four and now two mages were a powerful distraction. From the corner of his eye, the general noticed a shimmering; he whirled and threw his short sword as a dagger at it; the Ancient known as Enith stepped calmly through this shimmer, halting Brennan's sword without touching it as he did so. With the barest smile of contempt, his open palm dropped it, and the metal clanged as it crashed to the tiles beneath Enith's feet.

The remaining pair of his mages stepped back like a parting sea as Enith passed them; his initial blast staggered the High Regent who cried out in agony. The general's eyes widened as he heard the words of the High Regent in his mind:

If you survive this, Brennan, touch nothing...

The Regent who guarded the Kingdom of the Bright Forest had time to say nothing else. Enith toyed with him, holding him back while his two mages finished off the rest of Brennan's soldiers and anyone else still living. Once done, the pair flanked their master and waited. The general came to his feet with a roar, but he was held fast by power he could not overcome. Enith bound the High Regent with painful cords of radiation and slowly turned him to face the general like a roasted lamb on a spit.

"Speak, High Regent," commanded the Ancient, "Give your High General your last pearls of wisdom..."

Sweat poured from the High Regent as his features bulged under the strain of holding Enith's power back.

"Touch...touch nothing he gives you..." gasped the High Regent finally, "Protect the royal family...with your life..."

In an instant, the mage known as Enith vaporized the nation's High Regent, who screamed briefly as he was released from all earthly pain. The three now moved to face the High General, who still struggled to break their grip on him.

Enith scoffed.

"Not much wisdom there, general. You've already sworn to protect the royal family. As to the rest?"

The Ancient gave Brennan a slight smile.

"You refused my hand, general, when first we met. I'd wager you have wisdom enough. How unfortunate for your king and High Regent not to listen to your sage and instinctive warnings..."

"Why do I live, sorcerer?" asked the general as he raged against his bonds.

"Fair question, general," Enith mused as he drew closer to Lord Brennan and with barely a motion, forced the general to open his hand and drop his sword. Enith held out his own hand and a dagger appeared in his palm. The general began to struggle in earnest as the two remaining mages looked to each other and smirked.

"Suffice it to say that I need you for the moment. I have a king, a queen, and a High Regent for this nation, but I have yet to find a High General with the qualifications to replace a man such as yourself..."

Lord Brennan feared the sorcerer would stab him, but this was not necessary for Enith's needs, he merely placed the dagger in Brennan's open straining hand.

The general screamed anyway.

The Death of Ordant

When news of his father's illness reached his son, Ghent was confident that Enith would grant his leave, and he was not disappointed. The regent was unaware that the mage was focused on his campaign to wear down the prince while his wife was in a state she could not return from.

He hated to leave Rasdeter's side, but the prince was adamant that Ghent should go.

As before, the regent took nothing with him but saddled his horse to depart before the mage changed his mind.

Yet there were many things on Ghent's heart as he rode to his father's house, and over the sound of his steed's hooves on the path, the regent thought of them.

First of all, the regent knew that eventually, Enith would win.

Upon returning to the palace after his last visit to his family, the kingdom's new High Regent was dismayed to find Rasdeter in possession of the Prince's Sword. Ghent viewed the despair and exhaustion on the face of Saramis and began to realize that the prince's wife was fighting for him on both the visible and the invisible worlds. By her fatigue, the regent also saw that she was losing.

Himself a man, Ghent could see the raw seduction of the world of power that the mage was offering Rasdeter; few men in his vulnerable position could resist it.

Ghent also knew that his own days were numbered.

It was clear to the regent upon his initial recovery that whatever happened to the prince would also happen to him. Ghent could feel the darkness of the shared infection of the enchanted blade on his body and mind. He was having thoughts that he'd never had before, and feelings that would shame him if he spoke them aloud. The regent also discerned this was one of the reasons that Enith wanted him to stay near the prince; it would help the infection spread faster.

These thoughts brought tears of rage and despair to his eyes as Ghent flew homeward; the wind streaked them across his face and away into the air behind him.

Once home, Ghent was quiet as his family and siblings came forward to greet him. His wife Dru was first to reach the regent and the lines of fatigue beneath her eyes alarmed him. Ghent pulled her into a tight embrace and kissed her hair. His brothers were openly weeping as they circled the regent and Ghent was convinced the end for his father had come.

He shook his head when they reached for his outer robe.

"Take me to him now, I pray you," Ghent said softly, and his siblings lead the way as he held on to Dru.

His father's eyes brightened when his eldest son entered his bedroom; Ordant weakly lifted his hand towards Ghent and his son grasped it firmly.

"I knew you'd come," he whispered as his son's eyes brimmed.

"You must rise, father," said Ghent sincerely, "...and sup with me; Dru says you won't eat, not even your favorite broth."

His father smiled warmly through his pain.

"I will dine tonight on something different, my son, such food the body cannot partake of..."

His eldest daughter turned to weep on her husband's breast, who tried to comfort her. His grandchildren knelt on the floor surrounding his bed, wiping their eyes on his blankets; Ordant reached out to Ghent's eldest and touched his cheek. The boy did not restrain his tears, Carn grasped his grandfather's hand in despair.

"You cannot go, grandfather," The child pleaded, "I've not yet come of age, and you promised to be there..."

The dying man gently pulled his hand from his grandson and touched Carn's face between his eyes, and then his heart.

"I will be here, and here," he said softly, "Sometimes a man makes promises he cannot keep with his earthly form. What you love of me is indestructible, it is this that will watch you grow."

Ghent's father now turned his face towards him.

"You have made me proud beyond reckoning," Ordant said as his son's jaw tensed, "I will take my place beside our ancestor Roane with joy..."

Ghent now wept tears his father would never understand; Ordant placed his hand on the regent's head and stroked his son's hair gently.

"Where is my wife?" he asked weakly, and Ghent's mother joined her husband on the bed. She wrapped her arms around him as Ordant pressed his forehead to hers and moments later gave forth his final breath.

Ghent stayed for the interment of his father and spoke the ancient ritual of completion of his forefather Roane's oath. They all watched as the stone masons carved his father's name on the wall beneath the list of names that followed Great Father Roane. Many of his family members came to quietly congratulate Ghent on this honor; the regent did not recall what he said in response.

They would all be shocked to know his true thoughts.

Can there be honor in this horror? Rest well indeed, father, for you have escaped. You stepped through the veil ignorant and happy, while I must bear the burden allotted to you! Had you been able to take on this monstrous evil, I vow you would not praise our ancestor, instead you might stand here tempted as I to spit upon his grave.

The ache in Ghent's chest was a constant reminder of the cost of compliance; his fingers rubbed at it absently as he struggled with his dark imaginings.

The night before the regent planned to return to the Bright Forest Kingdom, he had his wife Dru, and their three children follow him on horseback to the borders of Everet. They were grieved that Ghent was leaving early; they could not know that the magic spreading through him was making it difficult to remain near their innocence. He was beginning to fear that his suppressed rage over his fate might cause him to do his family harm. The regent found a secluded place where none would hear them and gave his loved ones these instructions as he held Dru's hands:

"Listen carefully to my words, my wife, and do not dismiss them; this is my life and yours..."

Ghent looked off in the distance at the darkening road behind them. His son Carn followed this line of sight and watched the soft colors of twilight paint the horizon.

"Do not return to the house..." he continued calmly and tightened his grip on Dru's hands as she moved back in concern, "...and if you see me again, for any reason, do not touch me, no matter what I may say to you."

His children began to whimper and cling to each other; the middle child Iason pulled his baby sister Midlin closer to him and stroked her hair as she threw her small arms around his waist.

"Ghent, husband," Dru whispered fearfully, "Why do you say these things?"

But her husband hushed her.

"Take nothing with you but the clothes you wear, and along the way buy more robes and burn these; keep nothing that can be traced back to our home..." his voice became urgent, "Promise me this!"

"I...I promise," Dru said breathlessly, "I swear it, only tell me why..."

But Ghent went on as though he didn't hear her.

"Should anyone ask or delay you, say that you travel to help our ailing aunt in the Unnamed Lands, but do not linger with her. Go straight away to the Circle of the Earth Kingdom, you'll be safe there for a time. When you feel it, you will know, leave those lands, and go somewhere I have never been, a place I cannot visualize..."

Dru pulled her hands from her husband and wept openly. Her eldest son came to comfort her, and Ghent stepped away from them.

"I've placed gold in your bags, and precious gems," he said almost to himself, "You'll find more at my aunt's, and still more when you arrive at the Circle of the Earth. You...you should want for nothing..."

His son Carn didn't understand, but he was trying to be brave. He approached his father, who went down on his knees and held his son's shoulders.

"But what of you, father; what will become of you?"

"I don't know, son, I only know that I want you free of whatever happens to me. My father is gone, and now I am the keeper of the blood oath. That power belongs to me, and with it I free you, Carn, from its bonds. Neither you, nor your children shall be bound by it; indeed, I exhort you to forget this bloodline, and begin another..."

His wife interrupted this with her arms crossed against her body, her face distorted by anguish.

"What have they done to you, Ghent, that you speak so," cried Dru, "What have they done to you?"

For answer, Ghent stood up and opened his inner and outer robe, exposing his chest. His wife and children stood aghast at the dark light glowing from his torso, how the web of it seemed to spread and grow before their eyes.

"Set fire to everything I have touched and wash your skin," he said quietly, "When you reach my aunt's, send men back to our home and burn it to the ground. I want nothing left that might lead them to you, do you understand? Nothing!"

Against his protest, they surrounded him then, seeking comfort. Already grieving their coming absence, Ghent went to his knees. The touch of their hands brought tears to his eyes and Ghent covered himself, so they would not press his wound. Their tiny kisses felt like warm water against the magic acid on his flesh. "Wash your skin," he repeated tearfully, "Burn your clothes..."

Presently, the regent urged his family to part from him. Once they began to gather themselves to leave him, Ghent spoke softly to his wife.

"Find another, my heart," he said in pain, "I release you from your vows to me..."

"No!" Dru cried in rage, "No!"

She flailed at him passionately; Ghent caught and held her arms.

"I swore a vow, and I will not recant, Ghent! You are my husband, and so you shall remain while I draw breath. Don't you dare say such to me, don't you dare..."

He crushed Dru to him and covered her face in kisses and grief. They clung to each other while the children wiped their faces. With a child's mind, they could not truly understand this parting was forever; hope was etched on their stricken glances as they looked to their parent's display of endearment.

"I will die loving you..." Ghent whispered against her cheek and they wept together. Then he pulled Dru back from him and turned her towards their offspring.

He spoke to his eldest.

"Watch over her," he said firmly, "Over all of them..."

His son Carn nodded and blinked rapidly.

"We love you, father," he said simply.

Ghent listened to the chorus of their tender voices as Carn's siblings affirmed their brother's words. His wife watched him silently, there was nothing more to say. Then they left him there at the borders of Everet and the Bright Forest. The regent stood on the road looking at the shadows of their departure and listening to the measured clipping of their horse's hooves until the darkness swallowed everything.

The Blood of Kings

During the period of High Regent Ghent's absence, the prince learned the major purpose of the wound in his heart. Unlike Ghent, the prince had been mostly protected from the ravages of the infection rendered by the enchanted blade. This protection came from his wife Saramis, who boldly interceded for Rasdeter by pouring light into his body and warding off the magic running rampant through his hapless regent. She battled with Enith over his nightly rest and kept his mind intact as best she could.

The first night of her unconsciousness Enith struck down her husband, determined to make up for the time the mage lost fighting her. He trapped the prince in dreams he could not wake up from, flooding his mind with images of carnage and blood. Rasdeter could not even scream; he thrashed about the bed violently, trying to escape. The servants moved his wife who did not stir; they did not know the prince could not harm her. After the second night, Rasdeter tried to remain awake; he walked the halls of the palace like one who had lost his spirit; his soldiers closed their eyes as he passed them. If he stayed awake until morning, the mage would let him rest; Enith wanted the prince to fear the setting sun.

By the third night, his regents convinced him to confine himself to his rooms. He was seen thrashing about on a couch in his hall, and they feared the people would believe he was possessed. Rasdeter summoned healers to make potions over the next few days and finally he turned to magic, begging for spells to keep him oblivious...nothing worked.

On the seventh day, Enith came to visit as was his habit. He found the prince sitting at his supper, unable to dine and barely able to hold his head up. When Rasdeter saw the mage, he was almost too fatigued to show anger.

"You are responsible for my lack of rest, mage," said the prince wearily, "And now I see why my wife lies senseless on her bed."

The mage's eyes shadowed at this comment.

"You have no fathom of what I've had to do in order to obtain you, Rasdeter," said the Ancient, "The precious things I've been compelled to give up..."

The building shook and rumbled on its foundations as the mage began to walk around the hall, and despite his lack of rest, the prince felt his heart pound in his chest. Finally, alone with his prize, the Ancient gave vent to his frustration.

"Were I able to find you as a child seven years ago, I would have raised you as a son to me. You would have grown easily into your glory, accepted your position as a future king! Though they raised you to be a warrior, the years you spent with those Wanderers has weakened you and filled your mind with thoughts of everlasting peace!"

Lightning flashed across the sky as Enith sought to still his breath.

"However, I must admit that without Saramis, you would not be alive now, and for that I am most thankful..." Enith's thoughts darkened when his mind turned to the prince's wife. She reminded him of Ashlan, and how his presence hampered the plans the mage had for his mentor, the powerful and now departed Eridon. And yet, like Ashlan, without Saramis there would be no prince for Enith to mold and shape to his will.

The prince came to his feet and pressed his hand to the table to steady himself.

"Whatever you would have done to me, Enith," responded Rasdeter with a hint of sadness to his rage, "You cannot change what I am, the son of a coward, a traitor..."

The mage made a dismissive sound.

"Your father was no coward, my prince, nor was he in truth a traitor. Your kingdom has stood for thousands of years, Rasdeter. Is it truly your reasoning that this line of royalty was passed down uninterrupted and peacefully from father to son without intrigue in the line of succession?"

At the prince's stunned expression, the mage continued his line of thought.

"What your father did was bold and magnificent, and at the end of it, Lord Altus did it for you. Had he succeeded in slaying both Valtus and Sumter, he would be no traitor, but the rightful ruler, and the throne would be handed to you once his reign was over. Be sure that the historians of your kingdom would write it so..."

But Rasdeter's mind had stopped on something Enith had just said.

"My...father intended to slay Sumter, his own nephew?"

"Don't be a fool," rumbled the mage, "Your father could not ascend the throne while Sumter lived. Lord Altus fully intended to hurl your cousin from his father's balcony to his death below."

The prince's eyes widened at this information.

"How do you know this?" he asked softly, "How do you know how Sumter was to die?"

Enith said nothing to this; he merely stared at the prince, who came to life with a roar.

"HOW DO YOU KNOW?!"

"You have been blind your whole life, Rasdeter," answered the mage quietly, "Blind to the relationship of your parents, blind to the relationship of your father and your uncle the king. No doubt you were blind to how much you think your cousin loved you..."

Weakened though he was, the prince drew his sword on the mage, who showed this display no sign of contempt, though both men knew the prince could not make good on this threat.

Instead, the eyes of Enith shone as he looked on Rasdeter.

"You are my treasure, Rasdeter," the Ancient responded with respect, "...and I have but two," he said as his mind turned to Iroh.

"Yet to answer your question, no mage who had anything to do with your father's downfall and death is still living. I have many means and methods to obtain my goals, my prince, and many powerful allies. If you will learn to trust me, I can reveal these things to you and much more you do not know. Come with me, now, I wish to show you something..."

As the mage once did when he first transferred the prince and his wife to the palace, Enith now with a quick gesture moved Rasdeter and himself to the lower dungeons of the outer kingdom where the condemned prisoners were held. The son of Lord Altus felt his chest pound; despite his tender words, this was an unconscious reminder of what the mage was capable of, and whose power the prince was under.

The pair walked in silence through the darkened corridors lit by scattered torches. Unlike the Far Isles, the prisons of the Bright Forest were not lit by day through slender windows. All who resided here knew the next time they saw the sun would be their last. The prisoners did not rail against their bars as the mage passed them, as they might the guards and rare visitors who came there. Though Rasdeter raised his brow in puzzlement at the scattered piles of undisturbed ash he saw in various cells he passed, the criminals were not ignorant. They moved away from their bars and sought shelter along the walls, away from Enith's line of sight.

The mage turned down a long corridor with only one cell in it. Large and well lit, the prince surmised it was for political prisoners or someone of value in a fatal game of intrigue. Yet, he stopped in shock when he viewed the fine robes that draped the lone prisoner inside. This was no regent or general.

Enith questioned the prince.

"Do you know who this is?"

At the sound of the mage's voice, the man within stirred himself and lifted his head slowly, unwrapping himself from the near fetal position he placed himself in on the thin cot beneath him. He could hardly be called alive, from the gaze he turned to Enith, yet alive he was, though it was clear he'd seen horrors to pale what the prince himself had suffered.

Rasdeter stepped closer to the wall where torches hung; he shook his head as the man dully met his eyes.

"He's a nobleman," the prince whispered, "Highborn, from his garb. He cannot be a regent, even a High Regent would not be robed so..."

The Ancient turned to meet the man's eyes.

"Can you tell the prince who you are?" asked Enith calmly.

In a brief moment of sanity, the man blinked and rubbed at his unkempt beard.

"You know who I am, mage..." he rasped. His gaze then slid to the prince who tried not to flinch.

The noble's eyes narrowed then widened.

"He's bound you," The man ventured, "I can see the darkness coming from you..."

Rasdeter cut short this train of thought.

"Who are you?" demanded the prince, "Speak forth your name..."

"I am no one, prince," The noble answered soberly, "Once, I was a person of note, such that you would not have dared raise your voice as you did just now. Men bowed to me and showered me with gifts and favor, offered their sons to fight and die for me, and their daughters to sweep my floors and change my bedding. I had a wife once, and children..."

The man sighed then and turned his eyes from the prince to lock them on the mage who stared at him with an unreadable expression.

"I am the fool who trusted a thing without soul or honor..." he looked away to the cold floor beneath him.

"You may call me Templin, prince," he said sadly to Rasdeter's horror, "For the short time I have left..."

As the prince stepped back in shock, he lifted his sword and pointed at the prisoner.

"This," he asked the mage incredulously, "This is King Templin of the Bright Forest?" Rasdeter stared about him at the meager appointments of the former king's captivity. "He's been down here in this cell for over a year?"

Enith scoffed.

"Should I move him to a tower where all the people can see him? No, my prince, he stays here. As he just noted, he won't remain here for long."

"What is your will regarding him?" asked Rasdeter.

"My will?" the mage echoed, "My lord, he lives at your leisure. Have you forgotten our last discourse regarding your father and your cousin Sumter, who now reigns as king? As long as Templin breathes, you cannot ascend the throne of the Bright Forest, and if you do not rule this nation..." the mage spread his fingers in a gesture of helplessness. "Men follow kings into battle, my lord, not princes."

Rasdeter was outdone by this frame of logic.

"What means this, Enith? You wish me to just...just execute him? Now?"

The mage crossed his arms and shrugged.

"Your cousin executed a man at age twelve, Rasdeter. He took the Sword of the Far Isles, a symbol of Valtus's legacy, and removed your father's head with it. Even as a child, Sumter understood the burden of leadership..."

With an unbridled roar, the prince turned and swung his sword against the mage. He struck an invisible barrier over and over, as the Ancient calmly watched him.

He finally chuckled softly at Rasdeter's rage and frustration.

"You would do well to use such hostility on the true obstacle to your ascendancy, Rasdeter," offered the mage, "It is Templin who stands between you and your goal of taking the Far Isles."

"Do you think you can just suggest his death and I'll eagerly comply?" said the prince in angry disbelief, "I'll not slay at your whim, mage."

But the mage nodded in the affirmative.

"Oh, but you will, my lord," responded Enith, "Once you realize that with Templin's death, the pain and lack of sleep you suffer nightly will stop..."

The implication brought the prince to silence.

The Ancient walked past the stunned Rasdeter and paused to smile briefly at his royal prisoner, who was beyond the need to feel surprise at this turn of events. At the end of the corridor, the mage turned again to look at the prince.

"I grant you, my lord," said Enith, "Take as much time and as many days as you deem necessary. I only ask that once you are ready, do leave enough to recognize, we'd like to call it an execution, at least for the official records..."

The prince gazed in despair at the blade in his hands. When he looked up at the former king, Templin returned to his cot and resumed his fetal position on it. The prince went down to his knees as the sounds of the prisoners screaming indicated the absence of the mage.

After this horrid sequence of events, the prince made a nightly vigil between his rooms and the cell of the former king. The first evening as Rasdeter fought the need to sleep, Templin spoke to him in curiosity, and the prince began his tale. They engaged each other well into the early hours, and as the weary prince began to stagger off in search of his bed, he chanced to ask Templin a question.

"Pray tell, my lord," asked Rasdeter tiredly, "What became of your wife the queen, and your children?"

The features of the king darkened for a moment, then he stared blankly at nothing.

"Ask the general," he answered heavily, then turned away.

The second evening, the prince did not fare as well; all efforts to remain awake failed him. Templin watched spellbound as the prince slowly slumped to a sitting position; he made a last attempt to rally, then rested his head against the bars of the king's cell. Soon, he was completely sprawled out on the ground. He but rested a moment or more, then spent the rest of the night thrashing about on the floor, trying desperately to wake up from the terrors in his mind. The king pressed himself to the wall, unable to take his eyes away. He knew it was morning when the prince came awake with a loud gasp, flailing as though something chased him.

His chest heaving, Rasdeter gazed on the king with eyes shot red like blood. Templin shook his head.

"Fear not for me, prince," he offered, "Do what you must, for I am already dead."

The prince wiped his face.

"It is my soul I fear for, more than anything, King Templin..."

"Then strike, and take your rest, for he has your soul, and will not return it..."

At these words, the prince came to his feet and walked the long way back to the entrance doors of the prison, where his soldiers waited for him. He took to his rest near his wife and did not rise until late in the day. Tired and shaking, Rasdeter shared his thoughts with Saramis, who could not hear him.

"I've failed you," he whispered, then covered his eyes. After a time, he spoke again aloud.

"You've given me my life and yet that was not enough; I asked for your life and you offered it freely. Now I have brought us to this place, and I cannot escape from it..."

Rasdeter sat with his forearms resting on his thighs and hands clasped. He could feel the movement of the sun behind him and the prospect of the night before him had his mind searching for release through death. An image of the Great Elder came to the prince and his chest constricted in pain.

"I think of Mother, yet I can no longer find her, Saramis. She warned me, but at that time such words to me were impossible. It feels as though I've stepped too far away from her and have lost my way..."

Rasdeter paused to still the heaving of his chest as he contemplated the impossibility of escape from the path he saw before him; to slay a man to regain the ability to sleep.

"There's such darkness in me, beloved. There's blood before me; it feels like I'm hurting others and they are hurting me. It overwhelms me, so I fear to sleep, yet sleep is all I think of, it seems to be the only way out..."

The prince reached out and gently stroked the hair of Saramis, spread out over her pillows.

"Oh, my beauty, my goddess, I fear you should never have saved me. I think of the mage Enith as the monster, but now I surmise that the monster is in me..."

A glint of metal caught the corner of his eye; the sword Rasdeter now felt he had sold his honor to possess; the blade shone with fading light from the horizon.

"All I wanted was to go home, Saramis. I swear to you, that's all I wanted..."

Heartbroken, and alone but for his unconscious wife, the prince placed his face in his hands and wept bitterly as the sun behind him began to set.

* * *

It was the third evening, and the exhausted prince made it to the cell of the king before collapsing; his hands still clenched to the bars as he sank with a cry to the ground. As before, Rasdeter was but deep asleep for mere moments, then his body thrashed and flung itself about as his mind tried to escape the terrors it was entrapped in. Templin came dully to life as the sounds of the prince's struggle intensified. He watched the prince in dread, pressing himself again to the wall at his back.

Finally, the king roared a command into the empty air.

"Enough, mage! I say again, enough!"

The Ancient appeared instantly inside the king's cell as though he had anticipated Templin's summons.

"Greetings, King Templin," said the mage in grim amusement, "Are you so eager to depart from this life that you call me forth to assist you?"

"End this travesty, Enith," replied the king gravely, "How can you enjoy such evil?"

The mage gazed soberly upon the suffering of the prince.

"I do not enjoy it, my lord, but I do find it necessary for my purposes. Be certain that it grieves me to submit the prince to dark forces, yet his destiny requires it. As you well know, it is not a simple thing to let blood from a relative..."

The king shook off his lethargy and came to his feet.

"Nothing is sacred to you, Enith; it makes one doubt you were once human..."

The mage chose in this moment to redirect the path of the conversation.

"When he wakes, he will slay you, Templin. I thought it was your oath to live to see the downfall of Brennan."

The king closed his eyes and breathed deeply at this, when he reopened them, Templin focused on the Ancient.

"Brennan will stride into hell for what he's done, mage, I am confident of this, as will you. My family waits for me, so I do not fear the prince's awakening; he but sends me home. It is the living I pray for, though you are not among them."

The mage scoffed.

"I have seen empires fall again and again, my king," said Enith with a shrug, "So many that most of them I do not recall. The Nine Kingdoms will be dust and forgotten long before I join you, so do not wait for me..."

As the mage waved his hand towards the prince, it was the king's turn to scoff.

"There is no time on the other side, mage. No matter how long you live, when I open my eyes again I will see you and laugh..."

Enith's eyes narrowed at this.

"Stay careful, little king," the mage said softly, "Though the prince strikes with his blade, your death need not be quick."

Chastised, the former king stepped back from the Ancient, who now approached the prince and spoke to him through the bars of the king's cell.

"Let it be as morning for you, my prince," said Enith, "Awaken and join us."

A moan escaped the suffering Rasdeter as his body relaxed and his mind hurled forth from the cage around it; he turned bloodshot eyes to his master, not sure if he were in the cell or on the other side of it.

"Let me die, mage," The prince whispered in despair, "I cannot survive another night of this..."

"The end to your suffering is here, Rasdeter," replied Enith, "Templin stands ready to receive the blow that will cease everything."

The prince could feel his soul cry out in protest, but the voice of the former king spoke over it.

"Stand, Rasdeter, and fear not; yours is but the hand that will send me home. I am ready..."

Nearly mindless with agony, the prince staggered into the king's cell. The mage conveniently brought forth a tree stump, such as used for beheadings in the king's courtyard. The mage gave his future king the energy to stand as Templin quickly knelt and laid his head and neck upon the tree. Before Rasdeter swung the Prince's Sword, he paused.

"Forgive me, Templin," he rasped.

"Granted," responded the king firmly as he closed his eyes.

The future King of the Bright Forest made fast and true his mark, and the king's head dropped to the dust on the floor. But the prince tumbled to the ground as he felt the weight of the nights terrors lift, only to be replaced by a new pain deep in his spirit as he watched the blood on the blade snake up the length of it and sink into his hands and arms, shooting swiftly for his wounded heart.

"No..." The prince gasped as the blade fell with a clatter from his hands and he desperately tried to wipe away the stains from his skin and clothing, overcome by guilt and grief.

But the mage did not respond to this; Enith stood perfectly still in an instant of time. The boast of the former king had irked him, and for vengeance he held the second that had passed for Rasdeter as he sliced his sword into a ten second interval so that Templin would feel the blade longer than humanly possible. The murdered king twisted in agony, and as his eyes slid pleadingly in Enith's direction, the mage narrowed his own.

He spoke into the king's tortured mind.

You will not laugh when next you see me, little king.

And just for spite, Enith added ten more seconds.

The Trial of Saramis

She was called a Woman of the Woods, a wise one who communed with the Earth and sometimes, she commanded the elements the planet was made from. The four major houses of fire, water, earth, and air were home to Saramis and the dimensional segment that governed the chemical reactions between these elements called time was her servant. What some called the fifth relationship element, Ether, was also under her conscious control.

From childhood Saramis recognized the atoms, molecules, particles and waves that moved the universe through vibration, heat, sound, and form. With a thought she became one with the dance of these things and they in turn, responded to her movements. The elders respected the mastery of Saramis and trained her to offer the peace of her learning for the good of all others.

Yet there were more things Saramis needed to learn before she could move from the lower segments of the heart into the higher realms of true mastery.

She recognized on a spiritual level her soulmate from a previous life and failed to allow him the experience of the choices he made, and she suffered for it. She compounded this error by protecting him from the consequences of his future decisions. Saramis collapsed under the weight of her burden.

You cannot live another's life and you cannot give your power to them. You may try to, but eventually, you will fail.

Her body could no longer support the constant strain of standing in Rasdeter's way. Ignorance of the Law is no excuse, and yet Saramis knew the Law. For those to whom the Law is given, far more is expected than those who are ignorant.

Pride cometh before the Fall.

So, fall she did.

Now her spirit walked far away from her physical form and roamed the dimensions. Because all places are one Saramis had no destination. It could also be said that because she was already everywhere her spirit did not move. Yet because it amused her infinite mind to imagine it, Saramis walked a path that stretched out before her and disappeared behind her. Eventually, the prince's wife saw a figure in the distance standing beside a huge tree. Before she drew closer Saramis already knew who it was.

"Mother!" she cried.

The Great Elder's arms were already open; Saramis rushed into her embrace.

"I'm so happy to see you," said the Woman of the Woods, and her mentor chuckled.

"Of course, you are," she responded, "Happiness is a natural condition here."

These words brought thoughts of the prince to Saramis, and when her eyes misted, Affi-Tosla tightened her arms gently.

"Do not think of Rasdeter in sadness, Saramis, or you cannot remain here," offered the Great Elder, and her former student tried to smile.

"I fear I have failed him, Mother," Saramis began, but the elder shook her head slightly.

"Failure is not possible on the path you walk, so speak the truth of your heart in this place."

Saramis took a deep breath as she looked away into the Infinite.

"Then it is myself I have failed, by taking on a battle that was never mine."

Affi-Tosla chuckled again.

"Oh, the battle is yours, Affi-Saramis, but you must re-think the weapons you have chosen for defense."

"Weapons?" echoed Saramis.

"Pride, Arrogance, Judgment, Sloth, and Wrath, just to name a few," answered the Great Elder. "A worthier selection would be protection that requires no defense, so that attack is impossible. Can you tell me what they are, Woman of the Woods?"

Saramis made a self-depreciating sound as she responded.

"Peace, Love, Faith, Trust, Compassion, and Certainty, Great Mother," said Saramis quietly, "None of which I have armed myself with or identified myself to be..."

The Great Elder spoke with love to Saramis.

"You can be none of these things in the emptiness, Saramis, you know this."

"Are you asking me to leave him, Mother?" she asked in despair.

"I am not the one who is asking you, Saramis, yet ask yourself; Will the prince go with you? You've been given too much to remain where you are..."

"But the Ancient, Mother," said Saramis in pain as her mind turned to Enith, "I cannot overcome him..."

For answer, the Great Elder began to glow with light; so bright that Saramis was forced to shield her eyes with her hand.

"This is why despite your abilities and raw potential, you are a perfect match for Rasdeter, Saramis. All the Law, Light, Love and Knowledge that has been poured into you and yet still you believe the darkness has power over you?"

The light surrounding the Great Elder blazed away all shadows and the landscape around Saramis vanished. Though it appeared that she was alone, the Woman of the Woods knew this was not true. As confirmation, Saramis heard the words of the Great Elder coming in deep tones from everywhere:

"There is no darkness in you..."

Once these words were spoken into the Infinite that was her mind, Saramis woke up.

Council of Kings

The road to war is not a simple one. Rarely will kings come to battle over border disputes, theft of livestock, or the execution of an emissary, although a disagreement like this can be the fuel to finally light a long simmering fire. The embers that lead to such a roaring blaze typically begin after years of unresolved conflicts and even actual skirmishes that leave a beloved general or regiment dead. Regents lost over border raids, noble women taken under armed escort or the death of a revered prince or princess can bring the thought of resolution through war to the forefront of a ruler's mind.

Even the High King of the Nine Kingdoms found himself in the position of diplomat between nations when the Kingdom of the Golden Round refused to lend financial aid to the Kingdom of the Northern Walls to build a new seaport along the routes between them. Sumter opened his coffers himself to honor his alliance with King Garrin and Queen Orsa, to the relief of all parties. In time the seaport became a gold mine of revenue for both kingdoms, although King Barron soon learned the price of his non-participance; a higher tax on his shipping exports.

One day a marriage alliance between the two kingdoms would soothe the ruffled feathers of King Garrin and the infrequent clashes between their soldiers would settle into an occasional fight. Little did Sumter know that in his future, a dispute between himself and the Kingdom of the Southern Arc would impact him personally for the rest of his life. The king would come to learn firsthand the rumblings of discontent between nations that could easily lead to war.

As the ancient sorcerer Enith had noted during the Council of Pacine, the Nine Kingdoms were rich, prosperous, and mostly unsupportive of practitioners of magic. If this were not reason enough to plot their downfall, these kingdoms were made stronger by their alliances with each other, agreements that have stood for thousands of generations. If you add to this the presence of the powerful creators, it was almost impossible to use magic to foster dissent and turmoil between these allies.

Yet for reasons unknown, Lord Brayten was not always present in the Nine Kingdoms. The Master Creator could be absent for years at a time, and at last the great patience of Izar bore fruit, and the highest nation on the planet was brought to its knees.

But this victory was not enough.

Even with the child of prophecy now walking the Earth, the magicians who wished to control mankind grew bold in their plans to overtake and subdue the Kingdom of the Far Isles.

The seduction of Prince Rasdeter was merely the torch eagerly thrown into a vat of waiting oil. Regents from the Nine Kingdoms were disappearing in numbers to cause alarm. The Lourdes Clan, unconsciously sensing an increase in the lower vibrations of strife and adversity, raised up a new leader and began attacking the borders of Sumter's kingdom with aggression. Rumors were spreading that the dreaded Broken Meridian had recovered from their harrowing defeat from the Far Isles years ago and now were marching across the northern hemisphere bringing death and destruction to all on their path. There was no uncertainty in anyone's mind as to where they were headed as they moved towards the western part of the world, allowing mercenaries to join their mostly red-haired forces.

And what was the mind of the High King of the Far Isles on these things?

Regents traveled between the Nine Kingdoms; back and forth with warnings of impending war and preparations for same. King Sumter met with all his generals to assess the defenses and borders, he sought planning strategies to push back the deadly Lourdes Clan. Foremost in Sumter's mind was the name of the king who wished to make war with him and the reason for it. Diplomacy was the first offering and if that failed, the terms of engagement. Men who tilled the ground were advised to store the surplus, and livestock were constantly herded in from the outer lands to provide food for the soldiers who would soon give their own lives in defense of their people.

Despite the protest of High Regent Polymus, King Sumter drafted a summons requesting the recall of all regents and officials dwelling in potentially hostile kingdoms.

"If they are seen as spies and slain for conspiracy of corruption, what then do I say to their families, Polymus?" asked the king.

"It is but a part of the risk of diplomacy, my lord," answered his High Regent, "An oath they swore to offer both life and limb in your service."

"Have I asked any of them to spy for me, Polymus?" said Sumter quietly, and his regent knew what true question he asked, if Polymus had ordered such in his name.

His High Regent had the grace to flush before answering his lord and king.

"Once the letter arrived from King Garrin..." The regent halted and inclined his head in a helpless gesture. Of course, Polymus had acted discreetly but immediately to protect the interests of his king.

The king sighed deeply.

"So, then, if I recall any of them, the ones who are left--"

"Fall under immediate suspicion, my lord," Polymus finished the king's half-sentence.

Sumter turned away from his beloved advisor in frustration; he did not like the feeling of powerlessness this act had invoked in him. Families torn apart by war was the cost of running a kingdom, but this had never set well with the king, for obvious reasons. This reluctance to increase the loss of life was why Sumter was much beloved by his subjects and why most were ready to die for him.

He stood gazing out at the tall windows from his library, where he made most of his important decisions. At last, the king crossed his arms before his chest. Ever a sign that the king had made up his mind and his High Regent knew that the next thing that Sumter said would be law and unchangeable.

"I realize, High Regent, that your intention is for me to know as soon as possible when this enemy king or kings will move against me," began Sumter thoughtfully.

The king turned around to face his chief advisor.

"However, since this decision usually heralds the death of any regents then considered the enemy, I will see the needless slaughter of the innocent along with the guilty..."

Then the corner of Sumter's mouth lifted slightly, and the regent who knew his lord well barely withheld the need to groan.

"So, I have decided that you, Polymus, will dream up some event or celebration that will require the presence of all regents who serve my kingdom. With this declaration, two things will happen: either all my regents will be sent home safely, or some will be detained by some excuse of urgency. By the ones detained we will know who to watch for, and the rest will come home to their families..."

Polymus placed one arm across his chest and rested the other against it, his finger absently stroking the corner of his mouth.

"And if some kingdoms are clever enough to see through this ruse and send them all without disturbance?"

"Then we will wait a spell," answered the king, "Perhaps six months or more, and send them back. You will document the reception, whether warm or cool, and we will know who is under the influence of the enemy, and who is not."

"Well done, my lord," said Polymus with not a small degree of pleasure, "It is well to know you did not sleep through all your lessons on politics..."

The king laughed aloud at this backwards compliment.

"Begone, High Regent," said Sumter with a smile, "Tax that fine mind of yours to come up with an event worthy of the recall of my regents and draft it for my seal straight away."

"As you say, my king." Polymus bowed swiftly and departed.

The young ruler turned and lingered at the window, his mind again seeking for answers to the growing mystery of his cousin's improbable survival. If the prince had somehow been spirited away by a creator's hand, why would they not return with him? All Sumter had known of creators were their benevolence towards mankind, and their sympathy for the struggle of the common man against the forces of darkness.

How could this have changed?

Lord Brayten had refused to show the young king his cousin's last moments in the general's mind, and now a man, Sumter saw the wisdom of this. The creator did speak of it, however, and even the telling of it had haunted the king for most of his life. As he thought again of Rasdeter standing with his back to the tree that his blood would soon be shed on, the words of Lady Irisella came back to Sumter:

"Could you watch a grown man slay a child and do nothing?"

No...if someone had saved his cousin from General Aton, they would not bring the prince back to his kingdom to be somehow slain by other means. And how would Rasdeter trust no harm would come to him if he believed that Sumter himself had ordered his death?

The king's chest constricted in pain at this thought. How differently the world might be now if the general had simply obeyed his new king's command. Yet Sumter remembered the general's words in the throne room:

"If he had lived, he would have risen against you..."

King Sumter silently shook his head, even as his heart agreed that if the prince had lived, he would have reason now to turn his back on their former fondness for each other. A High General had sought to murder the prince on his father's lands.

How much persuasion would Rasdeter really need to believe that Sumter now hated him?

These musing brought the king's thoughts to a time when the boys were together, sharing their understanding after one of Regent Polymus many sessions on politics and how kingdoms were run. Both almost seven, the boys were debating what should be done once young Sumter became king.

"Why do we speak of these things, cousin," said Prince Rasdeter finally with a shrug of his shoulders, "When you ascend the king's throne, everything will be yours, what does it matter if...well, you cannot just give me an annexed kingdom to run, can you?"

The prince did not mean to sound hopeful in that moment, but his cousin heard it so and wished to ease his friend's pain.

"Well, we're related, aren't we?" answered Sumter with a child's reasoning, "Why can't we just rule together; wouldn't that be delightful?"

Rasdeter laughed, but Sumter noted how his eyes twinkled at the thought; perhaps it was a good idea.

"Come," the prince and heir said excitedly, "Let us both speak to father about it, maybe we can make it a proposition now that we can change to law later."

Rasdeter's face changed at this and became somber. It was one thing to speak lightly of ruling together when alone, but to mention it aloud to others was to make the concept real, and the prince was suddenly afraid.

"No, Sumter, we mustn't speak with Uncle Valtus of it..."

But his cousin took his hand and pulled at him urgently. His father denied Sumter nearly nothing, it was this assurance that moved him forward.

"Of course, we should, cousin," said Sumter confidently, "Why would father say no?"

So, the boys ran without pause to the king, who received them in his outer rooms. Valtus, who loved to drape himself in ceremonial robes was being fitted for yet another official dinner; Queen Inka dismissed the servants as the two cousins entered breathlessly from an apparent race.

"Sumter, Rasdeter," Inka said with mild displeasure, "Do remember your station in life and refrain from thundering down the halls in front of the servants."

But the king chuckled deeply at their foolishness.

Sumter was his only child and heir, there was little he could do wrong in his father's eyes. Soon enough Valtus would have to teach his child the limitations of his world as future ruler; he wanted Sumter to enjoy his illusions for as long as he could. But as his son began to share his latest aspiration, his father the king felt the full weight of how little time he actually had left before he must shatter Sumter's lofty dreams.

"So, father, what are your thoughts?" asked Sumter brightly, "Should not I rule half the kingdom and Rasdeter the other, or should we both rule all of it together?"

Queen Inka forced herself to breathe while her beloved son and prince spoke the words of a child who does not yet understand the world around him. Rasdeter stood a few paces away with his hands clenched together and feeling very small while he waited for his uncle's response.

But Valtus looked up at his nephew and opened his free arm towards him. Rasdeter ran to the king with relief and hope in his eyes as Valtus embraced him and pressed his lips with affection to the prince's dark hair.

"I see that you both bear a deep love in this wish to share all things with each other," said the king calmly to their happy faces as they turned to grin at one another and quickly bring their attention back to King Valtus. "And as you grow, it is my fondest hope that you will continue to love and protect one another as brothers, like Lord Altus and myself..."

King Valtus again brought the two boys into an embrace, sighing as he did so.

Then he came to his feet.

"Come with me, my princes," said the king kindly, "I'd like to show you something."

Valtus looked back to his wife as the young cousins tumbled out of his arms and out the door ahead of the king, already forgetting the queen's admonishment. His eyes were sad as they met hers, and Queen Inka brought her hand to her throat.

King Valtus led the young princes to the throne room.

The boys entered the room in awe. In the past, the few times they were allowed inside, the huge room was filled with people. Now it was empty except for the ever-present soldiers who lined the walls, so far from the throne they seemed like children themselves.

Two chairs rested on a raised platform with high and numerous steps; it was the intention of the throne room to intimidate visitors. Both chairs were large and ornate, but the king's chair was higher at the top with a carved image of the crown on it, enlarged and brushed with gold, silver, bronze, and precious gems. The seating and arms were padded with lush purple fabric, huge diamond and amethyst stones weighted down the hem and rested on the floor.

The King of the Far Isles ascended the steps and looked down at the two princes.

"Sumter," said the king, "Come up here."

Young Sumter's eyes were huge as he obeyed his father. The king rested his hand on his son's shoulder.

Valtus held out his other hand to Rasdeter.

"Come, Rasdeter," said Valtus gently, "Join us..."

Rasdeter tried not to tremble as he followed his uncle and cousin up the steps.

Once they were all together on the raised platform, the King of the Far Isles began to speak.

"This throne is thousands of years old, and only Lord Brayten remembers the day it was fashioned for our distant ancestor and all his bloodline. Every king or queen of our nation has sat upon it and ruled from this chair. It has seen every birth, death, marriage, expansion and war concerning this land, and one day in the far future, it will seat our last king..."

The king's hands tightened on the shoulders of both boys, who were still unable to make a sound as they listened to his words.

"It represents the heart, bones and blood of each and every subject of the Far Isles, and it is a metaphor for all we live and die for..."

Then King Valtus gently nudged his son forward.

"Take your seat, Sumter," said the king.

Sumter looked up at his father, his pupils wide and full, then he took the few steps from his father's hand to the throne.

It looked enormous, and at almost seven years, the boy had to grasp the arm of the great chair and climb up into it. Sumter's blood pounded in his ears as he sat back, his small feet dangling at the edge of the seat. He looked out and gasped; he could see across the huge room and into the lands sprawling for miles away through the vast columns that held up the roof of the king's hall. Sunlight covered everything, and all the boy could see was the bright blue of the sky and lush green of the land. He looked to his father and blinked rapidly as Valtus smiled.

The king held out his hand and Sumter nearly tumbled in his hurry to return to his father's reassuring arm.

Valtus then nudged a stiff and frightened Rasdeter.

"Now, you, nephew," said the king kindly, "Take your seat..."

Rasdeter hesitated when he reached the throne and looked back to his cousin first then his uncle, who gave an encouraging nod. The young prince cautiously took his seat and turned as his cousin did, his hand flying to his mouth as he saw the gorgeous vista stretched out before him. His eyes brimmed as he gazed again at his uncle, whose own eyes were now saddened. Rasdeter slipped down from the chair before his uncle asked him to, and ran back to Valtus's arm, shaking.

The king gently stroked Rasdeter's hair before speaking.

"Go back to the chair, now, both of you," said Valtus, "See if you can fit upon it..."

Soon enough, the boys were seated together in the chair, looking about and at each other in awed delight. When they began to giggle and squirm, Valtus indicated they should both come back to him, which they did.

Then the king took his seat.

The boys stared at the king, shocked to silence. Valtus sat there a moment more, until his message sunk in clearly and the two cousins flushed to their feet.

"How many kings can seat this throne, my princes?" The king asked quietly, and Rasdeter hung his head while his cousin Sumter felt his eyes brim.

"Come to me," Valtus said softly, and the two boys walked mutely to his side, where the king again placed his hands on both of them.

"A shared throne is a boy's dream," continued the king in hushed tones, "One that I myself held when Lord Altus and I were small as you both are now. But once you gain manhood, you will know that only Sumter can rule this kingdom. And like my brother and I, you will find other ways to show your love for each other, but ruling the Far Isles together is not one of them..."

The king then kissed the hair of both boys and shook them roughly, to help them control their feelings.

"It breaks my heart to show you this, as once my father showed my brother and I, but it must be clear and understood, yes?"

"Yes..." The two boys whispered together.

"Off with you now, "said the king firmly, "You may practice music with Lady Irisella until supper or archery with General Aton; which shall it be?"

The princes looked to each other in delight and shouted in unison.

"General Aton!"

The boys ran down the steps and out of the hall quickly before the king remembered that it was truly Lady Irisella they should be spending time with. Sumter, of course, would not know that his father remained seated on the throne after his departure, his feelings bittersweet after delivering to his son a first hard lesson in kingship.

How sad to realize he only had four more years to teach his son anything.

Now both man and king of his father's lands, Sumter began to realize why he had resisted so long the idea of his cousin Rasdeter's survival. It was not only because he believed the general had slain his cousin, because Sumter did believe this. It was because if Rasdeter had truly survived, he would remember sitting his uncle's throne as a boy.

And there was only one way he would ever sit it again.

Protection without Defense

The regents of the Bright Forest and the mage known as Enith had finally agreed completely on one thing: The coronation must take place, with or without the nation's new queen. Further delay would only destabilize an already shaky kingdom; the fate of King Templin and his family was still unknown by the vast majority of the population.

In the morning before he left the rooms that now were his, Rasdeter visited his yet unresponsive wife and kissed her brow as he did at the beginning of every day.

Even though he knew Saramis could not hear him, the soon king was reluctant to share with her closed ears that he was off to be crowned the monarch of the Bright Forest. He should be excited, he thought, but without his wife, the event was hollow. Rasdeter gazed down at his hands, which he felt were still covered in Templin's blood.

"How can this be a day of joy for me?" he wondered aloud.

As Rasdeter entered the throne room, followed by seventeen of his regents, the nobility came to their feet with a roar. Dressed in his huge coronation robes, the train of which was carried by six young pages, he looked every inch a ruler. The new king had requested that gold thread be spun into his dark red and sable brown colors, his only concession to the purple he could not have. The results were impressive, and every nobleman and lady in the hall was thinking of how swiftly the changes could be made in their own robes. Now in his mid-twenties, his youthful manly beauty and warrior's physique reassured his new people. Former King Templin had not been an old man, but the sight of Rasdeter's sharp profile and robust form gave his subjects confidence.

Enith and Keoni shared a sideways glance of triumph as their bound pawn strolled past them. It was the mage who had sent out rumors and gossip about the new king long before he was ready. Enith wanted the nations to be frightened and on the alert; to his mind it didn't matter what preparations they made. Only one death mattered, and that was the fall of Sumter, the High King of the Far Isles.

* * *

Saramis opened her eyes. She felt the complete absence of sound as she slowly looked about her, reluctant to let go of her vision of the Great Elder and the deep peace her words had brought her. Saramis had experienced such overwhelming joy as the light surrounded her, dispelling all shadows and contrast. The sense of being in a body was completely gone. It was difficult to describe to herself as she scanned the room and its now meaningless contents. Her eyes were drawn to the light at the window; how pale and insignificant it seemed against the memory of pure brightness that was quickly fading from her consciousness as Saramis accustomed herself again with a physical world.

"Mother..." she whispered, and felt a warmth cover her; Saramis sighed.

Finally, the prince's wife began to notice that she was not in the rooms she shared with her husband.

"Rasdeter..." she said softly, and suddenly, her mind was slammed by the memories and experiences of the prince and his recent entrapment by the Ancient. The interval Saramis had spent in the company of the Great Elder had enhanced her abilities significantly and the former Woman of the Woods gasped. She sat up refreshed and lifted herself from her bed without pain.

Saramis wandered unnoticed into the king's inner rooms and retrieved the box which held her headdress. She unfolded it and lightly ran her fingers across the fine fabric. When she looked up and saw her reflection in the polished mirror that graced the room, she stood before it and wrapped her hair in the traditional manner of her station in life as a Woman of the Woods.

With a look of determination on her face, Saramis left her bed behind her and sought out her husband, the future King of the Bright Forest.

* * *

Saramis heard the sounds of the coronation ceremony before she beheld it; the trumpets blowing and the subdued hum of voices coming from the nobility. The soldiers made way for her, but she stilled the page from crying out her name by a touch on his arm. Stunned by this honor, he fell silent as she passed him. A minor regent approached her with a white cloak made from ermine and studded with pearls and white polished stones; Saramis allowed him to drape her but shook her head at the red sash he offered for her shoulders.

It was the duty of the nation's High Regent to place the crown of the kingdom on the head of the new ruler. Both men stared at each other in awe as Ghent and Rasdeter experienced something neither man had truly grasped the significance of. As the soft fabric that protected the wrought metal of the crown touched his brow, Rasdeter felt the weight of this symbol of power and the world around him faded away.

King.

He, Rasdeter, a former Prince of the Far Isles, was now king of his own nation, The Bright Forest. He was a ruler, holding the highest position of government that a man was capable of on this planet. His hands unconsciously gripped the arms of another symbol of his authority, the throne he sat upon. Although the new king tried to fight it, thoughts of his father Lord Altus hammered at him. His father had coveted the place his son now sat, and never achieved it. Yet Lord Altus had wanted this, for himself and then his heir. Rasdeter could not help but wonder if his cousin Sumter had felt this way when he gained the throne of the Far Isles. Then Rasdeter felt his own thoughts scoff at him.

Had Sumter slain a man to reach his father's throne?

Pain ripped at Rasdeter; he would never feel the same as Sumter, no matter what throne he occupied. The new king found the eyes of his master on him and Rasdeter was again startled to find nothing of contempt or dismissal in Enith's gaze. The nod of encouragement was slight but discernible, and Rasdeter felt himself breathe a little easier. Just as quickly his heart saddened again, the new king braced against a loneliness and need for his absent wife. Suddenly, Rasdeter noticed a warmth around him, he looked to his left as his longing was fulfilled at the sight of his lifemate.

Rasdeter came to his feet as he noticed her entrance, breathless at her health and beauty. High Regent Ghent turned and bowed to her, as did all others, even Enith, who watched her entrance with a wary eye.

The new king held out his hand to Saramis.

"My queen..."

Saramis accepted her husband's hand and bent her knees in a small curtsey; the assembled guests began to sigh in appreciation. But when a page approached her with the queen's crown and scepter, the new queen shook her head. She turned to her husband the king.

"Permission to speak, my lord," Saramis asked, and Rasdeter smiled and kissed her hand before releasing it.

"Granted, always..." he said lovingly and Saramis returned this love with her gaze.

Then she turned and addressed the people.

"First, I wish to thank you all for your love and acceptance of my husband Rasdeter as your king..." began Saramis and found herself rewarded by a wave of appreciation flowing from the gathered nobles and common folk. Saramis then deliberately glanced briefly in the direction of Enith and Keoni before continuing; the mage clenched his fists beneath his robes at this subtle warning.

"It comes to me that many of you are wondering who governs you; how we two have ascended the throne of the Bright Forest from what may seem to be nowhere..."

She looked to her husband who turned pale at her words yet did not falter in his gaze; Rasdeter trusted Saramis completely. His nod for her to continue was almost imperceptible, but it was there. She breathed deeply and lifted her chin slightly as she returned her gaze to her subjects who were now spellbound to hear her next words.

"His name as you know is Rasdeter, which means 'To rule with determination.' His father was Lord Altus, Prince of the Far Isles..." Saramis paused at the collective gasp that filled the room. She looked again to Enith who also paled and flushed at the same time.

"Many of you have heard this as rumor, some of you were persuaded to belief by some promise of land and the spoils of war. I stand before you as proof of the truth of my husband's heritage, for it was I who unknowingly saved him as a child from the hand of Aton, High General of the Far Isles..."

Saramis paused at the sudden clamor of voices that flooded the chamber. She looked again to her husband who blinked rapidly as his breath quickened and his pride at her words rushed into his eyes. He felt defended and vindicated by her; she smiled her love to him and turned back to gaze upon the assembly. She held out her left hand which began to glow with light and the people were stunned to silence.

"To save his life from those who might exploit him," she said directly to the fuming Enith, "He called himself Pax and grew up among the Wanderers of the Plains. Since then, my husband was discovered and brought to your nation by the intrigues of sorcerers. This you know, for King Templin and his family have vanished..." Saramis now glanced at High General Brennan, who blanched in dismay. "The full story of this has yet to be told, yet I wish to assure you that you have not bonded yourself to a pretender, but to a man of royal blood and honor, the true son of Lord Altus, born a Prince of the Far Isles."

Rasdeter took his wife's hand again and kissed it as the nobles shouted and raised their swords. High Regent Ghent now motioned for the royal page to approach with the cushion holding the queen's crown and scepter, but the new queen raised her hand to give him pause as he neared the steps leading up to her throne.

"My name is Saramis, which means a valuable essence, in some languages, a woman of high rank, even a wandering brook in others. Among my people, it simply means female minister."

"In truth, I am a Wanderer of the High Plains, and a Wise Woman of the Woods..."

At these words, a quiet murmuring began among the people, and Saramis acknowledged this with a smile.

"If you know what this means, then you know that I follow the deeper mysteries of creation and life itself, as once did my husband Rasdeter, who is now your king..."

The new queen held out her hand to the page who now hurried up the steps; she took the crown into her hands and displayed it before the people.

"My first loyalty is to you as a people, not of a particular nation or boundaries of land, but as inhabitants of this planet. Therefore, if you know what I am, then you also know that I will never sit an earthly throne..."

Saramis turned and placed the crown and scepter on the queen's throne. When she again faced the people of the Bright Forest, they stared up at her in awe.

"My husband is your king, and mine. We have both sworn the same oath to serve him in war and in peace. Yet I would not have you ignorant of my function as your queen. I love each and every one of you with all my heart, my soul, and my mind. Should you need anything to ease the burdens of this world, you have but to ask, and as a Wise Woman, you shall have of me an answer..."

The new queen turned to her husband, King Rasdeter and curtsied again.

"My lord king," she said softly, and the people stomped their feet and staffs on the tiles to signal their approval. Rasdeter held out his hand for hers, then held it up before the people.

"I give you Queen Saramis of the Bright Forest!"

The halls shook as the assembled nobles and common folk roared in unison. Enith and Keoni spoke to each other in stunned voices.

"Saramis might have made a fine regent," said Enith as his jaw tensed, "She has blamed us for King Templin and exonerated her husband for all rumors in the family's disappearance, all while offering proof of his bloodline. Well done..." he concluded with narrowed eyes as he watched the royal couple receive well-wishers in the hall.

"Did she just declare herself queen yet refuse to sit as queen in the same breath?" murmured Keoni incredulously to his master's nod.

"And quite cleverly declared herself the spiritual head of the kingdom at the same time," bristled Enith under his curled fingers to hide his rage.

"What can be done?" whispered Keoni in muted amazement at the new queen's boldness.

Yet the mage Enith did not answer this query from his servant, he was too concerned with keeping his rage in check and his thundering energy from vaporizing everyone around him. With barely a sound the mage vanished, quickly followed by a surprised Keoni.

Only High Regent Ghent took notice of their absence.

The magic poison of Enith was rising and cresting through his body and the regent found it difficult to hear anything else. Ghent was beginning to realize that the poison had a purpose beyond keeping his baser nature at the forefront of his mind. The mage wants more than for me to watch as he damns the king, thought the regent in despair, some horrid transformation awaits.

As the waves of love and happiness that Saramis poured over the gathered company washed over Ghent he actually felt nauseous; he excused himself from the other regents and made his way back to his rooms. The distant son of Roane pulled his robe over his chest as his heart pounded fearfully; his own body felt strange to him. Ghent tried hard in this moment not to think of his wife Dru, to wonder where his children were. Instinctively, he knew that to imagine their whereabouts would be to direct the magic in him to search for them and he wanted them safe. The regent cast about desperately for a distraction and his mind turned to his second love, the law, and his books.

Ghent staggered into his suites and was surprised to find a young girl in his rooms arranging his things.

"What are you doing in here?" he demanded, and the girl started at the tone of his voice. She clutched her basket of linens and cleaning feathers to her bosom.

"My lord, the mage Enith bade me design the room to please you..." she faltered.

At the sound of his master's name, Ghent could not disguise his irritation and fear of the mage's intention. Feeling the magic coursing painfully through his veins, and fearing what he might do as a result, the regent shouted at the trembling servant.

"Get out!"

The web of poison around Ghent's heart suddenly gathered and launched itself across the space at the girl in obedience to his will; she screamed briefly as the darkness struck her and she crumpled to the floor.

"No...no!" Ghent cried out in horror and ran to the girl's side. He gingerly touched his fingers to her neck and nearly sobbed in relief as he detected a faint pulse. The regent gazed up and noticed another servant cringing against the drapery.

"Summon a healer," Ghent said urgently, then shouted again as the servant made to obey. "Wait! Take her with you; get someone to help her, but don't leave her alone with me..."

Ghent nearly stumbled in his haste to carry the girl outside and place her in the arms of a nearby soldier, who hurried with his burden and the other servant to find a healer. The regent did not wait until they were out of sight, he immediately slammed the doors to his rooms and sank against them, fighting against the temptation of madness.

"What has befallen me?" he wondered aloud, "Where does the terror end?"

* * *

The coronation ceremony and celebration lasted well into the night, and would go on for at least a week, so the new king and queen bid their guests goodnight and retired to their rooms. Once alone, Rasdeter embraced Saramis as though he would not release her; his joy at finding her whole knew no bounds. It was her intention to comfort her husband after so long a parting and at her touch the constant dread the new king felt was temporarily dispelled. He shared everything he suffered with her, holding nothing back, though he feared such honesty might drive her from his side. These thoughts of course, were unfounded, and the new king fell into a deep sleep as Saramis brought peace to his rest.

The difference was in her changed spirit, and the Woman of the Woods felt no strain as she ministered to the man she loved. She stroked his hair lightly as he slept, and her fingers drove the thoughts of blood and fear from his mind. She too, took her rest without concern that the darkness might slip past her. Yet she did not deceive herself. Saramis knew that without a true change of heart, her husband would once again fall prey to the intrigues of Enith.

Rasdeter confirmed this as the early morning rays of light brought him back from the realm of sleep. Bathed and refreshed, they donned their robes as they prepared for the morning court and the ongoing festival of the king's coronation.

"I feel lost and trapped, my wife," said Rasdeter in despair, "King Templin said the mage Enith has bound me, and by Templin's death at my hands, the mage has my soul..."

"Husband, this is the deepest kind of foolishness," answered Saramis passionately, "No man can possess another's soul. It is not a thing to be possessed, only your guilt and remorse makes it feel so. Enith is using your emotions and desires to make you think there is no other way to reach your goals. You need only turn away from him; resist without force and he will flee from you..."

"I want to believe you, Saramis, but you don't understand what I've done..."

The Woman of the Woods placed her hands tenderly on either side of her husband's face. She smiled as even now all she could see was the innocence still locked inside of Rasdeter, struggling to get out. He met her eyes, and she could sense the muscles of his body relaxing as he saw the love in her gaze, his own shadowed by doubt.

How could she still love the man he had become?

"Listen to me, beloved," Saramis said softly, "And do not dismiss my words. How do you think a magician is made? Not one of them is born the way you see them now, full of malice and discontent towards others. Every one of them was born innocent; it is the only way to enter this world. Like yourself, and even Ghent, a magician starts out full of hope and dreams for the future. It is our decisions that determine our steps, our choices. Every compromise, every attempt to bargain against your true nature will bring you to a darker place than before."

Saramis held her husband firmly as remorse crept into his deep green eyes.

"Every magician believes his power is obtained outside of him or taken from others. He believes he is forced to do what he does and the harm he brings is beyond his control. The stronger a magician becomes on the outside, the weaker is his moral core. One day, he will believe that evil is his nature, and he must feed this evil to survive. If you follow this course, my love, one day Enith will not need to coerce you, and the time will come when you will show the teacher how much you have learned. This is how magicians are made..."

"I want to believe you, beloved," Rasdeter said finally, "I'm trying so hard to accept your words of comfort..."

The young king was shaking as he drew his wife closer and held her tightly. Rasdeter closed his eyes so he would not see Templin's blood on Saramis robes. The Prince's Sword had bound him to the deed of innocent spilled blood, and he could not free himself from the guilt he felt around it. Rasdeter began to see it everywhere; on the curtains and tableware, even on the faces of his soldiers. It seemed not to matter that the former king had forgiven him before the blow was struck, the new king would not forgive himself. He tried desperately to hear his wife's words, but his visions precluded it. He breathed deeply as he gazed above him at the huge, vaulted ceilings that faintly dripped blood on the floor. He knew that Enith would offer only one solution to his horrid guilt.

***

The Seduction of Ghent part I

The acceptance of one's own failings is the beginning of wisdom, and the mage known as Enith realized his weakness was anger and what it might prompt him to do while under the influence of it. Saramis had returned with a vengeance for the havoc Enith had rendered while she was asleep, and the mage had difficulty reminding himself of his promise not to destroy her. The Ancient found it best to focus on things he had control over; the gathering of kings and alliances he would need to bring war to the gates of the Far Isles was one of them.

Also, the mage was aware that the progress of Ghent's transformation was slower than he wished despite the fact that the regent was not directly protected by Saramis. It must be that somehow her light interfered with the growing darkness; the mage was surprised to learn the girl he sent into Ghent's rooms as an unwitting sacrifice was found alive.

Enith bade his servant Keoni summon the High Regent.

The mage noted with satisfaction the haggard features of Ghent as he entered the Hall of Mages. Other than this, the kingdom's High Regent was well appointed for his station, and his robes were clean and properly adorned with the embroidery of the Bright Forest. Enith could see clearly the darkness surrounding the hapless regent and smiled slightly at Ghent's new habit of lightly gripping his robe over his chest and then smoothing his fingers on the fabric.

I cannot help what I am, the mage shrugged inwardly, I knew his fate was sealed when I appointed him. Now I must hasten the burning off of his innocence; there is much to accomplish before we march westward to King Sumter's doom.

"I need you to accompany me to the Unnamed Lands, High Regent Ghent," said Enith, "The High King N'Goth must give his approval before I can successfully woo the lower kings to follow."

Ghent nodded.

"As you wish, my lord," responded his regent with hollow eyes, "I will prepare for the journey."

But as Ghent made to leave his master's presence, his voice stopped him.

"This will entail a protracted absence, Ghent," said Enith with a touch of wonder in his tone, "Have you no desire to see your family before we depart?"

Ghent placed his hand over his wounded chest before turning to gaze upon Enith.

"Yes...but..." and for a moment, a fleeting glance of true longing crossed the regent's face, and then his eyes shadowed. "No, my lord," he said finally in despair, "I have a thought I might frighten rather than comfort them...with your permission, I'd rather not be seen this way. Perhaps I'll feel better on my return..."

The mage crossed his arms over his chest and nodded. Ghent bowed slightly and moved painfully away to make his arrangements. Enith rested one elbow on his arm and placed his hand to his face as his eyes narrowed.

It made sense for the regent to avoid his family in his current state of mind, thought the mage, and yet...

Keoni appeared at his master's silent summons.

"Do you know where the family of Ghent resides in the Kingdom of Everet, Keoni?" asked Enith thoughtfully.

"I believe the majority of his relatives live around or near the tomb of his ancestor Roane, my lord," replied his servant as he watched Ghent descend the steps of the outer courtyard.

"Find them, Keoni," said Enith softly, "Bring them to me; the wife and all his children. I believe they number three, yes?"

"Yes, my lord," answered Keoni with a slight smile, "Two sons and a daughter."

"Make haste," said his lord, "I'm certain that Ghent will appreciate my generosity when he finds his family waiting for him in the Unnamed Lands."

Keoni grinned broadly.

"As you say, master."

Signature of Kings

Several weeks later, it was High Regent Sathdan of the Unnamed Lands who greeted Enith and the men of the Bright Forest at the inner gates leading to the main palace. A minor regent who stood behind Sathdan lowered his eyes respectfully as Enith approached and passed him. A nod was given and returned by Keoni then the regent gazed smugly at High Regent Ghent until his eyes fell briefly on the near invisible radiation coming from his chest. The regent then cautiously stepped closer to Sathdan whose own eyes widened slightly as Ghent greeted him cordially according to his station as an equal. Sathdan returned this courtesy and moved to guide the group forward, his face now a mask against the tumult warring inside him.

His master Iroh had not warned Sathdan that the new High Regent bore the mark of Enith. All tales before that moment spoke of a promising regent from the nation of Everet who survived an audience with the Ancient. Ghent was known for his command of the law; he was rumored to possess no skills in magic. Sathdan had not expected to deal with Ghent as a true equal; he had prepared small snares of illusion to entrap the regent and bend him to his will during the summit proceedings. His schemes disrupted like dandelion seeds; Ghent was fully capable of moving independently unless Enith deemed otherwise. It was important to both his master Iroh and Enith that the High King N'Goth be persuaded to encourage the gathered kings to follow King Rasdeter into battle against the Far Isles. Now High Regent Ghent appeared to be immune to coercion.

What was the endgame of Enith?

Oblivious to the intrigues flowing around him, the suffering regent was focused on the pain that ravaged his heart. Each step required his full concentration, and Ghent felt the reaction of Sathdan was more due to the gauntness of his face than the darkness consuming his every thought. He began to entertain thoughts of self-destruction; anything was preferred to the hammering of his physical body. As though aware of his thoughts, his master Enith temporarily eased the constant pain so that his regent could at least respond to those around him. Of course, Enith did not know Ghent's thoughts, but he sensed the near collapse of his body so the Ancient measured his assault on his servant's defenses.

His plans for Ghent, though long term, were better served if the regent could assess his excellent understanding of government law in order to present a clear response to N'Goth. Though brutal in his physical dealings, the High King had a sharp mind. He was no dullard susceptible to scholarly musings. It was one of the things Enith admired of King N'Goth, and frequently helped the Ancient quell his urge to kill him when he found himself at odds with the king's viewpoint.

As High Regent Sathdan made certain of the accommodations for Enith's staff and soldiers, the Ancient met with his former protégé Iroh, to speak of their plans.

"I must warn you, Enith," said Iroh, "The king was not entirely satisfied with my explanation as to why King Rasdeter did not come himself to plea assistance in this venture."

"Yet, you spoke the truth, Iroh," answered the Ancient, "The King of the Bright Forest has been ill for some time; his whole kingdom speaks of it. He'll need time to recover; surely N'Goth will hear this reasoning. It is customary for regents to present such proposals at the beginning..."

"N'Goth is no one's fool, my friend," offered Iroh gently, "He knows Rasdeter is your pawn, and your methods..." The master sorcerer's voice trailed away as he shrugged.

"My hand has been heavy by necessity," responded Enith as his mind turned to Rasdeter's wife, Queen Saramis.

The Ancient gave a sigh as his former pupil comforted his past teacher.

"You will prevail, as always," stated Iroh confidently, "Despite all setbacks, the five kings are here, are they not? They will listen from curiosity and hope of opportunity, as all men do."

"I must allow Ghent his moment," said Enith resolutely, "Afterwards, I will speak with the High King should he require it," the mage concluded, and Iroh nodded his approval of this course of action.

Both men stood silent then, each caught up in his own thoughts. Presently, the Ancient chanced to speak to his friend.

"Will the High King be joining us this evening to sup?" asked Enith and watched as Iroh shook his head.

"Eventually, yes," responded Iroh, "Perhaps tomorrow. He's gone to meet his son Prince Arbu on his return from the Golden Round Kingdom..." The mage paused and then noted with a touch of irony, "It seems the Crown Prince has found his princess. He awaits N'Goth's approval with some trepidation."

At first the Ancient's eyebrows flew upwards, then Enith became very still, and Iroh knew his former mentor moved ahead of the king to spy on the cause of his concern, his future daughter-in-law. Iroh calmly turned away to order a servant to bring wine and bread in case Enith had cause to linger. The Master Sorcerer Iroh rarely reacted to the changes in the king unless it directly affected his plans for the Circle of the Earth Kingdom. That the king's son desired to marry would naturally cause anxiety; it was a reminder of the plans N'Goth would carry out in regard to his family, and his fear that Prince Arbu had somehow learned of it. Yet Iroh was well ahead of all fears, and he waited patiently for Enith to end his trance. Iroh had nearly finished his first glass of wine as Enith stirred again in the present moment.

Their eyes met.

"The princess is barren," said Enith thoughtfully then tilted his head at the calmness of Iroh's gaze. "You?" asked the Ancient and marveled as Iroh smiled.

"She will remain infertile until the plans of N'Goth come to fruition," said Iroh as he raised his glass to his lips, "After that, of course, it doesn't matter..."

Enith looked doubtful.

"The king is unpredictable, Iroh," replied Enith carefully, and watched as his former pupil shrugged.

"Whatever he thinks of it, N'Goth will not move against the princess on the open road," offered Iroh, "The king would have to slay everyone, including his son, and that would surely reveal his hand to all who watch him. He will wait until he has her behind private walls. Furthermore, he will approach me for such sport. Despite what you believe, Enith, N'Goth wants Prince Arbu to retain his illusions up until the very end. He would never want his son to think--Well, let us simply reason that even in his madness, N'Goth wants Arbu to love him..."

The Ancient then sighed in resignation and moved towards the poured wine that waited for him.

"You seem to have determined everything to the letter, Iroh, and I trust your judgement," said Enith finally.

His master pupil released a soft chuckle at this compliment.

"As you have taught me so long ago, I've placed a fluid time bubble around my favorite king. Should N'Goth prove unpredictable, I will have time to react and save both the princess and his son from his madness."

"Excellent," responded Enith. "So, what of Sathdan? Has he replaced his assistant whom the king slew in one of his rages?"

Iroh's face darkened for a moment as his mind turned to N'Goth's High Regent.

"No," Iroh said slowly, "Now that Princess Lisha is under the protection of her grandfather King Barron, there is no need for a surrogate to retrieve the energy Sathdan craves from her. It seems the threat of death is enough to curb his addiction for now."

The Ancient savored the fine aroma of his dark wine before speaking again.

"Perhaps you could redirect his needs to another?" offered Enith coyly, and the visage of Iroh darkened again.

"Possibly," conceded Iroh, "But then I would need to explain to the king why I destroyed Sathdan for such loathsome behavior. I'm afraid our High Regent will need to control this on his own."

"Let it be as you say," agreed Enith, "Shall we join the others?"

"Yes," said Iroh, "I'm most anxious to meet your new acquisition; High Regent Ghent, I believe?"

"He is," answered the Ancient, "I have a king, a queen and a new High General, Brennan by name. More than enough to complete my intrigues for the Far Isles and High King Sumter. With the exception of yourself, Ghent will make a most powerful tool, one that I plan to use long past the lifetime of King Rasdeter…"

The pair walked silently for a time through the corridors, the mage known as Iroh correctly felt that Enith had more to say, and he did.

"…I confess that I marvel continuously at the timing of it; how the distant son of Roane came to me in a moment of crushing defeat, and restored to me not only the son of Lord Altus, but himself, bound by a Blood Oath to serve me…"

Enith gazed at Iroh thoughtfully.

"It would be wise for me to return to the past and see again how it all came to be, Iroh. Memory is treacherous to an Ancient; I remember Roane and some of my dealings with him, but not the oath itself."

"Was the Blood Oath made from love or fear, Enith?" asked Iroh.

The Ancient shook his head.

"It is a point of reference that I do not recall in this moment," answered the mage honestly. "Roane's love for me was misguided but true, and I remember using the soul blade against him as opposed to his destruction and then extending his lifetime for centuries. Nothing else will come to mind; I don't know why I fashioned his tomb or why he bound his bloodline to me."

"Yet such details are important to the present moment, my lord," concluded his friend.

"Just so," agreed the Ancient, "It is well to understand a tool before using it. I can detect a natural resistance in Ghent, one that his father Ordant did not share. If it is in the bloodline, perhaps I can bend or refine it..."

"As always, I stand ready to assist you as you require it," offered Iroh sincerely, and his former mentor smiled in appreciation.

"Of this moment, Iroh, I only require that you continue to restrain me from slaying N'Goth and ruining our well laid plans," answered Enith with a sigh, and Iroh made a derisive sound as he accompanied his former mentor through the halls to the dining rooms.

A Matter of Blood

Prince Arbu hid well his alarm from the woman he hoped to marry when he received the parchment from his father King N'Goth instructing him to wait before advancing to the crossroads between his home and the Kingdom of the Golden Round. None knew better than Arbu the unpredictability of his sire and most of all the prince feared his father would not approve his choice for a bride.

But what was he to do? Prince Arbu was a grown man and a Crown Prince. His father N'Goth had never guided him in the ways of women and it was expected of him as future king of the Unnamed Lands to find a suitable mate to sit the queen's throne. Arbu was literally afraid to broach the topic with his father; either reference or thought of his mother Queen Reamath was inevitable.

A light touch on his hand as Arbu gripped the reins of his horse interrupted his tense thoughts. He turned to gaze into the warm grey eyes of Princess M'Chaunt, who began to sense his dismay.

"All is well, my prince?" she whispered and Arbu gently brought her hand to his lips, which made her smile as her heart skipped a beat in her chest. The prince was a perfect combination of his mother's dark blond beauty and his father's rugged handsomeness. His appearance at the King's Summit was like a summer storm on delicate flowers; the young noblewomen nearly fainted in awe. That Arbu was unaware of his own comeliness made him even more attractive; his father N'Goth was not one for appearance over function. Once Arbu's grandfather King Barron placed his grandchildren in the attire marking them as royalty and presented them to the collective court, many a blushing lady or princess beseeched their parents to consider the prince an acceptable match.

However, Princess M'Chaunt dashed all hope without much effort.

It was the princess who unknowingly saved him from Mora once Arbu's unmeasured challenge to King Ruan brought him under her sister's scrutiny. Mora had begun to scan the prince's thoughts when he chanced to gaze away from Ruan and met M'Chaunt's deep grey eyes across the room. For a second, the prince forgot completely his express scorn for the king as he took in a vision of the princess in her muted robin's egg blue and soft lilac gown. She, in her turn, blushed profusely as she realized that the Crown Prince had halted in mid-sentence while staring at her.

Recovering, Arbu reddened and stammered an apology to King Ruan, who followed his line of sight and wisely decided to silently allow the prince to step back from her rather than cause an international incident. As Ruan lowered her sword, both Mora and Quin instantly came between her and the prince, who also wisely turned away and used the opportunity to approach the stunned princess, who then boldly moved towards Arbu over the whispered protest of her mother.

"It seems you have saved both my life and my reputation, my lady," offered the prince quietly as he took her gloved hand and touched his lips to it, delivering a brief shock that caused the future pair to nervously laugh. The smiles, however, faded as they continued to look at each other, and Arbu found himself flushing again as the princess looked down and then hesitantly met his eyes again.

"Well met, my prince," M'Chaunt answered breathlessly, "Who knows what else I may do?"

Before the Summit was over, the princess showed herself to be bold in ways unforeseen, and Arbu was smitten. Reluctantly, he parted from her after his father King N'Goth requested that he alone return home from the King's Summit, but Arbu could not forget the princess. At the first opportunity he visited her kingdom and then the enamored couple exchanged a flurry of letters, each more ardent than the last. Finally, the prince nervously asked M'Chaunt's father, who was king of a much smaller nation, for her hand, which he granted. One day Arbu would be High King of the Unnamed Lands and his daughter would be High Queen, what father would fail to say yes?

These thoughts were of small comfort to Prince Arbu as he listened to the thundering of the king's soldiers and men. The princess gasped as the huge troops and regiments surrounded both her retinue and that of the prince. The High King of the Unnamed Lands came into view and Princess M'Chaunt received her first glimpse of the man who would be her father-in-law.

Prince Arbu was nearly thirty years of age, so his father King N'Goth would be anywhere from fifty to sixty years of age, yet there was no grey at his temples and no softening of his arms or torso. His eyes were clear and his jawline taunt and without sagging; his hair was still lustrous, black, full, and long on his shoulders. You would be more tempted to think Arbu a brother rather than son to him, and the princess stiffened to prevent herself from staring back and forth between them.

N'Goth's gaze as he appraised his future daughter-in-law was un-readable; he could well be looking through her, and M'Chaunt felt her hand gather the fabric around her cloak. Neither the prince nor his intended could know that N'Goth was thinking in this moment of what he must do if the princess is found to be already with child. The king had counted in advance the cost in human lives his plans would ask of him and he was loath to add an unborn child to his guilt, but if so, then so be it.

Then the king turned his gaze on his son, who kept his back straight. M'Chaunt blinked rapidly as Arbu's hand tightened on hers.

N'Goth, as always, was direct; he pointed at Princess M'Chaunt.

"Is this your choice for a queen, my son?" asked the king quietly as the princess blanched in dismay.

"Yes, father, with your permission," answered Arbu as bravely as he could. Though he felt it, the prince knew better than to appear indecisive or afraid before his sire.

The king nodded slightly and sighed.

"I've neglected you," he said bluntly, "As my father did me. This was not a decision that should be left to desire and physical beauty, which your princess is not lacking in, but strength of character and ability to rule, which we cannot know beforehand. Yet..."

The road was quiet as the king sat his horse, thinking.

The prince's heart constricted in pained amazement at his father's confession of neglect. Sadly, it was these small admissions, far and few between as they were, that fanned the flames of hope in his son's heart, hope that his father would change one day. This veil of blindness prevented Arbu from correctly seeing his father's madness, a kind of madness of Arbu's own, passed down undiluted from his mother Reamath, who died for her distorted belief in her husband's love.

There was a part of King N'Goth that admired what his eldest son had done. It reminded him of how he himself had defied his own father to marry Princess Reamath without King Osolum's permission and how N'Goth had refused to set Reamath aside once his father asked him to. *The cost of my disobedience has been high*, mused the king. *Now I must in my turn deny to you what my father denied to me, a future.*

"It seems you've not forgotten your mother all this time," continued N'Goth as his eyes fell again on the princess, who was beginning to wonder if she'd made a mistake falling in love with a man who claimed such as he for a father. M'Chaunt had thought the rumors of the High King's brutality and madness exaggerated: How could such a madman have produced a son so loving and kind?

"You have her father's permission?" asked the king, and his son reached inside his robe and produced a parchment of agreement in writing.

"He has signed to it, my lord," replied the prince quietly as his heart pounded.

"Then you have mine," stated N'Goth simply. "Ride with me, both of you."

The king turned his mount, and his men followed this movement as though they were a part of him, closing in around the royal couple and company.

As the hooves of their horses thundered on beneath his thoughts, the prince was struck again by his father's words. The slight flash of pain in the king's eyes was so brief only his son could detect it, and only because the prince realized in this moment that he'd spent almost his whole life looking for it. Arbu's eyes fell on the sleek sheath of M'Chaunt's blond hair under her scarf and partial veil. Queen Reamath's blond hair had been thick and wild, her eyes a deep and startling blue, but her quiet demeanor hovered over M'Chaunt's grey soulful gaze and straight white blond locks.

"...you've not forgotten your mother..."

The prince took a shaky breath and released it. The face of his younger brother Loan came to mind with its almost eternal cover of grief. Arbu hid his anguish of his mother's death in loyalty of the love he wished to gain of his father, but he felt it all the same.

I mourn her daily, father, the prince thought in despair. I believed I buried it deep from your sight, but now I see I wear it as distinctly as my brother does. Yet I will accept what comfort I can.

The road sprang to life again as the sound of the king's horses faded in the distance.

Signature of Kings, part II

High Regent Ghent was possibly the only man in the assembly who was glad of King N'Goth's brief absence; it gave the regent more time to prepare. Ghent was able to study the kings who gathered to support whatever decision the High King should make; their loyalty placed a great degree of pressure on Ghent to persuade the king to war. Ghent could feel the watchful eye of his master Enith as he moved between the Hall of Regents and the Hall of Mages. The throbbing of Ghent's wounded heart reminded him constantly of the mage's ambition, and the regent could but pray his family was truly beyond Enith's reach if Ghent should fail.

Five kings awaited a speech from the High Regent of the Bright Forest, each a possible match for the kingdoms of the Four Directions. The High King himself, the Bright Forest, and the Broken Meriden would have to account for any of the remaining kingdoms that might come to the aid of the Far Isles. Seven major kingdoms against Nine, it seemed the entire planet would be at war.

The Unnamed Lands were called such by its first High King, who made a mockery of the Delegation of the Four Worlds Council thousands of years ago when the Nine Kingdoms were named. Within the Unnamed Lands were seven major kingdoms, named for the seven major failings of man:

The Bright Forest(Pride)King Rasdeter
The Ardant Road(Lust)King Pilard
Rim of the Sea(Greed)King Jian
Sealed Gates(Wrath)King Cassum
Sky Vault(Covetousness)King Telugu

Worm's Hollow(Sloth)King Mrinal

The Broken Meriden(Envy)King Bokmal

The High King's lands were almost borderless where it swallowed the others and encompassed them. The beginning of it spread over a thousand miles from its peak to the borders of The Bright Forest then all the kingdoms in between until you reached the bleak lands of Worm's Hollow and the Broken Meriden.

Of course, Ghent noted ruefully, the kings of Worm's Hollow and the Broken Meriden wouldn't attend the gathering, they were too suspicious by nature. They sent envoys who vouched to obey the wishes of King N'Goth. The truth? They also feared and respected the High King, in that order. The death of the powerful mage Azanth by the king's own hand cowered Mrinal, King of Worm's Hollow, who preferred intrigue and treachery by magic to gain his ends. Bokmal, the King of the Broken Meriden would only follow and respect the lead of one as brutal as himself and N'Goth's brutality was legendary.

Ghent himself was no warrior. Yet despite his wound from Enith, the regent was a man who was used to commanding the respect of others. Ghent was no fawning servant who cowered at a word from the mage, even though his master could destroy him. This the kings could detect easily and so they would listen and then decide.

The regent's dilemma, however, was clear:

How could he foster the idea of war when he was against it?

The evening before his speech to the kings, Ghent sat to dine with the regents. Enith was there only briefly; from time to time the regent found the gaze of his master quietly watching him, a finger lightly touching his lips as though Enith studied him. Sathdan gained Ghent's attention as Keoni entered the room and bent over Enith and whispered; Enith's eyebrows raised in amazement then the mage became very still. When his servant continued his comments Enith lifted his hand in a gesture for silence. Keoni blinked rapidly as he straightened and crossed his hands in front of him. Sathdan chanced a glance at his own master Lord Iroh who pointedly did not return his gaze and the High Regent of the Unnamed Lands controlled his breath.

He spoke quietly to keep his fellow High Regent's attention.

"Our High King is very interested to hear tomorrow what you have to say about the possible conquest of the Far Isles, my lord," said Sathdan as smoothly as he could under the circumstances.

This comment made Ghent immediately tense. However, when his eyes turned to his master's chair, the regent noted with relief that Enith was gone. Keoni remained, his hands yet folded before him, his face a mask as his gaze locked on Ghent, who looked away.

"I, too, am interested in what I have to say, my lord," replied Ghent wryly, "And highly interested to see if one word of it will matter..."

Sathdan chuckled nervously.

"As you say, my lord," Sathdan agreed, "As you say."

* * *

The next day all five kings elected to listen to Ghent in the late afternoon, before the evening sup. Servants hurried about placing mead and bread at the tables while regents from the various kingdoms earned their keep organizing parchments for the kings to read; most of which were shoved to one side as High Regent Ghent entered the hall. Enith appeared late and took his seat near Iroh who covered his surprise. Enith was punctual to a fault; Iroh could only surmise that whatever delayed the Ancient was of vast importance. But he could detect no emotion from his friend, so Iroh turned his attention again to Enith's High Regent, who cleared his throat in preparation.

Ghent bowed first to the High King, then all others, and waited for permission to speak.

To the astonishment of all present, King N'Goth came to his feet and crossed the space between himself and the High Regent, who wisely gathered himself inwardly and held the gaze of the king.

N'Goth slowly circled Ghent, and finally stood in front of him with crossed arms.

"You look at me as a man does; and that is well," said the king gruffly. "You're no warrior, but you have the gaze of one who's not accustomed to being beaten like a dog…" and here the king paused and stared at Ghent's chest and then back to his eyes. "Yet you reek of magic, regent…" and now N'Goth turned his head and looked straight at Enith, who blanched in rage and shock. "Speak to me honestly and tell me why you are here, High Regent."

Ghent breathed deeply; this was the last thing he expected, though he had been warned the High King was unpredictable. Instinctively, Ghent knew that King N'Goth expected him to look to Enith before speaking; the regent lifted his chin slightly and held the king's eyes. He saw the barest hint of approval as the king's gaze narrowed. This was no man who desired flattery and smooth words.

Best to lead with the truth.

"As you stated, my king, I am now High Regent of the Bright Forest. I was born and raised in the Kingdom of Everet, which is now annexed to the Bright Forest. And I am here because my ancestor Roane bound his family to a Blood Oath over sixteen centuries ago to serve the mage Enith for whatever tasks he may require…"

The king's eyes both lit and shadowed at the words 'Blood Oath'. N'Goth had never shared a common bond with anyone; he suddenly felt a grudging respect for this man who would give his own life to keep the word of a long dead ancestor.

N'Goth interrupted Ghent.

"I know something of Blood Oaths…" said the king almost to himself, and N'Goth decided in that moment that he would hear the regent out. But not without testing him further. The king leaned against the table behind him, his arms still crossed as he spoke with Ghent as though they were alone in the room, to the ire of Enith and the amusement of Iroh.

"If you know me, you know that I am a man of direct speech. We are here to speak of war, regent. You have no High General Brennan with you to advise me of terrain and pitfalls on the road, and the count of men who will die for me and the kings of five nations under me. I am High King of the Unnamed Lands and I have my own plans. Why should I care what happens to the High King of the Far Isles?"

Enith felt himself tense as the five kings leaned forward unconsciously. N'Goth had said aloud what all of them were thinking. The Nine Kingdoms were practically on the other side of the world. Though the eastern kingdoms had no love for Sumter, a dispute over the lineage of the Far Isles was low on a list of shared priorities. This enterprise was the mage Enith's dream, why should they lend their blood and might to it?

Ghent sighed; at this point he felt he had nothing to lose. The parchment he was holding in his hands as the king was speaking Ghent now rolled lightly with his fingertips then placed on the table beside him and pushed it aside.

"As it stands, I agree with you, my king," said Ghent to the shock of all present, "You shouldn't care what happens to King Sumter, and you shouldn't care what occurs a world away from your concerns. War has never made any sense to me in all of my life, and there is not an argument presented that will ever make sense..."

Now the regent stepped away from the king and began to thoughtfully pace the tiles.

"Thousands of years ago, men thought it good and right and fair to rule over one another. This, as you know, created a need for land boundaries and hierarchies of government with a ruler of all men at the very top. Women were required to surname their children and exchange their freedom for rights to land handed down to mostly male generations. Then it became necessary to deny access to rivers and soon some metals from the earth were deemed more valuable than others. One day, men fought and died over land rights and we called it 'War' and defined it as a planned event; a course inevitable in order to settle disputes. Men such as yourself and all present were designed to carry out these conflicts, to such an extent that now none can recall any other way to accomplish what we call peace. Ironically, those assembled at the Council of the Four Worlds believed all of this was a temporary measure..."

Iroh covered the lower half of his face to conceal his admiration of Ghent's intellect. To suggest that the king not consider war was a far better tactic than to insist he should. N'Goth will bring the arguments himself and answer his own questions, and the ones that Ghent could not possibly know.

Well done, thought Iroh, Humility forswears arrogance, which would never have worked with N'Goth.

The High Regent of the Bright Forest continued thinking aloud.

"Now we know that war is the legacy of the reasoning of men. Destruction is the resolution of disagreement, a sure protection for what we leave for our children, who must take up our grievances and pass them on to theirs. In this manner we wish to be remembered as the victor, the one who overcame and vanquished all others."

N'Goth's eyes narrowed as his mind turned to King Sumter, High King of the Western Hemisphere. Many people thought of Sumter as the only High King in the known world, in effect the highest king in all the lands. It had never occurred to King N'Goth before that this was a subtle insult to his own rule. He'd been too consumed with his personal agenda to consider a larger picture. Should there be two High Kings?

"You are indeed High King," said Ghent quietly, as though he spoke aloud the king's thoughts, "All the men in this room recognize you as such, as well as those kings that are absent. And there are none on this side of the globe," and the regent slightly emphasized the word 'this', "That will not bow the knee to you, so your legacy is assured. Yet what else will you be remembered for, my king?" asked Ghent, "That you left a temporary legacy of peace for your son, Crown Prince Arbu? Or that you conquered the known world before your death?"

King N'Goth blanched and walked away from Ghent as his words sank in. The king couldn't look at his son, couldn't view the love and admiration N'Goth knew would dwell in Arbu's eyes. What, indeed, would he be remembered for? The willful slaughter of two kingdoms, or a glorious world conflict, that would be remembered throughout all time?

A war erupted within the king's own mind, a battle of his inner madness. He must not die before keeping his word to his dead mother, yet in this moment N'Goth wanted to be remembered for more than an international murder-suicide. If he conquered the whole world first, no one would care what he did afterwards. And it would give his children more time...

Prince Arbu started slightly as he felt his father's eyes on him. As always, loyalty gleamed behind his blue irises and his father stared through Arbu to his own father King Osolum, who smirked at the idea that his son might accomplish more than he.

The king spoke to Ghent as he looked through his son Arbu to the shadow of his father.

"I have considered your offer, High Regent Ghent," said N'Goth, "And you have cleverly brought to my attention that perhaps there should only be one High King, and that should be the King of the Unnamed Lands. The plans I have for my own kingdom can wait a few years..." N'Goth now looked away as his eldest son openly beamed his approval of his father's words. "Bring your parchments and reports tomorrow; I will sign your accords. All those who wish to join me can do so, or no; let every king decide for himself."

Prince Arbu came to his feet and joined his father; pride bounced in each step. The assembled kings also rose and slammed their cups on the tables in agreement; the accords were all but assured. Ghent thought in this moment that he would view the pleasure of Enith, but his master was gone. Lord Iroh accompanied King N'Goth and Prince Arbu as they departed the hall and the regent watched as Keoni quietly made his way towards Ghent; they would leave together.

Ghent knew he should feel triumphant, but he did not. He knew it was not his words that persuaded the High King, but the thoughts within N'Goth, and whatever his hidden desires were for the outcome that moved his mind. The regent looked down at the papers before him and felt he saw the blood of thousands of men dripping from his fingers to the parchment and the table beneath it. Whatever happened next, Ghent could not deny he had a direct hand in it:

The Unnamed Lands would bring war to the Far Isles.

The Seduction of Ghent, part II

Ghent felt a deep weariness in his bones as he followed Keoni through the torchlit corridors of King N'Goth's Hall of Regents. Once within reach of Ghent's appointed suites, Keoni chanced to speak.

"I confess I have envied you, High Regent Ghent," offered Keoni quietly.

"Envied me?" echoed the regent in confusion, "To what end, Keoni?"

The mage placed his hands behind him, and his face took on a pensive demeanor.

"Most of my life as a sorcerer I have sought the approval and favor of our master Enith. I have advanced myself by toil and struggle, cleverness and even I venture some measure of trickery to achieve my aims. It has grieved me that in so short a time you have won both admiration and respect from him with so little trouble..."

Keoni now paused and glanced pointedly at the darkness pouring from the wound in the regent's chest, but Ghent was yet unclear on the aim of their discourse.

"I have not wished you well, Ghent," Keoni said honestly, "Yet in this moment, I find myself uncertain as to whether I should rejoice or grieve at the turn your life has taken..."

"You owe me neither grief nor mercy as I see it, Keoni," replied the regent, "The only audience I deem necessary to view my fall is but myself, for this path follows me no matter where I place my feet."

The mage looked at his confused and unknown rival strangely for a moment, then inclined his head towards Ghent's door.

"Let it be as you say, High Regent," Keoni responded and stood to one side as Ghent opened his door and stepped inside. The mage's face was unreadable as Ghent nodded his goodnight and closed the paneled door.

He turned around as he noticed he stood in complete darkness. Ghent's brow furrowed; he knew his servant had lit the lamps in his rooms. As he reached to touch the draped wall to his left and perhaps feel his way to a candle, a torch suddenly blazed to life and Ghent saw Enith standing at the entrance to his sitting rooms. The candle in Enith's hand spilled light on the face of the person standing next to his master.

It was Ghent's wife, Dru.

"Enith..." Ghent began as his face blanched, but his master raised his hand for silence.

"It was my hope that you might be pleased at the trouble I endured to arrange a visit with your wife, regent," said Enith rather pleasantly. He then placed his arm over the terrified and trembling Dru, who blinked rapidly as she stared mutely at her husband.

The Ancient made a sound of pretended dismay.

"Yet I see perhaps I've fallen short somehow. No doubt you would prefer to see your children as well. Come, Ghent, let us see if they can be found..."

"My lord, I beg you..." said Ghent desperately but his master made a slight clicking sound with his teeth.

"You need not beg me, my regent," answered the mage in a conciliatory manner, "In truth, you've done nothing wrong. I gave no orders nor made any demands in regard to your family, so no transgression has occurred. You've merely brought to my attention that perhaps I was remiss in not doing so..."

Ghent quickly followed Enith into his sitting rooms, his mind reeling in fear of what the Ancient might do in either spite or jest. The doors moved back of themselves to reveal his children, Carn, Iason and Midlin huddled together with Carn's arms protectively around his siblings. When the children saw Ghent, they cried out as one.

"Father!"

They tried to move forward but encountered an invisible wall. Midlin began to weep and her brother Iason hushed her and pressed her face to his arm. With a wave of his hand, the mage transferred Dru to another part of the room where she too, could not move in Ghent's nor her children's direction. Dru placed her hands on this invisible wall and gazed in agony back and forth between her children and her husband.

Enith sighed deeply.

"I've misjudged you, Ghent," said the Ancient, "I thought you merely gifted and intelligent when in fact, your mind stretches easily into the realm of brilliance."

The mage walked around the room, studying the regent's children and then his wife. When his eyes came back to his servant's, they nearly twinkled.

"You whisked your family to safety, then burned down your house, all from a distance, with your father barely cold in the earth. Imagine my surprise when I learned this. Magnificent! I had mages searching for weeks while we rested here in the hospitality of King N'Goth, and they found nothing. Every single strand of DNA was gone, there was nothing to trace, no clothing, no items of sentiment, not even a shard of pottery. No witnesses, every member of your near relatives was completely ignorant of your movements. And each day you sat to dine with me as though none of these things had occurred. You have a mind to rival my own, Ghent--"

"You have me, Enith..." Ghent grasped his robe over his heart, "Your poison has bound me to you. Should I wish such a fate for my family? You have no need for them to ensure my service, I have done all you have asked of me, have I not? The fault is mine; they only obeyed my will. Have mercy..."

The mage continued as though his regent had remained silent.

"--Almost. My lifetime measures in the millions, regent. I have seen and foiled many schemes designed to overcome my aims. Yours, however, was succinct and sublime. So clever your artifice that I was forced to intervene and search myself..."

The mage stretched forth his hand and a scorched, dirty doll hovered in the air above his palm. Dru gasped in dismay and little Midlin pounded her tiny hands on the barrier, shouting the only word she could clearly speak:

"Mine!"

"Yes, little one," The mage agreed with a smile, "Yours. The only thing left with father's touch on it, the one thing I could use to trace and find your family. Now what did father tell you to do?"

"Wash our skin," said Iason sadly, "Burn everything..."

Carn shouted in frustration at his tiny sister who pouted, too young to understand how grave their plight.

"How did you find it?!?"

The boy whirled to face his father who showed his son only love in his gaze. "I threw it into the fire, father, I swear it!"

"It's alright, son," declared Ghent passionately, "It's alright, you've done well..."

"Don't hurt them, my lord," pleaded Dru, "Whatever punishment you have, I beg you; place it upon me. Please don't hurt my babies..."

Enith turned at the sound of Dru's voice as a thought occurred to him.

"Yet your husband's ancestor Roane swore a Blood Oath of your family's service to me, Lady Dru. This would preclude any attempt to flee from me. It is a point of dishonor, yes?"

Ghent sank to the tiles.

"Enith," he cried, "My life is in their breath. The fault is mine..."

The mage blocked out all sound for a moment as he watched his regent grovel for the lives of his family.

"You love each other," The mage said to himself. "This is clear to the blind, regent. So strong a love even my enchanted blade cannot overcome it. How then, do I bend you fully to my will?"

The Ancient next materialized behind the wall and next to Ghent and Dru's children who now fell silent and afraid.

Enith gazed at each child in turn.

"Your parents would each eagerly give their lives to protect you, so it would do me little good to slay either of them. Yet, what of you three? Would you die to protect one another?"

For answer both boys placed their arms protectively around their little sister, who still reached for the doll floating in the air above Enith's hand. With a smile, he allowed it to drift down to Midlin, who grasped it tightly to her cheek.

"You've taught them well," Enith said graciously as he continued to study the three.

"It would be too obvious to make example of the smallest, I think," The mage said as he pondered. "...and I have her to thank for finding you, so that shall not be my selection."

The mage stared at Iason whose pupils widened as his older brother fiercely embraced him. "Ah, the middle child, and a son. I've a feeling though your father loves you dearly, you may be your mother's favorite..."

The children could not hear their parent's cries from behind their barriers, though Enith could and smiled as his eyes finally lit upon Carn, the oldest, who stepped bravely in front of his siblings. Enith looked in silence on the child who did not turn away his eyes; then the Ancient grinned broadly.

"There are years between you and your brother Iason, Carn, son of Ghent," said Enith, "And even more years between you and your sister Midlin. It occurs to me that perhaps you think because of this that the younger ones are more precious, more important, in the eyes of your father and mother. You've outgrown much of their youthful foolishness and taken on more responsibility and now you feel closer in age to your parents..."

Enith now looked pointedly at Ghent, who placed his palms against the barrier separating him from his family. His gaze promised everything to the Ancient, who now narrowed his eyes as he turned back to Carn.

"But you're wrong, Carn," said the Ancient softly. "You are the most important. Look to your father."

Carn obeyed and looked at Ghent on his knees with tears brimming his eyes, and his own blinked rapidly. The mage was right, Carn had never seen himself as important, only as the eldest. He stared at his father in wonder.

"You are the first, son of Ghent, "said Enith sincerely. "The one your father pinned all his hopes on, his dream of immortality. No matter how many children followed, Ghent has loved you first and always..."

Now the Ancient allowed the children to hear their father's words.

"My soul for his, Enith," pleaded the regent tearfully, "I rest you, my soul for his..."

Lifting his chin, Enith dropped the barrier between the children and Ghent.

"Go to your father..." he said quietly, and the children began to run to Ghent.

Iason and Midlin fairly plowed into their father, who still on his knees, fell back on his legs and held them tightly. They covered him with sobs and kisses, and he fiercely kissed their hair and cheeks. Ghent looked up and noticed that Carn stood still, halfway between his father and the mage while Dru looked on from the other side of the room. She found the eyes of the Ancient on her and began to look around urgently to find what he silently called her attention to.

When she saw it, Dru screamed behind her invisible barrier.

Between the mage and her son Carn was the tiniest silver filament, smaller than the circumference of a human hair. What she could not see was that the other end of this filament was inside the child's body, tied around his blood veins, spine, and nervous system and as Carn reached the end of it, the filament tightened and squeezed his insides together between his neck and heart.

The boy could feel it; such pain that he could not speak. He reached out his hand towards his father, who began to shout in horror.

"Go back, son!" roared Ghent. "I beg you, go back!"

Carn paused and looked painfully behind him where Enith stood gazing at Carn as though he did not hold the boy's life in his hands. Carn took a step backwards and the agony in his body eased. He looked to his mother on his left, who cried out and gestured wildly for him to return to the mage. The boy swallowed with difficulty and tried to breathe. Then he looked again at his father, who hurled himself forward and crashed into the restored invisible wall. His siblings cowered behind their father and Midlin who understood nothing began to weep at the distressed emotions flowing around her.

Iason shouted at his older brother.

"Go back, Carn," he shouted. "Brother, go back!"

But Carn didn't want to go back to the mage.

Something happened inside Carn's mind, and in that moment, all he wanted was to be in his father's arms. He regressed somehow into a memory of being younger than his sister Midlin, and he saw his father encouraging him to take a step towards him on his shaky legs as his mother held up his chubby arms and prepared to let him go. He remembered how his father held him and looked at him with such love as he stumbled and fell. Ghent was his hero, the man Carn looked up to and wished to become one day. He'd tried so hard to act older and wiser, so he could continue to please his father when all he really wanted was to be a little boy who could do no wrong.

Carn looked down at his feet. Just one more step...

"No, son, don't..." cried Ghent with his heart in his eyes, "Please!"

The boy opened his lips to speak but couldn't. Carn felt blood trickle down the corner of his mouth; he touched his face and stared in confusion at his fingers. He could only hear the shouting around him as a roaring in his ears. He looked up at Ghent.

I want my father...

Carn stepped forward and tumbled to the ground like a limp doll. Enith watched dispassionately as he released all barriers and Carn's parents and siblings rushed to his side. The snapped filament floated in the air unnoticed as the family of Ghent wept unrestrained in the quiet of his inner rooms.

The Seduction of Ghent, Conclusion

The following day King N'Goth inquired after the Bright Forest's High Regent. Enith sat in the morning court where the assembled kings were ready to sign and commit to war and the division of spoils should the Kingdom of the Far Isles fall.

"This is his moment," said a bemused N'Goth. "Because of his wisdom we all stand ready to move forward together and yet Ghent is not among us?"

The Ancient gave a slight smile as he responded.

"Our esteemed High Regent is with his family, if it please you, my king," said Enith. "The long months of separation necessitated an unexpected reunion. Be assured Ghent will join us shortly."

The High King of the Unnamed Lands made a gesture of dismissal.

"He has earned my respect," said N'Goth grimly as he came to his feet. "We will sign the accords on his return."

The High King was not one for ritual and airs, he glanced at his son Prince Arbu, who was already rising from his seat. They left the morning court together as his High Regent Sathdan smoothly took over with the expected protocols. The mage Iroh who was used to the king's ways, merely shrugged, and returned to his previous conversation with the king to his left. Iroh was not aware of what had transpired in High Regent Ghent's rooms the night before. But Keoni was and his face was a mask as he looked to his master who also showed no outward sign of his feelings.

Inside his mind, however, the mage Enith seethed. There were moments when he regretted not slaying the High King when he had the opportunity, and this was one of them. N'Goth was unpredictable and unswayable once his mind was made up regarding certain things and he was now focused on the welfare of the regent who earned his respect. Ghent was in no shape to appear before N'Goth, and thus the plans the mage had for his pawn were again moved up ahead of Enith's personal timetable.

"Stand fast," he commanded Keoni in a voice no one could hear except him.

The mage needed to think and ponder his next move so instead of simply vanishing from the assembly, Enith came to his feet and silently left the morning court.

A Discourse with High General Brennan

During the absence of Enith, Keoni and High Regent Ghent, the new king requested the presence of High General Brennan. Rasdeter decided to dine with his general and speak of things political and mundane. But after the speech of the new Queen Saramis, the general was wary. What topic could be of more importance than the disappearance of the previous royal family?

Yet the king was alone when Brennan arrived; he tried to hide his sigh of relief. The two spent the early evening in light conversation, yet the general was not deceived. Brennan knew his king was but searching for the words needed to turn the discussion in the direction he desired.

"I have a confession to make to you, General Brennan," said Rasdeter soberly. "And it is my hope that you will render in kind."

"You are my king," said Brennan simply, yet his heart thundered at the term 'confession'. "I am not a man of fine words, yet what I know I will speak of to you."

Rasdeter nodded, then studied his cup as he slowly rotated it on the table. Yet whatever Brennan thought he was prepared to hear, the king's next words stunned him to silence.

"I have spoken with King Templin," said the new king as his servant flushed in dismay, "...and asked him of things that were troubling me, and he mentioned your name."

The general suddenly found it very difficult to breathe. He blinked rapidly and decided that diplomacy suited the moment even though it was not his best ability.

"Pray tell, my lord," said Brennan carefully, "What would you ask the king that he himself would not know?"

"I inquired after his wife and family, Lord Brennan and his direct response was: 'Ask the general'..."

Sweat gleamed on the general's brow. He tried to see King Rasdeter's face but couldn't; in that moment, he wasn't sure if he would soon be dragged from the hall in chains. But he heard no sound of mailed boots marching in his direction, and the face of his king was not dark or angry. In fact, the new king merely looked puzzled.

The general decided to speak what was uppermost in his mind.

"Is the king well, my lord?" Brennan tried not to stammer and failed.

"As you surely know, he is dead, general," replied Rasdeter. "No coronation of the Bright Forest could be done while he lived."

The new king looked uncomfortable for a moment, then returned his gaze to his general.

"I, too have little use for fine words, general..."

As though his mind was made up, the king came to his feet and using both hands, Rasdeter parted his robes before the stunned Brennan and bared his chest.

It was the general's turn to come to his feet as he stared at Rasdeter in astonishment. Brennan was a military man who had survived numerous battles and full-blown wars. He'd seen many wounds in his life, gruesome, fatal, and life-altering ones that left men scarred in both body and spirit. But to gaze upon a man with a deadly blow to the heart who yet breathed and stood before him made this soldier's skin pale. After a moment, the general barely whispered.

"Enith…"

Rasdeter nodded.

"Despite the blow, I did not die, Brennan. I am not some abomination returned to life by sinister means, if such a thing is even possible. Yet, I suspect you and I have something in common…"

Blinking rapidly, the general also nodded and used his left hand to remove the glove on his right, revealing a horrifying burn on his palm that refused to heal. The king lifted his chin and tightened his lips.

"We do, my lord king," The general whispered again. His chest heaved with restrained emotion. He, too, had made up his mind.

"I will tell you all I know."

How Magicians are Made

Of necessity the mage had once again separated Ghent from his family. The dark poison in the regent's heart made it dangerous for him to be near them while consumed with grief. Indeed, when Enith finally located Ghent in his rooms he was curled up on the floor in a near catatonic state. Enith had placed barriers around the regent who could not contain the flares of dark magic bursting from the wound in his chest. Enith crossed his arms and stared down at his regent with some measure of regret that he had been forced to break him so.

A thought of his servant Keoni who was jealous of the attention the High Regent received from Enith caused the mage to smile grimly.

How urgently he seeks my love, thought the Ancient as he gazed at Ghent. And now that Keoni sees what I render to those I do love, I but wonder does he want the prize so desperately still.

Darkness thundered against the walls of its cage around Ghent and the mage's smile faded.

Whatever respect I may have for a good man, I cannot yet keep one near me without making him over in my image, grieved the mage as his thoughts turned to Ghent's ancestor Roane. I know of no other way to be, no other options appeal to me. You must suffer or flee.

"Believe me, Ghent," said the mage aloud, "I completely understand what compelled you to save your family from my influence. Yet, you still must be punished for it; all must fear both my love and my hate..."

A strange thing happened to the regent upon hearing the voice of the mage. Ghent's eyes flew open and he shook off his inertia and came to his feet, his eyes filled with a mixture of defiance, grief, and hatred. Enith noted all of this with a somber gaze.

"So...your hate has finally outstripped your fear of me, regent. Good..."

Darkness flared from the regent's chest as the mage continued speaking.

"But let your rage be tempered with wisdom, Ghent. You yet have three more reasons to truly fear me..."

Ghent pressed his back to the wall behind him as his mind turned to his wife and remaining children.

"You've slain my son on a whim, Enith," said the regent with a voice that cracked from strain. "What is there to prevent you from slaying us all as it pleases you?"

The silence lengthened between the two men before Enith spoke again.

"I do nothing without cause or consideration, regent," replied the mage. "Although it is true my rage can test my judgment. You have something I want, Ghent, and despite your seeming betrayal I shall have it. You and King N'Goth have both forced my hand--"

But his regent was not finished hurling his despair at his tormentor.

"I will fight you, Enith, you know this, until the ceasing of breath to save those I love from you..." The regent drew a ragged breath. "What you've done to my son Carn has assured it..."

The regent tore back his robe to reveal the horrid magic seeping out from his wound.

"Do you think I want this for my family, for Iason? No loving father would pass on such a thing to his offspring!"

The mage held forth his fist and tightened it; Ghent gasped in shock and pain as his wound collapsed and squeezed his heart. He sagged to the floor as his knees buckled.

"You have no idea what I am capable of, regent, even now," said the mage quietly. "Do not provoke me from the course I have set for you, I can make the process far more painful than you could ever imagine."

Enith stood silent while his servant tried for several moments to catch his breath without agony. Once Ghent's labored breathing subsided, his master spoke again.

"I have something to show you before you meet again with King N'Goth," said the mage. "Come with me..."

The pair walked the long corridors to the Hall of Mages, Enith opening all doors before them with a slight wave of energy. They finally entered the mage's personal chambers and deep within the suites of the Ancient's rooms, a large marble slab rested on stone and granite. A single light from an opening in the ceiling illuminated a shrouded form on top of it.

It was the body of Carn, son of Ghent.

The regent rushed to his son's remains and pulled back the shroud. Carn's slightly bluish face looked ethereal in the soft lighting, tiny motes of dust floated around his blond hair and lashes.

"I'm sorry, son," Ghent whispered. "I'm so sorry..."

The Ancient said nothing as his servant wept again without shame. Ghent wiped his face on his sleeve and clenched his hand to keep it from trembling. He gazed up and down his son's form as though to memorize it one final time; the shroud bunched under his fingers. Then Ghent leaned forward to press a kiss upon Carn's forehead and stroke his shining locks.

The kiss lingered, then Ghent straightened up in amazement. He turned to stare at Enith whose face was now unreadable. At the lack of response, the regent turned back and pressed his hand firmly against Carn's arm; he recoiled in surprise. Then Ghent placed both hands on either side of the boy's face and rubbed his son's cheeks with his thumbs. He shook his head and still holding his son's body, the regent stared at Enith.

Ghent barely whispered.

"His body is warm..."

Still the mage said nothing. Ghent gathered Carn into his arms and crushed his unresponsive form to his chest, sobbing aloud at the possibility of life.

The mage spoke as his servant's cries subsided into muted joy.

"We will bargain now, High Regent," said Enith quietly. "And whatsoever you and I agree to will be bound and sealed by Carn's life..."

"Yes...yes..." nodded Ghent as he desperately held his son against him, "I will not break it..."

"...and to be certain, Ghent, I will show you my resolve," continued Enith. "Should you break your word to me at any point in your life while you still draw breath, I will go back in time to the moment Carn moved forward, and I will allow him to complete the step I prevented by snapping the filament myself. Be sure what this means, regent. Even if your son is older than you are now, with his own wife and children, I will take him back to that moment, he will step forward and erase his entire bloodline from the earth. Children, grandchildren, great grandchildren, thousands of generations gone in an instant. Are we clear on the terms, High Regent?"

"Yes, my lord, yes," gasped Ghent as he cradled Carn in his arms like an infant and sank to the tiles. He wiped his tears on his sleeve again, then returned to stroking his firstborn's cheek and kissing his eyebrows. Ghent's heart thundered in his chest. He knew he would do anything to save his child and his descendants.

"Very well, then," responded the Ancient. "I will give you time to consider your offer, and what you will render me in exchange, regent. When I return to these rooms we will seal our bargain."

Ghent rocked back and forth holding Carn's body as he reasoned what he would do. Enith left the room satisfied that his servant would indeed hand over his soul in exchange for his son.

The High General's Tale

"In the moments following the High Regent's death," said General Brennan, "Our ambitious mage Enith wasted no time on formalities. With a wave of his arm he transported everyone, the king, his queen, and children into the Hall of Mages. It was his plan to slay the royal family in secret; he used mercenaries who were paid for their silence..."

Brennan's mind replayed old images he would never forget in his waking hours. Enith entered the main hall with an enthralled High General Brennan behind him, followed by blood soldiers. The mage wanted the confused King Templin to believe that his general had consciously betrayed him. Enith had placed an enchanted sword in the general's hand, which fused itself painfully into his burned flesh. Templin stared about him in shock until his eyes met those of the general whose face was contorted by the searing metal in his palm. The Ancient had moved the king's family to a raised platform with broad steps leading up to it that served in times past as a reminder of the throne room. There were no chairs on the wide floor but a huge table with all sorts of instruments of defense lay atop it. Behind this table and against the wall were hung swords and axes.

Instinctively, Templin placed his queen behind him while his sons searched desperately for weapons they could use. They were nearly too young to be considered men, though their father had years ago begun their training. Still, they would be leaves in the wind against the seasoned warriors who calmly marched to the bottom of the steps, awaiting the attack order from the mage. The king's eldest, Princess Merick, pulled the two youngest into her lap and calmed them with sweets. The queen paled as she watched her daughter but said nothing, her hand at her throat.

Her husband however, questioned the two men before him.

"Enith, Brennan," said Templin as he glanced between them, "What means this? Why did you bring us here?"

"I warned you, Templin," growled the general as he grimaced in agony. "I warned you not to trust the mage!"

King Templin began to pale as he realized the danger his family was now in. They needed protection from the magic of the Ancient, and his mind went to the only source he knew.

"Where is the High Regent?" The king asked although he knew what the answer must be. Templin's gaze landed on the mage, who barely suppressed a smirk.

"Like any good High Regent, his last thoughts were of you and the royal family, my lord," answered Enith. "Be content that every single sorcerer faithful to you has given his or her life in your service..."

Enith smiled slightly as he forced Brennan to raise his sword and point it at the king, who blanched in outrage.

Templin drew his sword.

"Explain yourself, Enith," demanded the king. "You swore to protect our kingdom!"

"I did so swear, my king," replied the mage easily. "And I will protect the Bright Forest. But we did not specify you or your bloodline, although I'm sure the High General would prefer the queen at least should live…"

Templin's shocked gaze fell on Brennan, whose own dismay mirrored his. But the king's High General did not deny the mage's words. Brennan opened his mouth, but no sound came forth. Then King Templin's jaw locked; his hand tightened on his sword and the general knew his king looked on one he could only see as a traitor to his own kingdom.

"I'll see you dead for this," growled Templin to Brennan, "If the deed itself sees my last breath!"

The two princes had short swords they always carried on their person, but they knew it would do little good against grown men armed with long blades and axes. They found full swords hanging on the walls like trophies, the young men dragged them down quickly. The eldest brother kicked a sword in his sister's direction, but she did not look up, so focused was she on her younger siblings.

Yet she heard her younger brother's whisper.

"Whatever you do, Merick," he said urgently, "I pray you do not allow me to behold it…"

Princess Merick lifted her eyes to her brother.

"Have I not always promised?" she answered. "I will see you soon…"

Merick turned back to her young charges, both toddlers who reached for the heavy sticky sweets that clung to her fingers. She fed them both by hand.

"Remember what Mother taught you," The princess said softly. "Chew slowly until it is gone…"

The babies did as their older sister bid them, then slumped in her arms. She kissed their closed eyelids and bundled them together on their blankets, arranging their limbs to embrace each other. Merick then wiped her hands on their clothing and reached for the fallen sword. Her eyes hardened, and her jaw set as she came to her feet. The queen looked at her daughter with hollow eyes that shifted slightly past Merick's shoulder. The princess barely acknowledged this movement, but her mother knew she'd seen the table with the quiver full of arrows. The queen wanted to move towards her children, but her husband's hand prevented her. In return, she caressed his fingers; it would likely be the last time they touched.

The king stepped forward to engage his general and cried out one word.

"Guards!"

And the doors burst open as the king's men poured into the room. Enith calmly moved to one side as he prepared to watch the open spectacle of King Templin's last stand. He allowed the princes to arm themselves because he knew it would not matter. They faced battle ready men. But the princess knew something the mage did not. The Kingdom of the Bright Forest had a Guardian, trained, developed, and perfected by the previous High General.

And her name was Princess Merick.

She tore away the fastening of her skirts to reveal chain mailed legs and boots. Merick became a whirling mass of arms and legs as she launched herself between her younger brothers and the swarming men running up the steps. Brennan rolled to the ground as she hacked away at the startled warriors in front of herself, pulling an extra blade as she beheaded its previous owner. The men found themselves sandwiched between her and the palace guard. Merick at one point dove beneath their flailing swords, separating joint from thigh as she appeared at the other end of bloody screaming men. She came to her feet near her objective, the table, and quickly switched to arrows, bringing down those nearest to her and her siblings.

But the High General could only surmise these movements, he was busy trying to keep his king from taking his life, while the mage looked on in amusement.

"So, Brennan," said Templin darkly, "You play the innocent, yet you meant to replace me, and slay all my children?!"

"The mage you trusted has turned you against me for sport, Templin," countered the general desperately. "You must see this is true!"

"You led them here," growled the king. "Do you take me as a fool?!?"

Templin swung true and disarmed the general, but as his arm came back on a deadly arc that Brennan could not sidestep, Enith easily held the blade from the general's neck.

But only barely.

The two men's eyes met, and Brennan could not hold back the guilt behind them, but not for the reason the king believed. Templin brought his gaze to Enith filled with contempt.

"He protects you," said the king with distain, watching as the mage brought the general's sword to his hand again. Templin's eyes flickered as he noticed the burn on Brennan's palm, but his anger dismissed it.

"I'll guide you to hell, traitor," spat the king, "And kick you through its gates!" and he rose his arm and blade against the High General, who almost moved too slow to defend himself as his eyes met those of his queen.

The look on her face alone was enough to slay the general.

As her husband engaged Brennan, the queen shrank back and turned to her daughter, stretching out her arms.

"Now, Merick," The queen cried, "It must be done...!"

Blinking back tears, the princess obeyed her mother and planted an arrow in her chest. Without hesitation, she whirled again and fired at her brothers, one of whom was already dead, the other groaning from a mortal wound. As promised, she ended his pain then running straight on, Merick leaped on the back of a soldier and boldly vaulted high above the dead and dying men to bury her last two arrows in the chest of the general and her father the king.

But the mage was now ready for her.

"Magnificent!"

Enith bellowed in admiration at her craft as he froze the princess in mid-air. Brennan blinked rapidly and felt his jaw lock as he stared at the arrow halted only inches from his heaving chest. The general lifted his eyes in shock to Merick who yet hovered in the air above him. As she looked at Brennan her usual calm demeanor shifted, and raw hatred blazed for a second before a stoic mask again covered her face.

King Templin, strangely enough, was not afraid of the missile fired from his daughter's bow. He reached out tentatively to touch the tip but could not reach it. The king glanced around him in despair at the sight he'd prayed all his life he would never live to see: His wife the queen and their offspring scattered dead on the ground. He nodded almost to himself as he beheld his two youngest wrapped tenderly in blankets by Merick as though sleeping. At least they did not suffer, he thought as he struggled to hold back his grief.

The distracted Ancient gazed around him; every single person other than Templin, Merick, Brennan and himself were dead. It was the outcome Enith desired. There would be no witnesses to this story, no one else to tell the tale of what happened. The mage would not have to convince the general to remain silent; to speak of it would mark him as traitor and subject to be put to death.

As Enith lowered Merick to the ground she reached out swiftly for Brennan's face, who quickly tilted his eyes away from her grasping fingers.

King Templin moved forward to embrace his daughter, but the mage blocked this intimacy.

"I have plans yet for your father, my princess," said the mage, "So I dare not trust such talented hands as you possess. And now possibly, I have some plans for you. A princess, and a trained assassin; it is beyond the realm of thought. What an unexpected treasure you are..."

But the princess did not respond to this. Merick turned to gaze in misery at her father the king, whose eyes brimmed despite the carnage surrounding them.

"I'm proud of you," Templin choked. "You have not failed me, Merick..."

The princess slowly lowered her head and silently vented her grief.

In the event of a successful coup, it was her duty as the Bright Forest Guardian to ensure that no member of the royal family would be left to suffer kidnaping, torture or humiliation. The fate she imagined that awaited her father at the hands of the mage was more than she could bear.

King Rasdeter spoke into the deepening silence after the general finished his tale.

"Does the princess yet live?" he asked, trying not to sound hopeful and afraid at the same time.

The general shook his head.

"She died the same night. The king's men searched her for weapons like a soldier, not an assassin. The poison she meant to gouge my eyes with was yet on her fingers, and I surmise once alone she but needed to insert them into her mouth..."

Brennan's lips tightened.

"Each one of them died believing I betrayed them..."

The general's chest heaved but he managed to control the sounds that might accompany this action.

Rasdeter spoke again quietly.

"Were you in love with the queen, Brennan?"

The general hung his head in pain before looking up and to his right.

"No one knew," he replied at last. "Not even her. I cannot fathom how he learned it..."

The king shrugged as his mind turned to the Prince's Sword, and then to the enchanted blade that Ghent once embedded into his heart.

"The knife he placed in your hand, general," offered Rasdeter with a sigh. "The one that burned you. Through it the mage will learn all your past thoughts and desires. Be thankful the princess slew her family before the Ancient could think of some coarse amusement to subject you to, something that would pain your soul far worse than now..."

Brennan lowered his head again and placed his hand over his eyes, gripping them tightly as his mind came back to the place he could not leave from. It was the look on the queen's face as she witnessed his seeming betrayal. She went to the grave ignorant of two things: The general's innocence and his love for her. Yet one thing was certain:

The Ancient was very good at introducing men to hell.

KING OF THE FAR ISLES

"The day science begins to study non-physical phenomena, it will make more progress in one decade than in all the previous centuries of its existence."
~~~Nikola Tesla

The migration to the west began almost two years before the actual conflict. All towns, villages, and migrant cities along the expected march of soldiers from the east were being systematically evacuated. No farmer or tradesmen wished to be found undefended with their families when hungry soldiers and mercenaries made their way past their homes. Word of the men of the Broken Meriden now marching south and westward was more than enough to frighten sensible men. Those too stubborn or slow to reason soon became tales of caution for all others.

Like the Lourdes clans, the soldiers of the Broken Meriden were brutal and uncaring towards those they perceived as weak. A man might be forced to watch his wife and daughters tortured in unspeakable ways and their sons killed for sport. The ones who waited until late fall or winter to flee were pressed to leave their livestock behind and fields unharvested; speed was of the essence when the ground began to tremble beneath armored boots. The armies absorbed these gifts of abandoned cattle, birds, and even horses left out to pasture. Some villagers left roasting venison buried under flaming stones or turning on a spit; a temptation designed to slow down hungry men who might prefer to dine before pillaging and murder.
~~~

The Nine Kingdoms opened their gates to as many as they could; the rest were forced to flee into the mountains or make their final homes on the barren rocks leading to the ocean below. Many of them feared death at the hands of the brutal Lourdes clan, but it seemed during the same two years that clan had vanished much like the regents disappearing mysteriously from the Nine Kingdoms. The camps of refugees grew like small cities all over the continent.

It is said that the sun rises on the Kingdom of the Golden Round and sets on the Kingdom of the Far Isles. The Far Isles is nearly impenetrable by land because of this; an enemy kingdom would have to conquer every nation between it and its goal. And for this reason, every king who sat the throne of the Far Isles from its inception focused in some way on strengthening their marine forces to protect it from attack by sea.

From the beginning of his reign, High King Sumter followed the advice of his regents and generals and made steadfast improvements to the defenses of the Far Isles, but never in his reign, or the thousands of kings who sat the throne before him had his nation faced a threat like this. Seven kingdoms that made up over half of the planet were marching against him. Though all nine kingdoms would provide a united front, not one of the eight kings were deceived as to what would happen to them if Sumter fell. Should the Kingdoms of the Unnamed Lands succeed and overthrow the Named Lands, there would be only one High King, and his name was N'Goth.

Who, then, by nature of his victory would be proclaimed High King of the Earth.

King Sumter stood waiting on one of the steep cliffs overlooking the sea when his High General Marcus joined him.

The king wasted no time on formalities.

"What is the current head count, general?"

"Over one hundred and thirty-three thousand refugees, my king," responded Marcus. "About sixty percent of them are men;

but of that number, only fifteen percent know how to hold a weapon..."

The king sighed.

"They'll be wormwood for the mercenaries," he said heavily. "But at least they'll have a chance to die on their feet..."

Sumter turned away from the sight of the teeming refugees far below them.

"Spread the word, then, Marcus," he ordered. "Those that train and fight with us have first portion of the shared food for their families. The rest?"

The king shrugged in resignation. "Perhaps the Boatsmen Clan will have mercy on them and teach them to fish."

As the two reached the crest of the peak and began the walk down the rocky path towards fairer ground, Sumter spied High Regent Polymus and a retinue of regents making their way up the slope towards them. The king quickened his pace, his soldiers instantly hurried to stay close to him. Even on their own lands, the soldiers of the Far Isles never relaxed their guard.

But their king was alarmed: Polymus would not approach Sumter outside of their normal setting; the king's own library unless the communication was of grave importance. Sumter's mind flew quickly over a mental list: His son and heir Prince Asscher was safely again within the gates of his home, having completed his last visit to his mother, Queen Amara of the Eastern Crest. His maternal grandparents, King Garrin and Queen Orsa were well according to their previous letters, and his foster mother Irisella was safe in the Hall of Women. His thoughts went briefly to the former child of prophecy, now called the Dark One, but he had never feared for her, at least not directly. She had proven on more than one occasion that fear rightfully belonged to those who faced her.

Yet the death of Lord Brayten had driven home the point that anyone in this world of pain could leave it suddenly, and the young king found himself controlling his breath as he descended the hills leading to his home. Sumter had only realized a few short years ago that the feelings he had for The Dark One were more than brotherly and protective. It seemed that she fled from the king rather than address the obvious and in his fear of rejection he turned from her. But if the impossible had indeed occurred...

As his High Regent bowed deeply Sumter's heart raced; the news was grave for certain. He spoke more sharply than he first intended.

"Speak, Regent," he said tensely. "What news?"

"My king," replied Polymus quickly in a tremulous voice, "Your envoy from the Unnamed Lands has returned alive and with a response from High King N'Goth..."

The young king breathed deeply in thankfulness for his unfounded fears. His tone softened towards his favorite regent.

"This is well, Polymus. Where is my envoy?"

The emissary, who had heard the king's sharp tone, was terrified. A king holds the power of life and death over his subjects and a ruler's displeasure is not a thing to be taken lightly. The emissary stepped forward with the document and held it forth to the High Regent, afraid to come closer. Polymus retrieved the parchment from his shaking hands and offered it to the king with eyes downcast, whose brow furrowed at this subtle indication that the words of King N'Goth should not be read aloud. Being the head of all the king's communications, of course Polymus knew the contents of the missive. The winds of the cliffs gently disturbed Sumter's dark gold hair as he silently read the parchment:

High King Sumter:

According to the established Protocols of Engagement from the Council of the Four Worlds, you have asked of me if I would provide proof of the King of the Bright Forest's identity, if he is indeed your lost first cousin Rasdeter, Prince of the Far Isles.

Receive then, my answer:

You may meet with the new King of the Bright Forest at a place of your choosing and decide for yourself.

Or I can send his head to you for discernment.
N'Goth.

The King of the Far Isles felt the ground move beneath his feet as he read again the King of the Unnamed Lands response. When his eyes lifted from the parchment and met those of his envoy, the man threw himself to the ground and cried aloud:

"Mercy, my king, mercy!"

Even Marcus stepped back from his king; he had not seen such a look on Sumter's face since he slew a prince of the Lourdes Clan. But King Sumter was not looking at the cowering envoy; he was looking right through him to King N'Goth, who stared back unblinking at the challenge he hurled with contempt at Sumter's face.

Sumter gained his self-control with difficulty; he turned and near growled under his breath to his High General:

"All of my generals, of every rank, high or low, in my morning court: NOW!"

With exception of his personal guard, the soldiers of the king scattered like ants.

The Cost of Freedom

The rooms where Enith kept Lady Dru and her remaining children captive were tastefully appointed. The tiles were cut by hand and polished; the drapery was heavy and spun with beautifully dyed thread. The glasses that trembled slightly from the breeze by the window were blown by a master glassmaker; not a bubble could be found in cup nor stem. Trays of fruit and fine cheeses lay on the tables full to overflowing yet Lady Dru noticed none of these things. All she could focus on was the absence of her firstborn son, Carn.

Sight was no longer possible, nor was hearing. Unconsciously mirroring her husband Ghent, Dru lay on the floor at the foot of sumptuous seating and chairs, her hands covering her eyes and face.

Like most mothers, Dru blamed herself for what had happened to her son. She'd done as her husband asked to the letter and completely destroyed the life they'd built together. In secret and in haste, Dru erased every shred of physical evidence that might connect her to Ghent. There were things he had given her, things that could not be replaced. Dru faintly heard the crackling and popping of wood as she kissed her husband's rings before propelling them through the space between her and the hungry flames. It was just as difficult with the children's things, of course. Midlin had stood quietly by as things were thrown into the blazing fire until her brother Carn tossed her precious dolls and it registered onto her consciousness that they were being rendered into a state they would not recover from. Ghent's daughter shouted her protest:

"Fa-fa-da!"

For little Midlin, 'Fa' meant 'father' and 'Da' meant 'doll'.

They were the dolls mended by her father's hands and that made them special to her.

Midlin rushed forward to retrieve them and turned viciously on her brother when Carn tried to prevent her. Dru hurried to restrain her daughter who screamed and thrashed herself about, refusing to be comforted, even by offered sweet reeds. Carn rubbed at his scratched and bleeding arms, amazed at Midlin's determination.

They would all learn to their sorrow just how determined little Midlin could be.

In her attempt to perform all the things asked by Ghent, Dru failed to notice the bulge in her daughter's clothing. Midlin's new robes were layered for warmth as they traveled thus the whole family appeared bundled so Dru paid her no mind. Lady Dru had done what most wives fail to do when following instructions from their husbands: Take each detail more seriously. It was not that Dru was not impressed by her husband's wound, of course she was. The memory of it added haste to all her movements.

The error was that Lady Dru believed she knew of magicians.

Like many people of Everet and its sponsoring nation, the Bright Forest, Dru had grown up around sorcerers and mages and believed she knew what to expect from them. She'd seen the results of spells and destructive forces both fair and evil and held the common opinion that mages were mostly practitioners of magic with varying levels of expertise. The people of her time had rarely heard of ancient magicians and no one she knew had ever met one. Even the story of her husband's ancestor Roane and the Ancient he served so long ago was treated with skepticism by learned men. Such things belonged to the realm of myth and tales to frighten stubborn children to sleep.

Lady Dru believed that with time Ghent's wound would heal and she could reunite with the man she loved and build again everything they had lost.

All the illusions the wife of Ghent ever cherished blew away like leaves the moment Dru saw the Ancient waiting for her and her children at the crossroads between the Unnamed Lands and the Circle of the Earth Kingdom.

The gulf between a magician and an Ancient is so wide and deep and broad it cannot be measured. Like comparing a snowflake to a winter storm or the light of one candle to a raging fire in the mountains. Power stormed from the mage and it seemed the trees bent back from his path and the clouds vanished from the skies.

As Dru met the eyes of Enith she knew that Ghent had not stressed enough to her the price of one mistake.

Never in her life had Dru been so afraid as she drew her trembling offspring to her chest. She could still feel the imprint of Carn's head against her ribs, her fingers beneath his chin. It was a warmth, a sweetness she would never feel again.

Now Lady Dru knew fully the cost of what she overlooked, and she could not forgive herself or return from the moment Carn dropped lifeless to the tiles of her husband's rooms. Endlessly it seemed Dru's mind imagined how Midlin's doll fell into the flames and apparently tumbled through and to the other side. There must have been a hole it rolled and rested in, a place a little girl determined to have something of her father's touch could find. In this dread retelling Dru saw her daughter pull the singed cloth toy from the earth and stash it in her robe, away from her older brother's sharp gaze.

A dirty doll for the life of her son.

Oblivious to the pain of her family, Midlin wandered around a section of the room that was lit by candles as her brother Iason kept himself busy pulling his sister from harm's way. Time and again the boy tried to rouse his mother Dru and failed. He was trying to act as he thought his older brother would; the boy silently wiped his face as he stopped Midlin from tipping the edge of a tray over and onto her head.

Midlin did not understand physical death. She cried because her older brother was badly hurt, she could tell from how her parents and brother threw themselves over his body and wept. When Carn was carried away, the separation alone registered. That she might never see her brother again was an idea that would not hold on Midlin's consciousness; Carn must be with her father, who was also missing. Hungry and curious, the child returned to familiar activities; exploration, and destruction. As he watched his younger sister immerse herself in happy oblivion, Iason never realized before how much he relied on his elder brother's guidance. Carn had seemed invincible; watching him tumble to the ground had shaken Iason more than he knew. He felt only misery as Iason beheld the sight of his mother Dru curled up into something broken and tiny on the cold tiles beneath them.

A crash behind him reminded Iason that he'd forgotten his wayward and curious sibling. The sound also roused at last his mother Dru who raised herself up and beheld her daughter sitting in a pile of fruit and broken cheese wedges. Midlin popped a grape in her mouth and grinned.

But Dru did not return this affection; her eyes found a bulge in Midlin's robe, no doubt the frail and tattered toy that had cost them everything. As she came to her feet her son noticed the look in his mother's gaze and the press of her lips.

"No, mother," cried Iason, "Please don't…"

Lady Dru could not heed her son's words. She reached out and roughly pulled the offending object from her daughter's robe, who now screeched in dismay as her mother began to rip her precious doll in half.

"This is all your fault!" Dru said in anger. "If not for you, my son would be alive!"

Midlin screamed wildly and came to her feet to try and retrieve her doll, then fell back to the tiles crying as her mother continued the toy's destruction. Iason placed his hands together and wept, unable to step into his brother's shoes and calm his grieving mother.

A voice from the doorway was barely heard above the din.

"Dru…"

Despite her overwhelming misery, Lady Dru lifted her head to see her husband Ghent at the door.

"You mustn't blame her, my wife," continued Ghent softly. "All blame and guilt belong to me…"

Sobbing full on, the regent's family came forward into his waiting arms. Midlin threw her arms around her mother's neck as Dru lifted her and kissed her hair.

"I'm sorry," Dru crooned against her daughter's cheek. "I'm sorry…"

Iason wiped his face.

"I tried to do it, father," he said in sorrow, "I tried to be bigger like Carn, but I can't…"

Ghent lifted his middle child easily and held Iason tightly to his chest.

"You don't have to, Iason, you're fine just as you are…"

The regent then reached out for his daughter with his other arm who came to him eagerly and placed her tearstained face against

Ghent's robe. He kissed the top of her head and then said something that at first sounded strange.

"It's alright son, you can join us..."

A rather weakened Carn moved gingerly around the corner and met the startled gaze of his mother who drew in a huge breath of disbelief and heartbreaking joy.

"Carn!"

Dru almost fell as she rushed to her child; she barely heard her husband's admonishment to be careful. Ghent tried to hold on to his other screaming and struggling offspring then relented with a bittersweet smile as he lowered them to the ground where they also hurried to add more bruises to the ones Carn suffered from his mother.

But the boy didn't mind.

Carn could not recall in his life a moment where he felt happier. The fabric of Dru's robe felt like satin against his cheek and the painful tightness of his brother's arms about his waist felt wonderful as he pressed a shaky hand to Iason's head. Midlin was jumping up and down, pulling on Carn's clothes as she demanded to be picked up by her eldest brother, who could not reach her, engulfed as he was by his weeping mother.

For his part, Ghent enjoyed this reunion of those he held most dear. A shadow lingered over this moment of happiness, and soon the regent regained the attention of his family.

"There are things we must discuss, my loved ones..." Ghent began quietly. Suddenly subdued, his family returned to his side and stared up at him anxiously for his next words.

"The mage is going to release you all and let you go home..." Ghent began, and Iason let out a whoop of triumph that Midlin followed, not knowing any other way to react to news she did not fully understand. Dru and Carn, however did not share this reaction, both being old enough to realize that Ghent did not name himself among those who would be freed. As the regent continued to explain the things that must be done to accomplish this, Lady Dru found herself blinking rapidly and clenching her fists to restrain her emotions. For different reasons, Carn did not. He watched his father carefully and listened to his words. The boy looked sadly at his celebrating younger brother and opened his arms to his sister Midlin who loved being carried about now that she was almost too old to.

"We must have words, my husband," offered Dru quietly, and Ghent nodded, drawing his wife aside while their son Carn returned to what he did best, caring for and distracting his younger siblings while his parents talked.

Ghent sighed as his beloved wife pressed her hand to his arm. He'd longed to hold her again even as the regent dreaded what those same emotions might cause him to do.

"I cannot fathom what you promised the Ancient in order to restore Carn and obtain our freedom," said Dru in despair. "And I fear to ask. Will this deed truly separate us forever, Ghent; am I to live my life and our children's lives without you?"

For a moment, the regent could not disguise his need for his wife, but the hunger that fleetingly crossed his face was also tinged with a darkness that would forever be a part of him. Dru's pupils widened as her love for him was suddenly infused with a hint of fear.

"I could ask you to stay with me," responded Ghent as he struggled. "But this request would mean forever, my love. A forever that would include you and our children, that may eventually require that you, and they, become as I am. Should I ask this, loving you as I do?"

Dru bowed her head to Ghent's chest and covered her face. After a moment, the regent carefully placed his arms around her. She would never know how much he warred within himself to be with her and his treasures. Of the horrid things the darkness in him suggested he do, things of blood and destruction. They would be better without him now and remain the shining memory of goodness he needed to face what lay ahead.

Ghent noticed his eldest son looking at him and nodded that it was safe to approach. Dru reluctantly released him and turned to Iason and Midlin who yearned for her attention still. The regent went down on his knees as his son came near and wrapped his arms around his father's neck. Ghent thought his child merely wished to give a final goodbye until Carn turned his head and whispered into his father's ear.

"I know what you promised for me, father, for us," Carn said softly as Ghent tightened his arms around his son in surprised grief. "I heard every word..."

The regent's son explained that the mage placed him in a state of suspended animation, so that although the boy could not respond, from the moment Ghent first entered the rooms of the mage until the bargain was sealed, the child heard the entire exchange.

Lady Dru looked up anxiously as she heard her husband sob uncontrollably as he gripped his son's robes. When she made to move towards them, Carn looked at his mother and shook his head slightly. Instinctively, Dru obeyed her son, though she flushed in dismay at this turn of their roles. The look in her child's eyes had changed forever, the hopeful joy that used to rest behind his gaze was gone. Carn looked more like his father Ghent in that moment of pure sadness and Dru felt her heart tighten in pain. Yet whatever father and son shared, in this moment it did not include her, and Dru knew she must respect this.

Carn continued to whisper.

"You must not do this, father," continued the boy quietly. "You must not give in to such evil, not for me or who I may one day become. I don't care what he does to me; he's a monster..." and now Carn began to restrain his tears.

"He's a monster..." The child repeated in despair.

Ghent wiped his eyes with the back of his hand before looking up at his son.

"You are already a better man than I, Carn," his father choked. "This will comfort me for what lies ahead."

"No, father…" began his son but Ghent shook his head and his child fell silent as his eyes began to brim.

The regent unwrapped his arms from his son and placed his hands on both sides of his child's face.

"One day, when you hold your own firstborn in your arms, whether a son or daughter, you will feel and understand what I have always felt when I looked at you. This is why I freed you from the family blood oath. I must keep my word, even to a monster. A man must keep his word, or he is nothing on this Earth, do you understand me? Nothing. And now, I will bind you with another oath, in exchange for your life, which you know I have done for you. Will you do this?"

Carn nodded as he gazed solemnly at his father.

"Take your mother and siblings from this place and do not return…" at his son's sound of protest, Ghent gripped Carn's shoulders tightly and brought his eyes back to his.

"…and most importantly, do not allow your family to search for me or seek me out, Carn. This is your life and theirs. I fight against this evil wound daily, and I cannot risk what might happen should my concentration fade for even a moment…"

The father of Carn turned his mind's eyes to the innocent serving girl who entered his rooms and nearly died for displeasing him. His fingers trembled on his son's arms.

"Why…" Carn stammered as he searched his father's face. "Why do you say, 'My family'?"

"Swear it," repeated Ghent forcefully, and his son at last saw the darkness behind his father's eyes.

"I will not allow my family to search for you," whispered the boy, "…and we will not return to this place. I swear it…"

Ghent nodded at this and rising, he turned quickly away from his firstborn who now moved towards his mother and embraced her. Iason and Midlin milled in confusion at their brother's behavior; they gathered around their mother and sibling in disturbed wonder. The wound in the regent's heart caused the darkness to surge in symphony with his emotions; Ghent realized he had now reached the moment where he no longer could rein in the urge to release his destructive power. Of course, the Ancient had promised he would not harm Ghent's family, very soon Ghent would do this himself. The High Regent of the Bright Forest now faced away from his former family and did not look at them as he spoke again.

"Your things have been gathered for you and await you at the inner gates. I've assigned a half regiment to escort you as far as the borders between the Unnamed Lands and the Circle of the Earth Kingdom. Beyond that..." he hesitated as a fine sheen of sweat broke out on his brow from the strain of holding back.

Ghent controlled his breath with effort.

"Beyond that," he finally continued, "It would be best if I do not know where you are."

Dru attempted to move towards her husband but her eldest son stopped this movement with a firm grip on her arm and pleading eyes. Carn's mother tried to understand his actions but couldn't.

Her husband closed his eyes as the woman he loved spoke in a pained whisper.

"Ghent..."

The regent felt the darkness surge in him, and he used it to form a dimensional hole in the air in front of him that Ghent then stepped through without hesitation.

Dru screamed.

"Ghent!"

Even though he could no longer see them, the regent heard the cries of his two youngest as they realized their father was gone.

The former regent of the Kingdom of Everet stood awhile in the gathering darkness. Ghent did not know where he was, he merely asked the darkness to take him away from his family, a place where he could do them no further harm. He stood in the clearing of a forest and watched heavy grey clouds chase away the faint glow of a weakening sun. After a moment, the regent noticed he was not alone. He looked around at the hooded men who watched him in silence, their dark robes billowing gently in the evening breeze. Strangely, Ghent felt no fear of them, of the magic he could clearly sense that caused the ground beneath his feet to hum. The burning wound in his heart had already explained it:

He was now one of them.

Ghent understood in this moment the words of Keoni and the expression on his face when last the regent spoke with him. The regent had never seen Keoni or any other magician he knew of surrounded by or in fellowship with a loving or devoted family. Never seen the heart connections that would keep such a man or woman grounded in a world of unrelenting power and dark desires. The higher levels of the craft would not allow it: Ghent realized that men like Enith or any other powerful mage would use those connections as a weakness only useful to exploit or control. Separation was the only safety for a man like himself. Ghent mused briefly on how many broken-hearted family members this gathering of men represented; the hundreds, perhaps thousands of shattered connections made to keep them from harm, both from without and from within.

He himself had just added four grieving souls to that number.

Almost absently, the regent pulled the pieces of his daughter's doll from his robes and studied it. With less than a thought, the darkness had brought it to him, every fiber and stitch of it. Ghent smiled sadly as he spied the invisible skin cells of Midlin attached to it; co-mingled with his own. How easily it must have drawn the powerful Enith to where his family travelled on the road to possible freedom.

He drew his breath in sharply as he detected the cells of his wife on the doll; where Dru used her hands to rend it. His heart then lurched as Ghent's longing for Dru roared to the surface of his thoughts. Crushing his fingers together Ghent vaporized the offending object before the darkness in him summoned his wife to his side.

The regent doubted he would be able in that moment to send her away again.

Still silent, the men turned away from Ghent and began to walk the deep path that revealed itself, a path that led to the Hall of Mages located in the Kingdom of the Unnamed Lands.

The regent followed his new brethren.

* * *

Signature of Kings part III

As it came about, the High King of the Unnamed Lands had one more stipulation before signing the accords: He must meet King Rasdeter and High General Brennan face to face. It was not possible that such a protracted enterprise of men, food, weapons, horses and time, years of it, necessary to obtain victory would be offered to a man unknown. Royalty or not, Rasdeter must pass inspection or all is lost.

Enith agreed with his own proviso: The journey from the Bright Forest would take weeks by horse. He would bring the new king and his general by way of magic, in order to save time.

But the High King was only beginning his testing of Enith.

"You have the power to display his features; Iroh has demonstrated this," said N'Goth confidently, "Show me, then, this king you place all your hopes on."

Enith, of course, bristled at this request, but Iroh calmly produced the image of King Rasdeter at his coronation in the air before them. Less than a moment of scrutiny and the High King scoffed.

"This man will not slay his cousin, Enith," stated the king in a matter of fact tone, "Unless you use some horrid magic on him..." and this was said after turning to stare at the Ancient, who despite his anger could not meet the truth in the king's eyes.

N'Goth made a wave of dismissal at the image of King Rasdeter.

"There's too much softness in him," continued the king dispassionately, "He reminds me..." and here the king stopped as an image of his son Arbu mentally superimposed itself over Rasdeter's features. Unaware of his sudden inner turmoil, Iroh and Enith mutely watched as N'Goth unconsciously tightened his fist at the sight of a crowned and happy Arbu greeting his people. This would never happen if all his plans for both his kingdom and the Circle of the Earth Kingdom come to fruition. The king forced himself to see Rasdeter again in his proper setting.

Then N'Goth's eyes fell on the image of Saramis.

"She still lives?" asked the king to turn his mind away from his doomed son's unlikely future.

"For now," promised Enith, as Iroh raised an eyebrow. His mind went to Paza and the wishes of The Magician and Iroh said nothing. It was not the first time someone stood in his former mentor's way, and the Ancient was quite clever in finding ways to achieve his objectives around all obstacles in his path.

"What will you do to your pawn, Enith," asked the king, "Once he faces Sumter? They are children no more, and Sumter is an accomplished king with his own bloodline to protect; he will slay Rasdeter for Prince Asscher's sake."

"Sumter will hesitate, High King," offered the Ancient quietly, "I need less than a fraction of a second..."

But King N'Goth shook his head.

"He will not, if it comes to it," countered the king to Enith's now darkened features, "But it matters little. Play your game, mage, and when Rasdeter falls, I will slay Sumter, and at last, you will have what you wish, a High King to mold as you will..."

The two mages were stunned to silence as the king drained his cup of dark mead and without a glance behind him, left the room.

Finally, the elder mage spoke.

"Asscher..." said Enith in wonder.

Master Iroh nodded.

"It seems you have little to lose no matter the outcome, my lord," agreed Iroh, "Should Sumter fall, his son will be too young to remember him, or the High King's feelings of magic..."

"And I will be the only father Asscher will know," concluded the Ancient as he clenched his fist in expectant triumph.

The shadows shifted from the flames of torches before Iroh spoke his thoughts aloud.

"Poor Rasdeter," mused Iroh, "A pawn to the end. A perfect mirror of his father, Lord Altus, who never achieved his dark dreams of glory..."

"Rasdeter may yet rule the Far Isles," countered Enith, "I will keep my word. I have already made him a king, have I not? Asscher will be the foundation of a new plan only if his cousin falls despite all my efforts, and that same effort will be mighty indeed..." The mage could not hide the flash of pleasure in his eyes at the thought of how small his margin for error had now become.

"Your choice of High Regent for the Bright Forest was also masterful, my friend," said Iroh as the thought occurred to him, "Our High King has fully embraced the idea of becoming High King of the Earth before he dies. We are yet within our timetable for the demise of the Circle of the Earth Kingdom and the complete destruction of the prophecy; all seems to be well."

Enith made a sound of assent.

"I may have to revise my stance on the true value of our precious High King N'Goth," admitted the Ancient, "It is not often that an angle I myself have not considered is revealed to me. I begin to appreciate more your fondness for him..."

"Until the next time he irritates you," countered Iroh dryly, and watched as his former mentor raised his hands in an unaccustomed gesture of surrender.

King Rasdeter and High General Brennan were finally able to convince Queen Saramis to remain with the people while they traveled with Enith to meet the High King of the Unnamed Lands. Enith wisely remained silent as the couple said their goodbyes; he waited in the courtyard with the general who tensely watched the Ancient from the side of his eye.

"You must not fear for me constantly," the king gently chided his wife, "Who will trust me to rule?"

"Forgive me, husband," Saramis responded to his tender jest, "The mage has given me little opportunity for trust…" she kept her gaze from the courtyard beyond them with difficulty. "You are correct, of course; I wish for everyone to trust you as I do…"

Rasdeter smiled broadly at his wife's words and brought her hand to his lips.

"I will miss you," he said deeply; his words bringing her love for him into her eyes. Rasdeter turned from Saramis before she could speak to this; she breathed calmly and clasped her hands in front of her. As the new king's feet stepped onto the courtyard, he, Brennan, and the mage disappeared.

My heart pounds as though something dreadful will happen, thought the new queen in despair. Yet I must trust that only what must happen, will happen. Saramis thought of the Great Elder and tried to keep her eyes from brimming.

Is it my destiny to save him, Mother, or to watch as he destroys himself?

There was no answer to this thought, and Saramis stood on the steps leading to the courtyard until her servants called for her attention.

The Sport of Kings

It is evident that the world Rasdeter grew up in was dominated for the most part by men. You would think that such a world would be kinder perhaps to men in general, that all men would flourish within these structures, but this was not the case. Just like women, a man who cannot be easily placed in the boundaries of civilization will find himself outside of it, and likely to his detriment.

Strangers are normally thrown in the prisons of the kingdoms they are not wise enough to avoid, that is, if they are not simply slain on the road by thieves, mercenaries or soldiers escorting precious cargo between the lands. Sometimes, if a man is skilled enough, they are absorbed into a kingdom's military, a fate much preferred to execution or being thrown to wild animals for a bored king's sport.

An incarcerated man has time to ponder these things, and a group of such captured men who now languished in the jails of the Unnamed Lands found themselves with time aplenty to reflect on how they came there.

Each day was the same as the one before it: The sun moved by on its path, unconcerned by their plight. The nights were warm from the day's heat; most of the jails were underground as was the custom. Some days included food pushed through a narrow opening on the floor between the bars; some days didn't. There were days the men heard the sounds of struggle as a doomed prisoner was removed from his cell for trial or execution. Very rarely was a man returned to his cell; his removal simply indicated the need for space for a new prisoner.

But the very worse sound was the creaking of heavy rusted gates early in the morning. The newer prisoners heard the shouting and cries of the older ones, and they soon learned to dread this weekly ritual:

The jails of the Unnamed Lands were dug into the ground near a diverted river, and once a week the dam was lifted to rinse away the filth and waste of unwashed men.

Sometimes, the dam was lifted by guards who felt compassion, either for some prisoner they knew or someone they felt the military could use. This meant the dam would lift slowly and gradually, allowing the men to brace themselves or secure any meager thing of value to them. Other times, it was lifted by lazy guards who resented the task, who thrust back the dam gates and allowed the powerful waves to roar into the cells, slamming the unprepared into the unyielding walls. Those caught sleeping or who lost their footing would be knocked unconscious and drowned.

After one such weekly bath, an experienced prisoner began again his ritual of retrieving from the bars of his cell the items he had bound in a cloth shirt. During the flooding, this cloth caught the air and held it underwater, a ploy he sometimes used when the guards callously walked away to amuse themselves while desperate men tried to keep their heads above the rushing waters at the top of their possible coffins.

"Wolfkiller," asked the man hoarsely in the next cell, "Do you live?"

"Yes, I live..." responded the man and the one who asked said no more; he knew by now the man he called 'Wolfkiller' would say nothing else until the next flooding.

The Wolfkiller, who was actually a hunter, laid out his boots to dry, then removed his clothing and spread them out as well. His fingers ruefully stroked his ragged beard; prisoners must release all notions of orderly appearance. He rung the water from his hair and bound it in a knot as he sat the floor of his cell and stared at the opening above him to the uncaring sky.

Once his cell was dry, he would return to his daily ritual of exercise to keep his now sedentary muscles from atrophy. Should his fate be, to provide crude and deadly sport for some loathsome king, the hunter wanted to ensure he sold his soul at a high price. As a man, he was fast and strong, but fate can overcome any advantage. He came to the jail months ago, and marveled that he still lived. Often, his mind went back to the day he found himself trapped between roaring winter snow and the deadly Lourdes Clan.

But a man must hunt to live, and he was alone.

Of the known groups of people who dwell outside of kingdoms: The Lourdes Clan, the Wanderers, the Boatsmen Clan, and the Healers, it is the Lourdes Clan who are the most dangerous. Even mercenaries and trained soldiers treat them with respect and avoid them at any cost. They do not barter or trade, and they will not communicate or use diplomacy of any kind; if you cross their path you will be attacked. In rare cases, if you come across a group of them, and you are recognized as a warrior, one of them will challenge you. If you slay him, they will allow you passage.

Yet the day ended differently for the hunter.

The Lourdes are called so because of their tendency to capture wolves as pups. They raise the pups and train them to battle alongside them and slay the horses of travelers. The hunter who would soon be known as Wolfkiller watched as his horse died early in the attack. He leaped from it before the flailing beast could hurl the hunter from his back in its panic to avoid the slashing teeth of the wolves. The hunter came to his feet too far from his sword, he had only his dagger and a wooden boa. He quickly placed himself before a tree that allowed his back to be covered.

There were six of them; three warriors and three wolves. As the first wolf lunged for him the boa struck its skull and red blood and brains splattered the bright snow. A Lourdes warrior came rushing over the wolf and the Wolfkiller slammed his staff into the man's chest, stopping his heart and cracking the ribs around it. The warrior fell atop his wolf and died without a sound.

The snow drifted softly in the air as the remaining Lourdes warriors paused as though considering, then clearly decided this battle did not count as a challenge. The hunter braced himself for a grisly death as the pair first gave silent signal to the wolves to flank him. One warrior stood at the back of the other; he suddenly stiffened and looked behind him:

A lone man approached this standoff, marching purposely through the snow.

The hunter dared to look up from his attackers and also stiffened to notice a silent contingent of soldiers had gathered to watch his last battle. The Lourdes warrior furthest away from him gave a short whistle and both wolves immediately moved away from the hunter and charged the man who boldly and foolheartedly interfered in their bloodplay. It was clear the warrior was listening for the sound of tearing flesh and the cries of a dying man; seconds later, he whirled fully around:

The first wolf sprinted ahead of its brother and leaped into the air at the man who without breaking his stride punched the wolf in the face with all his might, smashing the cartilage of its muzzle and driving this and shards of its skull into the wolf's brain, killing it instantly. He caught the second wolf by the throat. That beast barely had time to change from growl to whimper as the man crushed the wolf's larynx and neck muscles and shook it like a rat before hurling it to the ground without so much as pausing as he walked the snow.

The warrior who set the wolves on the mysterious man howled as though he were one of them, and fearlessly charged him with two blades drawn. The man drew his sword and swung twice, once to separate the warrior from his arms and again to effortlessly shear him in half. During this time, the hunter had broken the shoulder of the remaining Lourdes warrior with his staff and then bashed in the side of his head on his returning swing.

But not before the warrior slashed the hunter's face; a poor trade for his life.

The hunter retained his defensive stance as the man approached him; uncertain if the man came to aid him or fight him. Yet the hunter knew he could not defeat such a man, if indeed he was one. Who could do what he did and be human?

They studied each other a moment; the hunter and the man, no doubt the leader of these soldiers who silently awaited his will.

Black hair whipped about his bearded face and the blue eyes that held the hunter's gaze were merciless. He was tall, massively built and like the Lourdes warriors, it seemed the man was making up his mind about what to do with him. The slight tensing of his body was a familiar signal; the hunter swung his boa in his defense, but the man was impossibly fast as he was strong. The hunter shattered his staff against the man's arm and then he saw nothing.

When he woke up, it was in the cell that was now his home. The soldiers who dumped him there called him 'Wolfkiller', and the name stuck because he would not speak or offer another. He recovered from the injuries endured from the mysterious man who captured him as the months passed and the weather grew warmer. The hunter was sure, however, that he would die as the months grew colder. Surely if the river were released before it froze over, they would all die from lack of warmth.

Execution was preferred to that, the hunter thought grimly.

All sounds in the jails ceased as the metal gates whined in protest and the hunter came to his feet, his heart thudding as he looked down at his wet clothes and boots. The dam had never been released twice in the same day.

Would the men now all die to make room for others?

Mailed boots clicked and echoed on the damp tiles as soldiers, not guards made their way past the silent men, some of whom pressed their naked bodies against the jagged walls in dread. Someone was leaving to a fate unknown, and usually execution. Despite his thought to face his fate bravely, blood pounded in the hunter's ears as the soldiers came to a halt in front of his cell. The man who spoke in the deafening silence looked to be their captain.

"Wolfkiller," said the man flatly, and pointed at him. Another soldier quickly stepped forward and pushed a bundle of dry clothing through the bars of his cell.

"Get dressed," the captain barked, and the hunter did so, marveling that the clothes he donned fit his large frame.

Then the captain jerked open the doors of his cell and the soldiers poured in and smashed his struggling form against the walls. A few soldiers went down before he felt a blade at his throat and instinctively ceased his physical protest. As they chained him and restrained his legs the hunter began to regret not forcing them to slay him. Execution was the only other option he could imagine, but the moment to die on his feet had passed. He glanced regretfully at the small things he would leave behind that had value to no one but him; a necklace and beads from someone gone and but not forgotten.

The captain lifted a pair of dry boots and grinned at the hunter.

"Now you can put these on," the captain said as he tossed them to the floor in front of him. A soldier assisted the hunter and then they dragged him to his feet and marched him out of his cell and down the hall. As he left, he looked into the eyes of the man who lived in the cell next to him for months, whom he had never seen before.

They didn't know each other, but both men seemed to appreciate the opportunity to finally see another human being, someone who had suffered as he had before death.

"Farewell, Wolfkiller," The man whispered.

He held the bars of his cell and watched the hunter until he could see him no more.

* * *

Signature of Kings, part IV

The mage known as Enith and the High General of the Bright Forest flanked the new king as Rasdeter entered the Hall of Regents in the Unnamed Lands. Enith brought his troops in the colors of the Bright Forest to make the king's entrance more dramatic; Rasdeter must not be seen as a supplicant, but a ruler. Rasdeter chose not to wear his official robes and crown but to have them carried by a page. A wise move on his part, for the High King was not impressed by airs and showmanship.

It was a fine line the new king walked. Rasdeter thought of Regent Polymus and sighed; in hindsight, it would have been well to have had more years with him. But his thoughts turned to Ghent and brightened; he had one of the best regents in the eastern hemisphere to guide him.

Still, Rasdeter's heartbeat increased as he entered the main hall to find not only the regents of the Unnamed Lands waiting for him, but five kings who turned to stare at him in silence of his approach. Ghent stepped from the group to greet his lord, and Rasdeter narrowed his eyes at the stark changes in his friend and High Regent. The king could detect a faint hum coming from Ghent and his own heart wrenched in pain as he noticed how it now beat in tune with the regent's shared wound. Ghent seemed to acknowledge this as he bowed to Rasdeter and then met his eyes.

"My king," said Ghent and Rasdeter responded under his breath.

"We will speak of this soon, regent," said Rasdeter and Ghent nodded.

"I will introduce you, my lord..." began the regent, but the High King interrupted.

"The introductions can wait, High Regent Ghent," said N'Goth as he projected his voice over the assembly, "All know who King Rasdeter is. Now is the time for words between kings and men..."

Enith looked to Master Iroh, who tried and failed to restrain an 'I told you so' type of glance at the Ancient.

"Is there no rule of protocol N'Goth will not break?" Enith could not keep himself from uttering underneath his breath.

The High King snapped his fingers and one of his pages almost ran to King Rasdeter with an offering of wine, which the new king graciously accepted. N'Goth then raised his glass, a movement his son Crown Prince Arbu and the other kings followed; Rasdeter noted this with a raised eyebrow, N'Goth made a clear point regarding the loyalties of the five kings.

"We will drink together like men and speak as kings," said N'Goth, then pointedly indicated High Regent Ghent.

"I am impressed with your High Regent, who has persuaded us to consider war with the Nine Kingdoms, Rasdeter, yet the question remains: Why do you want the throne of the Far Isles?"

The young king caught his breath at this directness but recovered quickly.

"I am entitled to it, my Lord High King," responded Rasdeter, who began to speak further but N'Goth interrupted him.

"You are not the heir, Sumter is," said the High King bluntly as his blue eyes nailed Rasdeter's green eyes to his, "And your father killed his father when you both were children; so how has High King Sumter wronged you?"

Spots danced before the new king's vision. He had expected diplomacy, even from such a man as N'Goth, and now he felt a child before a parent. His face flushed as he drank from his cup and gathered his thoughts for response.

"As you say, my lord," replied Rasdeter evenly after a moment, "My father Lord Altus did slay King Valtus when Sumter and I were children, and then this child king did send his High General Aton to cravenly take myself as a child into the forests of my father's estates to slay me..."

High King N'Goth nodded to this and had his wine refilled before responding.

"Then you have cause indeed for personal grievance, King Rasdeter, but not a royal one," concluded N'Goth. "Your father was a traitor to his nation; his whole family was under penalty of death for treason, including you and your mother. General Aton did what was right to save King Valtus' bloodline; it would be the same if Lord Altus were king; it would be Sumter who would die."

Rasdeter paled as he recalled his dream as the Wanderer called Pax, where Pax was the child king and General Aton drew his sword against his cousin Sumter.

Iroh tensed his jaw as the High King spoke; he could only imagine the reaction of his friend Enith to this discourse. Drunk or sober, King N'Goth was a force to be reckoned with; his knowledge of law and secession was indisputable.

But his next words changed the tone of the meeting which, up to this moment all seemed to be in question as to whether the endeavor would proceed.

"This does not mean that we will not assist you in this enterprise, King Rasdeter," said N'Goth with a rare smile, "Nor should you expect a High King to lightly give up his throne if you ask kindly for it. But it does mean that your own resolve as a man will be tested..."

"I stand ready to do what is needed, my Lord High King," said Rasdeter firmly, and King N'Goth noted the look in the new king's eye.

"I believe you..." said the High King finally, and Master Iroh realized the tightness in his shoulders as he released his breath. King N'Goth was taking the lead against Sathdan's and Iroh's own advice and he knew the king would not relinquish control to a mage, no matter how powerful. Iroh knew he would have to speak with Enith immediately afterwards to keep the Ancient from throwing all caution to the steep winds and vaporizing N'Goth.

The king was a man by all standards, and a man who is not afraid of his own death is dangerous indeed.

"Your mage has explained that though untested as a king, you are a warrior, which is good," said N'Goth as he looked to High General Brennan who stepped forward with maps of the Nine Kingdoms and the roads leading to them from the Unnamed Lands.

"But the difference between a king and a warrior is more than mere defense and battle. Any warrior can defend his home, but a conqueror must be the one he defends against," stated N'Goth as he pointed to the maps of the Nine Kingdoms.

"You must slay thousands of men without mercy," said the king quietly, "Women, children and the infirm; all who cannot defeat you or halt your advance. Burn down their homes and destroy families; watch your men rape and slay all that stands between you and Sumter..."

Rasdeter's eyes blinked rapidly; the High King was describing something that was against everything the former prince had stood for: The sanctity of life and family, love, and relationships. He closed his eyes as he recalled the savage dreams the Ancient had bombarded him with; now Rasdeter saw that Enith merely showed him all that he must do. The symbolic blood that ran down the tapestries of his rooms was in fact a mirror of all the blood that he himself would spill as he marched towards the Far Isles.

The High King interrupted the new king's thoughts and brought his worried eyes to him. N'Goth locked his gaze on Rasdeter and crossed his arms.

"And now I must test and challenge you, new king," said King N'Goth dispassionately. "Show me you are ready; that you can kill a man for the sheer pleasure of killing him and I and all these men and kings will follow you until you slay High King Sumter. Will you do this?"

Slay a man? Echoed the young king's thoughts, Wantonly kill someone who did not threaten him personally or his way of life? As his wounded heart thudded rapidly in his chest, his mind answered: Either this or back down and allow these gathered men to see that no true spine upholds your body; that you will weave in the wind to whatever direction it takes you.

What remained of Rasdeter's soul screamed silently as the young king locked his jaw and responded:

"I will stay the course, my lord," answered Rasdeter boldly, "If this is all you require, bring him forth."

Sathdan looked to the regent standing closest to him, who then hurried to the heavy doors leading to the corridors beyond the hall. The soldiers opened the doors for the regent, who could soon be heard directing the men standing out of view.

"Remove his shackles, and hurry! No, leave his hands bound for now, the king wants to see him immediately..."

The sound of chains dropping to the tiles rang from outside the hall and then the guards flung the doors wide and a group of twenty soldiers directed the bound man to the front of the hall, five soldiers across marched in front, five on the sides and behind him. The soldiers paused a distance away with the prisoner as they approached their king, who smiled at this precaution; there wasn't a man in the entire building who could harm N'Goth.

High Regent Sathdan spoke.

"As you requested, my king, the 'Wolfkiller'..."

The soldiers in front stepped aside and Rasdeter met the eyes of the prisoner; both men started in amazement as they recognized each other.

The hunter spoke in a tense undertone to the soldiers standing next to him.

"Unbind me..."

Rasdeter's eyes narrowed as the High King turned to look at him in confusion.

"You know this man?" asked N'Goth.

But the young king did not respond. Rasdeter reached for the Prince's Sword that hung from his side, the blade singing as it came forth in a rush from its scabbard. All things faded from the new king's sight as the memory of a young boy fighting for his life came into focus. His jaw set, the King of the Bright Forest moved forward with purpose and remembered rage blazed behind his eyes.

The hunter spoke again, his voice urgent and commanding.

"Unbind me...!"

The soldier nearest him stepped back and drawing his short sword, sliced downward at the ropes binding the hunter's wrists together; another soldier lightly tossed a sword to the hunter, who barely had time to plant his feet and swing the borrowed sword upwards to meet Rasdeter's deadly blow.

The Prince's Sword whined as the blade went down the length of the hunter's weapon; the man was staggered by the ferocity of the king's attack. The soldiers fell back, and the kings came to their feet as the men dueled silently and swiftly across the room.

It seemed the young king was possessed; Iroh turned in wonder to Enith who mirrored his dismay.

"I've done nothing..." said Enith in amazement as he watched the king fiercely battle the hunter.

"Who is he, the prisoner?" asked Iroh as he tried to keep up with the frenzied swordplay.

Enith gathered himself and searched the former prince's past memories; after a moment, he answered Iroh.

"He calls him...Bowman Kha..."

N'Goth followed the battle, grimly keeping stride with the men as they continued their deadly contest across the tiles of the hall. His eyes lit in new respect for the young king as Rasdeter demonstrated without falter his ability to give in to his bloodlust. It was clear to everyone in the room that the young king had no intention of showing mercy as he brutally fought the man who had terrorized him as a child.

Again, and again the hunter known as Bowman Kha of the tribe called Human attempted to stand his ground and halt Rasdeter's advance but found himself unable to. He fought for his life, matching blow to blow but Kha felt the righteous rage of his former rival overcoming him as he began to tire.

His borrowed blade was no match for the Prince's Sword; Rasdeter disarmed Kha and sent the battered sword flying from his hand. The impact caused Bowman Kha to lose his footing. Without hesitation, the young king swung back and brought his hands together to impale the hunter to the tiles. But as the blade struck, Kha disappeared in a brilliant flash of light that rumbled the ground.

Rasdeter went to his knees as he followed the blow, then shook his head as the red haze cleared and he beheld no slain foe beneath him. There was no sound in the shocked assembly but the new king's labored breathing.

Then Rasdeter came to his feet and his eyes met those of Enith. He pointed at the mage.

"Did you save him from me?" he asked as he panted.

But the Ancient said nothing as he appraised the young king.

Rasdeter's face darkened.

"Did you save him?!?"

Master Iroh quietly interceded between the king and his master.

"Your foe was not removed by magic, my lord," answered Iroh, and Rasdeter's face changed from anger to amazement as he continued to stare at Enith.

"Not...not magic? Then...what..." His face cleared for a moment, and then Rasdeter's eyes blinked rapidly.

"No...no, she wouldn't..." He whispered to himself, "She wouldn't..."

The High King strode over to Rasdeter and clapped him firmly on the shoulder.

"It matters not who saved him from you, young king," said N'Goth gruffly, "It only matters that someone had to..."

N'Goth turned to the assembly.

"I believe we've found a man in this prince turned king. What say you?"

The King of the Sky Vault enthusiastically raised his cup, spilling some of its contents.

"I'll follow you into battle, Rasdeter, and may the hounds catch any who fall behind you!"

The hall erupted into roars and laughter as each man of war agreed and seconded the king's words. Crown Prince Arbu now came forward and grasped Rasdeter's forearm at the elbow in a universal gesture of welcome. The young king returned this manly ritual with a bemused smile as he tried to turn his thoughts away from this seeming betrayal at the very moment of his triumph.

The two master mages watched these events with a practiced eye that was focused on the future. The success of the king's assembly and the signature of the accords meant all their plans and schemes were assured. Yet the disappearance of Kha, while shrugged off by the men and kings present, had brought an unaccustomed tang of fear into the hearts of Iroh and Enith. As powerful as they were collectively, they could not prevent the hunter being whisked away to safety; it was a reminder of how carefully they had to tread.

"You know who Rasdeter believes has done this," said Iroh evenly.

"I do," replied Enith as his eyes narrowed, "...and I will allow him to continue believing as he chooses...for now..."

To Live Forever

Naturally, Rasdeter was ready to leave the Unnamed Lands as soon as he caught his breath, but his High General reminded him that the accords still needed to be signed by all the kings, including himself.

Once all formalities were completed and the young king had graciously thanked each king who pledged his men and money to Rasdeter's cause, the business of how the spoils would be divided were presented by the regents of each country. The King of the Bright Forest followed the lead of the other kings and left the tedious haggling to the regents and generals, who would then present their best offers to be approved by each committee.

These proceedings made Rasdeter groan.

He never imagined he would find himself looking forward to dining in the evenings with Enith as he waited for Ghent to end his day, but he did so. The raised voices and muted discussions of the regents reminded the former prince of his days of studying government with Polymus, and how he longed to do almost anything else. The young king enjoyed his own debates with Ghent over points of law, but that was due to how interesting the regent made his findings. Ghent had a way of making the study of law come alive; his love for it apparent in every sentence. Rasdeter looked forward to the summary his High Regent would offer, couched in a way that caused him to marvel that it had taken the entire day to come to these now concise conclusions.

The regents of the collected kingdoms debated for a week; during this time Rasdeter joined the Ancient and master Iroh in one of N'Goth's many dining halls.

Rasdeter found himself fascinated to observe how Enith interacted with Iroh, his former student. The Ancient's respect for Iroh was evident; in contrast to his tolerance of Keoni and utter disregard for those mages beneath Keoni's rank. When his mind turned to Ghent, the young king noted with a start that for the most part, Enith treated the three of them, Iroh, Ghent and himself as a father would his sons, albeit a controlling abusive one to he and Ghent. Enith's treatment of those with little use to him was quite sobering, and when Rasdeter thought of his shared wound with Ghent, he began to wonder and not for the first time, exactly what might be the endgame of the mage.

The two mages suspended their discussion at the king's approach, and Rasdeter seated himself across from them, waving off a dish of sweet breads offered by a servant and indicating a cup of wine be filled for him. Enith and Iroh were surprised when the young king began a discussion of his own.

"I find myself curious as I look at you, Master Iroh," said Rasdeter, "I have never asked Enith's age, because I'm told as an Ancient, he would not recall it," and watched as the mage gave bemused confirmation.

The king now looked to Iroh, who could not hide his interest.

"Compared to my former teacher," responded Iroh, "I am less than a child just learning to walk. I've lived through three eons, roughly seventy-five thousand years."

The young king could not hold his own amazement; Iroh appeared a man in his early thirties.

"Be not amazed at such things as appearance, my lord," said Iroh with a smile, "Once you master the human body, it obeys you and becomes whatever physical age you wish..."

"What compels you to walk the Earth so lengthy a time?" asked Rasdeter.

"The Earth holds wonders that will astound you easily for millions of years, my king," said Iroh earnestly, "I've not begun to plumb its depths and marvels..."

"Yet what sustains you, Master Iroh?" asked the young king in curiosity, "Is it magic that lengthens your years?"

"More science than magic, my king," replied the sorcerer, "As you know, the cells of the human body renews itself completely every seven years, so that essentially you are designed to live forever. With the proper training it would take a man such as yourself but a nudge, and the body would follow its programming and renew itself so long as you desire it to..."

The former prince seemed to gaze off as he absorbed Iroh's words, and the sorcerer found himself accessing the young ruler with new eyes. The conversation had a similar effect on the Ancient, who had never shown interest in the thought system of his pawn any further than he had use for.

"Do you wish to live forever, Rasdeter?" asked Enith in genuine wonder.

At this, the new king paused again as though truly giving the matter thought. Rasdeter swiftly went over the events of his life and then with a sad smile, he shook his head.

"It may be a flaw in my character, masters," Rasdeter responded, "But as I think of all those I have lost or left behind in my life, my parents, my uncle, indeed, my entire existence appears to be one of constant separation. And as I believe that once I leave this earthly plane, that I will have a moment or more to see them again, it is not meet that I should tarry so long a time as seems comfortable to you, Iroh..." and now the king's eyes fell on Enith.

"For you, my lord, it may be that time is a blessing, for you no longer recall those who once cherished you, and their faces no longer haunt your night at rest. It is my hope that one lifetime is enough to mourn and regret; I would not wish to bear such pain forever as I walk this planet. Perhaps I embrace the philosophy of my fellow men who deem life sweeter for its shortness, and I will release all bonds at the end of this journey."

"Let it be as you say, young king," replied Iroh solicitously, and the men fell silent as the first courses of food were served. Later, their talk turned to mundane things, but Iroh found himself lapsing from time to time as they spoke. Rasdeter's words brought the memory of Iroh's first mentor, Lord Rannea, to the forefront of his mind, whom the Master Sorcerer would never forget, in all the long eons he felt might be in front of him. The new king's simple longing for those who loved him struck at Iroh's heart. He recalled the words of Enith not long after he saved Iroh from the insane Ancient who killed his friend and mentor Rannea:

"I respect your grief, young Iroh, but the pull and longing of union is almost impossible to resist if you continue to yearn for their company. You will not last another eon if being with Rannea is your fondest wish..."

Iroh reminded himself in this moment that it was Rasdeter's longing for home that brought all the trouble he suffered.

The Master Sorcerer sighed.

I will never forget you, Rannea. It is my comfort that no matter how long I live, you await me on the other side.

For Enith, however, the conversation with Rasdeter had a completely different effect. It had not occurred before to him to lengthen the king's life as he had Roane's. The Ancient reasoned that this steady consistent influence could hammer home the acceptance of magic through centuries of Rasdeter's rule, and his descendants would be conditioned to it through constant exposure.

Enith's thoughts turned to the king's wife, Saramis.

Perhaps the best outcome would be that you would die of a broken heart, rather than suffer at his side for hundreds of years, mused the Ancient. Either way, I have won.

This train of thought vastly improved the mood of the mage.

It came about that all were lost in such thoughts when Crown Prince Arbu burst into the hall with news; trailing behind him were regents waving parchments like flags. Because of Arbu's station as the Heir of the Unnamed Lands, all sound ceased, and all eyes were drawn to him as he spoke:

"Great news, my lords," exclaimed the prince, "We have confirmation from King Sumter and the Nine Kingdoms, they will meet us on the ancient battleground of Arin-Clath! We are at war!"

The hall erupted into roars and back thumping; servants hurried from harm's way as the more inebriated guests came to their feet with swords drawn and the cultural war songs of their various people on their lips.

Enith easily contained the flare of energy that shot out from King Rasdeter's heart at the mention of his cousin's name. Their eyes met, and Enith startled the young king by offering an encouraging nod. Seconds later, Rasdeter's heart leapt again when Prince Arbu leaned over him and placed a parchment with the seal of the Far Isles on the table.

"The courier was given strict instructions to deliver this unbroken to you, my lord," said Arbu quietly, and the young king caught a glimpse of compassion in the gaze of the Crown Prince before he turned respectfully away.

Rasdeter's face was hot and his fingers numb as he reached for the document; his thumb rubbed across the purple wax imbedded with flecks of gold. After a moment, the new king slid the yielding cloth into his robes to read later when alone. Master Iroh and the Ancient exchanged glances as the king excused himself from the table and headed for his rooms.

Iroh studied the carvings on his half-drained cup before speaking in an undertone.

"Familial love is a powerful weapon," mused Iroh, "It cuts both the intended target and the one who wields it..."

"And I feel the bite of it, Iroh, rest assured," conceded Enith with a sigh. "N'Goth is correct, hounds take him; for all my work to be undone by a sealed parchment..."

"Rasdeter does not wish to slay his cousin, Enith," said Iroh as he stated the obvious, "Yet he wants to go home, despite the impossibility of it...his longing for it hammers at me..."

"Yes," replied the Ancient, "It is the only reason he will stay the course; I am most gratified that I need not force him to go. But when he arrives at the battlefield..."

Enith thoughtfully traced his own mouth with his fingers.

"I must ensure that Rasdeter does the one thing that will ensure he can indeed go home."

Servants came forth with the next course of steaming delicious food; the sorcerers returned silently to their meal.

The End of All Means

Bowman Kha sat alone in front of the settlement firepit after the people had mostly turned in for the evening, using his new hand blade to whittle a soft branch of wood to nothing. He was nearly a year's distance away from his parent's tribe, whom he had become separated from while searching farther out than usual to hunt. Since leaving Saramis behind, Kha had begun to roam in solitude more and more, refusing company and nursing his hidden wounds. It was this developed habit that had led to the encounter with the Lourdes Clan and King N'Goth, his imprisonment and then near death at the hands of the man he almost killed as a boy.

It was the closest Bowman Kha had come to seeing Saramis again, and a part of him once refused to see that he was still looking for her. Yet Kha had almost died for a glimpse of her and the hunter was beginning to realize that.

He felt rather than heard the Great Elder standing behind him.

"Why did you save me, Great Mother?" Kha whispered and heard Affi-Tosla make a derisive sound as she stood over him.

"You know why," she answered.

Bowman Kha felt the fingers of the Great Elder lightly stroke his hair and he tightened his jaw to hold in his emotions.

"I have not released her..." he said finally and Affi-Tosla nodded though the hunter could not see it.

"You seek Saramis everywhere except where she truly is, Bowman Kha," said the Great Second Elder, "Therefore it will be impossible for you to find her."

The hunter sighed.

"I was born knowing these teachings, Great Mother, but I have not followed them, not truly, or things would be different..."

"Or things would still be as they are, and you would be different," offered Affi-Tosla gently.

"Why do I want so desperately to save Saramis from him, Great Elder," Kha gasped, "The need for it drives me so I cannot rest."

The hunter looked up towards Affi-Tosla as he heard her chuckle.

"The three of you so love to ask what you will not heed," she said finally. "Salvation is not your function, Bowman, you know this. Your attempt to force what you cannot change will lead you down the path such decisions must give, so you will continue to try doing what cannot be done..."

"Is it so wrong to wish to see her, even from afar, Mother?" The hunter asked in despair.

For answer, the Second Elder stepped in front of Bowman Kha and as she drew his eyes to her, Affi-Tosla opened her hands. Kha gasped and then squeezed tight his eyes and made a fist as the Great Elder offered him the necklace and beads he left behind in King N'Goth's prison.

"This may be the closest you will ever come to Saramis in this lifetime, Bowman," said the Elder quietly, "Is it enough?"

Kha could not answer while he struggled with his emotions. Affi-Tosla sighed as she pressed the childhood memory into his now yielding hand.

"It is merely a trinket you have given meaning to, Bowman. In the greater scheme, you know that it means nothing..."

Only the sound of the firepit crackling and spitting sparks of burnt wood shavings in the air continued for a time. The soft pressure of the beads against Kha's palm took him back to the moment a young Saramis had offered these things to him as Kha began his training as a warrior. Such gifts were common at this time but for some reason when the young healer draped the necklace around Kha's neck and placed the beads on his arm, their eyes met, and he felt something stir in his heart. Saramis flushed at his suddenly stern gaze and moved away from him. The elders later told Kha he had recognized the girl from another life and other experiences. The future hunter gave this information a meaning that made sense to him; Kha vowed to protect the young healer and soon this emotion evolved into feelings of love.

Bowman Kha's face appeared an open book to Affi-Tosla as she read his memories. Then the Elder watched as the hunter's gaze hardened in the light of the flames.

Finally, she spoke to it.

"You have removed my protection Kha, in this moment, and so I will honor your request. But know that in this lifetime it is Rasdeter who wears the mantle of destiny on his shoulders. And should you step again on the path between him and Sumter your story will end..."

Now Kha met her eyes boldly and spoke his heart.

"And what must I do, then, Great Mother? Return to my parent's tribe and live my life, knowing he will lead Saramis to destruction?"

The smile of Affi-Tosla was so gentle and so loving that Kha caught his breath and looked away from her.

"Were I to tell you these things only to preserve your physical life, Bowman Kha," the Great Elder whispered, "I would have no worth as a teacher. This flesh..." and now she gently patted his arm, "...is but the smallest part of all you are capable of becoming. Instead, it may be of greater use for you to lose your body in this endeavor... it may be the only way for you to learn that you can never die."

The hunter did not respond for a moment, then he reached for her hand and pressed it to his lips. Kha sighed as Affi-Tosla leaned over to kiss the top of his head. Then he came to his feet and bowed to the Great Elder, who smiled slightly and remained unmoving as the hunter first stepped back a few feet from her then turned and walked the path to his tent.

Second Elder Zema, who is never too far away when the Great Elder is present, came across the common area to join Affi-Tosla. They both watched as Bowman Kha vanished into the darkness.

"The Bowman's tent is dismantled, Great Elder," said Zema, "I fear Kha will leave us in the morning..."

"He was always planning to go, Zema," responded Affi-Tosla, "It was the direction he was not sure of until now."

"Kha should not travel alone, Mother," mourned Zema quietly, "It is not good for brothers to travel thus so close to the kingdoms."

"He will not be alone," responded the Great Elder thoughtfully, "Many of our brothers will go with him, and though he knows it not, Atoli will be among them..."

Second Elder Zema started in shock at the Elder's words. Atoli was the leader of the warriors, now that both Bowman Kha and Pax were gone.

"Our warriors will follow Bowman Kha, aware that he is leading them to war?"

Now Affi-Tosla turned to gaze on Elder Zema with compassionate eyes.

"For Atoli and the warriors, it is a battle for the heart of Rasdeter, who is a brother, Zema. Yes, they will go, and some will not return."

Overcome at the thought, Second Elder Zema covered her face with her hands and wept. The Great Elder sighed deeply and returned her eyes to the darkness that Kha surrendered to.

"Yes...to weep now would be appropriate," she whispered, "This is but the beginning of sorrows..."

Ursa Roars, part I

Rasdeter changed in the time he was away in the Kingdom of the Unnamed Lands. His demeanor towards his queen was more somber, brooding, and quiet. Gone was the young man who could not wait to hold his wife, his treasure, and whisper things in her ear that made the normally calm and reserved Saramis giggle unrestrained. The king would not speak of what had transpired while there and the young queen noticed his gaze upon her at intervals when Rasdeter clearly thought Saramis unaware of it.

She recalled his words of love before leaving her and the tiny stripes of pain she felt widened into jagged rips as Saramis remembered how Rasdeter marginally greeted her on his return, a cool and casual acknowledgment for the display of those of his subjects who were present and watching. When her gaze chanced to fall on Enith the mage had returned her look evenly, but his cruel eyes were shining. The king spent most of his waking hours in the company of the men who would soon accompany him to war; when his wife gently asked if anything was amiss between them, Rasdeter shrugged off her fears.

"I feel the burden of kingship, Saramis," the king responded in an even tone of voice, lacking the warmth he usually reserved for her.

"This is a far greater responsibility than a few warriors roaming the plains in search of timid game," he continued, coolly observing as her face flushed from such an unwarranted attack. His words were a direct reference to his time spent with the Wanderers, and with Saramis.

The young queen tried to gather herself and recover.

"Perhaps..." Saramis tried to catch her breath and keep the hurt from her eyes, "Perhaps it is not well to speak with you at this time, my lord..."

But as Saramis turned away, her husband came to his feet.

"Why, what is this, my queen," said Rasdeter in a voice of pretended dismay, "Do you relent so easily?"

Now the king's voice gave a mocking tone as his wife moved back in shock from him.

"I once believed it your life's mission to save me...!"

"Rasdeter...husband..." Saramis gasped, "Why do you wound me without cause?"

She now noticed the repressed rage behind the king's eyes; Saramis shook her head in confusion. "What means this?" she whispered.

"Perhaps it is not I you truly wish to save," said Rasdeter through clenched teeth, "But another!"

The queen searched her husband's eyes for reason and found none.

"What--" her brow furrowed, "Please tell me what you speak of, Rasdeter, I know not what you mean...!"

"Now you seek to deceive me, Saramis," Rasdeter replied darkly as he thrust his forefinger at her, "'Perhaps'", he declared with emphasis, "You have been using your power against me all along, allowing me to blame the mage while you secretly fought for what you've always wanted...!"

Caught completely off guard by her life mate, Saramis felt her emotional body explode. She could never have foreseen that Rasdeter would render unworthy all the efforts his wife expended to keep him whole, to battle the mage Enith until her own life hung in the balance. The young queen expected malice from the Ancient; to hear such words of spite from the man she loved dealt Saramis a blow she had no answer for. Her own dismay at her maltreatment roared through whatever defenses the beleaguered Woman of the Woods had left. The elements responded to her mental state, and the earth rumbled and shook as the hall filled with blinding light.

"What...madness...is this?!?" Saramis cried out as she struggled to keep what little control she had left. Yet, her words went unheeded as Rasdeter pointed at the light behind her triumphantly.

"Yes!" he shouted in his turn, "Yes, it was you, Saramis. You used your power to save Kha. This is the light and power that removed him from my grasp!"

Confusion and comprehension warred in the queen's gaze.

"Kha...?" she echoed, "You...you've seen Kha in the Unnamed Lands? But how?"

The king's anger had outstripped reason; sanity fled as he roared at his wife.

"It was him you've always wanted!"

Darkness burst from the young king's chest and hurled across the space between them; Saramis threw up her arms and screamed as the malicious power coming from her husband's heart slammed against her light, staggering her. As the dust cleared, she lowered her arms and gazed at her jealous, unhinged spouse, trying, and failing to keep the tears from her words.

Her voice tremored.

"You..." she nearly sobbed in disbelief, "You attacked me..."

But Rasdeter felt his rage at her seeming betrayal justified; he merely stared at her coldly, his own chest heaving.

Undone, the young queen wrapped herself in light and vanished.

Moments later, the sullen king marched into his morning court; all the seated nobles came swiftly to their feet. Rasdeter looked to his High General.

"Brennan," asked the king tersely, "Are my men ready to leave?"

"Yes, my lord," replied the general, "They've been ready for weeks..."

"Then get them assembled," snapped the king, "We leave as soon as they're in formation."

The general bowed smartly and left the hall; a minor regent who overheard everything soon appeared in the Hall of Mages, seeking Keoni, who seconds later, appeared before his lord and master Enith.

The Ancient stroked his face soberly, a fierce light in his eyes.

"Misunderstanding is a fair servant, Keoni," said the mage in triumph, "I have no doubt that tomorrow, our king rides alone."

Sons, Cousins, Brothers, Kings

The Toddler Prince was unhappy with his confinement to his rooms, spacious though they were. Prince Asscher was too young to realize that his father the king was now anxious in general for his well-being, and their coming separation was difficult for Sumter. Asscher's high pitched shrieks of alternating delight and irritation could be heard throughout the suites as he ran full tilt, his harried wet nurses doing their best to corner the prince and keep him from harm. His father visited frequently to view his son's every move-ment since his safe return from the Eastern Crest, which did little to relieve the stress of the staff in charge of the prince.

Queen Amara of the Eastern Crest understood the High King's demand that Crown Prince Asscher remain in the Far Isles until the conflict was over, but she wasn't pleased about it. Couriers rushed back and forth for months with letters between the frustrated monarchs until High Regent Polymus gently reminded his lord and king that the roads were becoming increasingly dangerous for the envoys, the very argument he was using to assert his rights to his heir.

On the king's final day before leaving for war, Lady Irisella sent word of an urgent request to speak with her king, which of course was granted. There was little that the High King would not do for his foster mother.

As was his habit, the king held his final audience with his favor-ite subject in his library. Lady Irisella tried to restrain a laugh as the Toddler Prince dashed frantically about his father's huge chamber of scrolls and parchments, chased by servants while his bemused sire watched. Asscher was playing a game only he knew the rules of, gleefully striking Sumter's knee or thigh then flinging himself under a table before his wet nurse could prevent him. From there Asscher ran to every hiding place he could think of, then back across the room, to strike his father again and shriek in victory. Finally, King Sumter roughly caught his child and swung Asscher high into the air, who howled in delight.

"Again Fa-fa," the prince commanded at the top of his lungs, "Again!"

Sumter obeyed the commands of his prince until he sensed his overexcited offspring was tiring at last when the tiny prince rubbed his eyes and tried to wriggle from his father's arms.

"Enough, Asscher," said the king firmly and smiled proudly as his child immediately reacted to the stern male sound coming from his father and curled his arms around Sumter's neck, panting in exhaustion.

"A-nough!" Asscher echoed, and the adults gave in to laughter at his precociousness. Sumter rubbed and patted his son's back as his sleepiness deepened; soon the prince slumped against his father's chest. He'd been running all morning; the king pressed a kiss to Asscher's damp forehead; by the time he awakened, his father would be gone. Reluctantly, King Sumter handed his child to Irisella, who touched her lips to the boy's eyelashes, long and thick against his cheeks, and then his limp fingers before giving Asscher to the nurse to take to bed. Once the doors closed quietly behind the servants, the king and his foster mother commenced their talk.

Lady Irisella gave every argument, logic, reasoning, and plea she could but the one she subconsciously considered her son would not relent.

"You cannot go with us to war, Irisella," said King Sumter, "You are all the family I have left, and I will not risk your life..."

"But...Sumter," Irisella began again, "What if all is true, and Rasdeter lives...I would give much to see him well and alive once more..."

"As would I," said the king firmly, "But this is not the King's Summit, where all are sworn to do no harm. This is war, my lady, and you would be mere currency for threat or execution for vengeance. Is there anyone who does not know your value to me? Surely you must see that I cannot allow this to occur."

Finally, Lady Irisella gave voice to her fears.

"If...if it is Rasdeter," she began haltingly, "...and he fights you, and you slay him..."

The High King sighed as he mirrored his second mother's hesitancy.

"It...it is my most sincere hope that all of this is nonsense, Irisella," replied the king grimly, "...and I will bring low the pretender and hopefully prevail. If by some twist of fate my cousin lives, and they have enthralled him, of course I will do all I can to free Rasdeter from intrigue. But...if he comes willingly against me..."

The room was quiet as two suffering hearts beat together in dread.

"If my true cousin does come against me, Irisella," Sumter continued, "Then we two shall battle, and for my son Asscher's sake, one of us will fall. If it is me, then you will surely see Rasdeter, for he will come to slay my heir and sit my throne."

"I beg you not to say such," Irisella cried out, "My life is in your breath, yours and Asscher's...!"

The king continued almost to himself.

"...And if I prove victorious..."

Sumter gazed painfully into his foster mother's eyes.

"Then, yes, my lady, you will suffer from the realization that he both lived and died a world away from you..."

Irisella then came to Sumter's opened arm and placing her face against his bosom, wept.

A Stand for the Light

After the king's impromptu meeting with Lady Irisella in his library, King Sumter marched to his war room, his personal guard surrounding him. His High Regent Polymus stood ready with the signed parchment from the eight kings who followed him: King Andron of the Southern Arc, and uncle to Sumter's heir, Crown Prince Asscher. King Garrin of the Northern Walls, Sumter's grandfather. King Barron of the Golden Round Kingdom; King Sienne of the Eastern Crest, and stepfather to Prince Asscher. King Roe of the Western Hills; King Ruan of the Circle of the Earth, King Anshan of the Rim of the World, and King Madouni of the Deep Places.

Three kings and their armies were not present in this moment: King Ruan and her armies had agreed to march with the army of the King of the Rim of the World. The distance from the Far Isles and their proximity to the Unnamed Lands made it impractical to leave the joint kingdoms open to possible attack from the Kingdom of the Broken Meriden, despite the rumors that most of the army had already marched southward a year ago. Reports of the location of the Broken Meriden horsemen were unreliable, as were the presence of their feared archers.

The armies of the Eastern Crest were so massive as to necessitate more months than usual to gather; King Sienne committed nearly half to an early march. He and his wife Queen Amara, mother to Crown Prince Asscher, would bring in the rear forces with his horsemen. Despite the protests of both King Sienne and King Sumter, they could not persuade the former Royal Consort of the Far Isles to remain behind. The Crown Prince of the Far Isles was barely three years old, and the queen's fears for Asscher, should the Unnamed Lands prove victorious could not be calmed.

Though his brow was clear as he entered the chamber, the High King mirrored the fears of his former Consort; it was Sumter's fondest wish to be present as his son and heir grew up and took on his inheritance. His father King Valtus died when he was twelve; now a man, Sumter understood how tenuous the future could be, and more than his life hung in the balance of this future conflict.

Every man and woman in the room felt the importance of the moment, their eyes somber as they met the High King's.

High General Marcus held the Sword of the Far Isles; his second in command General Hesta held the king's helmet and shield. High Regent Polymus addressed his king.

"We await your will, High King Sumter," and a soft rumbling of assent filled the room then stilled.

As King Sumter stood before his assembled kings and leaders of his army, he spoke:

"It would behoove us to remember in this moment why we are here and what it is we stand and soon will battle for," he said quietly.

"Thousands of years ago, at the Council of the Four Worlds, the concept of nations and kingdoms with one figurehead as leader over governments were formed. Of those countries, the Nine Kingdoms were formed as spiritual and physical boundaries to uphold the best attributes of men: Faith, Knowledge, Trust, Integrity, Compassion, Truth, Love, Peace, and Strength."

"As you know, all names have power. It was the first N'Goth, and soon to be High King of the Unnamed Lands, who disrupted the Council and made mockery of the names and positions of power of the Four Directions and the Five-Pointed Star. He vowed to create an opposite to the Light; a tribute to the darker nature of man: Pride, Lust, Envy, Greed, Covetousness, Sloth and Wrath."

"Once these kingdoms were banded and formed, High King N'Goth waged war on the fragile alliances of the Nine Kingdoms, and the Prophecy of the Knot, a necessary alliance of the Unnamed Lands and the Circle of the Earth Kingdom was all that prevented his victory. This all happened thousands of years ago, and for all that time we have held an uneasy truce...until today."

King Sumter paused as an uneasy murmur came from those assembled. No doubt the thought of the writings of what some called the End of All Existence was uppermost in the minds of those gathered; a fear that the coming conflict was the herald of the darkest times possible.

The young king spoke aloud to these fears.

"Some believe that the present High King N'Goth is the rebirth of the first one; that he has come again to complete his unholy mission..."

Sumter saw the conviction of this belief in the gaze of some who listened to his words.

"I do not know the truth of this...nor do I care..."

The king began to walk the length of the huge room, looking directly into the eyes of the men and women who pledged to follow him.

"Many of us now standing in this hall will not return to our homes. The fallen will not know if we were victorious or if the Nine Kingdoms fell, that a millennium of darkness and ignorance will come and blanket the planet..."

Sumter paused as the king could not keep his thoughts from his son Asscher, in this moment. No man can live forever, he mused as the image of Lord Brayten came before him. What matters is what that life was lived for, no matter how long or short it is, and Sumter's mind came again to the small boy sleeping in his father's rooms.

"But those of us who do fall," the king continued, "Will fall knowing that in this moment, we stood as a Light that will not be bowed or ever conquered; that no matter how many come against us, we will reign. Mankind will remember, if only in their deepest dreams, that the worm of the dust is not our inheritance, a despair of man's purpose unfounded. We will rise and show the part of our nature that seems corrupt, we will not yield to it. We will hold the high ground and march higher, and ultimately, that sweeter light we aspire to will embrace us and bring our hearts to places undreamed of and unforgotten..."

With these words, High King Sumter held his place and fell silent.

High General Marcus, his second in command Hesta, and all the king's generals waiting with him began to pound both staff and shields in honor of their High Commander. The six kings present joined in, and all the regents, officials and even the servants pounded their cups and boots. The sound echoed and the soldiers outside the hall pounded their spears, which began a wave that carried until all the soldiers in the palace joined in, launching a roar from the assembled mounted men in the courtyard.

King Garrin of the Northern Walls lifted his sword and shield and roared:

"To Arin-Clath! Let every soul make his mark and set it high!"

Marcus and Hesta hurried to adorn their king, who then wordlessly turned and marched out the hall, followed by the assembled kings and all present.

The people outside the inner gates came running to the main road. They knew that soon the king would begin his march towards war with the Unnamed Lands and all wished to catch a glimpse of High King Sumter, his assembled kings, and armies. They brought flowers and garlands and dried fragrant seeds to shower the kings and their men. The breeders of livestock brought small pouches of dried meats for the soldiers to carry on the road. Humble tillers of soil lifted their children with small bundles of dried fruit to offer those soldiers marching closest to the wall of humanity surging to offer prayers and hope for victory. The men all marched in perfect formation, accepting what they could without breaking stride. A series of empty wagons rolled in between the groups of soldiers and the people tossed their offerings into it, filling them up to overflowing.

On the open road, far from the final gates would be the refugees, lined up to cheer and encourage both the troops and those men of their own who joined the king's army over the last year. Mothers and daughters stood crying and waving on the path of the soldiers as they caught sight of the sons, husbands, sisters, and brothers who came bravely forth to offer their lives for their people's protection. Many women would run as far as they could with their children, weeping and laughing for a glimpse of the men they loved and hoped would return home.

* * *

Lady Irisella stood on the king's balcony wiping her face as the seemingly endless waves of marching men moved away from her. She lost sight of King Sumter hours ago, but still she could not move from the balcony. Her new husband Lord Orin came back to join her after dismissing the servants who attempted to offer supper; neither could eat.

The High King had also rejected Lord Orin's request to accompany him. The two spoke at length for alternative plans should Sumter fall; the survival of his son and foster mother were paramount among the things the king feared for. It was a faint hope: Sumter knew that if he perished, a multitude of mages and sorcerers would search as diligently for Asscher as they had for Rasdeter, and without a protector, his helpless offspring would be child's play to find.

Yet given the chance, Lord Orin knew his wife would be just as determined to give her life for Asscher as she had been for his father Sumter; Irisella had stepped boldly between the then child prince and his uncle Lord Altus, who had just slain his father. Lord Master Brayten had then saved them both, but now the Master Creator was gone. Irisella recalled her words to King Sumter years ago when the rumors of a Lost Prince Rasdeter resurfaced: would Lord Brayten's daughter be willing to help?

Lady Irisella did not know for certain what had passed between her king and the powerful channel known as The Dark One; she only knew the young woman had vanished and Sumter was unwilling to speak of her, even to Irisella.

"My wife..." said Lord Orin, and Irisella turned slightly away from the balcony to see her husband's worried gaze. She wrapped her arms about his waist, and he returned this embrace tightly to comfort her.

"What are your thoughts, beloved," he said kindly, "I know it pains you to watch our king off to battle..." Orin's voice trailed away as his own heart grew heavy.

"I fear to speak them, Orin," said Irisella, "Lest the words leap from my lips and take form..." The regent's wife pressed her face to her husband's chest as though she could indeed rest her cheek against his heart. Her voice tremored; Orin could feel the vibration of it as her lungs moved in and out around it.

"Such a horrid dream..." she whispered, "...and I cannot shake the sight of Sumter falling..."

Before Irisella could release her emotions in Orin's arms, they both heard a soft cry coming from deep within the king's rooms; the Crown Prince and heir was now awake and calling for his father. The couple gazed on each other with the same thought, that Asscher had never spent a night in his home without King Sumter's presence; all his short life had been mostly one of peace. This night was only the beginning of the Toddler Prince's changed world. In this moment he had neither mother nor father and Lady Irisella could not prevent the thought that she had suffered through this before. She could only pray this separation was not a lasting one.

The Battle for Discovery

Even a world war has many smaller battles along the way; the same held true for the final battle at Arin-Clath. High King Sumter had initially responded with three letters; one for the Regents of the Unnamed Lands, one for his presumed cousin Rasdeter, and one for High King N'Goth.

The letter for the regents was crafted according to policy and outlined the basic rules for engagement between the Nine Kingdoms and the seven kingdoms of the Unnamed Lands. Civilized men were required to use diplomacy before shedding blood and speak their intentions in noble language before ripping and hacking one another to pieces. Places to die were decided in advance; scouts and forerunners of armed forces could search for possible advantage on the terrain, giving those not directly involved time to flee for their lives. King Sumter agreed to Arin-Clath, Terranea, and the fields of Koa, disputed territories included Brith and the seas between Lorith and the Boatsmen Clan, for obvious reasons. These disputes would keep the delegates and regents busy while the opposing forces marched towards each other, shaking the earth.

To the High King of the Unnamed Lands, King Sumter's answer was clear:

High King N'Goth:

As I have outlined to the council, I will meet with the King of the Bright Forest in Terranea and test his claim of legitimacy.

You and I shall meet soon afterwards.

No magic. No mages.

High King Sumter.

Laughter was an uncommon sound from King N'Goth; the constant pain from his unhealed wound and his generally unstable state of mind precluded mirth. Yet the response from King Sumter brought joy to his heart. N'Goth knew that any normal man would fear him, and any normal man that did not know of him, soon would. So naturally, he had high regard only for those who stood up to him, despite his fearsome might and brutality.

"You have earned my respect, High King," said N'Goth under his breath, "Which is rare. I will not use my full strength against you, that I might savor the memory of fighting a true man before I slay you..."

Even in battle, most sensible men give King N'Goth a wide berth; his eyes lit up at the memory of the last man he fought without using all his power, one of his own soldiers. He was a man who faced death bravely, not cowering and pleading for mercy, even once the king disarmed him. N'Goth granted the soldier a burial, even though the man had failed his mission; the rest of the soldiers the king slew himself and left their bodies for scavengers and wolves to dine on. The man's family later received an unwarranted stipend, which they were wise enough not to question. The soldier died never knowing his last act would provide for his family forever.

King N'Goth crushed Sumter's parchment and tossed it to the floor, where a nervous page hurriedly scooped it up and placed it on the surging fireplace on the king's right.

"Bring me a fine dark mead," said the king to no one in particular. "A cask of it..."

As his servants and pages scattered, the king's eye fell on a group of females carrying soiled dishes from the hall; one of them was wearing a brightly colored scarf.

"You..." The king spoke and everyone in the hall froze.

"The one with the orange veil; you will stay..."

The young woman's steps halted; her eyes darting around in fear. Her friends did not dare to turn back to look at her; a servant who happened to be standing nearby quickly gathered the burden from her arms and walked away. Her closest friend crushed her ceramic bowls to her bosom, heedless of the stains she pressed against her garments. She stifled a sob as she turned the first corner of the corridor leading to the kitchens; she'd warned her foolish friend not to wear distracting colors in the palace.

But the two women had been called in unexpectedly from the gardens, where it seemed reasonable to wear small things the headmistress could use to distinguish one person from another. Neither friend remembered the scarf until the king's eye fell on it.

The woman in the veil turned and walked back to the king; disobedience was not an option. She stared at her feet as she stood in front of N'Goth, and her mind reeled from all the terrifying stories she'd been told about him. Safe in the kitchens, she would listen to the gossip with her hands over her face; now she would be one of the tales they told.

She went to her knees as the king touched her arm.

"No need to tremble so," N'Goth rumbled, "I won't hurt you..."

The young woman knew this would only be the case until the king was drunk enough; she closed her eyes at the sound of the huge cask being rolled on a rack into the chamber. She spent her time on prayers as the pages delivered the first cup of dark mead and set up the cask to easily dispense more as the king needed it. They vanished as quickly and silently as they came.

"I'm in the mood to celebrate..." N'Goth said aloud to himself as he lifted his cup.

The king's eyes fell on his guards who swiftly left the chamber and closed the heavy doors. They knew to remain outside, no matter what sounds came from the king's rooms. The king drained the large cup easily and poured himself another.

"Tell me your name..." asked the king as the young servant removed her scarf and finished her prayers.

* * *

King Rasdeter retired to his rooms for the evening and left word for his High Regent to leave him undisturbed. He was surprised at his own reaction to receiving a direct communication from his cousin; the young king was no longer able to sit and converse with the mages on mundane topics. Rasdeter listened to the sound of his boots as he paced the suites, the frightened pages mistook his impatience for something amiss with the firestones or the temperature of his bath; he shooed them away. He waited until all tasks were complete before reaching for the wax seal on the parchment; surely his cousin Sumter had pressed it with his own hand. Rasdeter seated himself at the edge of his bed, the veins in his ears throbbing and erasing all his thoughts. Finally, with a determined breath, the king broke the seal; bits of shining wax fell to his evening garments and the tiles beneath his bare feet as Rasdeter began to read:

To King Rasdeter of the Bright Forest:

According to the protocols laid out by the Council of the Four Worlds, you have made claim by right of blood to the throne of the Far Isles. You have claimed before witnesses to be Rasdeter, my first cousin and son of Lord Altus, who was brother to my father, King Valtus, the former High King.

As the High King and legitimate heir of the Far Isles, and father of Crown Prince Asscher, I have exercised my right to confirm your identity by means of diplomacy in an effort to save lives where possible... therefore, we two shall meet in Terranea, where the matter of legitimacy will be settled to the satisfaction of both parties.

The letter was written thus far in the customary formal writing; this was expected. It was the following words that made the young king catch his breath:

If you are truly my cousin, you will have answers to the many questions that have plagued me these long years apart, as I will have answers for you. And if you have succeeded in deceiving all around you, know that I will not be among those, for I know my cousin and I will avenge his memory to any who desecrate it...

The new king's hands began to shake as he read the last words:

My cousin would not come against me in this way, King Rasdeter. If any has ensnared you by magic or devious means, know that I will move heaven and earth to free you, this I vow...

In all truth, High King Sumter

Men do not weep as easily as do women, nor is there any fault in an expression of emotion. Rasdeter's heart opened fully at this offering from his cousin; an olive branch for pain remembered and mutually shared. His mind reeled from the revelations; Sumter had a son whose life he feared for, his determination to avenge his lost cousin's memory, and Sumter's vow to free his childhood friend and near brother from the intrigues of magic.

Though alone, Rasdeter pressed his face into the pillows and cushions of his bed, overcome. He could not convince himself of the reasons why he wished so badly to return to a former life that no longer existed.

"You cannot assist me, cousin," he whispered, "I am beyond all help..."

The young king drifted off in uneasy slumber, and the parchment fell from his relaxed fingers.

Who I Say I Am

A few weeks later, King Rasdeter and his troops reached Ter-ranea, a place where earth, sky, and water meet. Huge arches of grassy soil and stone rise from the sea miles high into the air to catch low drifting clouds. The stunning beauty of this land helped distract the young king from the heaviness threatening to choke his heart and depress his spirit.

All that High King N'Goth had warned King Rasdeter of had come to pass as his army marched southwest. He'd been forced to watch the burning of cities and villages, the deaths and destruction of people too slow or defiant to move from his path. High General Brennan felt sympathy for his monarch each time Rasdeter's face paled; mercenaries and former criminals bolstered their forces, and the horrific acts these men performed against helpless men, women and children kept the former prince from sleep.

"Brennan," Rasdeter asked one evening as they made plans for the days ahead, "We march towards eventual battle which may be months away and these men see rare conflict from any who can resist our forces. Can we not direct the lower generals to restrain such men to more honorable actions?"

The general considered his words.

"I can advise the generals to keep these men further away from your line of sight, my lord," answered Brennan, "But in all truth, no more than this can be asked. They march to their deaths, my king, in your name. Without promise of coarse rewards, most of them would scatter throughout the land, wreaking havoc with no direction, and we cannot afford to divert men to control them."

Rasdeter shook his head to contain his disgust.

"It would be well then to send such beasts to the front of the footmen," said the king wearily, "To give our more noble soldiers a chance to live out the days ahead."

High General Brennan smiled grimly.

"Of course, you will send them to the front of the army, my lord," said Brennan, "Every king does this to conserve his own forces. This is why, in a crude way such animals feel compelled to rape and slay everything in their path; they know the dogs die first in battle."

The shocked new king had no answer for this; Rasdeter reached for the latest ground reports and wondered why he had ever longed to be a king or leader of men.

When the king's thoughts turned to his wife, his heart grew heavy. As the miles marched away beneath his feet and lengthened the distance between them, Rasdeter could not hold on to the anger and sense of betrayal he'd felt when he first returned to The Bright Forest. Once his need to share the pain he suffered was spent the young king regretted his actions; surely, he could have given Saramis the opportunity to explain...

But when the king's thoughts turned to his once rival, Bowman Kha, Rasdeter felt himself spiral off again into hateful imaginings. High King N'Goth remembered both how he came across the hunter and where he found him. It was a path only miles from those the Wanderers would take to avoid the kingdoms; Rasdeter knew it well from years of walking the same byways.

That the Bowman was seeking some sort of contact with his queen was plain to any man with eyes to see it, reasoned the king, the question was, would Saramis welcome it?

Finally, Rasdeter decided they would speak of it on his return, he had plenty enough to concern his waking hours as he marched towards Sumter and his former life.

Enith did not accompany his king to this meeting, nor did he allow Iroh to. Rasdeter did not know that the Ancient feared to cross the path of the Dark One, who was rumored to visit the Far Isles, as had been the habit of her father Lord Brayten. Instead, he watched from afar and sent Keoni to marshal his defenses, and unknown to his loyal servant, to die in his stead if need required it. The mage had not forgotten the fearsome signature of creation that saved Bowman Kha from King Rasdeter's death blow, and he was smart enough to remain from harm's way.

High Regent Ghent insisted on traveling with his king for more reasons than he could give a number to. Keeping his thoughts from his once family being the most pressing concern, second was the magic seeping from his heart. Enith had fashioned a special garment for the regent to wrap around his torso to prevent him slaying those around him. Now that Ghent was infused with magic from the Ancient, he was now an asset should Rasdeter's army be waylaid by sorcerers. However, the formerly powerless regent still fought a battle against the darkness in him; a part of Ghent was looking forward to the moment he could give away some of the pain he suffered. His knuckles whitened on his reins as the regent fought off visions of spilled blood and agony.

The armies of the Bright Forest rumbled as they moved over the lands leading to the coast, and Rasdeter felt confident until he saw the armies of the Far Isles waiting for him across the plains. He could see no end to them, he felt as though they covered the earth and mountains like a blanket of purple and gold.

"Brennan..." the young king's voice trailed away as his jaw set, but his general's response was measured and calm.

"King Sumter is a man of honor, my lord," said the High General. "This show of force is meant to intimidate, as our is. He will only attack by right if you are not found to be a blood heir to his kingdom, and then after battle lines are drawn."

As Rasdeter turned his head to gaze in concern at Brennan, his general steadied his mount.

"Our lives are now in your hands, my king," said the general quietly. "We have all placed our trust in who you say you are..."

Sick to his stomach, Brennan's king could say no more; the weight of this entire enterprise was upon him. The trio of Rasdeter, Brennan, and Ghent silently watched as the envoys from both kingdoms rode out to greet each other. Soon, a swarm of men from either side came forth to erect a huge tent for the kings and generals to meet peacefully; Rasdeter dismounted and was surrounded by his personal guard. Far away in the distance, he saw this action mirrored by the enemy soldiers and knew one of these men approaching was his cousin Sumter, High King of the Far Isles. Shields were raised high over the kings as they marched forward, and Rasdeter saw this was a common precaution.

Though the meeting was peaceful, an archer could be tempted to have a place in history as the man who killed an enemy king and set off a world war.

Rasdeter could hear nothing but the blood hammering through his temples as he neared the huge tent; his lower generals held the flaps aside for his entrance. A man stood across from him, flanked by stern and anxious soldiers; Rasdeter imagined his people looked the same. The man slowly reached for his helmet; a subtle reminder to the young king that he was yet wearing his. Rasdeter removed his helmet, placing it in the crook of his arm and the two men looked at each other.

Both men flinched; though years had separated them, their eyes had never changed.

Rasdeter felt his hand tighten on his helmet as Sumter's gold eyes flecked with amber stared at him; the king could still be eleven years old and anxious to celebrate his twelfth birthday. Sumter's eyes widened in astonishment as he met Rasdeter's vibrant green eyes muted by gold, the dark brown hair still wavy and untamed.

His body went rigid; this must be magic...

That the two men recognized each other was clear to everyone in the room. When Rasdeter tore his eyes from Sumter and met those of Marcus, the High General of the Far Isles felt an electric shock. He knew Rasdeter, and if one could ever imagine the boy growing up into a man, this would be the image of him. Marcus felt Hesta tense up beside him and realized that if this was indeed an illusion, it included more than him.

As Rasdeter turned his gaze from Sumter, the High King's eyes fell on Ghent, Rasdeter's High Regent. His eyes widened in alarm as he detected magic coming from the regent, despite his shielding garment.

Ghent bowed deeply and backed away as Sumter's soldiers moved in front of him.

"Forgive me, my lord," said Ghent sincerely, "I will wait outside..."

The gaze of the High King was now skeptical as they returned to Rasdeter, who made a derisive sound.

"Sumter, cousin," said Rasdeter with a slight smile, "Do you truly believe I need magic to convince you of who I am?"

Recovering, the High King of the Far Isles shook his head in wonder. Though the tone of the voice had changed with manhood, the manner of speech and the facial expressions of the man standing across from Sumter mirrored his childhood memories.

"If it were possible..." the king mused, "For my cousin to be taken from my memories and fashioned into a grown man, there could be no better magic than this."

Sumter placed his hand firmly on Marcus, who reluctantly moved from in front of him. "We will have words, then, Rasdeter," continued the king, "Sufficient to remove all doubt from either of us..."

"Yes," replied Rasdeter with a strong voice, "As you have said, I have questions for you as you have for me, these long years away from my home..."

King Sumter noticed the tremor in King Rasdeter's voice as he spoke with emotion that cannot be pretended; he answered with his own.

"How can you be alive, Rasdeter?" Sumter asked in pain, "Was Lord Brayten deceived as he viewed Aton's memories?"

But King Rasdeter shook his head.

"I will speak of this only with you, Sumter," stated his cousin firmly. "These are things only you and I would know the truth of...have you not heard enough lies and half-truths?"

Ironically, both High Generals leaned in closer to council against leaving, but both cousins responded in the negative.

"Clear the tent," commanded Sumter, and Marcus, his most loyal soldier and general obeyed reluctantly, as did Brennan to Rasdeter's nod.

***

The two kings talked at length; Rasdeter shared his tale of being saved by Saramis, and Sumter's heart constricted in his chest, both for his cousin and for Aton, who died for his intention of slaying Rasdeter. It was not the first time Sumter also mourned Lord Brayten, whom as Irisella reasoned would have soon ascertained the truth and perhaps saved both Rasdeter and Aton.

"You may have forgiven General Aton, cousin," said Rasdeter darkly, "But I will not."

"I did not forgive him for trying to kill you, Rasdeter," replied Sumter firmly. "You see this now...and if the place I have given Aton grieves you, I will take it down myself to calm your heart."

Rasdeter had no answer for this offer, and the look of sincerity and determination on his cousin's face disarmed him for a moment.

"Why didn't you come home?!" asked the High King in despair, for he knew the answer his cousin would give.

"Were you in my place, would you have done so, Sumter?!?" responded Rasdeter in frustration, "Everyone has told me it would be logical and reasonable for you to try to kill me...!"

Neither man was aware that as Rasdeter became more agitated, the wound in his heart throbbed in sympathy. As always, memories of General Aton brought Rasdeter's fears and anger to the surface. Ghent forced himself to move further away from the tent as an unreasoning hatred for Sumter flowed through him.

Keoni observed these movements and silently conferred with his master Enith, who was a world away in the Unnamed Lands.

Enith, who stood with Iroh in an empty dining hall, looked through Keoni's eyes to spy Ghent moving quickly towards the horsemen of the Bright Forest and away from the tent. Iroh easily projected the thoughts and visions of Keoni onto the wall of the room.

"Why is Ghent so far away, Keoni?" asked Enith.

"As High Regent of the Bright Forest," reasoned Iroh, "Ghent should be at the side of his king, assisting with diplomacy should emotions run high..."

"High King Sumter requested no mages near the council, my lord," replied Keoni in a whisper, resulting in a sound of frustration from the Ancient. The mage moved away from the earshot of others, so he could speak louder without his words being overheard.

"Gaze again on the tent where they gather," directed his master, and Keoni obeyed. Once there, Master Iroh had questions of his own.

"Is everyone outside the tent, Keoni?" asked Iroh in curiosity, "Our High General Brennan should be inside to protect King Rasdeter..."

"Both High Generals are outside the tent, my lords," replied Keoni. "In fact, there doesn't seem to be anyone within the tent but the two kings..."

Inside the tent, Sumter paced the perimeter while Rasdeter stood in misery.

"It is true, then," asked Rasdeter hoarsely, "What the mage said, that my father killed my mother...for yours?"

King Sumter also paused at this painful reminder.

"Poison..." he answered quietly. "Lord Brayten spoke with Lord Altus who confessed as he read his memories..."

Where he had railed and raged against Enith for the words of truth he spoke, Rasdeter stood mute before his cousin, who yet held his love. Images of the two boys running and playing around their mothers, who were truly helpless to control them without the firm and loving hand of Irisella, stirred his mind. The young king saw again his father, Lord Altus, strolling through the corridors of the palace, his uncle King Valtus' home. He'd always assumed that his father spent so much time there because of his many duties as second in command of the kingdom; with a wrench of his heart, Rasdeter realized that Lord Altus sought the company of his brother's wife.

"Your father also said no one knew of his feelings," added Sumter. "Even less my mother, Queen Inka, which eased my own soul, though she died of a broken heart less than a week after my father…"

Rasdeter could not help but think to himself how these events mirrored what happened with General Brennan and King Templin. As he pondered this in the silence that followed, the king continued.

"Lord Brayten said these feelings Lord Altus had were a weakness the forces of evil were eager to exploit. Your father was…possessed by the mages, Rasdeter," offered Sumter in a subdued tone. "They stabbed him with an enchanted blade through the heart to control him…"

Rasdeter's face whitened at these words.

"Brayten slew the one behind it…A star being known as Izar, The Twins…"

King Rasdeter was speechless; his hands bunched the cloth over his tunic as he recalled the look on his father's face when last he saw him, feverish and pale…like himself.

His cousin, the High King, who did not know Rasdeter's thoughts, went on with the speaking of his mind and heart. Sumter's words were healing his own pain as he gave them forth; his mind now set on how he could redeem these sad events and bring his suffering relative home to the Far Isles.

"There must be something we can do, cousin," said Sumter resolutely. "Without you, they have no cause for war." The High King stopped his pacing and turned to King Rasdeter. "If you truly wish to come home, Rasdeter, there must be a way, for you and Queen Saramis. Lady Irisella wishes desperately to see you again…"

The image of Lady Irisella's face loomed before the young king and memories of her kindness and love hammered at Rasdeter.

"Irisella…" he whispered, "She is well?"

The king gave a sound between a sigh and a chuckle.

"She begged me to come; to see you for herself. Of course, I could not allow this..." Sumter sighed again at Rasdeter's understanding shake of his head, "Polymus is too old for the journey, though he is High Regent..."

"Polymus..." said Rasdeter wistfully, "I remember his lessons still..."

Now it was King Sumter's turn to glaze his eyes in memory.

"I'm not certain what the protocol is for a foreign king to return home," mused Sumter. "Or even if it's been done before now. You might declare yourself a Fallen Noble, but for your troops and generals; surely they will not leave Terranea without you..."

The King of the Far Isles made a self-depreciating sound.

"We may well have to fight our way out of here..."

Rasdeter heard these words of welcome from his cousin with longing, but behind the need was a darkness he had yet to share with his childhood friend. Sumter was startled to see his cousin lift his head and meet his gaze with brimming eyes.

"I wish so much to return home, Sumter," said Rasdeter in sorrow. "You may never understand what these words we've shared have meant to me..."

The young king shook his head, wracked in agony of the soul as his mind turned again to Templin, whom he could not forgive himself for slaying and Enith, the one he hated, who controlled him, as his pawn.

"But you don't know what I've done to reach this place, cousin...you shouldn't trust me..."

A world away, the Ancient immediately became still, and Iroh knew Enith was searching Rasdeter's past memories to see if the two kings were alone. In seconds, he met the gaze of Iroh with a start.

"They're completely alone..." said Enith in disbelief.

Iroh spoke urgently.

"You must strike now, Enith!"

Keoni whirled at the sound of his master's name.

"What is your will, my lord?" he said earnestly.

"Stand fast, Keoni," shouted Enith, "This is not for you to do...!"

The Ancient reached out, and thousands of miles away, Ghent fell to his knees, his fists clenched in blinding pain. A whisper escaped his grimaced lips.

"Kill him..."

A strobe of darkness roared from Ghent's chest and hurled through the air towards the tent occupied by Sumter and Rasdeter. King Sumter gasped in amazement as the strobe pierced the fabric of the tent and blasted into the chest of King Rasdeter, bringing him to his knees with a groan.

"By the hounds," shouted Sumter in rage, "I said no magic...!"

Unknown to the king as he rushed to his cousin's side, the Ancient known as Enith had eliminated all sounds coming from the tent. Neither Marcus nor Brennan who were listening for raised voices heard anything as Sumter knelt to assist his cousin. A blade materialized in Rasdeter's hand which came swiftly up, aiming true for King Sumter's heart.

"Kill him..." the young king echoed with misted eyes, and the High King heard the voice of Enith behind his cousin's.

Sumter used all his strength to catch Rasdeter's wrist, grunting as the tip of the diverted blade drew blood from his shoulder. At the king's touch, Rasdeter cried out and dropped the blade as something unexpected happened; creation flowed up from the ground and through Sumter into Rasdeter, who grasped his chest and slipped again to the ground.

Rasdeter reached for Sumter's hand and held it weakly.

"Don't trust me, cousin," gasped Rasdeter, "Or the love I bear you and my home..."

The King of the Bright Forest slipped into unconsciousness.

The High King could not say later why he reached forth and pulled apart the robe over Rasdeter's chest; Sumter's face drained of blood as he beheld the scars over his cousin's heart.

"Sorcery!" King Sumter cried, and then quickly covered his cousin as the guards of both kingdoms came into the tent at the sound of his voice. The king came to his feet.

"Stand back," the king commanded as Marcus and Brennan squared off. "I've not harmed him, your king has been struck down by magic; the protocols of this meeting are yet in force..."

"Rasdeter is our king, my lord," said Brennan tensely as a reminder. "As High General of his troops, you must release him to me..."

King Sumter was reluctant to leave his cousin so soon after finding him, but he knew he had to. Rasdeter was now a leader of his own kingdom; he was no longer a subject of the Far Isles and his cousin had no authority to claim him. And while unconscious, Rasdeter could not speak for himself and make known his will.

Shielded by his guards as he strode back to his army, Sumter felt angry and helpless.

So long I felt your death was among the worst things that have happened to me, the king thought. *Now I find you alive and ensnared by loathsome magicians, who wish to use you to destroy me. And should they succeed in turning you completely against me, one of us must die in order to save my son. Would I had listened when they first spoke of you, cousin. Had I found you first...*

Then the young ruler shook his head.

Now I indulge in fantasy, Rasdeter, for it was I who thought to exile you and save your life. This would have only made you easier to find for those who wished to use you.

King Sumter's mind now turned to Saramis.

A great debt is owed for the years you've added to his life, Queen *Saramis, yet even you were unable to save him from the mages. Is there any part of this path that does not end badly?*

The guards standing in front of Sumter's tent held the flaps open for the king's entrance. He waved away the healers trying to bind his wound, the bleeding had stopped almost immediately. Sumter's High General stood by in misery; his gut had twisted when Marcus entered the council tent to find his king bleeding from a surface wound from King Rasdeter.

"What say you, Marcus?" asked his lord kindly, so his beloved general could speak his mind.

Marcus took a deep breath and sighed.

"Had you asked me as soon as he removed his helmet," said Marcus, "I would swear on my life that it was Rasdeter returned from the dead. But now that he's raised his hand against you…"

"It is he," replied Sumter firmly. "He shared things with me that no one but Rasdeter could know…" and the king's mind turned to Rasdeter sharing the story of Valtus and the shared throne, down to what he and Sumter were wearing. Things about his mother Princess Erami and even Lord Altus that only two boys who grew up together would share. The fabrics Sumter selected for his birthday celebration that never happened, hunting with Lord Altus and all the mischief the pair had done and gotten away with; things no adult in Sumter's world would know.

"…and he told me not to trust him, Marcus, just before the bolt of energy struck him. Would one trying to deceive you do such?" Sumter said in conclusion.

"No, my lord…" answered Marcus, but his expression was doubtful. The king stepped closer and roughly grasped his friend's shoulder.

"I know your loyalty lies with me, Marcus," offered Sumter, "So I will not ask you to agree with me. But I believe him to be my true cousin, so I must do all I can to free Rasdeter from sorcery."

"And if he comes against you, my lord, despite all these things?" asked Marcus quietly.

King Sumter turned from his friend and general and crossed his arms.

"Asscher must live to rule," responded Sumter resolutely, and his general nodded; for Marcus there was no more to say. As High General, like Aton, he was committed to Sumter's bloodline; if it came to it, Marcus would not waver.

"In this moment, Marcus, all I can recall are the words of General Aton..." Sumter began, and his general finished for him:

"'If he had lived, he would have risen against you'...," quoted Marcus. "Lord Altus set forth a chain of events with few choices to the outcome, my king."

"Hounds take him..." whispered Sumter.

There was silence in the king's tent as he gathered his thoughts. Marcus felt himself dismissed; he bowed quickly and left.

Sumter gazed at his bed in the opposite corner of his haven with a rueful smile; he knew there would be no rest for him tonight. He sat down in his chair and twenty minutes later realized he had dozed off.

"Summon my generals," the king barked in the direction of the tent's opening and heard the boots of his soldiers hurrying away. Sumter walked over to his war table and ran his fingers lightly over the piles of maps and reports.

There will be war, he thought darkly, and it matters not which one of us falls, cousin, the earth will be soaked with blood.

The king paused as he felt the ground tremble beneath his feet. He gave a slight chuckle.

"Great lizards," he mused aloud. "And probably near the mountains. Surely, the coming battle is not enough to concern me; now I must consider how to keep them from trampling my men and disrupting our war."

Several sleepless hours later, after his discourse and strategy with his generals, the king would be exceedingly grateful for the Great Lizards, that one day would be called dinosaurs, trapped in the mountains. Their presence would yield an unexpected meeting with The Dark One, and a rout of King Rasdeter's forces, including the distant Enith and Iroh, who missed their opportunity to end the war early by reaching their objective, the death of Sumter.

The king's own personal war with The Destroyer would take a surprising turn, finally offering both insight and advantage.

But all these things were yet to happen; the King of the Far Isles sat down to his desk and rendered stain on parchment, to send news of his cousin to his foster mother, news that would gladden and then sadden Lady Irisella's heart.

Honor and Recovery

The discovery council at Terranea succeeded and failed at once. Sumter sent word to the council of regents acknowledging King Rasdeter as his cousin and blood relative third in line to the throne of the Far Isles. Crown Prince Asscher was named as the Blood Heir; this meant that Rasdeter could only ascend the throne through the death of both Sumter and Asscher.

King Sumter, however, did not exercise his right to battle his cousin to the death at Terranea.

The king disclosed to the council:

After the intrigues of magic displayed at Terranea, it is my summation that this is not a battle for the throne of the Far Isles, but a battle for dominance by magic over the hearts of men. Should I prove victorious and slay my cousin the conflict will continue, for what is wanted is the prize of the Nine Kingdoms; not one throne, but eight more. Therefore, we will meet the Seven Kingdoms of the Unnamed Lands at Arin-Clath and strive to free all souls from tyranny and return men to personal choice.

In All Truth, High King Sumter

Unhappy with the outcome between the two kings, the Ancient kept a suspicious eye on his prize, the King of the Bright Forest. After meeting with his cousin at Terranea, the former prince's emotions were becoming more difficult to control. Enith viewed again and again the moment when Sumter grasped his cousin's wrist and stopped Rasdeter's deadly thrust for his heart. The battle at Arin-Clath was only months away; the advancing armies of Rasdeter took shelter at the palace of the Kingdom of the Sea Gates; it was there Enith decided to make his most daring move to subdue his king.

Suspicious to Vicious

Since that fateful day that Rasdeter met with Sumter, the young king was feeling regret for all his previous actions. He read Sumter's letter almost daily and relived the moment when his cousin tried to help him and the shameful reward Rasdeter had rendered.

The King of the Bright Forest prepared for rest with a heavy heart. Rasdeter began to wonder if there were some way out of this massive conflict; some way he could be at peace with his homeland, even if he could not stay.

If I truly changed my mind, he reasoned, I could return to the Wanderers, become Pax again. Surely the Great Elder could protect me from Enith...

The young king drifted off into slumber, dreams of home returned to his mind.

A few hours later, Rasdeter was stirred from his rest by a sound in the room with him. He opened one bleary eye and furrowed his brow as he noticed the parchment from King Sumter floating in the air beside his bed. He then sat up quickly as he beheld the cloth beginning to burn at the edges.

"No..." he said aloud and thrust back the sheets to reach for the precious document.

Rasdeter whirled as the air to his right shimmered and parted; the Ancient burst through an opening in the dimensions, accompanied by two mages on either side of him. The wax melted as the parchment fully exploded into flames.

"No!" the king shouted as he came to his feet. "Enith, you dare not!"

But the Ancient's eyes shone with malice.

"I dare as I please, Rasdeter," answered the mage. "It is well that I happened to peruse your recent thoughts and felt the weakening of your heart towards your cousin. You will not foreswear me, little king!"

Instinctively, the young king lunged for his weapon, the Prince's Sword. Enith did not respond to this action; instead, he stood silently watching Rasdeter with narrowed eyes. The mages with the Ancient were fiercely obedient; they would not move without a word from their master. Rasdeter took a defensive stance, his heart pounding. He did not know what had provoked the mage, but he knew the Ancient would not hesitate to enforce his will.

"Why do you approach me in rage, Enith?" asked the king to distract the mage. "What offense is between us?"

Enith did not answer; it was clear he was attempting to control his anger. A storm had begun to whip about the chamber and the king could see everything rolling around and crashing into the walls as the winds released it. The sounds of porcelain and glass shattering echoed everywhere.

The king's mind raced through his past thoughts before sleeping; when he remembered his emotions on the subject of his cousin, Rasdeter's hand tightened on his sword. It seemed every father figure in his life had either betrayed or manipulated him; his own feelings of frustration and resentment roared forth.

If he died, so be it; Rasdeter would die in defense of himself.

"You're all the same," the king cried as he charged the Ancient. "Trying to control what you do not love or understand!"

The Ancient thrust his arms forward and Rasdeter felt himself lifted and hurled against the wall behind his bed. He cried out from the impact and struggled against the invisible restraints on his arms and legs. The mages who stood next to Enith were silent, awaiting his will.

"Release me, Enith," demanded Rasdeter, "What madness is this?"

The Ancient's voice, however, was tense with wrath, and the young king began to pale as he listened to the mage's words.

"I imagined it enough to stab you through the heart and darken that same heart with the guilt of Templin's blood; to taint you with the bloody use of the Prince's Sword. But no...still you fight me with the disgusting emotions of love and compassion; the desire for union as opposed to separation. No more, Rasdeter! I've gentled you enough, now you will learn the true use for the Blade of Twin Souls..."

Enith stretched out his hands in the air, placed them against each other with the palms facing outward; he curled his fingers and with a slow motion, separated them as though pulling something apart.

The young king screamed mindlessly as the Ancient callously reopened the wound over his heart. In another chamber, High Regent Ghent gasped and gripping his chest, fell to the tiles, senseless. Brennan rushed to his side, but was unable to rouse Ghent, whose mouth gaped, and half lidded eyes stared at nothing. The general looked up to Keoni, whose usual smug demeanor dissolved into horror as he gazed down on his former rival.

The mages on Enith's left and right suddenly shimmered and appeared transparent; at a nod from the Ancient, they folded themselves dimensionally and entered the ruptured flesh and embedded into Rasdeter's heart. Rasdeter spasmed and dropped to the floor as Enith released him, his eyes dim and sightless.

Iroh appeared in the king's rooms to find the Ancient standing over his quarry, his own chest heaving from exertion.

"By the heavens, Enith," said Iroh in apprehension, "What have you done to him? I had to blanket the sounds of his screams from the entire palace!"

"He forced my hand, Iroh," replied the Ancient in a near whisper, blinking rapidly to cover his own dismay. "I had no other option; he'd almost completely changed his mind...I would have lost him forever. Thus I pushed the blade deeper and sent two mages to guard it. Hounds take him..."

Iroh gazed in wonder at the king's face, sunken and lifeless.

"Is he alive?"

Enith nodded after a moment, then spoke.

"Yes...if not for Ghent, he would be dead..."

"And your High Regent, Enith?" asked Iroh incredulously, "You cannot slay them both...!"

The Ancient stood breathing deeply then chanced a sideways glance at his former pupil. "I will need your assistance, Iroh..."

"You have it," answered the sorcerer. "What must be done?"

The two mages conferred quietly amongst themselves over Rasdeter's unconscious body.

Ursa Roars, part II

Queen Saramis endured many sleepless nights as she waited for news of her husband's progress on the road to war. Not the least of the things tormenting Saramis were the words exchanged between them before Rasdeter departed, leaving her despondent and yearning for his company.

The only people who could enlighten her as to what changed her husband had accompanied him; High Regent Ghent and High General Brennan. It puzzled Saramis that Enith remained in the Hall of Mages with Keoni. Why the Ancient would pass on the opportunity to see his plans come to fruition gave the young queen much to ponder.

All questions, however, were answered weeks later, when during the middle of the night the Ancient vanished. The queen felt her rest disturbed when the unrelenting low vibration of the mage's power lifted, and she felt a calmness settle over the palace. Saramis returned to sleep, only to be devastated by a power surge she could feel a world away. As the queen sat up in her bed, her immediate thoughts were of her husband the king. Saramis drew her hair back from her face ruefully; her braid had become undone during restless dreams.

Still sleepy, Rasdeter's wife reached out with her mind to sense his heartbeat and brainwaves, which should be at rest.

But she felt nothing.

Saramis leapt from her bed, summoning her robes in terror about her. Gone were the feelings of hurt from his wounding words and stern glances, Saramis only knew she must find the man she loved and quickly.

I will gladly accept your coldness over your absence, beloved, she thought in agony, Only tarry until I am again by your side.

* * *

Master Iroh and Lord Enith had just laid King Rasdeter and High Regent Ghent on separate beds alongside each other when they felt a shift in energy; they both turned in time to see Queen Saramis materialize next to her fallen husband. Unable to even speak, the young queen reached out over Rasdeter's chest but did not touch him; she stood gazing at the vacant stare in his eyes; he looked as one dead.

When her eyes lifted to the mages, Enith unconsciously stepped in front of Iroh.

"Enith…" began the master mage, but his former mentor was resolute.

"Leave us, I pray you," asked the Ancient, who had little regard for the Queen of the Bright Forest.

"As you say…" responded Iroh doubtfully but obedient to his friend's wishes. The master mage could sense that there was something the Ancient did not wish for him to see as Enith dealt with Saramis. Iroh couldn't help but notice there was something different about how the former Woman of the Woods gazed on her husband's tormentor, but he couldn't place it; with a shrug, Iroh turned and vanished.

They faced one another over the unconscious King of the Bright Forest, his master, and his wife. The Ancient huffed sarcastically as he felt the earth rumble gently beneath his feet.

"Now comes the expounding of the virtues of good over evil," stated the Ancient, "The salvation of a supposedly 'good man'…"

"Does it?" responded Saramis softly as she locked her gaze on Enith.

This calm answer gave the mage pause; his eyes narrowed as he appraised the king's wife. He began to circle Saramis, who slowly rotated to his orbit in silence.

"You speak to me thus because of the safety of Paza's protection, 'Woman of the Woods'," continued Enith. "Your fragile assurance that I will not harm you..."

"Do I?" said Saramis, and the Ancient stopped his pace and rendered the young queen an incredulous gaze.

"Are you...Do you challenge me, child?" said the Ancient in wonder. "Your paltry might is nothing compared to the ages of power I wield!"

The silence lengthened between them as they stared at one another. Finally, Queen Saramis responded.

"Is it?"

Rage and disbelief blinded Enith; his promise to Paza forgotten in an instant, he raised his hands and pulled his power together. Yet the young woman did not falter or raise her own hands in fear. Instead Saramis brow cleared as she repeated her words.

"Is it?"

For answer, the mage hurled his might towards the queen, who placing her hand on her husband's chest, pulled the radiation pulsing from both Ghent and Rasdeter and sent it roaring through her other hand to the Ancient. Struck by his own combined might, Enith flew backwards and slammed into the wall behind him. The Woman of the Woods watched as the Ancient's face contorted with anger and became unrecognizable. He spoke with contempt.

"I...will...annihilate you...you...Wanderer!"

Saramis stepped calmly away from her husband and friend and faced the mage directly. Enith now heard the quiet resolve underneath her somber tone.

"Can you?" She asked as she met his distorted visage.

It had been eons since the Ancient had pulled this much power from deep within himself; ages since he faced another like himself in pitched battle; yet Enith had won. He measured himself only to be certain he focused on Saramis; she would become as dust and shifted into the air; there would be nothing left for even Paza to save.

But the young Woman of the Woods did not defend against Enith's wrath; instead Saramis began to glow with light. Her mind became a prism for the light she knew existed from her vision with the Great Elder, a light that had no end and no shadows. As the darkness hurled forth from the Ancient her form disappeared, not into darkness, but into a Light that cannot be countered or held back; everything vanished and from a faraway place, what was once known as Saramis heard the Ancient cry out in agony.

"Can you, Enith?" the Light asked again; the battered mage and the two who hid in her husband's heart fled from her presence.

Sound ceased for a time as the Light coalesced into Saramis as the Woman of the Woods remembered herself. Breathing deeply, she opened her eyes and looked on a world without shadows or darkness. Eventually, normal vision returned, and the young queen moved again into the space between her husband and the regent. She realized that Enith would never threaten her again, but this was a small comfort, for Saramis knew she could not prevent the mage from using magic against Rasdeter as long as the king believed Enith could. In the silence following the mage's departure, the queen gazed down in love on the man she lived for and could not save.

"I understand you now," she said gently to Rasdeter's vacant eyes. "You cannot consciously see that you will not turn from this path while this body you wear holds breath...and you have just shown me that although I do see the dangers before us; I also will not leave you while I draw breath..."

Saramis turned her head slightly towards the comatose Ghent and smiled in compassion.

"The mage has separated you from life and family, Ghent, because you believe he can do so, and the faith we give power to is all that drives us..."

Her mind turned to the Great Elder, who taught Saramis that every action or reaction involves choice whether conscious or not, and that thought returns fulfilled and never empty.

The young queen sighed as she looked down at the two men of importance in her life.

"We are in agreement then, to walk together to the end we are all determined to experience; to know every dark thing that is possible to know, to the point where it seems light can no longer find us..."

She raised her hands above the chests of both men; Saramis closed her eyes.

"I have chosen you, Rasdeter, and I will not repent my choice," she said with brimming eyes. "I will go with you, my husband, my love, my heart, until I have no body to move with and no eyes to see with, until nothing that can be hurt is left..."

With these words, the woman known as Saramis, Woman of the Woods and Queen of the Bright Forest, placed her hands firmly on her king and her regent, and shuddered as she brought the rumbling power of creation up through her body and into theirs.

* * *

Paza Returns

Later that same evening, when the young king opened his eyes, his gaze first fell on Saramis, his wife. But the king said nothing, he simply gave her his heart in his eyes, and she gave him hers. The queen's presence told Rasdeter everything he needed to discern; he had not expected to return from the dark place the Ancient had sent him to, and the forgiveness he saw in her eyes left no reason for explanation or apology. For long moments they gave each other no words while Saramis gently stroked Rasdeter's dark and wavy hair. Then the king reached up and tenderly began to release the bindings of his queen's headdress and sighed at her loving smile.

Rasdeter's High Regent, however, came to consciousness alone in his private rooms in the Hall of Mages. Ghent's limbs felt heavy and he struggled to recall what passed before. Soon the regent realized he was no longer alone; Ghent carefully turned his head in the direction of his window and saw the Starchild Paza gazing up and out at the planets and burning orbs in the night sky.

"Great Mistress…" Ghent struggled to speak, and his words faded as he beheld Paza hold out her hand towards him.

"Please join me, High Regent," said Paza kindly. "I wish to show you something…"

Ghent found the strength to come to his feet and found himself surrounded by her power; it made walking easier.

Beautiful dark velvet greeted him, interspersed with brilliant blazing stars and nearby planets. Ghent sighed in appreciation at the belt of Orion, Ursa and her cub and all the constellations with their ancient and future names displayed before him.

"You've made them all brighter," He said happily, and followed the motion of Paza's hand.

"Now, watch, Ghent," Paza said, and the regent gasped as the sky shifted and all the stars changed pattern and position.

"What have you done?" Ghent asked in wonder, he now recognized nothing.

Paza gazed down at Ghent serenely.

"You are now seeing the constellations from the viewpoint of the star we call Sirius, Ghent," responded the Starchild. "I show you this to demonstrate the importance of where you are standing; how the influence of the planetary movements is determined by your exact placement in space and time."

The Starchild sighed.

"No ordinary person living, or dead has ever seen all of Creation, regent," offered Paza soberly, "It is infinite in design and purpose, that we may soon learn we mirror it..."

"Are you offering me hope, Paza?" asked the regent softly as his mind turned to Enith. "Are you saying there is power beyond the one who controls me?"

"I am saying that as Enith also strives to be greater than the one he follows; you can rise above the fear that holds you back."

Paza heard sadness beneath the wonder in Ghent's voice.

"Why are you telling me these things, Mistress?"

"All creatures that are bound seek freedom, regent," answered Paza thoughtfully. "Even those like me, who appear to be infinitely powerful."

As the two gazed together on the breathtaking spectacle of the heavens, the Starchild felt an unaccustomed emotion: Joy.

"For the numberless eons of my existence, I thought the key to my freedom from the First Brother was locked in the past, Ghent. Now I see it is before me, and soon..."

ONE HIGH KING

*'There is not anything returned to nothing, but all things return
dissolved into their elements.'*
~~~Lucretius, De Rerum Natura, 50 BC

The Final Conflict, part I

The King of Worm's Hollow moved prematurely against the King of The Deep Places, striking down the flank of his third division in the valleys leading to the agreed battlefield. The treacherous king decided to use his mages against the forces of The Deep Places, which contained footmen of the Far Isles and the refugees that had trained in the last year to fight for the freedom of their families.

"It is a king's privilege to reserve his forces for battle," said King Mrinal smugly to High General Azymbek. "What better way than magic to spare my own men?"

"To my knowledge, the Kingdom of the Deep Places have no true mages to defend themselves with, my king," agreed his general with a smile.

"Then the hounds shall feast well, general," replied the king. "Give the order..."

Unaware of these things, General Koa of the Deep Places directed his lieutenants and archers in preparation for arrival at the battle-field. Driken, a refugee from the Far Isles listened attentively, eager to obey and show his loyalty. Often, his hand wandered unconsciously to a small belt around his chest; within it stored a trinket from his wife Nard and small daughter Zarina. He shook his head
~~~

from the memory of Nard running alongside the marching soldiers for as long as she could for a glimpse of Driken, carrying his toddler offspring, who waved absently, unable to see him.

The soldiers cleared the way for a scout who came running with an escort to the general, breathless, and terrified. General Koa signaled for a pouch of water and the grateful scout rinsed the dust from his throat quickly and spoke in hurried gasps.

"They're coming, General Koa," the man cried, "Not soldiers, or archers, but mages from Worm's Hollow. Only three of them, my lord, and they slew every scout from here to the sea…"

In this moment, the general was thankful he was separated from King Madouni, whom Koa bid proceed him with the bulk of the army and his private guard. Mirroring his thoughts, his men spoke.

"All our own mages surround the king, General Koa," said a lieutenant urgently. "What can be done?"

"Run!" cried the scout desperately, "There's no help for it; run!"

Before the general could respond, a snaking beam of radiation surged between the standing men and vaporized the hapless scout before the man could complete a scream. The soldiers facing General Koa whirled to protect their leader and viewed a lone man in dark robes walking confidently towards them.

The robed man, whose name was Trikha, projected his voice to the general as he walked.

"I advised my brethren that in our haste to hunt down your scouts that one or two may have been overlooked." The mage stopped and burnt the grass beneath him as he crackled with power.

"How sad to learn that yet again, I was correct…"

"Ground forces!" roared Koa, "Attack!"

There are times when a group of trained men can overcome a magician. The levels of learning and skill varies not unlike any other profession, which is why many sorcerers will study and seek the protection of more skilled mages as a matter of survival. A practitioner of magic must master velocity, mass, trajectory, and distance along with time in order to avoid the varying speeds of swords, lances, catapults, and arrows hurled by a master of weaponry. The three mages (Trikha, the leader, along with Itzel of the east division and Kasi of the west division) commanded by the High General of Worm's Hollow were adept at repulsion of most manmade articles of defense and their concentration was unwavering.

At Koa's command, a wall of soldiers on both sides of the mage surged forward and bombarded him with everything they had while Trikha calmly focused on the small group of elite soldiers surrounding the general. The sorcerer pulsed his barrier of radiation and the wall of men around him fell screaming in agony. Driken watched as a full regiment of four thousand men came rushing between the mage and where he stood by General Koa.

The mage regarded these precautions lightly.

"You have called forth reinforcements, High General Koa," said Trikha by raising his voice unnaturally. "Yet, I have some of my own..."

The sorcerer's brethren, Itzel and Kasi appeared to the east and west of the division, effectively surrounding Koa's men in a triangle of heat and radiation. Koa noted proudly that his men remained in formation, raising shields, swords, and spears as they were trained to.

"We stand ready to resist and repulse you, magician!" shouted General Koa.

The mage made a dismissive sound.

"You stand ready to die, general," Trikha replied. "Your remaining divisions will be crippled by your loss. First blood goes to High General Azymbek."

The High General of the Deep Places did not respond to the mage's words, though his lips tightened at the mention of Azymbek's name. Koa had no illusions as to why he and his men suffered such a cowardly attack; the two High Generals shared no love for each other. The general took a defensive stance, raised his shield, and readied himself for death.

Raising themselves high into the air, the three mages amassed the burning elements to a level well past what the human body could safely withstand. Their hair and robes rose and billowed in response to the rapidly crashing chain reaction growing between them and aimed at the defenseless soldiers of the Kingdom of the Deep Places.

Driken braced himself for annihilation, one hand on his sword, the other on his belt, holding tightly the only thing of worth to him, a handful of painted stones from his daughter Zarina, who kissed them in her mother's palm before his wife placed them safely away in his armor. "For good fortune," Nard whispered as Driken held them both to his chest. His daughter's mind could not conceive of never again, so she looked at him as though the only thing possible was his return. Zarina reached out to touch his face; Driken felt the tiny imprint of her fingers for days afterwards.

His hands tightened on these things; a weapon, and a pledge of trust.

"I must see you grow..." He prayed as the blast of radiation struck and the men disappeared in a great ball of light. The Earth and sky shook from the sound like a sonic boom and the three sorcerers watched the cloud of dust rise past them to the heavens and spread to blot out the afternoon sun. As the leader turned to go, Trikha heard the amplified voice of his fellow mage.

"Should we leave the Deep Places short a division, brother," Itzel asked, "Or an entire army?"

The lead mage paused to consider these words as the clouds of dust began to dissipate to the point where they could faintly see one another.

"Well spoken," Trikha said finally. "Azymbek will only send us forth again from this victory..."

He took a deep breath, his lungs expecting to be filled with the stench of charred flesh and seared bone. He stopped in puzzlement.

"Dissipate the clouds, brethren," Trikha commanded.

Kasi, the mage facing the west waved his hand quickly and the wind followed this motion, blowing away the dust for miles.

The three stared in shock as they hovered above the plains, for the division of the Deep Places stood well and whole, the soldiers rising to their feet from where they perched behind their shields.

"Impossible…" marveled Kasi on the western flank.

"Again!" cried Trikha as he swiftly deflected lances thrown by the swarming army.

A High General is a trained observer of men. Once Koa realized he was still alive, and under the shouting of orders to his men to attack the mages, his keen eyes searched for a reason for survival. Koa noticed the pattern of energy surging from the sorcerers and his gaze caught sight of an energy field that protected his men and pressed back the radiation. Without hesitation the general ran towards the source of it, his guards moving with him as one. Marveling that he was not blinded by it, Koa detected an aura of blue light coming from one of his volunteer soldiers, a refugee. The general boldly reached out and grabbed the startled man by the shoulder.

"Soldier!" General Koa shouted over the next blast of power, "What is your name?"

The man turned to look at his commanding officer in awe but answered him promptly.

"Driken, my lord," the man replied in wonder. "General, what has saved us from the mages?"

The men all braced themselves and covered their ears as the now frantic pounding from the sorcerers continued. Then the general stared at the blue light coming from Driken's body.

"By the Great One," cried the general, "I believe it is you…!"

"Cease, brothers," said lead mage Trikha as his mind recovered from disbelief and he searched the area behind them in haste for traces of magic; he found none.

"What is it?" the mage Kasi from the west shouted in fear, "How can they have survived multiple blasts of radioactive energy? Is there an Ancient nearby?" he finished in panic.

"Allow me a moment," answered Trikha, "Do not yet fear, my brethren; there is only defense; we are not attacked..."

The mage from the east projected his voice.

"Behold, brother," Itzel said pointing in the direction of General Koa, "That light coming from the general, I've never seen such energy. Perhaps we should flee..."

"Stand fast, Itzel," demanded the leader, "Whatever his power, we can be certain he does not know how to use it--" Trikha pointed in his turn, "Focus now on the general...fire!"

Despite the energy protecting them, High General Koa gasped in pain from the combined attack and his hand slipped from Driken, who instinctively grasped Koa's arm, which he knew from his training, he should never do. But the contact enveloped the two men in a deeper blue light, and his guards stared in wonder, even as they raised their shields over their commanding officer and his footman. Koa felt the pain in his body recede as the light within him chased it away; he spoke hoarsely to Driken.

"Whatever you hold dear," whispered the general, "Focus on it, Driken, and do not turn your mind from it, or we shall all die..."

Koa's lieutenant spoke to his leader while he stared openly at the confused Driken.

"Is he a magician, my lord?" he asked, "To repulse such power?"

The general shook his head.

"There is no life in magic, lieutenant," said the general as his mind turned to the warmth that healed him. "Albeit I have never seen one before now, I'd swear on my soul that Driken is one of those we call creators..."

Driken could not speak for a moment as all the surrounding men looked to him in hope. Him? A creator? A legendary being of power? The refugee's mind whirled. He was a man without a home, or even a kingdom.

In his mind, he was less than nothing...

"But..." Driken stammered in doubt, "I don't know how to use it..."

As though in agreement with his words, the next blast from the mages brought a regiment to its knees; soldiers fell screaming and smoking to the earth.

"Yes!" cried lead mage Trikha, "He's weakening...more power, my brothers!"

Driken staggered from the onslaught; Koa grasped his breastplate tightly.

"Listen to me, Driken," said the general firmly, "Doubt and second thinking is death to a soldier; without faith in the outcome, a man is dead while still breathing. What means more than life to you?" Koa shook Driken, "What?!?"

"My...my daughter..." said Driken with brimming eyes as he stared and then tried to look away from the general, "...my baby girl..." he choked.

The general sighed as he tried to reason how the memory of a small child could save thousands of men. Koa was a man of war, not peace; he could not think of a single strategy to translate thought to physical might; how the seemingly nebulous blue light that protected them could be used for offense.

"I know little of creators, soldier," said the general as he shook his head helplessly, "Or how they are formed. I only know whatever they believe becomes real..."

Driken looked to the sky in despair. These were concepts beyond his grasp as a man of meager skills and no higher learning. The gulf he was trying to bridge widened as he reached for it; he was ashamed so many would die for his ignorance.

"I have pledged my life to you, general," Driken finally whispered with resolution. "The kings we fight for, and my family. I will give my best to it..."

The High General nodded soberly.

"There are worst things to die for, soldier," Koa answered quietly, "Far worst..."

The general looked to his men.

"Surround him," he ordered, "We live or die in a moment..."

Driken swallowed hard and turned to face the mages, who seemed to fill the entire world with unlimited power. He'd only learned to use a sword properly a year ago, and he had fully expected to die in the first battle. Now the lives of thousands rested in his hands and the refugee from the Far Isles had no idea how to save them or himself. Driken wanted his love for his daughter to be enough, and he knew that love had brought them all this far.

Whatever gave me this power for this moment, he thought, I dare but see me through to the end of it; I know not what else to ask.

A ball of fire blazed towards the division and Driken watched in slow motion as it roared through his defenses, aiming for his heart. He saw again his daughter bending from his arms towards her mother Nard to kiss the roughly painted stones.

The strength I have I send to you, my daughter, my breath...

A shadow fell over Driken as the blast struck and, in the same instant, he saw nothing.

The lead mage sighed in relief as he felt the barrier cave in under their combined might. The possibility of failure had frightened him; it couldn't be that an army of ordinary men, however enhanced, would render him defeat. Yet, Trikha raised his hand cautiously as his brothers ceased their hammering of the protective light on the remaining soldiers of the Deep Places; mage Kasi from the west again dispelled the dust of radiation and poison from the air.

Trikha could not see General Koa for the shields covering him. The soldiers were all kneeling beneath their shields, alive or dead; he lowered himself from his elevated position to peer closer. The mage drifted back in shock as he beheld one man standing. It was not the general, or anyone else he'd seen before.

The man looked to be a regent, but one from antiquity; the fashion of his clothing resembled a manner of dressing long gone. Trikha's own heart began to beat faster; this was an Immortal, the seal of his power flared over the entire company of men, and from the expression on his face, he was not pleased.

"I've never been fond of one-sided battles, sorcerers," stated the man coldly. "What say you, we even the wager a bit?"

The mages from east and west appeared immediately at the side of Trikha, crackling with burning energy. The leader of these two replied as cold.

"This is not your affair, stranger," said Trikha as he pointed to the blackened earth, littered with dead and dying men. "You've come a fair distance to feed uncaring crows and wolves..."

For answer, a blast of blue light, greater than seen before this moment, came from the unknown Immortal, and the three mages unconsciously shifted away from it.

"As I recall, crows have a fondness for magicians..." The man replied grimly as his hands blazed with power.

"Shall we?"

The ground shook as the opposite forces met, and the soldiers of the Deep Places were pushed back to their knees. General Koa came to his feet with difficulty, giving his men the guidance and direction, they needed to remain strong.

"Find archers!" he cried. "And anyone skilled with the lance; we must help the one who fights with and for us!"

The general knelt to the fallen Driken, who lay sprawled like a broken chalice in the ashes beneath him, his breastplate charred and smoking.

"Your daughter is proud of you, soldier," Koa said gruffly, "...as am I."

A voice above the general interrupted him.

"He's not dead yet, General Koa," grunted the strange man as he battled the mages. "At least, not as long as I breathe..."

What the general did not know was that it was Driken's immature display of power that drew the Immortal to their aid, and the strange man was determined to keep the fallen soldier alive.

The lead mage however, had his own problems with morale. His two companions, Itzel, and Kasi, already shaken by Driken's resistance, nearly came unglued by the stranger's obvious command of what the fallen soldier had been ignorant of.

"I've never seen such an energy before," cried the mage Itzel from the east. "I don't recognize it!"

"I tell you, he's an Ancient," declared Kasi from the west. "We're dead men!"

"Stand strong, hounds take you," shouted mage Trikha. "Observe his power, he's not an Ancient...!"

Yet the Immortal was strong enough to hold off the three of them and push them back. The trio began to feel the heat from their own radiation.

"We must pull everything together, and strike him with it," commanded Trikha, "Wait for my word..."

* * *

From the safety of his gates, King Mrinal of Worm's Hollow tensely followed the battle displayed on the walls of his court by his own High Regent Jadu. High General Azymbek clenched his fists in frustration; for his own reasons he was looking forward to witnessing the death of the Deep Places High General.

"What is he, the stranger?" demanded the king.

The High Regent narrowed his eyes.

"I know not, my lord," answered the regent slowly as he chose his words. "He's clearly an Immortal, you can mark from his garb. But..."

"Is he an Ancient?" asked Azymbek, and the High Regent paused before speaking again.

"No..." Jadu said finally. "I cannot sense in him the levels of magic required for such...yet, the blue light, the magnitude of it; he's combining them together somehow..."

Azymbek's eyes widened in unaccustomed fear.

"Is he a creator? The creatures of legend?"

But High Regent Jadu shook his head.

"I know not what manner of being he is..."

The combined blast from the mages shook the stranger, and the eyes of the High Regent lit up with determination. Jadu turned to his king.

"Allow me to join them, my lord," said the regent urgently. "With my aid we can turn the tide against the stranger and destroy him!"

King Mrinal turned a withering gaze on his High Regent.

"We've wasted enough resources on this fool's game," said the king firmly, "Should I lose my High Regent on the winds of chance?" Mrinal made a move of dismissal with his hand. "Let them fight their way out or die of incompetence, it's all one to me..."

As the king turned away in disgust, the High General felt Jadu tense up; he spoke under his breath.

"Don't be a fool, Jadu," Azymbek growled softly. "Stand fast..."

The High Regent's face went rigid. Trikha, Itzel and Kasi were among his most valuable and Jadu was loath to lose them in protracted battle. The task was meant to be simple, and without error; it had taken his breath away how quickly the errand had turned into a deadly one. He chanced a sideways glance at his king, who seemed distracted. With barely a movement, the High Regent caused a dimensional opening to form between himself and the images on the walls; as the general cried out, Jadu stepped through.

"Regent!" bellowed the general as the king turned back in disbelief.

Azymbek hurled his shield to the floor as the images dissipated with the disappearance of the High Regent.

"Blast his eyes!" swore the helpless general.

"Summon another magician," said King Mrinal angrily. "Let us see at least how the fools will fare...!"

The lead mage noted with satisfaction how their shared might shattered the defenses of the Immortal, causing him to stagger backwards. It seemed the power of the stranger was uneven in places, as though his focus or concentration wavered.

"Well met, stranger," boasted Trikha, "Perhaps the crows will wax immortal once they've dined on you..."

The stranger's eyes danced with anger.

"And perhaps you'd care to leave your perch and test my might directly, sorcerer," countered the Immortal, whose answer caused the mage's jaw to clench.

The mage from the east unwisely accepted this challenge.

"I will unbind you..." Itzel declared as he rushed forward, blazing with radiation.

As the two met, the Immortal grasped and hurled Itzel to the earth, who screamed as the blue light surged through and disrupted his mortal coil. The soldiers closest to the stranger raised their shields to cover their eyes as the mage disintegrated.

"Itzel!" roared Kasi, from the west.

"Wait!" cried Trikha but it was too late. The sorcerer Kasi launched across the space between himself and the stranger, who slammed the flat of his hand to his adversary's chest. The light within the Immortal followed this line of contact, and the mage flared brightly before transforming into shards of crystal dust.

"No!" cried Trikha, now alone. His eyes rose from the dark grey ash of his fellows to those of the stranger, who mutely raised his forearms and gestured with open palms for the mage to engage him.

But before the maddened sorcerer could accept this deadly invitation, the High Regent of Worm's Hollow stepped through the dimensions and blasted the Immortal with all his might, bringing the stranger to his knees.

"You've done well against these, my talented and treasured fledglings," snarled High Regent Jadu. "Now face the one who trained them all!"

Without hesitation, Trikha joined his master in battering the Immortal, who cried out, straining to maintain his protection of the general's troops and his own defense.

"Fight, damn you," General Koa roared. "If he falls, we all die by fire!"

The lancers and archers of the Deep Places darkened the skies with their missiles, then fell back in agony as High Regent Jadu, without turning his head, rained flames of radiation over them. The footmen offered what protection they could to these brave soldiers by flinging themselves and their shields over their bodies.

"Had you heeded the warning of mage Trikha to go your way, Immortal," growled Jadu through gritted teeth, "These men would have died quickly and without pain. Now I will see to it that they, and you, suffer things unspeakable!"

With a man's cry of agony, the stranger struggled to his feet, the blue light within him shimmering and fading. He marshalled himself and drew on reserves of power, hidden for such a moment.

Yet he knew it would not be enough.

"General Koa," said the Immortal with a shaky breath, "Forgive me..."

"There's nothing to forgive," answered the general grimly as he signaled to his men to prepare for the end, "It is an honor to fight and die with you...!"

High Regent Jadu drew a massive amount of air into his lungs as he pulled from deep inside his body every scrap of destructive power he possessed to strike down his adversary. The mage Trikha followed this example and waited for the signal to release their deadly force.

As the Immortal began to pull hard on the light within himself, Driken's eyes suddenly flew open and he came to his feet with determination, replenished by the energy of the stranger. As the High Regent struck, the soldier placed both his hands against the Immortal's back and closed his eyes. Power surged through the earth and into Driken, who unconsciously transferred this energy to the stranger, who then pushed it forward with all his might.

The radiation from the High Regent and Trikha smashed against the blue energy which became a wall of dense light, hurling back the repulsed force exponentially; the mage Trikha barely had time to raise his arms as he was vaporized.

The High Regent fell from his vaulted position to the ground and stumbled as he tried to bind the absorbed energy and maintain his physical form.

But he couldn't.

As he fell from his knees to the earth, Jadu began to crawl across the plains, blinded and clawing mindlessly at the scorched grass; the soldiers stepped quickly from his path. The Immortal almost felt compassion for him...almost. He repented the thought as his eyes fell on the men the High Regent had coarsely slain.

Finally, Jadu ceased all restless movement and lay still. In seconds, his body dissolved into dark grey ash.

The men of the Kingdom of the Deep Places were silent for a moment. Then as one, they began to roar.

General Koa pounded Driken's back and shoulders, who responded with a sheepish grin. The Immortal turned and offered his hand; in awe the soldier accepted it.

"My thanks, Driken," said the stranger. "Without you, we could not have prevailed."

"But it was you, my lord," protested the soldier, "I knew not what to do, only to help..."

"A mighty help indeed, were you both," replied Koa as he turned to the Immortal, "How thankful am I that the legends were true..."

The general's words brought a brief shadow to the Immortal's face.

"Would that I could tarry with you, my friends," said the stranger finally, "But I must return to my journey, and the one I seek..."

Soon the men shared their farewells and the troops of the Deep Places stood in crisp formation as the Immortal left their company. Driken spoke quietly to his commander.

"My lord," said Driken, "You did not ask the stranger who saved us for his name."

The general shrugged.

"He felt to me like a man who preferred to remain unknown, Driken...sometimes it's best to allow such a one as he, to keep his secrets..."

General Koa walked away with his lieutenants and Driken stayed to watch the figure of the Immortal grow smaller in the distance. Yet before the man vanished over the rise of the hills leading back to the sea, he paused and looked behind him in Driken's direction. The soldier could not see his face and could faintly make out that the man lifted his hand again in farewell. But as he turned and disappeared over the horizon, Driken stiffened as a name entered his mind; a name he was certain belonged to the stranger:

Thane.

***

The magician in the court of Worm's Hollow silently faded the scene of the death and defeat of the nation's High Regent, and the chamber was quiet as the king sat staring at the blank wall. High General Azymbek did not dare to speak; even the servants ceased their movements and swiftly fled the room.

The mage could not withhold a flinch as King Mrinal hurled his kiln-fired cup to the tiles, shattering it in pieces.

The king spoke tensely to his High General.

"How many men are currently awaiting execution, General Azymbek?"

"At least forty men, my lord," responded Azymbek.

"Bring them all to the courtyard. When you run out of stockades, release the wolves."

"Yes, my lord, as you say it," said the general sharply, who gestured to his lieutenant, who in his turn moved as though his head were next for the basket.

"General..." continued the king.

"My lord?" replied Azymbek.

"You will join me to watch the executions; we will need to discuss the next appointment for High Regent...preferably one who can follow orders," the king finished tightly.

The general bowed deeply and waited for his king to rise from his throne.

The Final Conflict, part II

Tales of the unknown creator who disrupted and destroyed the might of Worm's Hollow raced through the opposing kingdoms like a wild storm, bringing caution to the seven kings and a surge of hope to the forces of the Nine Kingdoms. General Koa bound his men and lieutenants with an oath not to disclose the name and actions of the soldier refugee Driken; like any maneuver designed to protect lives, the general felt it best if the soldier's abilities remained unanticipated.

The homeless soldier was stunned by Koa's offer to join the king's private guard.

"You're untrained, Driken," said the general truthfully, "...and the Far Isles has first rights to you, since you are loaned to us from their forces. Yet we are allowed to make this offer during times of war, and the king himself has promised that if we survive the conflict, you'll be promoted immediately, and I'll train you myself. You'll also reap the privileges of the king's personal guard; citizenship, a small estate with lands and staff for you and your family..."

Driken stared at the High General as though the man had pinned Driken to the earth with a spear.

He was a tradesman who lost everything when the Broken Meriden unexpectedly changed direction and matched through his people's lands, so small it had no name yet. Driken barely had time to grab clothing for himself and his family; his wife Nard quickly packed as many dried goods as she could with their daughter Zarina safely bundled to her chest. They ran in the dark past burning homes, set alight by their owners to discourage the soldiers. Driken led his family into the forest when they heard the terrifying sound of marching boots. Nard begged to rest in one of the many caves they passed but her husband said no; later that night, even miles away they heard the screaming and cries of their neighbors and friends found in the caves by the soldiers. Nard clung to Driken, silent and shaking; he felt her tears on his tunic as he pressed his lips to her forehead. Soft heat from his daughter's sleeping head against his chest made Driken wipe his eyes in the darkness.

The words of General Koa brought the refugee soldier back to the present moment. "You don't have to decide now," said Koa as he pressed his hand to Driken's shoulder. "Once King Sumter learns of your abilities, he may make you a far better offer; he is the High King..."

Driken gathered himself and shook his head.

"Your proposal is accepted, general," said the former refugee in humility, "We have already fought and nearly died together for the Kingdom of the Deep Places; I will not turn from you for promise of greater gain."

Koa could find no response for this; he stood silent with his men as Driken worked to continue his words.

"You are my home," he concluded hoarsely to Koa's pleased surprise, and the general's lieutenants surrounded Driken with happy shouts and manly pounding of his back and shoulders.

* * *

King Cassum of the Sealed Gates had an army to rival that of the Eastern Crest, so the King of the Ardant Road was content to march with him; Pilard felt his archers and horsemen were the envy of the Unnamed Lands and a fair compliment. Lady Irisella's homeland, the Kingdom of the Western Hills was their aim of destruction; King Cassum of the Sealed Gates cast lots for the privilege; none knew of his grudge with King Roe.

Not every king of the Unnamed Lands was evil, just as not every king of the Nine Kingdoms was without flaw. The point of dishonor between the two kings was unforgiven by Cassum, though his heart was divided on how the matter should be settled. His lower regents advised assassination for justice, but the king hesitated. His High Regent Kierion, a Master Sorcerer, advised caution.

"For your word, I would do it myself, my lord," she said quietly. "But your gaze would never again say peace to his queen..."

The king could not speak for a moment at the truth of these words, and he felt assassination too cold an act to match the fire in his heart.

"You may wait until the next King's Summit," continued the High Regent. "Where you may make an official petition before the gathered kings."

Cassum turned away from this suggestion, as his advisor knew he would.

"We will meet on the road to battle, or on the fields of destruction, Kierion," The king said finally. "I have tried reason and law to no avail with King Roe..."

Kierion sighed. The battle is in your heart, my king, she thought, and neither magic nor law has prevailed...

The armies of The Western Hills and The Ardant Road met at Lorith before the Sea, with a coming together so powerful the ground split for miles beneath the hooves of war horses and struggling men. King Pilard's High General gave a shout of frustration that went unheard over the cries of dying men when one of his ground generals moved before an agreed signal and the archers of King Roe darkened the skies.

A regent and mage who stepped forward to ward off the arrows was impaled by a javelin; one of his brethren pushed a wall of earth in time to defend the second volley of deadly missiles.

King Roe spoke quietly to High General Baynes as his sharp eyes surveyed the plains below them.

"Where is he?" And though Roe did not say his name, his general knew of whom he inquired.

"Our scouts were certain last week of the colors of the forces of King Cassum, my lord," replied Baynes, "At least another day's march from Terranea..."

The king sighed heavily.

"It makes me uneasy that his colors were spotted at all," said Roe. "Hold back my horsemen until I give the word; commit more ground forces."

"As you say, my lord," Responded High General Baynes, who looked to his middle command generals to send word to the ground generals.

King Pilard was visibly nervous as he looked to the hills overlooking the battle; King Cassum had separated his armies and split his forces a week ago. Promising to meet his allies at the borders of Terranea and Lorith before the Sea, he was now nowhere to be seen. Pilard wished to reserve his precious horsemen for the final conflict; his visions of glory as his mighty forces struck the plains faded into fearful imaginings of defeat against the clever strategies of King Roe.

Pilard began to search his mind for possible offenses committed against King Cassum over the years he had forgotten or overlooked. None seemed worth the annihilation of his forces, but in this moment, King Pilard was not certain.

"What is your will, my lord?" Asked his High General, who wished to press this advantage over Roe's footmen with his archers.

"Stand fast, general," Grumbled the king as he turned to his High Regent. "Enhance the horizon and the hills to the east, regent," Pilard practically barked. "What colors?" He demanded, meaning if the banners or standards of King Cassum could be spotted.

High Regent Dolat answered in a subdued tone.

"I've been searching all morning, my lord," The regent said as he brought the views closer to King Pilard's gaze. "There's nothing..."

A commotion on the fields below distracted Pilard: King Roe's men were overrunning the wall of turned earth as reinforcements surged behind them. Before Pilard's general could signal his archers, General Baynes sent a barrage of arrows onto King Pilard's screaming footmen.

"My horses!" Roared the king as the men on the field scattered; a wave of men descended on the unprepared cavalry, who turned back as their general caught an arrow in his chest.

King Pilard's High Regent was strained as he used magic to save the second line of horses, the first line was pulled down by arrows, lances, and roaring men. The momentum of this surging carpet of thousands of men struck the regent's wall of force, pressing it inward. Two regents stepped in to assist, but High Regent Dolat faltered.

"I'm not certain I can hold it…" He gasped.

The King of the Western Hills scented blood in the water.

"Give me two regiments of cavalry on their eastern flank, now!" Shouted King Roe.

"Do it!" Baynes barked at his generals, "And cover them!"

Pilard's High Regent went to his knees as this added contingent of men stormed and buckled his wall of energy; an aerial view of the plains showed the beginnings of an absolute rout of King Pilard's forces.

But…

From the southeast, a massive bulge of swarming men came over the hills and down onto King Roe's now vulnerable forces, forming a wedge that slammed between Roe and Pilard's men like the hammer of a master forger.

In the distance, a king stood overlooking the carnage. He did not turn to his High General as he spoke.

"Now…" said King Cassum with narrowed eyes, "Smite them."

King Cassum split and held back his forces for dual purposes: To fool the scouts of King Roe and leverage his attack with the most damaging effect. If he'd warned King Pilard in advance of his strategy, he knew the vain king would not commit his armies and Roe would be warned of his presence. And although Pilard had forgotten his offense, the King of The Sealed Gates had not.

The Horsemen of The Sealed Gates trampled the footmen of The Western Hills; thousands died under his mounted men. Even those soldiers able to drag down a warrior from his seat was struck and killed by the sword or hooves of another; it was a scene of complete bedlam. King Pilard shuddered in relief as his beloved cavalry was spared and his forces allowed to recover. He shook his head as he deemed King Cassum a better friend than foe; he knew why the king had not communicated his true plans.

For his part, King Roe felt his chest deflate as he watched the decimation of his armies. His gut had warned him, but the king had ignored the signs.

"Cassum..." growled Roe, "Hounds take you..."

Only the direct order of King Roe prevented High General Baynes from leaping into the fray himself: Soldiers ran like ants to give his shouted orders to the lower generals and lieutenants that were dying on the field before they received them.

"Turn back!" The middle generals bellowed.

The king dismounted his horse and moved quickly to his tent, followed by Baynes. Though it seemed he retreated, King Roe knew what came next and he hurried to anticipate it:

As the king stood before his tent and drew his sword, High Regent Kierion materialized, crackling with radiation. High General Baynes stepped grimly in front of his king.

"Kierion..." whispered King Roe and gripped his blade tighter.

Kierion resembled a dark sun as she stood before the king and his general. The colors of King Cassum reflected deep within her robes, muted garnet and blue. Her king gazed through Kierion's eyes to behold the administration of his will.

"High General," said Kierion, "I admire your bravery, but the debt that King Roe owes King Cassum is not payable by you, the end of your mastery is a waste..."

"Strike sorcerer," snarled Baynes. "Hounds take you; I'll not stand from your way."

The mage noticed the bare flicker of Baynes gaze and smiled slightly as arrows, spears and lances bounced off her field of force.

"You face not a mere practitioner of magic and spells, Baynes," declared the High Regent, "But a true sorcerer..." Her eyes lifted from the general to his king.

"His life is in your hands, King of the Western Hills..."

"Stand down, Baynes..." whispered the monarch as his hidden guilt betrayed him, and his general's eyes widened.

"No, my lord!" cried Baynes as he raised his sword against Kierion, who flared with dark energy to strike down the general, then paused as an armored figure stepped from the king's tent.

Queen Gara.

The High Regent drew her breath sharply as she heard her king gasp in the distance; Cassum believed the Western Hills Queen half a continent away in her palace. Kierion watched as the queen slowly drew the Legacy Sword of the Western Hills and moved to stand next to her king, and still his protest.

"What business have you with my husband, sorcerer?" Asked the queen as she narrowed her eyes at Kierion, who flushed in dismay.

"Withdraw, my regent," said the king softly as he stared through Kierion's eyes at the wife of King Roe, his heart pounding in pain.

"But..." stammered Kierion under her breath, "I can enforce your will without harming her..."

"Withdraw!" roared Cassum, and with a final glare in Roe's direction, his High Regent vanished.

In the silence that followed, the King of The Western Hills commanded his general.

"Oversee our retreat, faithful one," said Roe softly, "I will not count your disobedience against you...but for heartfelt loyalty to the death..."

"My lord, my king," said Baynes deeply as he turned, knelt one knee and struck his chest. He stood and bowed from the waist to his queen, then swiftly departed to enforce the king's will. A moment more of quiet between the two monarchs as they watched the movements of men, women, and horses on the plains of Lorith before The Sea below them.

"Gara," said the king in a muted tone, "I asked you to remain in our tent, to lead our forces should I fall. Now both my High General and my Queen have disregarded my words, how then shall I rule?"

The Queen of the Western Hills lifted her chin.

"As you have just stated, my lord, a dead man cannot rule us," answered Gara. "Should I stand mute and watch the regent strike you down, dishonoring the vows I uttered?"

Roe now turned to meet the eyes of his queen, who returned this gaze with an even calm. The king looked as though he would say more, then turned back to the fields below them. Gara moved back towards their tent, before she stepped inside, she heard King Roe speak.

"Thank you..." he said over his shoulder.

Now it was the queen's turn to pause with words unspoken; the king soon heard the sound of her retreating boots and sheathed sword.

The Queen of the Western Hills held out her sword and helmet to her page's eager hands, her mind locked on the fading image of High Regent Kierion. Gara controlled both breath and emotion, for she could see what her husband the king could not; the face of King Cassum through Kierion's eyes. It felt as though he stood before her and took every ounce of her training as a ruler to keep her feelings from her gaze. Gara had focused on Kierion and tightened her grip on her sword.

The queen's own words to her king came back to haunt her:

"...should I stand mute and watch the regent strike you down, dishonoring the vows I uttered?"

Queen Gara closed her eyes in pain. Her husband's artistry in strategy was not confined to military movements; Roe had never intended to leave her behind. Even his protest upon departing the Western Hills was superficial, she could see it now. Somehow Roe knew that King Cassum would find a way to cross his path and engage his forces; to repay Roe through battle what Cassum could not obtain by any other honorable method.

Gara removed her mailed gloves and waved off the page who hastened to assist her. She lightly ran her fingers over the metal rings with the colors of the Western Hills painted over the hands and wrists, recalling the muted garnet and blue woven into Kieron's robes.

I could never fool you, Cassum, she thought ruefully. That sad play was for my husband. And I know you will forgive me; I must remain what I am, a queen of another country...

"Gara..." called her husband the king from outside the tent, "We must make all haste..."

"Yes, my lord," she responded as she should, "I'm coming..."

Over the protests of King Pilard, King Cassum allowed King Roe's defeated army to retreat to the safety of the mountains and await help from the Kingdom of The Golden Round.

"You said you wished to reserve your precious horsemen for Arin-Clath, Pilard," stated Cassum tightly. "So if you wish to use them now, do so; but you will do it without my assistance."

King Pilard's jaw locked, but he said no more. He knew that even defeated, King Roe could repulse him without the aid of Cassum. Pilard left the tent of his ally, wishing he could melt it down with molten lava and all inside it.

* * *

The Final Conflict, part III

It was the most beautiful day that most people on Earth had ever seen, and for many of them it would be the last. The sky was a crisp and brilliant blue with fluffy clouds and sharp rays of light bouncing off the shaded ground.

The marching kings of the Unnamed Lands made their point of command at Arin-Clath the ruins of an ancient palace. Made of stone, marble and slate, the sprawling buildings housed the kings and their regents and generals; the troops camped on the grounds surrounding it. The regents made the place livable; servants worked day and night to care for the nobility, the pages and lower rank camp soldiers administered food to the armies.

King Rasdeter of the Bright Forest, whose quest for home had grown from one man to millions of people from all over the Earth, woke from his rest elated and disturbed; the tiny girl from his dreams returned with her offering of dandelion seeds. This time as he beseeched her to come to his arms she finally did so; but as Rasdeter drew her close the red tressed toddler burst into tears and would not release him. The young king rocked and crooned to her as he had seen many of his tribe do, but she would not be comforted. The dream seemed so real; Rasdeter could feel the softness of her red-gold hair and the tears on her cheeks. When she lifted her face to look at him the king was startled by the vibrant green of her irises; they matched his own. The sudden sharp pain of her tiny nails on his arm as she clutched his tunic shattered the dream.

"Did I cry out?" he asked in a gravelly voice; Saramis was gently stroking his face.

"You did," she affirmed, and her husband pressed her fingers to his lips at the sadness in her eyes.

Later that day as dusk settled over the plains of Arin-Clath, King Rasdeter comforted his queen before he rode out to battle.

"All is well, my goddess," He said tenderly as the king kissed her forehead. Saramis sighed.

"One day, Saramis," Rasdeter said as he pointed to the west, "I will take you to see my father's estates, and the homes my uncle King Valtus built for us. It will rival palaces, and high places. We will ride together on the roads to the Far Isles; I grant you have never seen such beauty as our lands, from the valleys of it to the seas below..."

As his wife gently pressed her fingers to his cheek, Rasdeter looked down on her smooth brows and softened lips, his gaze warm with love for her.

"You take my heart with you to the fields, husband," answered Saramis. "I will only breath again when you return it."

"My life has only been the better for your place within it, Saramis," mused the king sincerely. "Know that I will give back to you all that you have given me…"

His queen affirmed this promise.

"Let it be as you say."

Rasdeter lingered within his wife's embrace, and as he chanced to glance to his left, he saw again in daylight an image of the tiny girl who sweetly haunted his rest. Queen Saramis felt her husband stiffen slightly and spoke to it, but Rasdeter shook his head as he gazed down at her.

"It's nothing…" Then the young king sighed.

"Perhaps we will speak of it one day, my love, when all of this is but a memory."

As he walked to the edge of the porch and the broad steps leading to the courtyard below, Rasdeter paused and looked back at his treasure, his heart filled with happiness in this moment.

"Saramis…"

The light behind him blazed over her body, and the king admired her glory.

"Your hair, beloved," Rasdeter said as his eyes fell on her ceremonial headdress. "Allow me to see it unbound once more…"

The young queen remained still as the bonds of her hair unfolded and floated to the tiles at her feet. The sun stirred the red and gold light beneath her strands as her deep amber locks floated to her waist and glided slowly back and forth in the breezes on the wide porch.

Her husband the king smiled in pleasure, and Saramis saw the young Pax once again in her tent those long years and lifetimes ago, whispering the word 'Goddess' as he beheld her beauty.

As though he knew her thoughts, Rasdeter's smile deepened, then he turned and walked the steps leading down and away from her.

The winds on the porch brought Saramis a sudden chill as her husband disappeared from her sight.

* * *

Brennan and Rasdeter rode swiftly with a company of men to the wider fields that held the bulk of the king's troops. The king felt a peace uncommon as flowers and leaves spun through the air before them; he smiled as the mixed petals fell on his hands. Some were the whitish-pink blossoms his mother cherished; it was good to remember her on such a lovely day.

In the distance ahead, a lone man strode through the trees towards the open road in front of them; Rasdeter cautioned his men not to fire on the man because he recognized him. The company of men slowed the pace of their horses and waited for the man's approach.

Bowman Kha stepped boldly from the long shadows of the trees and onto Rasdeter's path. The king quickly dismounted, followed immediately by his general. Rasdeter gestured to General Brennan and the others to stand down. He knew the hunter would not attack him...yet.

"Greetings, Bowman Kha of the Wanderers," said the young king as he crossed his arms. But his High General drew his sword and stood beside his king in a defensive position.

"Greetings, King and former Wanderer," replied Kha sharply as his blood pounded in his ears. "As I long suspected, you were never a farmer's child..."

The man once known as Pax breathed deeply to control his anger at the memories the Wanderer brought forth from him; he answered in kind.

"And you were never a true believer, Hunter," countered the king. "For all your words of peace, here you are, seeking my life..."

These words stirred the men behind Rasdeter. The young king made a gesture of forbearance as he heard the bows of archers pulled back and swords drawn from their scabbards at this perceived threat. The hunter felt his body go rigid. His former adversary could simply have him slain on the road; his quest unfinished. Kha felt an unfamiliar tang of fear in his mouth.

"It is not your life I seek in truth," responded the Bowman honestly. "But that of Saramis, who has joined you in the snares and traps of the world..."

The King of the Bright Forest interrupted the hunter's words.

"So, you've come back for her, Kha," said Rasdeter with contempt. "No matter how many times she turns away from you."

The hunter forgot for a moment that he was surrounded by death as he responded.

"You will be the end of Saramis, Rasdeter," answered Kha firmly. "Surely you see that now. Allow her to come with me and live..."

The king stared at Kha incredulously; did he truly believe Rasdeter would just give Saramis to him for the asking?

"You've blinded her," continued the hunter darkly. "Made her a queen of the very civilizations Saramis swore to avoid."

Enough of this madness, thought the former prince as he made up his mind. This day our conflict ends.

"Will the Great Mother save you again, Bowman?" asked the young king as he drew the Prince's Sword. Rasdeter acknowledged the paleness of Kha's face as answer enough.

"Then you're alone, Kha, as I am. If you slay me," vowed the former Wanderer, "You can keep her..."

Brennan watched anxiously as the two men fought again for dominance. He was sworn to uphold the bloodline of the Bright Forest and although the general had witnessed Rasdeter's victory in the past, the present moment held its own truths. Brennan gripped his sword and followed the battle but unlike King N'Goth, if he saw an opening or weakness in Rasdeter's defense, the general would step in and slay the hunter himself to save his king.

This time, Kha and Rasdeter were evenly matched, though the battle was no less fierce since the prize was the honor of Saramis. No words passed between them, only the sound of grunts and the singing of metal. Despite his silent vow, General Brennan was a few seconds too slow when Kha caught Rasdeter's arm as their blades met and whipping his arm in two sharp circles, twisted awkwardly the king's wrist and The Prince's Sword flew from Rasdeter's surprised grasp.

"I will save her…!" cried the hunter as he swung his sword upwards to fatally stab the former prince once and for all. But the Bowman in his zeal over compensated and pulling his short sword, Rasdeter moved swiftly forward and without hesitation, buried his blade in Kha's chest.

Mere seconds stretched into eternity as the two men's eyes met, speaking silent volumes of pain, loss, and victory. Rasdeter roughly withdrew his blade; it made a sucking sound as Kha's rent flesh followed the motion of the king's hand.

Kha tried to speak as he dropped his weapon.

"I…"

As the Bowman pitched forward to fall at the young king's feet, General Brennan briskly waved his hand and one of his soldiers offered the Prince's Sword back to Rasdeter. The king marveled again at its beauty as the powerful weapon molded itself to his fisted grip. It drank the hunter's blood eagerly from Rasdeter's palm and the general acknowledged the darkness in his king's eyes.

"You have sired destiny, young king," said Brennan. "Now you must birth it…"

Rasdeter gave his former adversary a final glance then moved to join his High General.

* * *

In the stillness following the absence of the king and his men, the hunter shuddered and coughed up blood. His mind dimmed as his body was turned over, his limbs were no longer his own. Someone was holding Kha and speaking words he could faintly hear.

His eyes finally focused:

Saramis.

Drawn to the struggle by the aggravated beating of her husband's wounded heart and a twist of fate, Saramis saw only the fallen Bowman, her king now vanished in the company of his soldiers. The young queen stared down in dismay at her childhood friend who could not speak the final words of his heart to her; that same organ was beating the last of his blood into his lungs and swelling torso.

Kha could not feel her fingers on his beard.

"Oh, Kha..." Saramis whispered. "Why?"

His hand reflexively tightened on hers as the light faded from his eyes. When Saramis finally looked away from his dull gaze, her breath caught at the sight of her childhood beads and bracelet tangled in his fingers.

Then Saramis wept for the Bowman's shattered dreams.

Red, Sable, Purple and Gold

The Far Isles and the Bright Forest met at Arin-Clath, and the earth was soaked in blood.

The former Wanderer of the Plains had never seen bloodshed on this scale; from his protected position on a hill far above the conflict, King Rasdeter could not contain a gasp as the armies met. Thousands of men on foot clashed, sending a shudder across the ground that he could feel miles away. Though he was dressed in his official robes as King of the Bright Forest, inside him the man called Pax was still struggling to live. Rasdeter tightened his grip on his royal staff as he heard the sounds of men and women dying in his name.

He heard the voice of his High Regent from a faraway place.

"A soldier chooses to die for his king, my lord..." Ghent offered quietly, "They would not be here if they did not love and champion your cause..."

The young king tried and failed to keep the emotion from his response.

"And what cause is this, Ghent? Other than my foolish desire to ultimately leave them and go home?"

The High Regent of the Bright Forest breathed deeply, it was his duty to advise his king of all probable outcomes.

"Should you prevail, my lord, you will rule two kingdoms, and your offspring will seat two thrones..."

Rasdeter turned to meet Ghent's eyes in shock, this thought had never occurred to him.

"There can be no other outcome, my king," said his High Regent in compassion. "Yours will be the only bloodline left..."

The king's eyes were bleak as he returned his gaze to the battle below. Now he felt the bonds of the trap he laid for himself tighten; in his mind's eye Rasdeter saw the face of Lady Irisella change from love to horror as his armies marched to the gates of the Far Isles. The terror compounded as Rasdeter's mind turned to Enith. Though a king, he could not control the Ancient; surely Enith would slay his nephew Asscher if his father Sumter fell to Rasdeter's sword. And what of the people he grew up with and loved? They were loyal to the present king, the only fate before them was execution.

"Ghent," Rasdeter whispered. "What have I done?"

The shared wound throbbed between them, and as though he knew the king's thoughts, his High Regent answered him.

"If you renounce your claim to the throne, my lord," said Ghent so softly that none other could hear him, "...and refuse to meet King Sumter in battle, Enith will likely slay yourself and all those with you: Queen Saramis, High General Brennan, and myself. Then High King N'Goth will meet High King Sumter, for the right to rule us all..."

The former prince felt his face whiten and his whole body flush at the thought of his cousin meeting N'Goth in battle. The High King of the Unnamed Lands appeared invincible, surely his cousin would die in seconds. Rasdeter swallowed and nodded his head tightly.

"I will stay the course," he said in a barely audible tone.

"For myself," continued the regent, almost to himself, "Perhaps death would be a kindness; for it may offer my family freedom at last from the hell our Great Father Roane has sent us from his grave."

Then Ghent met the tortured gaze of his king.

"Yet fear not; I, also, have chosen to live or die with you, my lord. We are bound by more than dread magic; whatever is ahead for you, I am with you, this I know."

Rasdeter took his regent's shoulder, unable to say more.

The young king turned his eyes to his High General, who ascended the hill from a lower plateau.

"What news, Brennan?" asked Rasdeter.

"King Sumter is reserving his forces, my lord," responded Brennan. "To what end, I know not, for his armies outnumber ours..."

He's waiting for me to change my mind, but I cannot, thought the king in despair. I must convey the impossibility of it...

"Prepare the archers, general," said Rasdeter resolutely as his general raised an eyebrow. Brennan tried to keep the anxiety from his reply.

"That will but anger him, my lord," said the general.

"Yes..." said the young king, "It will..."

✱ ✱ ✱

The High King of the Far Isles stood in tortured indecision on the opposite direction of the conflict. Another king would surely have overrun the forces of The Bright Forest as soon as he saw advantage, which Sumter clearly did. He stood prepared to surround his lost cousin if necessary; to place him under his protection; he needed only a signal. His own High General waited in silence for his king to see the improbability of accepting Rasdeter's surrender. He was older than the king when Lord Altus launched his failed coup, Marcus remembered the horrid pallor of the former king's brother in his cell.

Altus' son Rasdeter looked the same when Marcus saw him in the king's tent after the attempt on King Sumter's life.

General Aton could not save your father Valtus, thought Marcus grimly. Hounds eat my flesh if I hesitate.

Marcus chanced a glance at his second in command Hesta, who returned his look evenly, and Marcus saw the steel behind her eyes. Their king would die atop their cold bodies or not at all. Hesta placed her hands atop her double blades and her commander nodded at her unspoken vow.

"Marcus..."

The High General of the Far Isles followed the direction of his king's gaze towards the distant hills where stood the colors of the Bright Forest. Marcus saw the tell-tale sign of archers marching forward of the cavalry. This move was deliberate; Sumter knew from this that his cousin would not surrender.

Regent Aeryn, who was groomed by High Regent Polymus to replace him on the battlefield spoke softly to her king.

"The signal for surrender was for the archers to retreat *behind* the cavalry, my lord..." said Aeryn as her voice trailed away.

"You cannot protect him, my king," agreed Marcus. "Even if we crush his forces, we have no answer for the powerful Ancient who has bound Rasdeter as his father was bound..."

King Sumter watched bleakly as Bright Forest arrows descended like rainfall on his troops. The young king had sworn to move heaven and earth to save his cousin; the thought of failure tasted bitter in his mouth.

"Then crush his forces, Marcus," said Sumter tightly. "Let us see if the Ancient can stop us all..."

King Bokmal of the Broken Meriden narrowed his eyes as he beheld the footmen of the Far Isles begin to surround the forces of the Bright Forest, who attempted to spread out and break the growing wall of surging men. Sunlight glinted on the vibrant red hair of the king and his High General, a color predominant among the people of this nation, whatever the color of their skin.

"King Sumter will grind the Bright Forest like wheat, my lord." remarked General Augury, but his king seemed to disregard this statement.

"Does General Marcus yet lead his main forces?" asked Bokmal as a breeze gently ruffled his long and generous beard.

"The one who slew the Red Bear all those years ago?" replied the general, who then answered his own response. "To my knowledge, Sumter made him High General..."

The year that marked Sumter's seventeenth birthday, the Broken Meriden engaged the Far Isles in battle. A respected and revered warrior called the Red Bear swore an oath to slay King Sumter, an oath broken when then Forde Marcus buried his sword in the Bear's heart. This left a wound in the mind of Bokmal that would not heal.

The King of the Broken Meriden was silent for a moment, then in a slow deliberate movement, Bokmal lifted his right foot and placed it ahead of his left. Without another word, High General Augury sliced the air with his right hand. His mid-level generals stepped forward, their regiments behind them. The will of the king was clear, and protocol be damned:

Attack the Far Isles.

The maneuver of the King of the Broken Meriden was brilliantly timed: The forces of King Sumter were already committed, and High General Marcus made an unconscious sound of dismay as he watched the colors of one of his favored middle generals vanish beneath waves of red-haired soldiers. Marcus looked to his left as his second in command General Hesta ran past him and towards the hills overlooking the southern flank of his footmen. The private guard and battle elite raised shields above Sumter as it became painfully clear the initial attack was a distraction; Sumter calmly watched as his footmen surged forward from the southeast and lower southwest to grind the soldiers of the Broken Meriden between them.

"Hesta!" bellowed Marcus.

A huge group of men at least a thousand strong broke through this defense as Hesta and the hundreds of men who followed her leaped over the barricade of rocks to meet the Broken Meriden and defend their king. The words of General Aton rang in Hesta's mind as she pulled her feared twin swords:

If you use no shield, your arms must replace it; you must whirl your invisible defense until nothing around you that offers threat still moves.

A huge man twice her size came roaring up the incline and Hesta rolled under his shield and came up with flashing blades that ripped arms and torso; he screamed as he fell, and she waded boldly into the next object that blocked her view of the battle. One of her soldiers cried out to warn Hesta as he backed into her and they viciously dispatched every enemy in sight. They both leaned forward as a circle of warriors separated the pair from their companions.

"Commander..." said the soldier at Hesta's back in alarm.

"Yes..." she answered in breathless agreement. "It ends now...get ready..."

Hesta marveled to herself that she could yet discern the voice of Marcus over all the clamor and shouting; she knew only one of them could leave the side of the king and she made the decision for him.

A thought came to her as the red soldiers moved towards them:

If you die now, he will never know...

She smiled grimly to herself as she raised her weapons and answered her fears.

Then it wasn't important for him to know...

Before Hesta and the soldier behind her could step away from time and into eternity, a swarm of men overran the confident footmen of the Broken Meriden; a feat made even more remarkable for the four-legged company they kept.

"The Lourdes Clan..." Hesta said in wonder as the fearless men of the Lourdes and their savage trained wolves plowed into the unprepared red warriors.

It quickly became apparent that the Lourdes Clan was only interested in the Broken Meriden; Hesta pushed at the shoulder of the man who stood with her.

"Back to the king, soldier...Now!"

As they leaped again over the rock barrier Hesta felt a painful thud in the shield on her back and rolled to the ground: Arrows from the frustrated leader of the Broken Meriden. The archers of the Far Isles answered, darkening the skies, and giving them cover. She looked to her right; the man who followed her bravely into the jaws of death still lived, his own shield peppered with missiles from the enemy.

"What is your name, soldier?" She asked.

"Shustak, commander," the man replied, "If it please you."

Hesta grinned.

"If you live through this, Shustak, I'll promote you..."

The soldier grinned in his turn.

"I'll do my best, general..."

As the two ran up the steep incline to the relative safety of the king's guard, Commander General Hesta met the eyes of her High Commander Marcus, whose face was a mixture of gratitude and frustration. He could not berate his general's decision or the outcome; Marcus was merely thankful he did not have to witness her final sacrifice to protect the position of their king.

She watched his jaw tense as he spoke to her.

"We move to higher ground, General Hesta," Marcus said tightly. "Our king is already above us..."

"As it should be, my lord," Hesta responded with a trace of a smile. "...and you're welcome..."

The High General opened his mouth as though he would say more, then clearly thought better of it. His treasured commander walked past Marcus and up the hill, breaking off the shafts of the arrows in her shield and pushing the sharp points through to the ground beneath her.

* * *

King Sumter noted the leader of the Lourdes Clan deliberately paused as his men charged through and brought to a halt the advance of the Broken Meriden. Their eyes met and the young king received the distinct impression that the Lourdes had been missing from the lands of the Nine Kingdoms this past year for a reason. His pupils widened as the thought came to Sumter that a war against the Far Isles would be the only way such a large contingent of the Broken Meriden would gather.

As though he acknowledged this thought, the leader of the Lourdes raised his axe, then slowly lowered it; another wave of the Clan came rushing down the hills and towards the reinforcements sent by the King of the Broken Meriden. Sumter's breath quickened as he recalled that neither his people nor any other nation had ever been able to accurately number the Lourdes, who before this moment, seemed only one of a number of wandering tribes.

The young ruler heard the voice of his High General.

"Should we engage them, my lord?" asked Marcus, but his king shook his head.

"No..." he replied thoughtfully. "It seems the Lourdes has a long-standing dispute with the Broken Meriden; best we allow them time to work it out while we recover our own forces..."

As he watched the leader turn and engage their mutual enemy, Sumter found himself thankful today that his kingdom was not the recipient of the Lourdes' apparent grudge.

The Far Isles was not the only ones who benefited from the distraction of the Lourdes. Atoli and his brother warriors of the Wanderers came to the field where three armies fought; the Bright Forest, the Far Isles, and the Broken Meriden.

Atoli searched the waves of straining colors and bodies for some sign of his brother Pax; he was not ignorant of the standards of the kingdoms. Once he found the bright white fabric, Atoli looked for the rich sable brown enlivened with vibrant red, when he saw it, he pointed.

"There, brothers," called out Atoli. "The colors of the Bright Forest; we will find our brother Pax Rasdeter soon..."

But as the warriors moved forward, a woman appeared between them and their goal; the men respectfully lowered their weapons.

"Affi-Saramis..." said Atoli in wonder.

"Where do you go, my brothers," asked Saramis gently. "You who have sworn to shun the world of men and hold fast to the teachings of the Humans?"

"And if a brother is lost, Mistress," responded one of the warriors, "Are we not to search diligently until he is found again?"

Queen Saramis stepped from the tree line onto the lighted path of dappled trees.

"I, too, once thought of Pax, now Rasdeter as one lost, yet...If one is blind to their choices in life, does this dispel the fact that one is still...choosing?"

"Then we are choosing also, Mistress," answered Atoli.

The Woman of the Woods looked off in the distance as her mind turned to another path on the road to her husband's destiny.

"Your brother Kha is done with choices, Atoli..." said Saramis but the brother of the Bowman was not surprised by this news.

"Yes, Affi-Saramis..." answered the leader of the people in sorrow. "My brother walked a path he could not willingly turn from." Silence covered the forest as Atoli remembered his brother. "It would be well to secure him here," he continued, "In the hope that at least one of us will be left to perform the proper rituals-"

Saramis drew her breath sadly.

"Leave him with me, Atoli...I will secure him for those who will honor our wishes..."

Atoli and Saramis stared at one another for a time, then Atoli voiced his concern.

"You...you have no faith in what unfolds, Saramis?"

The lips of Saramis tightened as she tried to meet the gaze of Atoli.

"I only know that whatever the outcome, I will not leave Rasdeter; If that is faith, then am I full to overflowing..."

The warriors carefully lay the burden of Kha on the ground next to the former Woman of the Woods as she moved from the open road. Then the men of the Tribe called Human gave their love to Saramis and their fallen brother; as they began to leave Atoli heard the parting words of Affi-Saramis.

"Give my love to Nea, Atoli, and all of our people..."

Atoli was not so far away that Saramis could not see the pain in his eyes.

"How do you know I will return to her, Mistress?" asked the leader of these brothers; the face of the woman Atoli loved hovered before his memory.

"That would be my faith, Atoli," answered Saramis. "At least, that is what I would call it..."

The husband of Nea had no response for this, other than to nod slightly as he again turned away.

As her former people faded from her sight, Queen Saramis felt the earth tremble beneath her feet as she drew on creation to protect the remains of Bowman Kha.

* * *

The King of the Unnamed Lands watched with growing disinterest the drama of King Rasdeter's former homeland; his High Regent Sathdan could feel it. The reappearance of the Lourdes and their wolves peaked the king's curiosity for mere moments; then Sathdan chanced a glance at a lower regent, who in his turn caught the attention of one the king's pages. The man quickly produced a skin swollen with dark wine; it would not do for the High King to remember his aching wound before offering him ease to it.

Of all the people in the kingdom of the Unnamed Lands, only Sathdan, Iroh, and Crown Prince Arbu knew of N'Goth's unhealed wound, and High Regent Sathdan was not privy to the details of how it came about. Prince Arbu knew because one day his father told him; after trying to kill Arbu during one of his unpredictable rages. Iroh knew of it because he watched King Osolum attempt to slay his only son and heir; a fact Iroh kept to himself when King N'Goth shared this horrid tale in private.

But those who worked closely with the king knew the signs of his disturbance; any servant who wished to retain life and limb learned these things as a matter of survival. Wine and mead eased the constant throbbing and spikes of agony; it was a belief system N'Goth cherished along with his madness. Transferring his pain through the shed blood of others was another distraction, as was forcing his will upon his subjects, something the hapless servant with the orange scarf had learned to her detriment.

But now King N'Goth was beginning to regret his patience with the unfoldment of King Rasdeter's war. The leagues of miles and months marched had offered little in the way of entertainment for the restless king; there were only so many burned and destroyed cities to savor before one began to resemble all the rest.

Yet his mind's eye lit up as his thoughts turned to the High King of the western hemisphere. N'Goth was in no particular hurry to slay Sumter, but he was certainly ready to kill something, many somethings...

The king easily drained the offered skin and gestured for an-other, which the page was wise enough to have nearby. N'Goth threw both skins to the ground empty and wiped his mouth.

"Sathdan..." N'Goth rumbled. "Send word to all armies to withdraw, including the King of the Broken Meriden. It's time for the cousins of the Far Isles to meet and fall together."

"As you say, my lord," replied Sathdan with a bow. To the men of the Unnamed Lands, it appeared the regent was staring at the clouds gathering in the skies as he moved away from his king; in truth Sathdan's gaze pierced the dimensions to where he knew his master Iroh and the Ancient known as Enith watched the unfoldment of destiny.

* * *

A shadow fell across the feet of King Rasdeter and his men: Keoni, who represented his master Enith and his wishes on the battlefield. The mage bowed respectfully to his king, who paled at his approach.

"What news, Regent Keoni?" asked the young king with difficulty, for he suspected he knew the likely response.

"The High King has spoken, my lord," said Keoni quietly. "You must meet Sumter on the battlefield, or lose all support for your cause..."

"Set it forth, then, regent," answered the king bravely. "Brennan, give word for the troops to clear the field as Sumter's men withdraw."

"As you say, my lord," responded the general firmly, and indicated that the king's personal guard should surround Rasdeter, which they did. "What weapons will you take with you, my lord?" asked Brennan, who offered his king the Legacy Sword of the Bright Forest, with an assortment of axes and spears.

Rasdeter could not bring himself to wield the Legacy Sword of his kingdom, to him it was still Templin's Sword and the energy of guilt he felt surrounding the blade made it heavy in his hands. The young king chose the weapons he deemed were truly his; the Prince's Sword of the Far Isles, his short sword, and the wooden Boa from his days as a Wanderer of the Plains. His pages quickly strapped the weapon to his back where the king could easily reach it if need be.

Ghent stepped forward, raising his hand at Keoni's solemn protest.

"You cannot imagine that I will leave him now, Keoni," said Ghent, "And surely it is your fond hope that I will follow him in death..."

"Yet I have never hoped for your death, High Regent," responded the regent and mage honestly as their eyes met. "And whatever pain I wished for you has been more than surpassed. Fare you well, Ghent..."

The mage watched as the trio, surrounded by guards and soldiers, made the deep descent from the hilltop to the bloodied fields below.

Keoni spoke aloud to himself.

"For it is true I do not expect to see you again..." he whispered.

N'Goth had himself transported by Sathdan to the bloodied fields; he stood with his High Regent as King Rasdeter passed him. Yet there was no contempt or judgment in the High King's gaze as their eyes met, for N'Goth saw only the future image of his own son Prince Arbu marching to his doom.

"Stay strong, my son," The king whispered as Rasdeter passed him, his heart thudding in his chest at the High King's words.

Rasdeter did not dare to think of his father Lord Altus in this moment, the one whose treachery set his feet on the path that lead to this stride past the dead and dying. So many had given their lives for a lost boy's dreams of a world he could not return to, even if he prevailed against every obstacle. Rasdeter saw again the golden casket of his father's promises; so empty it all seemed now that he was here.

"Will you meet me, cousin?" asked Rasdeter, his voice amplified across the plains by Ghent. He saw the familiar illusion of shields moving over the ground, and the king stepped forward beneath his own barrier of warriors. His senses heightened, Rasdeter thought every blade of grass beneath his feet as he walked was a brighter green, a deeper hue.

Why have I done this, he asked himself as he neared his goal, And what will I do if I win?

The two kings faced each other across a plain littered with the blood, bodies, and gore of dead and dying soldiers. The King of the Far Isles and the King of the Bright Forest, two cousins and former brothers, separated years ago and now brought together for a brief moment of destiny. The time for words of familial love and diplomacy had passed; there was only the question of who would live to save or slay the helpless Crown Prince of the Far Isles.

The Legacy Sword of the Far Isles shone like the sun in King Sumter's hand and King Rasdeter could not take his eyes from it. It's beauty and power dwarfed that of the Prince's Sword, as it was intended to, and for a moment, Rasdeter finally understood that all along he had wanted it: Sword, crown, and throne. But he didn't want his cousin or his nephew to die. The mocking words of High King N'Goth came back to haunt him:

"Think you that Sumter will hand over his kingdom if you ask kindly for it?"

High King Sumter also had a revelation in this moment, that he, too, had wanted unwisely all his life for his cousin to come home. That over all reason and sanity he had dreamed of it, and now that the dream had materialized the only payment required for this manifestation was the life of Asscher, his only son. His hand tightened on the legacy of his kingdom, the Sword of the Far Isles.

The two kings came together silently like lightning and crashed like thunder.

N'Goth turned away from the two cousins and walked back towards his own army, disinterested in the outcome. He felt certain that Sumter would prevail and then...the High King smiled grimly as he pulled his sword and waded into the hapless soldiers between him and his men.

Marcus and Brennan fought only those soldiers who came across them, anxious to keep eyes on their respective kings and protect their backs. Across the battling cousins, the general's eyes met briefly and without remorse; sworn to slay anyone who threatened the throne of their kingdoms. Hesta drew her double swords and viciously dispatched any enemy soldier foolish enough to approach Marcus; the deadly artistry of her mentor Aton shone through her movements.

High Regent Ghent stood not far from this tragic personal battle. He barely noticed how his heart now beat in time with Rasdeter's, rising and falling with his physical exertion. Ghent knew when Sumter would render the fatal blow to Rasdeter that he too, would fall, he merely awaited his freedom. As his gaze fell on King Sumter, whom Ghent knew fought for the life of his only son, Prince Asscher, the regent struggled to keep his thoughts from his own children, Carn, Iason and Midlin. Ghent also realized in that moment that perhaps the master he shared with Rasdeter would expect him to give sorcerous aid to his king against Sumter. Ghent watched the light that seemed to illuminate the King of the Far Isles, how it seemed to battle the darkness surrounding the King of the Bright Forest. The regent knew in that moment that he would never use magic against Sumter, who only wished to save his cousin from the dreaded Lord Enith.

As the High Regent stood musing on these things, he noticed a soldier moving with purpose towards him, wielding a huge axe. It would be so simple, thought Ghent as he closed his eyes; a moment of searing pain, perhaps a cry of agony and both he and his family would be free of the intrigues of Enith. Then his mind turned to the man he shared a heart with, fighting for his life and the woman he loved, Saramis, who was helpless to save Rasdeter from his destiny. For answer, the twin hearts throbbed between the two men erratically. The once regent of the Kingdom of Everet sighed and opened again his eyes as he conceded; he was bound by more than one vow.

Ghent watched in slow motion as the man and his company fought through the soldiers between him and the regent. The soldier dispatched the last man before Ghent with a sound blended into a grunt and a laugh.

The soldier of the Broken Meriden spat on the ground as he and his men circled Ghent.

"Only a fool would stand on a bloodied field without a weapon to protect himself, mage," said the soldier with contempt, "...and fools die..."

This man did not fear any possible magic Ghent possessed. He had slain men of magic before; many of them. His gaze glinted with the memory.

But the soldier had never faced a man sealed by the power of an Ancient.

Ghent slid his eyes sideways towards the soldier and felt his heart fill with rage. Unnoticed by the servant of Enith, his darkness began to burn away the constraints that protected those around him from the deadly radiation his master distilled in Ghent. Resentment, hatred, fear; all the emotions the regent had so diligently fought against overcame his thoughts, begging for release.

"This fool...has lost everything, soldier," whispered the regent tightly, "Wife, children, and family. To what end? So that men such as yourself can glory in these bloody works, the senseless acts of war?"

Without another word, the soldier swung his heavy axe towards the regent's neck and grunted as it abruptly stopped inches from the target. Each man then attempted to attack Ghent to the same end as they found themselves frozen in place. Confidence gave way to fear as the soldiers beheld flames distorting the regent's face and torso.

"I have never understood it, before..." said Ghent almost to himself. "What would drive a man to attack another for some nameless cause. But today..." and between heartbeats the regent felt the darkness boil his blood, "I give you both answer and understanding...!"

In obedience, the darkness in Ghent's heart pulsed, leaped forth and with dark fire obliterated the men who encircled him as the regent screamed forth all the rage and pain of his transformation. As his sight cleared, Ghent saw the circumference of his attack far passed the initial boundary of the men who circled him, and that the formerly powerless regent had slain both friend and foe. Ghent gasped in dismay at the bubbling stains and smoking ash that greeted his eyes; men from all sides of the conflict were running from him in terror.

Then the new mage fell to his knees in sorrow for his terrifying initiation into the forces of magic.

A *Series of Simultaneous Events*

Rasdeter tried to draw on what he remembered of Sumter's abilities. He soon realized that his cousin's exposure to constant, protracted battle was in sharp contrast to his own experience as a warrior of the Plains people, which was mostly defense against attacks that were far and few between.

Sumter, too, noticed his cousin was no true match for him. Several openings he saw that left his cousin vulnerable Sumter let pass; finally the grieving king disarmed his former brother as the Prince's Sword suffered a fine crack against the hilt of the Legacy Sword of the Far Isles.

Without hesitation, a desperate Rasdeter stepped back from Sumter and reaching over his shoulder, he drew the wooden boa staff from his back and took a defensive stance. Sumter halted in respect for the weapon in his cousin's hands; General Aton had trained them both. The king raised his shield in time for Rasdeter's expert blow and clenched his teeth in pain at the force of it. The boa was Rasdeter's mastery; it was a Wanderer's first choice to subdue or conquer an adversary. Sumter found himself on the defensive from the greater reach and power of it; he could only use his shield for protection and wait for an opening to bring his sword to bear; this time the High King would not hesitate.

The Ancient known as Enith watched the battle in dismay. He knew from Rasdeter's once battle against the hunter known as Bowman Kha that he was not attacking Sumter with all the expertise he was capable of. He faintly heard the voice of Iroh behind him.

"Rasdeter will die, Enith," said Iroh in urgent despair. "He does not wish to kill Sumter...!"

At these words, the Ancient experienced an unfamiliar sense of defeat and frustration, then his countenance cleared as a light came into the mage's eyes.

"You're right, Iroh," agreed Enith in wonder. "He doesn't want to kill his cousin..."

And the Ancient reached deep into Rasdeter's mind to bring forth the only man remaining that the young king would most wish to slay. Using his power of illusion, Enith changed the battling figure of Sumter into the former High General of the Far Isles:

Aton.

Rasdeter's gaze unhinged into madness at the sight of General Aton holding a sword and shield before him, a recurring dream of the general come to life. The young king, as before, forgot where he was and who faced him as his mind hurled back to the moment, he stood helpless before his death.

Sumter nearly froze as he witnessed his cousin scream insanely.

"ATON!!!"

The king rained down blows upon Sumter's shield as the two moved fiercely over fallen bodies. Sumter desperately swung his sword and sliced down the wooden Boa, which broke in half from his swing and without hesitation, he pushed forward to impale his cousin, but...

Rasdeter came upwards from the blow and the round end of the broken wooden staff struck the High King's wrist, releasing the Legacy Sword from his grasp.

"No!" cried Sumter as he brought his shield up in time to break his cousin's deadly swing. He tried to push Rasdeter back with it, but the King of the Bright Forest slammed his staff into the shoulder that once held Sumter's sword, and the King of the Far Isles felt that limb go numb and useless.

Without the ability to hold a weapon, Sumter knew it was only a matter of time as his cousin relentlessly battered him.

"I was but a child," Rasdeter shouted over and over to the illusion of General Aton. "I was but a child...!"

"Marcus!" screamed Hesta.

The world slowed down as Marcus whirled and swung madly at anyone between him and Sumter. Brennan also found himself separated from his king and viciously dispatched the soldiers before him to meet Marcus, whom he must prevent from saving King Sumter. But before Brennan could reach him, the general felt an arm across his chest that pushed him back and a sharp pain that stopped his momentum. As Brennan fell a shadow crossed him and his eyes clouded in wonder at the figure who leaped over him to intercept the battle between the kings.

Atoli and the warriors he had left to him ran through the gauntlet of straining bodies, pushing most from his way, and only engaging when necessary. The wooden boa was used to advantage by the experienced warriors; men found themselves falling like leaves before their artistry. Atoli's brother Pax and the king he fought were surrounded by a light that came from within them, and not the sun, that seemed to rush towards the horizon to stop this devastating conflict.

"Mother guide my aim..." prayed Atoli as his spear hurtled towards Sumter, only to be knocked aside by the shield of an equally determined Hesta, glaring at Atoli, who was too far away for engagement. The one who led the Wanderers reeled at the possibility that he would not reach Pax in time to save him. Atoli reached for his sword as he ran full out; he could hear himself shouting his brother's name as he saw those he could not know were Marcus, Brennan and another who leaped towards the cousins as they battled.

Sumter felt the slipperiness of the bodies beneath him, but he could not avoid them as he tried to move back from his maddened cousin. Time paused as his shield was battered away and he saw the deadly arc of Rasdeter's swing; he raised his arms to protect his head and chest, knowing the gesture would be futile.

"Asscher..." Sumter gasped in pain as the image of his small son came before his eyes. "I've failed you..."

But the crushing blow did not fall.

King Rasdeter grunted as two spears pierced his body: Marcus stood over his king, his borrowed spear entering Rasdeter's lung; behind the young king a spear ripped his back and through his wounded heart.

The red haze cleared from the stricken king as he looked down and saw not Aton, but Sumter at his feet.

"Cousin..." said Rasdeter weakly as his limbs lost their strength. His eyes rolled upwards, and he tumbled to the ground.

The warrior who floored General Brennan and impaled King Rasdeter removed the spear with a satisfied grunt and then returned to a defensive stance as High General Marcus released his stained weapon and drew his sword. Hesta dropped her shield, shook the blood from her twin blades and readied herself as her king rose slowly from the ground and spoke.

"Who are you, warrior," said the king in grief and rage, "That you raise your hand against a king and former Prince of the Far Isles?"

The warrior straightened and pressed the bloodied spear into the ground.

"I claim both vengeance and sovereignty, King Sumter," said the warrior calmly. "I am Merick, daughter of King Templin, a former princess and now King Elect of the Bright Forest."

The one who had avenged her father's death removed her helmet and gazed evenly at Sumter, who despite his anger signaled to Marcus and Hesta to lower their weapons from the new king.

Brennan, who had regained his footing stepped forward breathlessly. With Rasdeter brutally removed from his throne, the general knew he must follow his training and his own integrity to defend the ruling bloodline, even if his King Elect's first act was to execute Brennan for treason.

"As High General Brennan of the Bright Forest, High King Sumter, I confirm Lord King Merick's identity. She is indeed Templin's daughter, Crown Princess, rightful heir and now King Elect of the Bright Forest."

The High King tensed his jaw at his mixed emotions as his gaze shifted from the face of Brennan, whom Sumter recognized and Merick, whom he did not. It did not escape the king's mind in this moment that if Rasdeter had succeeded in slaying him, Merick would have killed Rasdeter anyway, to regain her father Templin's throne.

"Very well, King Elect," said Sumter gravely. "I will recognize both your sovereignty and your vengeance in this moment. But you will leave us now, to tend our dead..."

"As you say, High King," responded the new king respectfully as she retrieved her spear, but Merick paused at a question from Sumter.

"Merick," asked Sumter, "Is it your intention to endorse this campaign against the Nine Kingdoms and the Far Isles?"

The new King Elect of the Bright Forest made a derisive sound.

"The mage who raised your cousin against my father," said Merick as she pointed her spear at the fallen Rasdeter, "Did so because King Templin stood in his way. Think you I would stand in alignment to anything he deemed precious?"

Without waiting for an answer, the new king turned and marched away. Brennan, after a moment's pause followed her, after one last glance of remorse for the fallen king, who had done Brennan no harm.

"Rest well, King Rasdeter," whispered Brennan as his thoughts flew to the last time the general laid eyes on the former princess and the royal family, "No doubt I join you soon..."

* * *

High Regent Ghent of the Bright Forest had just risen from the dust and gore of the soldiers he'd slaughtered, wiping his face in grief when Merick's spear pierced King Rasdeter's heart. Instantly enveloped in blue light, Ghent staggered forward like a drunkard in a tavern, then fell wordless back to the blood soaked mud, his eyes rolled so far upwards as to almost appear completely white. Seconds later, his shuddering form vanished.

* * *

For Enith and Iroh, the silence that followed the piercing of King Rasdeter was profound and deafening. In seconds, the looming defeat and death of King Sumter changed as Enith's pawn fell by Merick's and High General Marcus' hands. The Ancient marveled as he wordlessly gazed on King Templin's offspring, a former princess...and assassin. He made a fist and cursed himself for not delving closer into the myths and legends of the Bright Forest. His contempt for the royal family was a critical error, as was his confidence in his own power.

Master Iroh stood respectfully silent as he measured what could be salvaged from this resounding defeat. He gazed over the battlefield to note that King N'Goth was too far away to be of assistance in this moment, a terrifying engine of destruction as he fought a garrison and the Lourdes Clan single-handed.

Iroh spoke into the quiet surrounding his stunned friend.

"N'Goth predicted that King Sumter would defeat Rasdeter..."

"...and that he would slay Sumter," Enith murmured in agreement, then the Ancient's eyes finally lit up with hope.

"Asscher..." said Iroh as he gazed again on the king conferring with his generals Marcus and Hesta.

Enith's face took on a look of determination.

"I'll not wait the King of the Unnamed Lands," growled the mage, "I'll slay Sumter myself...!"

But as the Ancient readied himself, the dimensions over the battlefield parted, and the former child of destiny, now called The Dark One materialized on the plains before King Sumter. Crackling with power, The Destroyer raised her head to the heavens and looking through the dimensions she stared directly into the eyes of Enith, who backed away in fear.

"Now, sorcerer," she said grimly, "Step again on my path..."

"NO!" cried the Ancient, throwing up his arms in unaccustomed terror as he recalled her promise years ago as a child of nine. Master Iroh swiftly closed the dimensions between them, his own eyes widening in fear as he realized The Destroyer could yet see them.

"Be wise, Iroh," she said softly, "...and go your way..."

The two scheming mages quickly vanished.

* * *

Queen Saramis stood watching the battle between her husband King Rasdeter and his cousin King Sumter, tears streaming down her face. She forced herself to stand still no matter the outcome, determined to remain out of the way of his eventual destiny. She slowed down time to behold every movement of each person on the field. Her body blazed with light as Saramis witnessed Marcus and Merick leap together over Sumter to stab the man she loved in the very moment of his dark victory.

"Oh..." She whispered softly. "...oh..."

As Rasdeter tumbled to the earth, Saramis rested there before him, his head rolled against her thigh as she enfolded him in her arms. She placed her hand over his re-opened wound, to staunch the flow of blood; the spear of Marcus slid from his body. The young queen leaned forward to kiss his brow, heedless of the stains that soaked her garments. When a shadow fell over her, the queen looked up into the face of King Sumter, distorted by grief.

"Forgive me, Queen Saramis," Sumter lamented, but with a tearful smile, Saramis touched his cheek with unstained fingers, and the remorseful king tightly grasped her hand.

"It was what he wanted, my lord," she whispered. "I have spent my life trying to keep him from it..."

They both looked down in wonder as Rasdeter stirred; only Saramis knew his shared wound with Ghent prolonged his fading life.

"Cousin..." Rasdeter choked as he tried to focus his sight on Sumter. "I ask for what is undeserved..."

The High King of the Far Isles saw only his childhood friend led astray and he spoke from this place.

"Stay with me," asked Sumter urgently, "There's nothing to forgive, my cousin and brother, just--"

The king turned to look upwards in hope at the former child of destiny, who shook her head.

"He doesn't want to stay, Sumter," S'ateegra said in compassion, remembering in this moment the king's mother, Queen Inka. She knew Sumter could not bear this coming separation. "I can only render aid if Rasdeter accepts it..."

S'ateegra gazed on Saramis, who only nodded sadly.

"Why, cousin?" asked Sumter helplessly. "Why can we not restore the years we've lost? The mage has released you; I'm trying to understand..."

Rasdeter's voice strengthened for a moment; he felt the warmth of his cousin's hand.

"Does the son not resemble his father?" asked the dying former prince. "Can a heart such as mine truly heal, or shall I be used again the next time it burns?"

Rasdeter painfully turned his head towards Saramis.

"My goddess..." He whispered as his strength began to fade; his wife stroked his cheek tenderly.

"You know I will not leave you, Rasdeter," she said simply. "...and where you go, I follow..."

S'ateegra knelt and mentally spoke into the young king's mind. He stared at her intensely and finally whispered a barely audible response.

His eyes locked again on Saramis, and the young queen took a sharp breath as Pax stared up at her through her husband's gaze.

"Take me home," gasped the dying king, "I want to go home. Take me..."

A second between heartbeats and a moment between breaths and the young king felt his spirit expand and compress at once. He looked down on his body where Saramis and Sumter leaned over it; with a start he noticed S'ateegra gazing serenely on him and not his body. There was a glow around her and everyone else. He felt a deep warmth to his left, when he turned to it, Rasdeter saw in the distance the Great Elder watching him. He focused on her face and she smiled at him.

"Mother..."

The young king wanted to go to her and feel her embrace once more, but now he realized that she was always holding him, and her warmth was healing his wounded heart. Affi-Tosla's smile broadened as though to acknowledge this thought.

Then she spoke to him.

"Run, Rasdeter..." she said softly. "...run..."

He turned again to see how his physical eyes were still locked on Saramis, the woman he knew he loved more than anything; then he felt a pull within him and turning from the battlefield, Rasdeter began to run.

As he ran, the men and women on the battlefield who had fallen came back to life. Their eyes as they looked on him were full of forgiveness and love; Rasdeter felt strengthened and he began to run faster.

He retraced every step he made; past the hunter Bowman Kha, who stood whole and strong, both palms resting on his sword. His eyes clear and full of peace, Kha nodded as the young king passed him. His brother Atoli and the warriors held up their spears as Rasdeter ran without stopping. Ghent, Enith, Iroh, Paza, Templin and Brennan; all stood watching in the distance as the king ran past his kingdom, The Bright Forest, and westward. At the borders, a small boy with a bruised face was laughing and waving wildly. The former prince looked down at his hands.

"The blood," he said in wonder, "It's gone..."

As he approached where the Wanderers first embraced him, he saw the Great Elder standing in front of the tent of his initiation; she pulled back the flap at his approach and Rasdeter ran through it.

On the other side, he saw again the tree on his father's estates, and his younger self facing Aton, who turned to meet his gaze with peace. As the younger Rasdeter turned his head away from the general and towards Saramis, Rasdeter stepped between them and saw Saramis about to raise her hand and release her power; her pupils widened as their eyes met.

"I remember you, Saramis," He whispered. "I've always remembered you..."

Rasdeter looked without fear on General Aton, who raised his sword in a salute as he passed him.

He ran faster than the horses bearing soldiers back to his father's estates, but he did not stop at his home, but ran straight to the palace of the Far Isles.

Sumter greeted him at the gates, a boy of twelve again and overjoyed to see him.

"Cousin!" Sumter cried, "You've returned!" The young prince took his cousin's hand in a burst of light and they ran together.

"He's back home!"

Rasdeter began to grin in pure joy. He gazed again at his cousin's face as they ran. Sumter's happiness could not be contained as he looked up at his heart brother and best friend.

Every gate and door flew open to allow their passage; as the two entered the throne room, he saw everyone he loved on the steps leading up to where King Valtus sat:

Lady Irisella, Queen Inka, great with child, Marcus, Hesta, Aton, Gervaise, his mother Princess Erami, and his father, Lord Altus, whose eyes shone with love at his entrance.

The young king and Sumter paused at the bottom of the steps, and his cousin released his hand as King Valtus rose from his throne and stepped aside. Rasdeter turned to Lord Altus.

"I don't understand..." Rasdeter said, but his father smiled warmly.

"It was never the Earthly throne, but the Light within it, that you've always wanted, my son," said his father.

Now Rasdeter could see it; the purple and gold throne of the Far Isles glowed and then faded into the light surrounding it; a Light so bright it dimmed the sun behind him.

"It's beautiful..." Rasdeter whispered.

He looked down again at his cousin, who embraced him with his arms about Rasdeter's waist. Sumter gazed up at him.

"You don't have to say anything," His cousin said quietly. "I already know..."

Rasdeter bent and pressed a kiss to Sumter's cheek; then stepped away from him. As Sumter touched his fingers to his cheek in wonder, Rasdeter looked up to what seemed a deep ladder leading up to the Light, his body blazing with it. Within the light Rasdeter saw the faint outline of Saramis who cradled on her hip a small child. The king could almost detect the faint hues of red gold hair.

Rasdeter threw back his head in a movement of pure joy.

"Home..."

He became a blur as he ran full speed up the steps.

* * *

On the battlefield of Arin-Clath, Rasdeter's body shuddered, and held by his wife Saramis, the Lost Prince of the Far Isles gave one last deep sigh, and he was gone.

A deep hush fell over the plains, and the sounds of war and strife receded. Dandelion seeds floated across the fields, catching as they drifted onto the eyelashes and breastplates of the fallen. Soft breezes caressed the young king's dark wavy hair; the brilliant amber and green of Rasdeter's once startling irises were already beginning to darken and dull from the absence of life.

Sumter came to his feet, unable to bear anymore; he walked away. Saramis took her cloak and covered her husband with it. Then she began to rock with him in her arms as though she comforted a child.

The Woman of Power spoke quietly to the once Queen of the Bright Forest.

"Why did you not tell him, Saramis?" S'ateegra asked in compassion. "Can you be so sure that Rasdeter would not stay?"

"Shall the offspring of Asscher contend forever with the children of Rasdeter?" Asked Saramis as she gazed on her husband with shining eyes. When the Woman of the Woods looked again at the beloved of Sumter, S'ateegra could tell the soul of Saramis was already far away.

"My husband calls for peace from the grave, LightBringer, with wise counsel from Queen Inka...the House of Lord Altus ends here..."

For answer, The Dark One felt a light go out from deep within Saramis and caught her breath.

"She's gone..." whispered The Dark One and covered her mouth in sorrow.

"Like her mother..." responded Saramis softly as she caressed the slight swell of her belly, "...I knew she would not stay long without him..."

The former Woman of the Woods caressed Rasdeter's cooling face and pressed her lips to his. Then she looked up at S'ateegra again and held out her hand.

Power flowed between the young women and S'ateegra placed the light from Saramis over her heart.

"Please give King Sumter this gift from us both: Memories of the years that were stolen from two boys who loved each other..."

"You have my word...fare you well, Saramis..."

Saramis then lay down completely on the ground, wrapping her arms around Rasdeter, and pressing her face to his. In the distance beyond earthly boundaries, she saw the Great Elder standing next to a tall and majestic tree with leaves that billowed in the wind. Grazing beneath the tree was a doe with her fawn, the perfection of its speckled coat marred by a bloodless sword thrust. The tiny fawn's dark eyes were deep with love for the Woman of the Woods. The gaze of her Master Teacher held only love and light.

"Well done, Saramis..." whispered the Great Elder.

In this moment, the former Woman of the Woods felt all questions she had were answered. Saramis sighed as the heaviness of her body sank deeper into Rasdeter's. Calling on the power of the Earth and the elements she loved, Saramis closed her eyes and released her spirit, so she could follow his. A cloud of dandelion seeds rushed to fill the spaces between the former King and Queen of the Bright Forest and S'ateegra flexed lightly, clearing the ground surrounding them of all blood except their own. She pulled flowers from the trees in the hills, white with pink centers on the petals and covered the two lovers with them, forming a barrier that none could cross.

Then S'ateegra left to find the grief-stricken King of the Far Isles.

* * *

What Remains

King N'Goth shook his head to clear the sweat and blood from it; as the pain in his spine seared him, he remembered King Sumter. Turning from a pitched battle of the Unnamed Lands and the

Eastern Crest, he marched back to where he last saw the cousins of the Far Isles.

With a grunt of satisfaction, he beheld Rasdeter and Saramis on the ground; he noticed the light surrounding them and shrugged, disinterested. N'Goth resumed his search for the High King of the Far Isles.

However, a prolonged search was unnecessary. Once the young king lifted his eyes from the monumental task of retrieving the fallen and spied the High King of the Eastern Hemisphere striding across the plains, Sumter set his jaw and reached for his sword.

His High Regent Aeryn cried out, which caused his generals to follow Sumter's line of sight.

"My Lord King!" exclaimed Aeryn, who of course instantly recognized the brutal High King of the Unnamed Lands.

For Marcus, recognition and action were one, and he left the heaps of the dead behind him as he ran to intercept, join, or die with his king. General Hesta, who was never far from either her High Commander or her king, ran full out to make up for distance lost.

"Commander!" shouted Shustak, who dropped the edge of the heavy fabric used to drag bodies intact across the hard ground.

"Have you lost your senses?" cried a page near him. "That is N'Goth, who cannot be killed! What do you think you can do?!?"

"What a soldier does," Shustak snarled without looking back. "I'll not cower and wait while my king needs me..."

He snatched a fallen shield from a woman who no longer needed it, running.

Marcus reached King Sumter first, resisting the urge to grab his arm. It was death to touch a king, even though Sumter often treated Marcus as a friend. He tried to step in front of Sumter, but the king would not stop his advance to N'Goth; Marcus was forced to nearly run beside him as he reasoned with his monarch.

"My king, I pray you, reconsider; N'Goth is not a man..."

"He is a man," Stated Sumter grimly as he increased his stride. "...and I have given my word that he and I will meet."

"Then I die with you, my lord, as I too, have vowed…"

"No…" replied the king as he finally slowed his pace and faced his general. "You will neither die nor avenge me, Marcus. If I fall you will remain and protect my son Asscher, who will be your king."

"Sumter," choked Marcus, who in this moment forgot himself. "You cannot ask this of me…"

But the young king's face darkened.

"I am not asking you, Marcus, I am commanding you…!"

Sumter whirled and faced General Hesta and his private guard, drawing his sword, and pointing it at his people.

"Stop!"

All of his elite soldiers came to a staggered halt. The king placed his weapon in his left hand and using his right hand, he reached for his High General's sword and with a stabbing motion, thrust the blade of Marcus deep into the ground.

"Any man, or woman," King Sumter growled as his eyes nailed Hesta's, "…who passes this point while I'm engaged with N'Goth I'll have executed. Do you heed my words?"

Though he saw their faces all drained of blood at his command, Sumter repeated it.

"Do you heed my words?!?"

"Yes, my king!" cried Hesta, as she went down to one knee; the others, including Marcus swiftly followed her lead and swore assent. Satisfied, the King of the Far Isles moved across the plains where King N'Goth had ceased his advance and waited for him.

The brutal king crossed his arms at Sumter's approach, his eyes shining in admiration for how the young king handled his subjects.

"There are few true men in this world, High King," said N'Goth, "It will grieve me to destroy something so rare…"

"For what you have cost me, High King," replied Sumter with emphasis, "I will grieve you not at all…!"

"Come, then, Sumter," said N'Goth with relish. "Let there be one High King!"

The legacy swords of the two kingdoms met, and the ground shook from the reverberations. King Sumter met King N'Goth blow for blow, Sumter being the better swordsman; the King of fog the Unnamed Lands relied more on brute force than skill. The exertion burned off the king's last inebriation and the pain of the wound in his spine seared him. Sumter braced himself as he saw N'Goth's gaze begin to gleam with madness; he'd just seen a similar look in his cousin Rasdeter's eyes.

In slow motion, the young king spied N'Goth's left fist coming towards him when their swords met; Sumter raised his own hand to stop the blow; from the tight grin on the older man's face he knew N'Goth was using his full strength to bring Sumter down.

But still...

Sumter stopped N'Goth's fist with his open hand.

Every soldier on the plains felt the earth shudder and rock beneath their feet; Marcus and Hesta stared at each other in wonder.

For his part, King N'Goth looked from his fist to Sumter's hand in amazement; not since N'Goth killed his father Osolum thirty years ago had any man ever withstood his strength. N'Goth dropped his weapon and stepped back, intending to swing his right fist when the young king stepped forward swiftly and struck N'Goth in the face with his Legacy Sword still in his hand.

King N'Goth fell to the ground.

Every king that was sitting came to his feet, and those astride their horses dismounted; no man in living memory had ever bested the King of the Unnamed Lands. N'Goth felt something warm on his cheek; he rubbed his hand across his mouth and looked at it.

Blood.

His wound forgotten; the king began to laugh.

A true man, indeed.

"Yes!" N'Goth roared and came to his feet while Sumter planted his own and waited. But something came between the two men; the young king could hear N'Goth shouting in deranged glee, but Sumter could no longer see him. The barrier seemed a solid fog that yielded to Sumter's hand but would not allow him to pass through it. The High King's puzzlement soon turned to frustration.

"The Dark One..." Sumter murmured under his breath. Only she had the power to turn the massively powerful N'Goth from his determined course. The question was:

Why did she come between them?

Sumter had little time to speculate. He breathed deeply as he felt every muscle in his body ache from facing the High King; his arm hummed from his hand to his back and shoulder. But Sumter felt the pain worth the victory he gave his fallen cousin Rasdeter. The young king turned and walked towards his soldiers and generals, who waited quietly for him behind the sword of Marcus.

* * *

N'Goth noticed a figure blocking his path, he only slowed his stride when he both saw and felt the power rolling off her. She stood quietly in silhouette on a rock above him, a light from some far-off place behind her. The king knew in that moment who he faced: The Dark One and Destroyer, who as a child brought low any and all who faced her.

He did not fear her, or his own death; his madness precluded it. The High king moved forward and stared up at the one all men considered the most powerful being on Earth since the death of her father, Lord Master Brayten.

Though shadows blocked her face, N'Goth could clearly see that she gazed on him without concern; indeed, it appeared The Dark One studied him as something under glass. Her hair and robes flowed about her from some unseen breeze, reacting to the staggering might that hummed from the very cells of her form.

His blue eyes narrowed.

Then the king lashed out with his legendary swiftness to strike upwards at The Dark One's face.

He struck her wall of creative force that unknown to him, S'ateegra branched out in front of her so that N'Goth would not break every bone in his hand and arm. His face cleared in amazement that he could not even reach her.

Then the mad king roared and began to pound her barrier with all his strength, something N'Goth was unaccustomed to doing. The king had never experienced resistance much less defeat before to-day and there was nothing in N'Goth that would not persist to the death to prevail.

S'ateegra silently watched this display of irresistible force as the king hammered at her creative wall, then her eyes darkened, and lightning lit up behind her gaze. She stepped forward and pushed the startled N'Goth back with her barrier.

"Learn today, High King," said The Dark One, "What an immovable object truly is..."

King N'Goth took a deep breath and swung at her barrier with everything he had.

This time, S'ateegra allowed the king to feel the results of his rage, and N'Goth cried out in sudden agony as he felt his bones breaking from his hand to his shoulder. Then S'ateegra's eyes flashed lightning again, and the High King of the Unnamed Lands vanished in a burst of light.

In the ensuing silence following N'Goth's departure, The Dark One could hear the clashing startled thoughts of the soldiers and leaders around her, who believed she had vaporized the brutal king. S'ateegra gave herself a rueful smile. Would that she could end his terrifying reign, but The Destroyer knew she did not have permission to interrupt the High King's eventual destiny.

She sighed as her thoughts turned to the High King of the Far Isles. Her meeting with Sumter was just as inevitable as the one with N'Goth, the only difference being that S'ateegra would rather face N'Goth again than answer the questions she knew Sumter would ask of her.

* * *

The maddened and injured King of the Unnamed Lands appeared miles and months away in the crumbling deserted palace the armies of the seven kings had used while plotting the downfall of The Nine Kingdoms.

N'Goth held his broken right arm with his left hand, whirling in disbelief at his surroundings. He roared into the silence.

"Sathdan!"

But neither his High Regent Sathdan, Iroh, or any other mage could come to his aid and return N'Goth to the battlefield. Every sane magician had already fled the presence of the one who wielded creation without limit. The king was forced to nurse his wounds and heal alone. By the time N'Goth's armies and fellow kings found the High King, the war for the Far Isles would be a distant memory.

Unfortunately, bolstered by these events, many men would die in the next few months challenging the High King's rule. They would soon learn that only King Sumter and The Dark One were the exception to N'Goth's feared might, and that other than this, all else remained unchanged.

The View from Sirius

The Starchild lingered at the low sloping window where Paza could see the changed constellations, holding the fallen Ghent in her arms and across her lap. From time to time, she absently stroked his hair. The Starchild had instantly pulled Ghent to her as he fell on the battlefield and still, she could see the power of S'ateegra surging through him. Paza saw clearly how The Destroyer had placed her seal on Ghent's life, which should have faded with Rasdeter's. She marveled at the deep blue energy coursing through the regent's body; how it healed his ruptured cells of forced radiation.

"Did I ever know this power," Paza mused aloud, "Was it ever a part of the dancing stars that rained their light on me?"

The Starchild lost herself in her thoughts.

How sad I once feared you, child of destiny, thought Paza, Now I love your name, Destroyer, for one day you will dispel all illusions...

"Come forth, if you are ready, Starchild," said a voice from the corridor leading to the halls.

"Yes..." Paza responded as she easily lifted the unconscious Ghent and placed him on a bed of rest, kissing his brow as she did so.

"May you find your own freedom from bondage, Ghent, as I will find mine..."

Moments later, Paza stepped across the threshold of the ruined palace and through the dimensions, entering the mountain retreat of the Ancient known as Enith. The Ancient's defenses of destructive energy did nothing to Paza as she strode through them; it barely registered on her awareness. She smiled at the immensity of his retreat; how it mirrored the vast halls of The Magician. Her gaze fell on the people in the distance on Enith's elevated platform: Keoni, Master Iroh, and the Ancient himself.

Enith hid as well as he could his alarm at Paza's sudden presence; no one else possessed the power to invade his home against his will, other than his master, and the thought of The Magician increased his dis-ease. This visit is not for company, thought the mage, may a question buy me time...

"Good morrow, Starchild," said Enith more courteously than he felt. "Have you need of me in this moment?"

But Paza did not respond; she instead admired the hall of the Ancient as she approached them, and Enith chanced a tense glance at Keoni, who instantly vanished, terrified by the power emanating from the Starchild.

Master Iroh was also afraid, but he would not leave the side of the Ancient. As with Rannea, Iroh was loyal to the death. He heard Enith's controlled whisper:

"Iroh..."

The Master Sorcerer shook his head slightly but firmly; he would not go.

Paza stopped at the bottom of the steps and gazed upwards at the sorcerer.

"You are Iroh?" she asked. "Who once served Lord Rannea?"

The Master Sorcerer drew his breath in sharply at how easily the Starchild tapped his thoughts; his chest constricted in pain at the memory of his teacher.

"How beautiful you are," she continued dreamily as she beheld the white and scarlet strands of his power, slowly orbiting Iroh's body on a light spectrum a normal human's eyes could not see. "No doubt you are Enith's great treasure..."

These words caused Enith's brow to sweat; he had not the means to stop the Starchild.

"Paza..." said the Ancient urgently, "I know not what you are about, joining us unannounced, but I pray you allow Iroh to remain unharmed, for he was once under my protection..."

A flash of heat and darkness heralded the entrance of The Rook, who smiled slightly as the composure of the Ancient abandoned him completely.

"I'm afraid the Starchild can offer you both no promises, mage," said The Rook, whose eyes were bright as he contemplated Enith's former student, "You will come with us to audience with The Magician...now."

"He's most anxious to meet you, Master Iroh," agreed Paza, "And to hear Enith's account of his failure to acquire King Sumter's throne."

The Starchild made a blanket of stardust to cover the four as they disappeared.

* * *

When the Light Changes

King Rasdeter and Queen Saramis would soon be laid to rest in the crypt King Sumter had prepared for his cousin at the time of

High General Aton's death. The High King one day would expand the marble building to include carvings of Rasdeter's life during his time with the Wanderers. Second Elder Zema, and the remaining members of her tribe including Nea and Aylin had followed Atoli and the warriors to the Far Isles to offer the ritual of the Completion of Life, a very different process from what we now call burials and funerals. This was granted by King Sumter, who despite the pleas of Atoli and Rasdeter's former people, would not release his cousin's body to the Wanderers.

"I respect your ways," said Sumter gravely to Elder Zema and Atoli. "But Rasdeter was born a prince, and crowned a king; he will rest in a king's crypt in the Far Isles."

Sumter walked over to Atoli and offered his arm, a great honor. For Sumter recognized Atoli as an equal, in recognition of his beloved cousin. Atoli accepted this, his eyes shining; he knew it would please Rasdeter if he did so.

Sumter continued with difficulty.

"You hold the years with Rasdeter that were denied to me, Atoli," said the king softly, "And gave him the love that I longed to offer him...allow me to possess what remains..."

"He was my brother..." began Atoli, then paused as he gathered himself. "But he wanted to return here; it was all he wished for..."

The High King turned to Elder Zema, and taking her hand, pressed it to his lips, then held it firmly in his.

"Thank you, Second Elder Zema," said Sumter, "For allowing Queen Saramis to rest with her husband; I know you have first rights to her..."

"She would never leave him willingly in life, my lord," Responded Zema as strongly as she could. "It would be wrong to separate them now..."

Nea gently comforted Aylin as she mourned the warrior she only knew as Pax.

Her grief, however, was twofold: Though it was true Aylin hoped Atoli and his men would save Rasdeter, the primary reason she traveled the miles with her people was because Aylin desired to reconcile with her brother Cord. She'd heard a rumor that he came to the conflict with another tribe; Aylin searched as far as she could, but she could not find her brother among the living or the fallen; and her heart was broken.

"This could be cause for joy, Aylin," offered Nea. "Cord may yet be found alive among our people..."

Aylin nodded to Nea's words, but she did not believe them. As she assisted her family, Aylin could not keep her eyes from searching the faces of the dead.

The king's soldiers assisted the Wanderers with the removal of their fallen warriors; Marcus himself helped Atoli with the body of Bowman Kha.

"I must send word to our parents of Kha's passing," stated Atoli quietly as he and the other warriors laid Kha down on a blanket and arranged his limbs in a position mimicking that of an unborn child. The young men began to groom Kha and the other fallen Wanderers; some dug shallow pits and placed their brothers within them with things they had treasured in life. Atoli placed the necklace and bracelet the hunter gave so much meaning to inside the curl of Kha's limp fingers.

"Bowman Kha was your brother?" asked Marcus in disbelief.

"All men are my brothers," replied Atoli thoughtfully as he met Marcus gaze. "But yes, we share the same father and mother..."

Atoli reached down to tenderly brush Kha's long hair from his face and braid it in the style he knew his brother preferred.

General Marcus stepped back with the others as Zema approached carrying a small drawstring pouch. The Second Elder poured a small amount of the contents into Atoli's hand; a blue-white crystalline substance. The king's general watched in amazement as the substance multiplied in the palm of each warrior Atoli offered it to; they then knelt and spread it over the bodies of their fallen brothers. Soon the bodies were completely coated; the warriors began to build a huge fire. When they were finished, Zema began to chant, and the Tribe called Human sang behind her words:

The Great One creates all things and all things return to It
The Outgoing breath is the Light that extends itself
The Inward breath is the Life returning fulfilled
We do not choose the path of the Breath
We but follow it...
In the ways our feet are held up and directed
And the Circle brings us Home...

Marcus could not know that in three days' time the crystals would penetrate the bone and transform it to powder; then absorb all the water and fluids of the human body, returning the few dry elements and minerals left behind to the earth, replenishing it.

Atoli spoke almost to himself.

"The crystal is like the dust of stars hidden in our bones, my brother," Atoli whispered. "I will keep watch with you until the third day..."

The High General of the Far Isles felt he had intruded enough on this ritual of mourning; he silently moved away. But he would not soon forget the image of Atoli holding his spear and standing over Bowman Kha's crystalline grave, and the huge flames leaping before Elder Zema's outstretched arms.

Sumter and S'ateegra watched the ritual from a respectful distance; further still stood General Marcus, who suffered for having dealt Rasdeter a fatal blow. That Merick had pierced the young king's heart did little to erase the thought that it was Rasdeter's heart Marcus aimed for. When the moment came, the faithful soldier had saved his king; this he did not regret. The thought that plagued Marcus was that once, a lifetime ago, he had remarked to Hesta that he could not imagine the pain that High General Aton had suffered to slay young Rasdeter; to do what the laws of the kingdom required, despite the consequences.

Now he knew.

Marcus felt more than saw The Dark One's gaze of compassion, he turned away, in a direction that had no destination.

* * *

High General Brennan, however, was quite clear on the way his feet should go; he marched resolutely to where King Elect Merick stood and first bowed then kneeled before her. He stretched out his arms to be bound, or his head separated from his body, he knew not which would follow.

But the face of his king was unreadable as she stood over him with a spear in her hand.

"Why do you kneel before me, High General Brennan?" Asked the king sternly. "What punishment do you think is before you?"

"I will accept whatever my king deems fit," choked the general. "And grant it sufficient release from all my pain."

The seconds between his answer and her response seemed eternal, but it was but seconds truly.

"Then rise, High General," said his king, "For your punishment is to serve me for the remainder of your natural life..."

Brennan's head snapped up in confusion as he met her eyes, but her gaze was unwavering.

"I know the truth of how you came to be under the thrall of the Ancient, Brennan," said King Merick softly. "You confessed it to me over my presumed grave..."

Brennan's jaw worked as he tried to speak, but no sound came forth. His thoughts rushed back to his broken tearful words alone over her rest. Thinking Merick dead, Brennan shared his despair that she died believing he'd had betrayed her, and his grief that his secret love for his queen had been made a mockery of; a secret Brennan wished to take to his own grave, in respect for the king who trusted him.

With a slight smile, his King Elect continued.

"Further," She stated, "I have you to thank for following protocol in the face of your grief. Had you buried me in the grave of a princess instead of the Bright Forest Guardian, it is possible I would not stand before you now, and my father's bloodline would in truth have ended..."

The King Elect said no more for a time, as her thoughts returned to conversations she once had with the previous High General on possible response to disaster. The poison Merick took had an antidote; one that required that she be buried in the crypt of the Guardian. Only Merick and the former High General knew of these arrangements, and he died before her. The former princess spoke to no one else of it; not even her father, that the secret be truly kept. What even Merick did not know was that the clever general had placed the cure in both crypts. That the antidote was halved accounted for the long time it took for her to recover; time for a preternaturally suspicious mage to turn to more pressing matters than the improbable survival of a princess assassin and the last of King Templin's bloodline.

Merick reached down to take Brennan's right hand and turned the palm upwards to expose the wound received from Enith. Already the flesh was closing, a good sign indeed. Brennan shuddered at her touch, a high honor; one he felt he did not deserve.

"For necessity, Brennan," the king said calmly, "You will not train the next Guardian, nor will you know their identity. The mage has no more use for you, but the Bright Forest Guardian is a position shrouded in secrecy, and you can see the reason for it. Now..." Merick smiled slightly, "Do you accept the terms of your punishment, or do you yet prefer execution?"

The High General remained on his knees in overwhelming thankfulness as he stared up at his king, his heart in his eyes.

"My life is yours," said Brennan hoarsely. "Command me, my king; I live at your whim..."

The King Elect lightly tapped both shoulders of her general with her spear.

"Rise, High General Brennan," said Merick strongly. "And command my troops."

Brennan came quickly to his feet and bowed; he stepped back from Merick and bowed again. Then the general paused as a thought just came to him.

"What of the Bright Forest High Regent, my lord?" he asked.

The face of his king darkened.

"We shall appoint another, my general," replied Merick. "Regent Ghent still bears the mark of his master; if he crosses my path again, I will slay him."

The general blinked rapidly as his face paled; he'd seen firsthand what his king was capable of; he doubted the hapless Ghent would see her coming.

"As you say, my lord," whispered Brennan, and strode away to obey her word.

The Tree of Experience

King Sumter took comfort in the company of The Dark One as the fires of the ritual burned. He'd lost her once before; the king savored this intimacy as S'ateegra stood next to him. When their eyes met Sumter did not, as in the past, keep his feelings from his gaze. He watched her pupils widen and her face flush before she looked away; the young king determined they must speak again privately and soon. As ever, it distressed him that she kept her name a secret from him, whatever the reason. But he would not press her now; his former impatience had cost Sumter more than he cared to admit.

"Destroyer," the king began, drawing her eyes back to his. "You've not yet explained to me why you came between myself and N'Goth...am I to understand that now creators involve themselves in the affairs of men?"

Sumter's eyes narrowed as he watched her expression change; she was about to tell him something of the truth, but not all of it, and S'ateegra, in her turn, was not fooled by his veneer of patience.

"You will see the High King again, King Sumter," She began softly, "There can be no doubt of it...and..." She continued wryly,

"You know I can do nothing without permission, or more accurately, I will not."

"Did you save my life?" He asked quietly, and heard her breath deeply, her face turned away from his; Sumter knew not what to make of this response. Her eyes were veiled as she looked up at him.

"Now you press me, my king," She offered, and noted the tenseness in his jaw. S'ateegra knew the phrase, 'my king', would irritate and distract Sumter; she was not a subject of his kingdom, a point the two had clashed on in the recent past.

Yet as the king appraised the young woman who had been a rare constant in his life, his brief irritation at her words faded into a poignant sadness. Sumter had no true father figure to guide him in the ways of women while growing up, which brought his thoughts without fail to Lady Irisella, to whom he must bring the sad news of Rasdeter's true life and death.

A memory came to Sumter in this moment and he spoke to it, rather than continue to debate royal protocol with her.

"My dear friend," He murmured soberly, a term that never failed to make her eyes soften. "You spoke to Rasdeter before he died; I could not discern the words you shared, but I heard my cousin answer, 'Yes'..."

S'ateegra did not speak right away, her gaze bittersweet as the flames danced in her eyes. She would not point out to the king that she said no words aloud to Rasdeter; she was having difficulty enough keeping from Sumter the many things he was not yet aware of. It seemed, however, his question brought out some hidden emotion; her voice deepened slightly, and Sumter's breath caught as she responded.

"I asked him..." She sighed before continuing. "I asked Rasdeter if he had a chance to do it again, would he choose differently..."

The crackling of the distant fire and the chanting came to the forefront as the young king struggled to respond.

"You've pierced my heart..." answered the king finally, who could say no more as his memories turned to the moment his cousin stood before General Aton, and Sumter accepted at last that he would not see his cousin again. King Sumter's throat tightened as the image of the window of the child Rasdeter's rooms displayed again the faint imprint of the prince's small hand. The king decided he would protect it still; a fragile reminder of Rasdeter's innocence and misguided love.

The pair remained silent, staring into the blazing fire.

Yet as S'ateegra watched, her vision parted the dimensions, and a leaf fell again from the Tree of Experience.

* * *

Affi-Tosla walked through the common area of one of her many tribes; most of the people greeted her with a smile but did not attempt to impede her progress. As she reached the center of the area, her steps halted; a young girl and boy were walking across the way from her; as the boy turned and met her gaze, he stopped.

The girl spoke in alarm.

"You mustn't stare at the Great Elder..." She said in an undertone.

But the boy heard nothing; all sound around him had ceased. Everyone paused as they noticed the child who dared to meet and hold the gaze of the Great Elder.

After a moment, Affi-Tosla opened her arms.

He dropped his baskets and ran to her, embracing her tightly. Her heartbeat seemed to fill the entire world, and for the first time, the young boy felt safe.

When he looked up at her, his eyes brimmed.

"Mother..." he said it without thinking, and Affi-Tosla smiled warmly down at him.

"So..." she replied kindly, "It seems you are not completely asleep..."

The boy with dark wavy hair and deep green eyes stared up at her a moment, and all the elders held their breath.

Finally, the boy spoke.

"I will stay with you..." He whispered.

All the people were stunned as the Great Elder, Affi-Tosla, and Sun Womb of the Earth, threw back her head and laughed.

Finis

ACKNOWLEDGEMENTS

First and foremost, this book, and those that follow would not exist if not for the teachings and presence of **Dr. Carolyne Fuqua, PhD.**, who gently, patiently and lovingly assisted me in freeing my true voice. These characters and concepts would yet be pleading with me for their freedom if Life had not placed my feet unerringly on the path that lead to Dr. Fuqua. Yes, and Thank You!

Lisa Diane Elzy Watson, who has listened to my tales from childhood, sitting on the tiles of our bathroom floor while I whispered them like secrets. Even today, she is the best person to read aloud to; her reactions are priceless. May the world one day be gifted with the stories you only shared with me. My sister Denise L. White, who inspired my creativity growing up; I still remember her early drawings and handmade books; our lively family discussions on all sorts of topics; political, scientific or mundane.

Many thanks and love to Team Dignan: to Phillip (Socrates) Dignan, who was among the first to support my work after a reading of the first fifteen pages of the Dark One Trilogy in Egypt December 2017. I highly respect your work and the standing ovation you gave is etched on my heart. Katherine Dignan, who, sight unseen, offered her considerable talents to edit this prodigious work during the future Kevin and Nadine Parks wedding cruise. You are a thoughtful and generous soul, Katherine.

Angela Hupp, Psychology professor and sweet friend, who also bravely volunteered her editing skills; who not only performed the first edits on the Trilogy, but actually asked for the rest of the document once completed. I am surrounded and supported by amazing people whose lives must prosper with their unfailing willingness to be of service. Moo Creamery in Bakersfield, the scene of many discussions. Nuff said.

Vionela Vaughn-Austin, who purchased the first copy of The Prince of The Far Isles before the edits were finished and after I submitted my final draft to Dr. Carolyne Fuqua, who as my muse, must be first in all things. Thank you, Vionela for your unwavering belief in the importance of the work.

My wonderful brother Willie D. Elzy, who always sends me financial support and never asks me why.

My nephew Paul Bristol, the first son I helped raise, who sent funds while I was still writing.

Mark David Warlick, my fellow warrior and Horus, who has always supported me in whatever I was into, no matter how outlandish. I appreciate you.

Jady Yuk Yu Choi, who described herself as the biggest fan of my work at the 2018 COLM conference. Your sweet and shining face is all the thanks I require. May this latest offering find favor with you!

I would also like to thank my Mastermind group, Women of Wisdom Walking the Path of Peace: Lisa Diane Elzy Watson, Vionela Maria Vaughn-Austin, June Kathleen Hannays, Rochelle Malone, Dr. Jewa Lea, special guest my sister Denise L. White and last but not least, Mae Conedy. Your support, love and encouragement has meant more than can be inscribed here.

Much love and thanks to family and friends too numerous to mention here. Don't worry, there's eight more books. Lol

And in case those of you that know me haven't guessed it by now, I must acknowledge my own Lost Prince, Dirk Turhan Austin Elzy. My once protector, who showed me how to climb trees, fight like a boy, collect comic books, go on spy missions, and re-discover the Lost City of Mu. I will miss our talks. And oh, yes, he was a Gemini.

BIBLIOGRAPHY & SOURCES

A partial list of books and sources that inspire, support, or compliment my work:

Dr. Carolyne Fuqua, Ph.D. The Keys to the Kingdom, A New Paradigm for Humanity vol I, vol. II, Circles of Light Publishing, Beverly Hills CA

Three Initiates, The Kybalion: Hermetic Philosophy, Yogi Publication Society, 1908; reprint Devorss, 1999.

Albert Einstein's 1912 Manuscript on the Special Theory of Relativity

Albert Einstein, The World As I See It, 1949.

Albert Einstein, Cosmic Religion: With Other Opinions and Aphorisms

Theodore Gray, The Elements: A Visual Exploration of Every Known Atom in the Universe. Black Dog & Leventhal Publishers New York, 2009

Nikola Tesla, The Eternal Source of Energy of the Universe, Origin and Intensity of Cosmic Rays, New York, October 13, 1932

Nikola Tesla, How Cosmic Forces Shape Our Destinies, New York American, June 5, 1915

Nikola Tesla, On Light and Other High Frequency Phenomena, Franklin Institute, Philadelphia, February 1893, and National Electric Light Association, St. Louis, March 1893

Nikola Tesla, The Problem of Increasing Human Energy, June 1900

Cover Photo: Carl Studna Photography

ABOUT THE AUTHOR

"One day She tied the Universe around her finger, and made a Knot..."
~~~T.M. Elzy

T. M. Elzy, also known as a Person in Love with the Cosmos, is a writer, poet, screenwriter and now author of her own vision of the Universe called the Hidden World Book Series, inspired by the teachings, science, and philosophies of Dr. Carolyne Fuqua. Beginning with the prequel Prince of the Far Isles and the deeper Trilogy entitled The Dark One: A Hidden History of a Previous Earth, the middle volume, The Destroyer: Battle for the Heart, and the conclusion, LightBringer: The End of All Shadows.

A staunch proponent of Speculative Fiction, T. M. Elzy is passionate about human potential and taking us far beyond the present reach of our abilities using science, quantum physics and the future Invisible Things we have yet to know. If she's not at home writing or driving through the Angeles mountains, you may find her in Egypt, Peru, London, Athens and maybe Bolivia if she missed her train.

∞

To learn more about these and other titles by the author, visit: https://linktr.ee/tanyamarieelzy
~~~